I0762285

GONE BY MORNING

A SPOOKY SHORT STORY ANTHOLOGY

ISBN Hardback: 978-1-7361363-8-6

ISBN Paperback: 978-1-7361363-3-1

ISBN eBook: 978-1-7361363-4-8

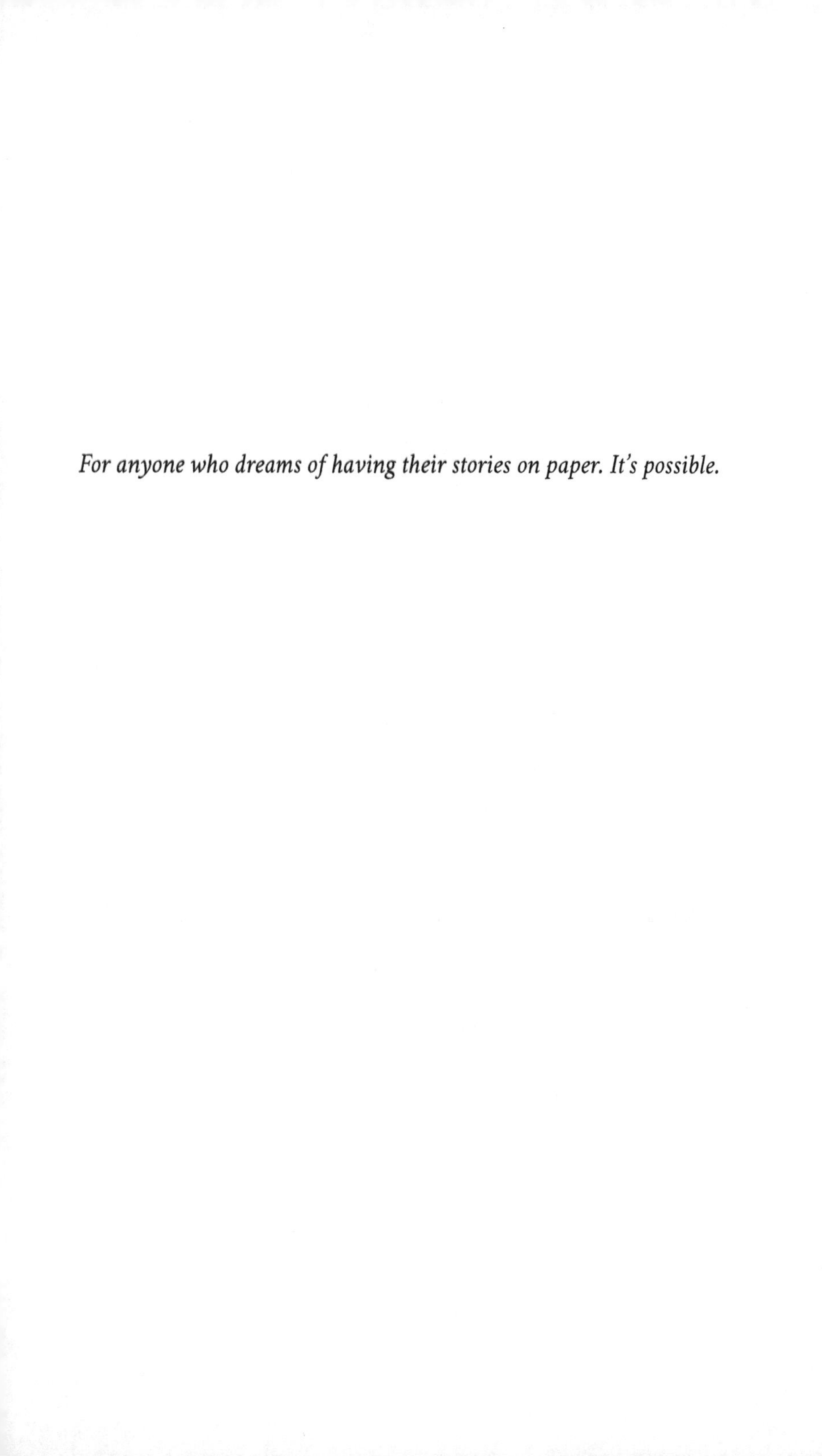

For anyone who dreams of having their stories on paper. It's possible.

TRIGGER WARNINGS

Nora's Box: Murder, death, car accident, body horror (skin lesions), estranged family relationships, language, gaslighting

A Dove's Song: Blood and gore, mention of sexual abuse/harassment, verbal and physical abuse, death/murder on page, language, violence

Skin and Bones: Suicide, mention of drug use, mental health (anxiety, depression, suicidal thoughts), language

The Pumpkinheads: Body horror, violence, death

The Oxblood Door: Gore, death

Heart of Thorns: Slight violence

Cemetery by the Bay: Suicide, death, body horror

One Last Tale: Death, blood, gore, gaslighting and fighting

Enchanting Emilia: Live murder, animal death

The Night Game: Psychological manipulation, terminal illness, language

A Crow's Call at Night: Body horror

Luck Run Out: Animal death, mention of murder and death

Tales of the Karsha: Body Horror

In Dark Corridors: Blood/gore, death, food and drink, murder, violence, attempted manipulation, language, drug use, paranoia

Them: Racism, death, violence

A Death's Ballad: Death, gore, language

The Skin Between My Teeth: Suicidal thoughts/urges/behaviors, self harm, body horror

Unhappily Forever Ever After: Vampires (blood, biting, etc.), explicit sexual content, mention of firearms

Not Just a Nightmare: Domestic abuse, body talk/fatphobia

NOTE

A translation glossary for *One Last Tale* by Hasfariza Hassan is provided at the end of the book.

1

NORA'S BOX

AMANDA HAVILL ADGATE

The headache clawed at the back of her eyes, the buzzing in her skull seeming to pulse with the hum of the fluorescent lights above their heads.

The run-down motel looked straight out of a horror movie. A shiver ran down Nora's spine as her dark eyes slid from peeling paint to rusted door hinges. Four other vehicles sat in the lot outside the window, ruined masses of twisted metal, as if parked there for decades. Everything was coated in a layer of desert sand and bruising afternoon sunshine, including the threadbare armchair shoved into the small office where she sat, as far away from the moldering fabric without appearing rude. The papers from the coroner sat on the desk before her, next to the final bill, the ink blurring on the page as she blinked back tears.

Why would her father spend his final days *here?*

The manager sat in a plastic lawn chair on the other side of a chipped desk, his long graying hair tied back in a greasy ponytail. His rheumy eyes met hers, expression dazed—from the trauma of finding a dead body in one of his rooms that week.

And, maybe from years of heavy drinking. She could smell the whiskey on his breath from where she perched.

Nora eyed the red plastic keychain, its surface covered in something sticky from a stranger's fingers and God knew what else, lying innocently next to the paperwork. She didn't want to touch it. Her stomach roiled at the thought. She couldn't keep from wiping her palm on her dark jeans, as if the gummy mess was already touching her.

Easton brushed a hand against her shoulder, a comfort she wanted to flinch away from. She glanced at her boyfriend, meeting bright blue eyes that cut sharply to the motel manager as if to say, *make him stop talking*. The man's nasally voice filled the room like a cloud of smoke, an irritating background noise that she couldn't comprehend. The thought of making him stop, of moving forward, made her stomach churn with dread. A few more minutes pretending to listen, delaying the moment she touched that key and walked to the place where her father took his last breath wouldn't make a difference, would it?

She didn't want to be at this seedy motel in the middle of nowhere, picking up her dead father's things. Something explosive burned inside her bones as she recalled the years spent, waiting for him to come home from his research, countless days ending with her crying in her bed in the dark, her heart splintering a bit more.

There was no longer a chance to make it right—a late night phone call from the college's president ended that secret hope, expressing his condolences in a staticky jumble of words. Nora replayed the moment that the corded phone slid through her mother's fingers, onto the linoleum floor in the kitchen, every night in her dreams.

And just like that, her father was gone forever. He would never come home again.

Her heart couldn't take it, having cracked and refrozen so many times. That final blow shattered it into a million pieces.

Before the sadness overwhelmed her like an avalanche, Nora clung tightly to the bitterness that soured her stomach, refusing to move an inch as she shoved that pain down into a box and locked it up tight. She couldn't let it escape. If she shared the feelings slowly poisoning her from the inside out, she was sure the rest of the world would begin decaying. It would open a can of worms she couldn't put back, spiraling out of control.

The bitterness only grew sharper when she realized it reminded her of one of the stories her father was obsessed with proving real. The reason he died in a motel room, five hundred miles from home.

Her mother refused to handle it when the motel called days after the funeral, complaining about the boxes taking up space, the unpaid bill.

So, Nora was forced to go in her stead.

Easton nudged her again from his spot next to the armchair, and she pushed down the annoyance that sliced across her skin. The relief she felt at his presence—that she didn't have to do this alone—was a comfort, but did he have to rush her?

Nora forced herself to interrupt the manager's long monologue on unpaid bills. "Yes, thank you, sir. We'll go get my father's things now and be on our way." The smile on her face was fake, and she knew she'd overdone it when the manager's eyes widened in confusion. Easton swiped the key off the desk and they headed for the door.

"Don't know if you'll be able to beat that storm, now—sky looks as black as death, it does. You can have the room for the night, ya hear? Since you paid up through today."

Nora couldn't stop the grimace that twisted her mouth at the thought of staying the night in one of the rooms in this motel. Unsavory types stayed here. People who probably lived inside a prison cell longer than they lived outside of one.

People who ran out on their family, who neglected their

daughters to chase an obscure reference from an ancient story, in the hopes it was real.

Easton waved a hand behind him to acknowledge the words, glancing at the chipped number seven on the key ring. "I hope there's not too many boxes."

"Don't jinx it, East." Nora nudged him in the ribs. "I want to leave this sketchy place as soon as possible." She glanced up, taking in the swirling clouds, their edges dark as an oil spill. Maybe the rain would hold off long enough for them to grab the boxes and go.

"Are you worried about some sleaze ball messing with you?" He puffed his chest out, his eyes flicking across the doors. *Four, five...*

"No, I can take care of myself, thanks." Nora's skin crawled as they stopped in front of the off-white door, marked with a rusted '7'.

Easton squeezed her hand, his expression understanding, before putting the key in the lock and twisting the handle. "Home sweet home," he sang out, thrusting the door open.

A musty smell hit her nose, a cough crawling up her throat. Waving a hand in front of her face, Nora took a step into the dark room, eyeing the shag carpet and peeling wallpaper with a pinched expression. The floral pattern on the plasticky coverlets was a lurid green and violent red, clashing spectacularly. The headache pounded a furious tattoo behind her eyes as she caught sight of a mountain of banker boxes stacked next to a tiny cart with an ancient television.

"Jesus." Easton shook his head. "There's gotta be more than twenty boxes here. We won't be able to fit them all in the truck. What the hell was he researching?"

Nora shrugged. She hadn't touched a single box and already she was tired. This was more work than she signed on for. "He *was* the Ancient Studies professor at Lloyd College, so I'm sure it has to do with a myth or something. Maybe some desert creature from a story–why else would he be out here, in the middle of nowhere?"

He scrubbed a hand through his dirty blonde hair. "Damn. I think you'll have to go through the boxes and get rid of some of his things here, Nor." A crack of thunder rumbled, shaking the room. "And they'd be ruined by the storm. I think that creeper was right—we're gonna have to stay here tonight."

Nora heaved a sigh and sat on the rickety chair in the corner. "I knew this was a mistake. Mom should've told them to throw it all away. I should've refused to come."

Easton watched her for a moment, concern flickering in his eyes. Nora glared at him, annoyance causing her to clench her hands into fists. She didn't want his pity.

"Stop looking at me like that, East. I'm fine."

He pressed a kiss to the top of her head. "I'll run back to the office and see if I can talk the manager into giving me a few trash bags or something."

The door shut behind him with a *click,* leaving Nora sitting in the dimly lit room, surrounded by the ghosts of her father's lifelong love. Always his work, and never her.

The wall behind the boxes was speckled with spots of brown water damage. A shudder slid down her spine—*why,* of all motels, had her father chosen this one?

She forced herself out of the room and into the bathroom. Flicking on the light, she caught sight of herself in the cracked mirror, all dark eyes and even darker hair. Bracing her hands on the countertop, she heaved a breath, pushing against the emotion clawing at her throat.

She couldn't do this. Digging through her father's things—the work that he chose over his own blood—was a punishment Nora didn't deserve. "Damn you, Dad." She snarled the words, glancing away from her reflection and toward the boxes. They taunted her, a reminder of the years he missed, stuffed into cardboard. The sooner she got the work done, the sooner she could leave this all behind, go home, and forget him.

Keep that box closed, shoved into the back of her consciousness.

Nora turned the light off and headed back into the room, selecting one box at random and dumping it over, a quick flash of her hands. Papers spilled across the bed; black spiral notebooks and cream-colored file folders muddled together, an avalanche of pain. Pages curled and bent over each other, some yellowed from the passage of time. His handwriting was everywhere, the spidery scrawl on nearly every page. Familiar words caught her eye—characters from the stories she heard as a child, heroes from Greek mythology, tricksters from Norse stories. Sketches of their faces or artifacts from lore filled the margins, the pencil strokes strong and clear. A pang filled her chest at the sight—her father always enjoyed sketching.

A memory rose from the depths of her mind: *his eyes glinted behind his thick-framed glasses as he laughed and tugged one of her dark pigtails, a pencil flying across the page in front of him as he drew her face. His tongue poked out of his mouth as he squinted at her playfully, darkening the outline around her face with a final flourish before holding the paper up.*

"There! My fair maiden, sketched and immortalized forever." His smile sparked her own, spreading warmth across her body like a warm breeze. She could still feel the kiss he pressed against her forehead.

Scrubbing a hand across her eyes, Nora glared at the pages. *Enough of this.*

One happy memory didn't erase the multitude of lonely ones.

It didn't matter if he once loved her. Her father made his choices, and she would never forget that. So many of her years, wasted on waiting for him, hoping that the next time he would keep his promise.

But no.

The thought of being in the same place, where he so recently slept, worked, and then faded away, brought a trickle of dread down her spine. Tension filled her bones until she was sure they would shatter from the force.

Shove it all down into the box.

Sorrow clung to her like vapor. She brushed it away as best she could. Her father spent his time as he'd seen fit—searching for stories that weren't real. It struck her then: she was doing the same thing, waiting for a father who never existed.

Nora picked up another handful of pages, determined to get through the box before Easton returned.

Nora's commitment to stay strong in the face of her father's greatest love was difficult to stick to, but she gritted her teeth and made it work. The steady pounding of rain on the roof became background noise as she picked her way through two piles of papers, throwing some into the box she designated the 'trash' pile—it was already close to overflowing. Absorbed in her task, she moved on autopilot, giving the pages in her hand an objective once-over and making a quick decision. She didn't second-guess, just moved on to the next set of papers like a robot completing its designated task.

The research was obscure, and Nora scanned the pages with the barest prickle of interest. There were reams of paper with rough sketches of a box, unremarkable with a latched lid, and a lot of characters in a language she couldn't read. So many pages of the box—why? She paused to study the drawing, thinking of her own mental box—how funny that they resembled each other. She must've seen this before, in her father's office at home as a child. Pandora was always a favorite of Nora's, their names so similar.

Another memory surfaced; her father's desk strewn with

pages as he rubbed his tired eyes. She, in an overstuffed armchair on the other side of the heavy wooden desk, listening as he lectured a student on a story about a box holding immense suffering...

She shrugged the memory off, refocusing on her task. Her father's handwriting covered pages from top to bottom, as if he jotted down frantic notes. She could imagine him sitting at this very table, a hand in his hair as he worked into the wee hours of the morning.

The door creaked open as she heaved the third carton onto the bed. Easton poked his head into the room. He shook droplets from his hair and stepped into the room.

"It's really coming down out there. Sorry I disappeared, that guy must never have the chance to talk to anyone. I couldn't get him to stop once he started." He sat down on the edge of the bed, taking in the mess. "Find anything interesting yet?"

Nora slung another notebook into the 'trash' pile. "Nope."

"Do you need any help?"

"No, I can handle this part." She glanced at him, pushing dark curls behind pierced ears with a jagged smile, false on her lips. "You're my moral support. I don't expect you to dig through old papers."

She could taste the thunderstorm on her tongue, mingling with the musty scent of the pages. Dust motes speckled the air. The sound of static filled the room as Easton turned the dial on the ancient TV, searching for something to watch before settling on a blurry sitcom. The laugh track echoed through the room as Nora chucked more pages into the 'trash' pile, papers spilling onto the floor, a flood of hurried words and smudged ink.

A couple hours passed, the only noise the laugh track and Easton's grumbled complaints. Nora worked her way through her father's belongings with ruthless efficiency. The empty boxes began to pile up and she paused to break them down, a thrill filling her chest as she destroyed something.

She pulled out a small wooden box with an intricate latch from the next carton. A jolt passed through her, sharp as lightning—it was the very box from the sketches she found earlier. No bigger than the palm of her hand, there was a primordial aura surrounding it, as if it was steeped in a mysterious substance that crackled with a barely-there frequency. She ran a finger across the faint etchings carved into the lid, her mind puzzling over the design.

"What do you think it is?" Her voice was soft, the question laced with hesitation, as if she didn't really want to know.

Easton looked over at her question, an eyebrow raised. "It's so small. Maybe it's for like, keepsakes or something?" He scratched his chin, eyes gravitating back toward the television. Annoyance flared in Nora's chest at his lack of interest. Before she could respond, he spoke again. "Does it open?"

A feeling not unlike dread pooled in her stomach as her fingers connected with the cool metal of the latch. Thunder cracked outside the door, and Nora paused, a prickling of awareness filling her senses. Thoughts skipped against the matching box in her mind, caressing the length of the wooden surface, the darkness inside pressing against her touch as if it were drawing breath.

But this wasn't *her* box. What could be so scary about a trinket?

Shoving her sudden nerves aside, she flipped open the lid in one smooth motion. Lightning flashed through the cracked curtains, and a bolt of blue electricity flew from the box into her fingertips, racing through her flesh with a sharp bite. She dropped the artifact with a yelp as the room went black. The television was thrown into darkness with a hiss and the slow fade of the screen, the fluorescent overhead lights flickering out with an abruptness that stole the air from her lungs.

Easton let out a curse while Nora pressed trembling fingers to her mouth. *What was that?* Her bones hummed with unexplainable energy, the air around her crackling.

"I guess the storm knocked out the power." His forehead creased in annoyance, Easton stomped over to the window to throw the curtains wide, barely giving Nora a glance. The murky light from outside spilled through the dirty window, leaving half the room in thick swaths of shadow. How his attitude changed, darkening like the storm-strewn sky, since entering the motel room. "The whole building is out. *Shit.*" He cursed under his breath again before shoving on his worn sneakers with angry movements. "Guess I'm going to talk to that weirdo again."

"Easton—" Nora began, attempting to get his attention—to ask him if he'd seen the eerie blue glow, if her eyes were playing tricks on her—but he waved her words away.

"I won't be long." He slipped out of the creaking door before she could say another word, into the raging storm without a backward glance. Leaving her alone in the gloom.

Nora paced the length of the room, her boots catching on the shag carpet with every jerky step. The sharp stabbing pain hadn't faded away yet, and her heart gave a lurch. Static electricity. It must be.

Some unexplainable instinct laughed cruelly in the back of her mind. *It was the box, you know it was.*

Impossible.

Heart racing, Nora turned toward the carton still perched on the bed, running through all the pages she read in the hours before. There was nothing about electricity, or conduction, or anything else close to what happened with the power.

The room seemed to close in around her. Without Easton there, invisible eyes followed her every move from the shadows. The room shifted in the corner of her eye, as if inhaling a breath. As if waiting to see what happened next.

She was spooking herself, she knew it. *There's nothing here.*

"Sure, my dad died in this room–and probably others, too, over the years–but there's nothing in here with me." She said the words firmly, as if speaking them out loud would still the quaking in her chest. She huffed a breath and raked her fingers through dark curls, the sharp bite against her scalp clearing the fear a bit. "Get a grip, Nora. Jesus."

She rubbed her hands together, moving closer to the window to see if there was a wound, something to explain the continued sensation curling under her skin. Her fingers looked normal aside from a small mark, like the after-image in a flash of light—would static electricity leave a mark? Her eyes roved over the delicate latch on the box again, a recollection snagging at the edge of her thoughts, a fluttering that was lost the moment she tried to grasp onto it.

Her mind whirled as she struggled to come up with a logical reason for what she experienced, for the mark it left behind on her pale flesh, but nothing made sense. The storm turned the unfamiliar room into a place where shadows lurked in the corners. The hair on the back of her neck rose as she squinted into the dark bathroom—was it her imagination, or was someone moving there?

"Calm down, you idiot." She dug her nails into her palms, willing her heart to stop galloping in her ribcage, and forced herself back to the bed. Something threatening lingered in the air, like the scent of smoke long after the flames burned out. She swallowed down the rising hysteria in her chest. "Focus on the boxes. Get through the papers. Easton will be back any minute."

The wooden box sat innocently on the bed, its lid shut tight once again. She nudged it with her foot, ignoring the voice in her head that scoffed at her childish fear to touch the thing again. Maybe there was a note in the cardboard bin that explained what that thing was.

It was difficult to see anything written on the papers in the darkened room. Her hands were clammy as she smoothed pages into a stack, at a loss at what to do to pass the time, to distract her frazzled nerves. The sound of rain echoed in her ears, the scent of mildew rising from the carpet as wind howled, thrashing against the window with a rattling bellow. The roof must leak.

Forcing a deep breath in her nose and out between her clenched teeth, Nora closed her eyes, willing her body to relax. The stress of dealing with her father's things, combined with the loss of power and the strange storm outside, overwhelmed her.

A loud scream rang out from the other side of the thin wall, and Nora froze, listening as the shriek turned into a cackling that grew louder, piercing her ears. Her heart began to race again, and before she knew what she was doing, her hand was closing around the doorknob and she was stepping out into the covered walk. The rain battered the worn motel, roaring down from blackened clouds, forcing her to hug the building as she walked the few feet to her neighbor's cracked door. Something must be wrong.

The '8' was rusted and dangled, upside-down, to cover the peephole. Nora knocked, barely able to hear it above the cacophony of the storm. Her stomach dropped when the door creaked open at her touch. She nudged the door open as another agonized cry sounded from inside.

"Hello? Are you okay in here? I heard a strange noise, and with the storm, I wanted to make sure…" Nora trailed off as she scanned the room, her eyes catching on a shifting shadow in the murky darkness of the bathroom. A woman stepped closer, her lavender bathrobe shining like a beacon in the gloom, her face still concealed in the dark.

"Oh, that was kind of you, dear. I was admiring my reflection when the power went out." The laugh sounded again, making the hair on Nora's arms raise. "But don't be modest—there's no need to lie to me. I know why you're in here."

Fear scuttled across Nora's spine. "What?"

The woman *tsked* and took another step forward. Nora could make out her hands clutching the top of her robe closed near her neck as she moved. "Now now, many have traveled hundreds of miles to see me—I'm not ashamed or afraid to admit to my great beauty. Come closer and you can see like you wanted."

Her feet moved without thought, her breaths coming in quick gasps. *Something wasn't right.* An acrid taste filled Nora's mouth as she finally caught sight of the woman's face, the need to scream clawing at her throat.

The woman was covered with lesions, weeping with pus, glistening as they caught the dim light. Her wild laugh rang through the room again as Nora stumbled back out the door and down the walkway, the need to escape searing through her veins. She slammed the door of her room shut behind her and dead bolted it, collapsing to the floor. *Where was Easton?*

"What the *hell* was that?" She gasped, her eyes wild as she pressed her back into the nearest wall, ignoring the paint that flaked off onto her shoulders. The woman must be sick. Yes, and the illness affected her mind, warping her reality. The image of the festering boils filled her mind again and Nora dry heaved into the corner.

She couldn't sit still, pacing the length of her room, straining her ears to hear any noise to indicate that the woman was coming after her, double checking that she locked the door after her. Her hands were trembling wildly, the ache in her skull sharpening with every beat of her frantic heart.

The door rattled, and Nora let out a yelp.

"Nora!" *Easton. Thank God. It was only Easton.* "Nora, why is the door locked? Open it up, I'm getting freaking drenched out here!"

It took her three tries to unlock the door with trembling fingers, and when she finally managed, Easton burst inside in a flurry of wet clothes.

"Damn storm." He grumbled, before frowning at her. "What the hell? Why did you lock the door?"

She launched into her explanation, telling him about the wild laughter and her decision to check that their neighbor was okay. She faltered as she told him about the woman's appearance, swallowing down the bile that tore at her esophagus. Easton's expression changed from annoyed to skeptical.

He muttered something Nora couldn't quite catch, raking his fingers through his hair as he released a long-suffering sigh, as if he were humoring her. "Well, I got some snacks from the vending machine for dinner, so there's no reason to leave this room again. We're gonna hunker down here, and as soon as this goddamn storm is over, we are packing up the truck and getting the hell out of here." He wrapped a damp arm around her shoulders and squeezed. His familiar smell, licorice and sandalwood, filled Nora's nose and her shoulders drooped, relaxing enough to take another deep breath. He pressed a kiss to her forehead. "I'm sorry, Nor, I bet that was terrifying."

Nora closed her eyes and let the heat from his body seep into hers, ignoring the water that dripped onto her skin. "I'm really glad you're here with me."

He held her at arm's length, studying her face for a few moments before responding. "You doing okay? I'm sure this isn't easy."

Nora wasn't sure what to say.

The room was dark when Easton closed the curtains. "Oh, shit." He fumbled with his back pocket for a moment before pulling out a small flashlight. "I did manage to find this—swiped it from the front office. He had one, so it's not like he'll miss it." He pressed the button, the weak beam of light illuminating his face, shadowing his eyes. Nora shivered at the sight, turning away to check the door was locked once more before sitting on the bed and rubbing her hands along the tops of her thighs, her nerves still on edge.

"Yeah. I'll get back to going through the boxes so we can get out of here in the morning."

Easton turned to peer through the curtains, his eyes on the dark clouds looming across the sky. "It doesn't look like it's going to clear up anytime soon." He turned back to Nora, a slight smile on his face. "Take a break and share some chips with me."

He turned out the pockets of his hoodie, throwing his treasure on the bed with a flourish. "Dinner is served, my lady." He bowed, making Nora laugh as warmth filled her chest. Easton always knew what to do to keep her afloat.

They sat, leaning against flat pillows and each other, sharing bags of chips and chocolate bars. Nora's gaze kept sliding over to the little wooden box perched on the nightstand. Her fingers tingled at the memory of its smooth wooden top, the flash of fire burning her, a moment before the lights flickered off. She rubbed the tender skin.

Her thought from earlier continued creeping in, hovering at the edge of her consciousness in the silence. *Had* the box caused the power to go out?

It was ridiculous, of course—the storm was the cause of the power outage—but the suspicion niggled at the corner of her mind, refusing to be dislodged. A tale she would've believed as a child. She poked and prodded at the memory of that moment; the box opening, the hinges shining in the lamplight for less than a second before everything fell into darkness.

Goosebumps covered her as the woman in the room next door—her lips cracked and peeling as she cackled, her eyes rolling in their sockets as the sores on her skin seemed to fester and ooze in real time—flashed in front of her eyes.

Nora forced the thoughts from her mind and snuggled back

into the covers next to Easton, his gaze trained on the screen of his phone as he tapped brightly colored tiles and watched them topple, points tallying rapidly in the corner. She yawned, her eyes drooping with exhaustion when Easton absently pressed a kiss to her forehead as the storm continued to rumble ominously outside the thin walls of their motel room. She would continue looking at her father's things in a few minutes —the papers could wait a little bit longer.

Blood covered her hands. Thick and congealed, Nora couldn't tear her eyes from the way the light in the room caught the ruby red, like gloves. There was no pain—was it her blood? Her mind struggled to make sense of the situation, turning over sluggishly as her skin crawled. She flipped her hands over, heart jolting in her chest at the sight of the small box in her palm, its pale surface speckled with bright crimson.

"Why are you touching that?" The voice sounded right next to her, one so familiar her stomach dropped to the floor. She turned to meet her father's dark eyes, his black hair silvered, just as she remembered.

"Dad?" His eyes didn't budge from the box lying innocently in her bloody hands, and for a moment, Nora struggled to come up with a reason, to explain why she was drenched in someone else's ichor. "I—"

"Don't touch it." His words were gritted out between clenched teeth, spectacles flashing in the light. His body was mottled with the purple and gray of decay, a far cry from its usual rich brown. One of his hands smacked into hers, the box tumbling from her grasp and onto the floor, the latch coming undone and cracking open.

"What the hell is your problem?" she snapped, fingers rubbing what was sure to be bruises.

Her father's eyes snapped to her face, his gaze hardening. "You already opened it, didn't you? *Answer me!"* He screamed the last, and Nora recoiled from him. This couldn't be real. Her father never spoke like that—he was calm, studious, a quiet man with a serious air.

He began pacing the room, hands tugging at his scalp. His nails clawed faster with each step, horror ballooning in her chest as strips of skin sloughed off, leaving his skull gleaming in the light. "What have you *done*? This is colossal, catastrophic—"

Irritation surged through her, even as her eyes widened at the sight before her.

He was *rotting*.

The words came, tinged in the frantic beating of her heart. "What the *hell* are you talking about? I thought you were *dead*—why am I even here in this disgusting motel room if you've been here this whole time?"

His feet faltered as he turned to meet her eyes, his face twisting at her words, his nails limned with vermilion. "Nora, Nora you don't understand. This isn't real, this isn't happening, I *am* dead—"

Her skull ached, a sharp stab of pain right in the center of her forehead. She wrenched away, shaking her head. "No, no you can't be dead, you're standing right here. What kind of game are you playing?"

Her father's face changed again, thinning out, skin stretched taut over his bones like a Halloween mask. "There's no game, Nor, there's only death." He pointed a bony finger at the box, still lying on its side on the floor, his eyes burning pits. "It's empty. You opened it, and now, you'll pay the price."

Her mind spun wildly. "This doesn't make any sense!" She couldn't control her voice, rising wilder, shrieking higher the more she spoke, as out of control as the fear in her belly. "It's a wooden box, it was in your things. How are you here if you're dead? Why would you have some harbinger of death?"

When he didn't reply, Nora stomped on her door. "Answer me, Dad!"

His mouth opened in a snarl as the door blew open—

THUNDER RUMBLED AND NORA GASPED, opening her eyes to the flashlight's weak beam on the ceiling. Easton let out a snore on her other side and turned his head away as she sat up, wiping a hand—no blood in sight—against her jeans, clammy fingers trembling.

A dream. It was just a dream.

The power was still out, there was no blood, and her father was still gone. Her chest ached at the knowledge, and she squeezed her eyes shut, forcing breaths out of her nose slowly. She could still smell it, the stench of her father's rotting flesh coating her throat like a film. Tearing herself from the bed, she crossed to the window and threw open the cheap curtains, struggling to calm her racing heart. The rain was still pouring from the sky, lightning flashing in the distance. The jagged bolt of light illuminated the courtyard, framing two figures standing at the edge of the building, saturated by the deluge. A familiar greasy ponytail was visible as the men moved around each other, like the earth orbiting the sun.

Nora squinted at them—what were they doing out there in the rain? A jolt exploded in her belly as she watched them surge forward, grappling with each other, their movements fierce and violent, punctuated by loud bursts of rumbling clouds. Flashes of lightning lit the world in shadow and white light, like a movie missing some of its frames. Horror rose in her chest as she saw a flash of silver—*a knife*—glint in the next flash of brilliant electricity, before the hand holding it collided against the motel manager's chest with a juddering twitch.

Bile rose in Nora's throat as she watched the man fall to the ground, blood seeping into the puddle of rain around him. The second man stood over the body, wiping the knife on his pants before tucking it out of sight. He glanced up suddenly, causing Nora to throw herself onto the moldering carpet at her feet, heart crashing wildly, so loud she was sure he could hear it over the storm. He saw her. He would kill her next.

A sudden noise came from behind her—Nora flinched before she realized it was Easton, mumbling in his sleep. She risked moving back to the window, glancing out only to see a bloody trail from the spot where the manager had fallen to the courtyard's entrance, over by the office door. The other man was nowhere to be seen.

Nora moved to the bed, nudging Easton awake. "East, wake up!" The words slipped from her lips, frantic, her fingers shuddering.

"Mmm, wha?" Easton opened his eyes blearily. "Nor, what's wrong?"

"There was a fight in the courtyard. We have to get out of here."

He blinked, expression clearing as he absorbed her words. "What?"

"I saw a man murdered, that's what I'm saying! Get up, let's go!" She shivered, crouched on the floor beside the bed.

Easton sat up. "Murdered?" He rubbed a hand across his forehead. "What do you mean, murdered? Are you sure you weren't dreaming?"

She shoved the lone chair underneath the doorknob, flinching at the metallic rattle. A chair wouldn't keep her safe. They needed to *go.*

Shaking her head, Nora pulled him off the bed to the window. Her knees trembled with each step. "I was already awake from a nightmare. Look, you can see the blood. It's still there—" She broke off, her eyes scanning the scene out the window. *Where was the blood?* She had seen it, soaking into the concrete, turning the rainwater dark as an oil spill. The man laid *there...*

Easton raised an eyebrow. "I don't see anything."

"They were fighting, and one man pulled out a knife and... then he *stabbed* the other guy. The motel manager! He collapsed, right there." She wrung her hands, mind racing in the silence that echoed with her yell. "Maybe the rain washed it away."

"Did the rain wash the body away, as well?"

"That's not funny, Easton. I'm being serious."

He rolled his eyes, and something in her chest fractured. *He doesn't believe me.*

"Nora, you had a nightmare. Stop stressing and go back to sleep. This place is freaking weird, and with all the stress you're dealing with, it's no wonder you're seeing crazy shit in your dreams." He tugged her away from the window, back toward the bed. "Let's go back to bed. It's like, three in the morning."

Allowing him to pull her back down to the creaky mattress, Nora listened as Easton's breaths evened back out, her mind replaying the scene again. Surety filled her—the two men fighting. The knife—it was burned in crisp technicolor in her brain — the body collapsing in a heap... It was *real,* the horror slithering down her spine as she watched. Her father's wild eyes flashed across her mind, his purple skin cracked and sloughing off like in her dream.

She moved before she meant to, shaking off Easton's touch and the scratchy sheets to pace the shag carpet in her socks. Static electricity prickled up her calf, feeling *so unlike* the sharp blast of whatever spilled from the box.

The bizarre dream swirled through her mind like a shroud, coating everything in a film of sticky uncertainty. This motel—this entire *day*—what did it all mean? The woman in the room next door, the storm, her dream...and the box, unmoved from its place on the nightstand. Awareness filled the stagnant air, turning her stomach and causing the hair on the back of her neck to stand on end.

Something was missing, some important piece of information tying everything together, but instinct told her that it *was* all connected. She caught sight of the stack of boxes, waiting like broken statues in the gloom for her to dig through their contents. Remnants of a broken man's life, the culmination of years spent researching. Surely answers were there, tucked between spidery scrawls and pencil smudges.

No time like the present.

Box after box, she searched in the faint watery light from the old flashlight. The pounding rain and Easton's soft snores were her constant companions as she dug through the pages covered with her father's writing, the familiar words blurring to an endless stream of inky black and grayscale marks. Nora pushed her hair back with her wrist, alert to any noise outside the crappy motel room as she pushed through the stacks of papers. Where did the man go, the murderer? Was he waiting outside the door?

Forcing a breath, she refocused on the last box, cursing out loud when her fingers scraped against the cardboard bottom. *Nothing.* She glanced inside as she moved to toss the box into the now-mountainous discard pile, her eyes snagging on a jagged paper tucked into the corner, caught between the edges.

Gingerly, Nora peeled the ancient scrap from the box, careful not to abuse the already ragged page, unfolding it slowly. There, in the center: the wooden box, inked with every detail captured, clear as a photograph. Her eyes darted across the room, comparing the drawing to the real thing, before scanning the faded words along the ragged page.

The box holds incredible—the rest of the line cut off, torn free from whatever book housed the words for years. The next line circled in Nora's mind, her skin prickling with nerves as she read it again and again.

Beware the power of the box. Do not open—

Her skull pounded with the words, her heart racing. Light peeked through the yellowed curtains, casting a long shadow behind the box. For a moment Nora was sure the shadow was writhing, shifting like dark flames, but when she blinked everything was back to normal. The paper—what did it mean *don't open the box?*

Again, her mind cast back to the story of Pandora, to the sketch of the box and the strange writing. The steady drone of her father's voice filled her ears like a distant hum, and she was back in the armchair in his office.

"Pandora unleashed plague and horror on the world. Disease and death, it followed her until she couldn't escape it. She poisoned the world."

TIME PASSED in fits and starts, and Nora sat, consumed by the threads of memory, unable to pull them into focus, to examine them closer, until a sound broke the haze in which she was wrapped. She blinked, looking up as Easton let out a loud yawn, and scrubbed a hand through his hair as he sat up. blinking at her with bleary eyes. "How long have you been awake?"

Nora turned back to the pages strewn across the floor, her hands automatically shuffling them into piles, stuffing them into emptied boxes and white plastic trash bags. "Long enough. I made it through all the boxes."

"Excellent." He crossed to the window, throwing upon the curtains with a grimace. "Ugh, so bright. The storm's gone, it looks like. Let's get everything packed up and get the hell out of this place, grab some breakfast."

Nora quickly finished collecting the pages and notebooks, throwing anything related to Pandora and the strange little box into a container. The rest she shoved into a big pile for Easton to take to the dumpster out in the parking lot. He pressed a kiss to her forehead as he picked up the last bag of trash. "This the last of it?"

"Yes. Then we can carry these two to the car and head home."

Easton left the room with a wink, and Nora turned back to the box, still sitting on the nightstand where she placed it hours before. Her stomach ached. What was she supposed to do with the damn thing? Assuming her father's story—and her memory—were accurate, that box was trouble. Guilt rushed over her, making her spirit quake.

Pandora's box. She opened the thing, unable to resist the box that so closely resembled her own—*Nora's box.* She swallowed down the bile that threatened to surface with the guilt.

She trembled with the possibility that it was her fault that the manager died, that the woman next door was covered in a horrific rash. Nora scrubbed at her tired eyes, willing it to all be a dream—a horrible nightmare.

She grabbed the box and shoved it underneath the mattress. No one would find it there; the motel room looked as if it hadn't been cleaned in over a decade.

Easton flipped off the ramshackle building as they loaded the final two boxes into the car, slamming the trunk shut and climbing inside the front seats. "Zero out of five stars. This place was a dump!" He put the key in the ignition and the car into gear, pulling out onto the empty stretch of highway.

Nora could feel the tightness in her chest loosening with every mile that passed, her breath coming easier. The nightmares wouldn't follow them—the box and all its contents could stay back there, at that shitty motel in the middle of nowhere. The ruined people and their ruinous actions, the ones that broke up families and destroyed lives.

Easton's stomach let out a loud rumble not ten minutes down the highway.

"I'm hungry. There's gotta be a place to stop and eat around here somewhere, hasn't there?"

Nora closed her eyes and leaned her head against the back of her seat, allowing her muscles to relax. The exhaustion was catching up to her. "I'm sure there's a diner or coffee chain where we can stop nearby."

The car rattled over a large bump, Nora's stomach dropping with sudden fear, her hands gripping the center console in a flurry of panic.

Easton chuckled, the edges dark, as if he were mocking her. "Still reeling from that nightmare, Nor?"

She ignored his words, pushing the flash of pain inside the mental box, adding it to her collection of misery. The memories buried there strained against the lid, and it took all her focus to force them back down, slipping the latch closed. She breathed out, turning her attention outward once more.

No more thoughts about boxes and the secrets hidden inside.

Her eyes alighted on the dark cloud at the horizon—another storm already threatening. Was it typical to see so much rain in this part of the desert? She couldn't wait to leave and never return. The woman with the weeping sores flashed across her mind once more, causing her to shudder.

"You okay?" Easton's voice pulled her back. She turned toward him, taking in his profile, hair light against the looming clouds ahead, and smiled, a wry twist of lips. The shadows lingering underneath his blue eyes.

"Yeah, everything is fine."

"I was thinking about your weird dream last night—your mind was playing tricks on you. That motel was the worst." He reached over and squeezed her fist, clenched on her thigh. She told herself that the weight of his fingers was reassuring, not restricting.

"I'll be glad to get home." Her words sounded brittle. Broken. Nothing had changed.

"Yeah, I can't wait to sleep in my own bed tonight."

Nora turned toward Easton, determined to make the long drive home fun—it was the least she could do, he came all this way to be with her—when she caught sight of the little wooden box, sitting innocently in the center of the backseat.

"What the hell?" Her voice shook as she breathed the words.

Easton looked in the rear-view mirror, and grinned. "Oh yeah, you almost left that behind. I found it on the floor, by the bed. You're welcome." He turned to face her fully, giving her a wink.

Sick churned her stomach. The nightmare wasn't over. She couldn't escape. She unbuckled her seatbelt, lunging into the backseat, the need to throw the box out the window consuming her like wildfire.

The car jerked as Nora bumped into Easton's arm. "Nora! What are you doing? Shit!" He righted their trajectory, throwing Nora into the side of her seat. Her fingers stretched, the box just out of reach. *So close...*

A prickling awareness slid across her skin. She looked up in time to see the red mack truck, barreling right toward them as Easton ran a stop sign. The driver laid on his horn, but it was too late. Easton moved in slow motion, his foot pressing toward the brake.

The semi struck their car with blistering force.

Nora heard the crunch of metal, the crystalline sound of glass breaking—

—and the little wooden box, simple and innocent, glowed with blue electricity, out of reach, the moment before the world went dark.

2

A DOVE'S SONG

AVA LYNN BECK

I – THE BEACH

The girl stares out her bedroom window. She admires the sunset, how its molten colors splay along the horizon until eventually, day fades to night and there's nothing left but the vast dark sea. Waves lap against the sand, foaming up the rocks, its rhythm like clockwork. It's disturbingly hypnotic.

The girl has never been fond of the sea. Perhaps it is the mysteriousness of the ocean itself, or the gloom it casts over her quaint coastal town. Regardless, the water discomforts her. It lies too still for something so triumphant. Its permanent state of calm drowns the girl in quiet.

The girl hates the quiet.

More specifically, she hates how it makes her think. She doesn't want to think. She wants a distraction, something to take her away from her cooped room and the paint peeling off its walls, the creak of the front door when her mother left for work.

Left her here.

Her mother hadn't locked her inside by any means. Rather,

she asked the girl to stay safe, away from the danger looming outside. This made the girl angry, but the fear in her mother's eyes churned her frustration to sympathy. Now, she's paying the price.

The girl does not itch to go outside. She considers herself more of a homebody than most. Unlike the rest of the town, she does not enjoy the wind knotting her hair, salt coating her skin like seasoned meat. She relishes in warmth and comfort. She finds none of that in being trapped. More than anything, she craves opportunity. At least venturing outside would let her experience something, anything other than the bubble in which her mother framed her.

Her mother has her reasons. After her father left, her mother had no choice but to worry. About the girl, about rent, about college funds and job cuts and grocery bills that seemed to grow more and more than the girl ever did.

The girl doesn't remember her father's face, nor does she want to. She doesn't want to know what he looks like, the same way she doesn't want to imagine any other man approaching her mother, admiring her the same way one might observe an open invitation.

It is another reason she agreed to stay. Bordering herself inside is the only comfort the girl can offer her mother while she's out, earning just enough for the pair to eat, drink, and bathe.

There were other methods, too. The girl used to work. She waitressed at the diner down the road, plastering her best smile in exchange for man-handled tips. She dealt with haggled remarks, eyes roaming her uniform, even the occasional grab for her waist or skirt when bussing tables. She convinced herself it was worth her paycheck, and a few extra sandwiches salvaged from orders she "accidentally" mistook.

Her mother hadn't been fond of it. She admired the girl's help. After all, their list of costs was endless. But at the expense of a daughter? Her mother wouldn't have it. The girl tried convincing her otherwise, but the deal was struck. The town just wasn't safe.

The killings made it worse.

The girl can't remember when they first began. Maybe it was the day she noticed a poster on her walk to the bus. *Charlie Flannigan*. The name was too common, but the girl recognized the face. The first boy who had tried kissing her behind the bleachers. To this day, she is grateful she said no, that the strength she gathered from hauling dishes and packaged meat helped her escape the boy's clutches. But that didn't rid her of her shame. Her slipping away freed Charlie to find another target, a new pursuit. Nancy Polick hadn't fled so easily.

The second time the girl saw Charlie was in the hands of police officers, an assault chained to his name. She hoped to never see him again, aside from maybe a mugshot. It was then she realized the poster she saw had the wrong label. It wasn't *rapist* or *offender* branded above his head, but MISSING, as if it was in her benefit to find him.

It seemed like a fluke. A mysterious disappearance, one that could happen to anyone. Until recently.

The killings have been going on for months. Posters adorn every telephone poll in a twenty-mile radius. Despite the fear her mother upholds, the rest of the town doesn't bat an eye. It's as if they don't see it, or frankly, choose to ignore it.

The girl sees it. She simply doesn't care.

Every morning, she watches the news, hears anchor after anchor spew about a predator on the loose. Every morning, she wonders why. Why worry about one when they should worry about them all? When will they notice the predators at their front doors? The fangs of their neighbors. The claws of their colleagues. Every man the girl has encountered has been more animal than friend, hunting women to satiate their lack of control. The killer has yet to attack a woman, and still, men choose to believe they're not in danger. Why should they when they create danger themselves?

Sometimes, the girl wishes the killer would never get caught. Maybe that makes her morbid. Or maybe it makes her sane. It doesn't matter. No one will know how she feels, not as long as she stays shut inside this house.

Aggravated, the girl finishes off her last slice of pizza. The burnt crust scrapes her tongue raw, but she ignores it. She can imagine her mother scolding, insisting she order take-out instead, but the girl doesn't carry fond experiences with delivery drivers. She doesn't want to add a new one to the list, nor does she care to wait any longer to satiate her howling stomach, so she tries, and fails, at operating the oven herself. She's gotten better at it, just enough for the frozen dough to turn edible. Swallowing the dregs of her water glass, she goes to head upstairs, when she hears a noise outside.

Her first instinct tells her it's her mother. The girl doesn't recall her mother's current job, only that the schedule is irregular. One day, her mother would come home in the morning and drive her to the bus stop for school. The other, her mother would be gone, leaving the girl to fend for herself with the heavy tin of her lunch box and the knife she kept strapped to her jeans.

Even if her mother came home tonight, it wouldn't be this early. The sun has hardly set, and yet, the girl is certain she heard a woman's voice. Soft and elegant, nothing like the grunts of drunken strangers roaming the beach.

Her mother would tell her to stay inside, but her mother also taught her to protect herself. This woman could easily be an intruder, and if not, she could be a victim. Low wails echo through the window. Whoever the woman is, it sounds as though she's in pain.

Rushing upstairs, the girl pulls the knife from under her pillow and stashes it in her pocket. She then hauls herself to the bathroom, snatches the pitiful excuse she has of a first aid kit – a Band-Aid, a half-used tube of Neosporin, and an open alcohol wipe tied shut with a rubber band – and leaves the house, trailing the withered noise until she hits the water's edge.

And finds nothing.

Maybe it was a seagull, she thinks. Her house's warped architecture distorts sounds all the time. The noise could have easily reverberated off the walls, morphing into something nonexistent. A woman who isn't real.

The girl turns to the sky, slightly annoyed, and shrugs. She ran out for nothing, but at least she's out. It's the first time she's skipped curfew in weeks. She'd be a fool to waste it.

She decides to walk along the beach. The girl relishes the cool night air, the sand crinkling between her toes, the rhythmic flow of the waves, when it dawns on her.

She left the door unlocked.

Her mother might worry about stolen trinkets, but not the girl. As far as she's concerned, her father took their valuables years ago. Their house is but a shell of who she really is. No, she fears her mother returning home, finding a stranger in the living room.

And if they had a weapon…

She can't leave her mother defenseless, not over a noise that she now knows was nothing but a measly bird.

The girl starts to race back when she hears another noise. It's the same one she heard before, only this time, it isn't weak or muffled. It's decipherable. She makes out words, clean and crisp, like the sudden pop of a soda can.

"Hello," the woman says. "And who might you be?"

The girl swivels, but the woman is out of sight. She hides her name deep in her throat. Her mother taught her to hold her guard for a reason.

She'd die if she didn't.

The woman repeats her question. The girl chokes out an answer.

"I live here." She tries to speak defiantly, but her words come out frightened. She hesitates before asking, "Who are you?"

"I am called many names," the woman responds. "You may call me Arina."

Arina. The name doesn't sound horrifying. If anything, the girl finds it enchanting. She softens at the word, perhaps from the power the knowledge gives her. She knows the woman's identity, meanwhile the girl's is kept secret. It's a relieving thing, entrapping someone when you know you're safe.

The power makes the girl bold. Demanding. "Where are you?" she asks.

"Look towards the waves, my child."

The girl turns. The ocean was empty before, but now, there she is. A beautiful woman wading in the waves. She wears a white chemise, the fabric rippling like water down her body. The girl blinks, confused. She scoured every inch of this beach and found nothing. The woman couldn't have appeared from thin air, and yet, she could have only come from the sea.

Her gown defies any science the girl knows. Despite where the woman stands, the fabric appears dry, as does her hair. Long black curls cascade down her back, untouched by the dampened sea. Her eyes are piercing green, emeralds shining like Christmas lights against her snow-white skin. Too white. If the girl squints hard enough, she swears it's translucent. A bluish tint runs over Arina's body following the path of her veins, and there's a sheen to her that in the right light reminds the girl of scales. Compared to the darker shades of the rest of the town, the deep tans of the girl, her mother, and the fishermen nearby, the woman looks unworldly. Her rarity makes her beauty terrifying.

She's too beautiful, the girl thinks. *Too perfect to be here.* And yet here she stands, tip-toeing her way to the shore.

The girl doesn't ask about the water or where the woman came from. She doubts she'll understand. Not as though it matters. This woman – *Arina* – exists. It's enough of a fascination to beg the question, "Why are you here?"

Arina tosses her a smile, her pearl white teeth framed in coal-colored lips. "Why should I not be?"

"What are you talking about?"

"You may live here, child, but you do not live alone." The girl tries to comprehend, but Arina deters her before she gets the chance. "Why do you lock yourself away?"

How – the girl's mind blanks. The woman can't know that, but then, if she truly came from the water, she would've seen the girl in her window, peering at the waves for hours. With the cable shut off and her books read twenty times over, staring at the sea is the only reprieve the girl has left.

Aside from watching the boy across the street.

But no one needs to know about that.

"It's not safe," the girl replies. "Mom says I shouldn't be outside."

"Then why are you now?"

The girl bites her tongue, afraid she'll sound stupid if she explains why. Thinking again, she assumes she'll sound stupid regardless, so she settles for, "I don't know."

"But you do." Arina assesses the girl from head to toe, then gestures to the knife in her hand. The girl tucks it defensively behind her back. Arina smiles. She circles the girl, cooing as if impressed. Unperturbed.

"You want to protect," she says.

The girl shakes her head. "No."

"No?"

"I want to not have to protect."

Arina's grin deepens. "You do not have to. That is why I am here."

"You know what's been happening? To our town?"

Arina nods. "You have nothing to fear, child. The danger in this city will not harm you. I will not let it."

The girl's hand hovers over her knife, just in case. She thinks for a moment, then says, "And my mother? You'll protect her, too, right?"

"Of course." Arina bends, tucking a strand of hair behind the girl's ear. "Our kind must stick together."

The girl wonders what Arina means by this when she notices a light reflecting on the water. It's a different color than the moonlight, a dull shade of yellow and one she knows too well.

She swivels to the house. Unlike earlier, the kitchen is lit. A shadow crosses the window, sending chills up the girl's back.

Someone's home.

"Go, dearest," Arina says.

The girl stills, surprised, not by her mother's appearance, but by herself. She doesn't want to leave.

"Will I see you again?"

"Perhaps," Arina considers. "But you mustn't come when you hear my song."

So that's what the noise was. It hardly sounded like a song, the notes of Arina's voice more strained than fluid. Maybe it sounded different to other ears.

The girl looks into Arina's eyes and shudders, finding slits where her pupils should be.

"Why not?" she asks.

"It is not meant for you." Arina smooths the girl's hair over her head. "Come after it has finished. Then, I will be waiting."

At her final word, the girl dashes off. She tries not to look back but for some reason, she can't help herself. When she turns, Arina is already gone, the wading sea like a dark pool in her wake.

Instead of using the front door, the girl climbs up the patio screen to her second-story window. She crawls under the covers right as her mother creaks open the door, the hallway light spilling into the dark.

The girl flutters her eyes, feigning exhaustion.

"I made pizza," she yawns. "There's some left in the fridge if you want it."

Her mother tilts her head. Her dark curls have escaped the loose bun she wore before. Food and drink stains cover her clothes, though the girl does not know why. She can, however, place the bruises on her mother's arms, the indentations of fingers pressed into her skin.

"I saw. Thank you, dove." Her mother leans on the door frame. "Did you have a good night?"

The girl nods sleepily, though this time, she is not pretending. Arina's voice plays in her head like a lullaby. Her muscles begin to relax until she feels herself sinking into the mattress, her senses intoxicated by the woman she met minutes before.

"I'm glad," her mother says. "I'll see you in the morning, then."

The girl barely has enough energy to say, "Goodnight," as her mother offers a soft smile before retreating to her room. It isn't until the lights are switched off, the moon casting shadows over the girl's wilted blanket that she remembers she didn't put her knife under her pillow.

It is the most gracious sleep she's had in weeks.

II – THE LANDLORD

The girl wakes to the smell of instant coffee and toaster waffles. Her mother slumps over the breakfast table, the bags under her eyes stretching dangerously close to her cheeks. The dial phone lies limp in her hand, the receiving end still ringing. The girl pads into the kitchen, collects a semi-thawed waffle from the toaster, and sits next to her mother.

"The landlord called," her mother says. "He's raising the rent again."

The girl needs no other details. They couldn't afford rent to begin with. It was why her mother took on another job, why the girl resorted to selling most of her belongings to the thrift store down the street, why her mom endured marks on her skin without so much as a grimace. Anything to get an extra dollar in their pocket.

"I'll have to see him after work." Her mother lays a calm hand on her wrist. "Don't worry, dove. We'll be okay. I promise."

Their rent didn't make the girl nervous. Nonetheless, she swallows her fear along with a dry corner of her waffle and paints on a smile.

The smile stays throughout the day. The girl dazzles it in front of teachers, classmates, even the neighbor boy whose cheeks flush every time she turns the corner. She refuses to let her smile drop, convinced if she keeps it on, her happiness will become more truth than lie.

When her mother picks her up, the girl recalls what she learned, distracting herself as much as her mom from the hungry gazes and comments thrown at them in the car line. Her mother eats it up, or at least she pretends to, her eyes glued to the road as they drive, drive, drive. They reach their street only to spot a thin, disheveled man waiting at their door.

"What's the landlord doing here?" the girl asks. Her mother doesn't answer, her attention focused on the man as they get out of the car.

His hair is wiry, his eyes a dark shade of whiskey, a distinct match to the stench of his breath.

"I called your office this morning," her mother says.

The landlord shrugs. "I was busy."

"I'm sure you were." The house keys shake in her mother's hand as she heads for the door. "Would you like to come in?"

"Come on, Lucina. You know that's not how this works."

Her mother stiffens. "I have to watch my daughter."

"I'm sure she'll be fine on her own for a few hours." The landlord shoots the girl a glare. "Won't you?"

It's the moment the landlord creeps close to the girl that her mother spurts, "Fine." She spins to the girl, squeezing her shoulders. "Stay here. I'll be home soon."

"But Mom– "

"Leave some food in the fridge for me, 'kay?"

Reluctantly, the girl nods. She watches her mother follow the landlord to his truck, the hard screech of its tires echoing in her ears. The girl tries to drown it out with music, movies, TV, but reruns of the local news only bring her back to the killings, the victims.

Her mother.

She waits on the couch, knees bobbing until the door peels open. Her mother's come home.

"We got an extension on the rent," her mother says. "It's a good start, but I'll have to cover more shifts to keep up." She tilts her head so the girl meets her eyes. "You'll be okay, won't you?"

"Of course," the girl says, but that wasn't the forefront of her worry. She watches her mother tug her sleeve, but the girl has already counted them. Fourteen spots. Ten more than last night, each one a deeper purple than the last.

"Be sure to thank the landlord if you see him," her mother says. "He would appreciate it."

Of course. It's their kindness, not their money that keeps their roof over their heads. The girl hates it, having to hold a front for survival. But what other choice did they have? What else could they do but pretend they weren't suffering in a world that so desperately wanted to eat them alive?

She doesn't know what to do, doesn't know what to think even as she buries her feet in the sand, moonlight casting over the tar black waves. Arina's melodic voice creeps into her ear.

"You've come back."

"You said you would protect my mom," the girl says.

"I have, dearest."

"Then *why* is she hurt?"

"There are many who have hurt her, child. I only know so much." Arina draws the girl to her chest. The girl feels comforted, like she is wrapped in a warm blanket, or guarded by a magnificent beast. "You have someone in mind, I take it."

The girl questions her words for a moment. She screws her eyes shut, then chokes out, "The landlord."

"Do you want him gone?"

More than anything. She remembers the signs posted around town, the list of missing boys and men almost never-ending. For all she knows, the landlord could be next.

Maybe this is for the best, the girl thinks. Her mother will be safe, they can keep their home, and the landlord...She doesn't care where he goes, as long as he's away from her.

Throat tight and burning, the girl nods.

She feels Arina smile against her cheek. "Consider it done."

III – THE SIREN

The girl walks downstairs to find her mother pacing in the kitchen. There's something different about her, unhinged in a way the girl has not seen before. Her mother buries her head in a stack of papers, bills, and documents the girl is accustomed to, but has yet to discover what they truly mean.

There's nothing in the toaster. No bitter sludge in the coffee pot. Only her mother with a disheveled top knot and spaghetti-stained sweatpants.

"I don't know what happened," she whispers to herself. The girl sits beside her, ignoring the growl of her stomach as she bears through the conversation. "There was no one else there. Who would have done this?"

The girl opens her mouth, but her mother cuts her off.

"The landlord is dead." She shakes her head then, correcting herself. "I shouldn't say it like that. He's not dead." She frames her words in air quotes. "He's *missing*."

The girl wants to know the details but can't find the words. Instead, she recalls what Arina said the night before.

She said she would take care of him.

She never said how.

"How did you find out?" the girl asks.

"One of the neighbors went to visit him this morning. To ask about the rent, like I did. He couldn't find him. No blood. No body. It was like he disappeared. He left his wallet, phone, even his keys. Who leaves their house without their keys?" Her mother sighs. "The police have been searching for hours, but they haven't found anything."

A flicker of light passes her mother's eyes, an expression almost too familiar to hope. The girl doesn't know how to react. She's shocked, appalled to see her mom wish well on a man so harmful to them both, and yet a sinking feeling takes hold of her, refusing to let go. She doesn't feel guilty over the horror inflicted on the landlord. Only that whatever it was, she wasn't made aware of it.

The mother squeezes the girl's shoulder. "Don't worry, dove. Nothing's going to happen to us. I promise."

The girl buries her dismay and nods along. It's easier for her mother to assume she needs comfort. Maybe then she won't notice where the girl ventures at night, how much she might be responsible for.

Anxious and aggravated, the girl waits until dark then pads to the shore. She doesn't need to see Arina to know the woman is waiting for her.

"What did you do?"

"What are you talking about, child?"

"The landlord," the girl says. "What happened to him?"

"You said you wanted him gone." Arina emerges from

behind a cluster of rocks. Her head lolls to the side, her dress shining as if covered in sea foam. "I've only done what you asked."

"Did you kill him?"

Arina stays silent.

"Did you *kill* him?"

"He answered my call."

"What's that supposed to mean?"

"My call lures those who wish to leave. Your landlord followed it here, to me."

"And then what?"

Arina turns to the water. "He followed me below."

Below. The girl tumbles back. She needs to grab onto something, anything to keep her steady, but she only trips, sinking deep into the sand.

Arina kneels to her. The wind blows through her hair as she drags a finger down the girl's cheek. It takes a moment for the girl to recognize the sharp sensation as Arina's nail, the under part of it caked with blood.

"Don't feel sad, dearest," Arina coos. "He is happy now."

"How could he possibly be happy?"

"He no longer carries the burden of life. He can rest easy beneath the waves. It is a gift, really. To offer someone that relaxation. The freedom to do and be nothing. They can simply let go."

"But you're..." The girl catches her breath. "You're lying to them."

"I do not speak to them as I do you. How can I lie if I do not speak?"

The girl buries her head in her hands. She tries to make a reason for it all but can't. What Arina's telling her now...she's a monster. But what kind of monster would speak so lovely or rub smooth circles up and down her spine?

Suddenly, her breathing eases. The girl lies into Arina's

warmth, letting her caress her hair, her face, until they are one but the same, gazing at the fractured moonlight above.

"You should have told me," the girl says.

"You never asked."

"I am asking now." Without meaning to, the girl grabs Arina's hand. "Please, don't leave me in the dark."

"I won't, my child." Arina brings the girl's hand to her face. Her skin is cold and wet, but it's the warmest the girl has felt in years. "We will walk through the dark together."

IV – THE BOY

Weeks pass. The town quiets. Each night, the girl visits Arina on shore. She listens to Arina speak about her culture, where she came from, what she and her fellow sirens do.

There are certain parts of her homeland Arina loves to share. The women. The music. The undersea coves they inhabit. Others Arina refrains from. How the sirens came to be, and particularly what they ate and drank, though judging from the frailness of her body, the girl assumes it is fairly little, anyway.

At one point, she swims the girl far out to sea, and the girl catches a glimpse of her tail. Thousands of silver scales gleam up at her, each leading to a pair of iridescent fins. It's magic if the girl has ever seen it. The near pitch-black water makes them hard to detect, but the girl brands their image in her mind, refusing to let the magic go.

The more Arina describes to the girl, the more enthralled she becomes. With her weapons tucked away and her windows open wide, the girl dreams of nights amongst the waves, can almost feel the fish swimming by, the ocean floor spread endlessly beneath her feet. She wonders how the sirens interact with other creatures, how their systems work, how they differ from the corruption breeding on land. Each night, she has Arina tell her more, but the siren's answers only spark more questions, more discoveries, more dreams than the girl ever thought possible.

The girl shows up at school, boggled with information she can't share. She ignores her classwork, too focused on making sense of what Arina's planted in her head. She almost doesn't notice the murders festering around her, the MISSING posters plastering every corner store, every step she takes from her front door to her mailbox. But she already knows this. Arina doesn't warn her of the disappearances before they happen, but the girl has her guesses. The snarky cashier with the side eye at the gas station. The fisherman who shoots her a grin like rusted roof tiles whenever she walks home. Her P.E. coach who insists on showing her the proper way to hold a football, though she's sure he can do so without his hands on her arms and his breath on her neck. One by one, they fade from the city, beckoned not to their death, but to Arina's welcome arms, then the tumultuous crashes of the sea.

Visiting Arina incites the girl to explore more of the city. Granted, it's far easier now, what with the once-dangerous bodies dropping like flies around her.

There are rumors, of course, but the girl finds joy in them, almost like it's a game. Everyone's playing, guessing who'll go next, a desperate attempt to avoid the obvious question, *What if it's me?* She feels like she's toying with ants, watching them writhe beneath her heels. It's fun, seeing them squirm.

"It's killing left and right."

"But there's never any blood."

"How are we gonna catch it if we don't have nothin'?"

"Maybe it's that Lucinda bitch."

"Nah, she's too timid for that."

"I dunno. She can get crazy when you want her to be."

"Anyone can go crazy if ya give 'em time."

The girl basks in the overcast skies as she walks to the cafe, the bookstore, then finally the bus stop where she meets not her mother– who would undoubtedly fold over if she heard where her daughter had been– but the neighbor boy.

He looks innocent enough with his floppy hair and doe-shaped eyes. The girl has seen the boy for weeks now, though she keeps this from Arina. The siren doesn't trust men, and for good reason. But the boy is just a boy, not a man. Not yet. He still has that soft, joyful smile, a warm tint to his cheeks from running outdoors, something the girl often watches from her window when she gets the chance.

The boy sees the girl and waves. The girl clenches her hands, squelching the nerves knotting her belly long enough to say, "Hey."

"Hey."

The boy and her talk about everything. Their hobbies. Their favorite ice cream flavors. Their incredulously long homework assignments they assume neither of them will finish. No matter the topic, the boy almost always derails into his own interests, mainly his runs up and down the coast. What he feels, what he sees, places he says he wants to take the girl someday. The girl dreams as he speaks. She imagines what lies outside the town, countries, and landmarks she might enjoy. What they might enjoy together. He asks her about her books. She asks if he will ever read them. When he says "Maybe", she tells the stories to him anyway, omitting the most exciting ones of all. The ones Arina shares at night.

The girl and boy wade into a routine. They walk the halls. They ride the bus. They hide their hands in their laps, too afraid to touch aside from the brush of their shoulders as they smush into the seats. When they stop, the girl's mother picks her up while the boy walks home, unperturbed by the supposed predator in the streets. Sometimes, he leaves her notes on her doorstep. Other times in the sand, knowing she will peer out to see.

Tonight, as the girl ventures to the shore, her porch is empty, the sand utterly vacant. She looks to the boy's house less than a block from hers. His usual glowing room is dark and grim, his light flickered off an hour earlier than expected. The girl buries her thoughts with her toes beneath the sand and listens to Arina.

"You like the boy."

The girl lets out a feeble, "Yes," and Arina scowls. Her eyes light with a fire no soul would believe came from the water.

"He is not good for you."

"Why?"

"None of them are good for you."

"You don't know him."

A spike of terror punctures the girl as Arina whispers, "I do."

The girl doesn't know what to make of this. There's not much to imagine other than the boy walking the beach before she arrived. Him answering Arina's call.

"You didn't."

"I did not," Arina says and the girl breaks with relief. "But he came just the same."

"That means nothing."

"Not all come to me, dearest. Only those with lustrous thoughts. It is what draws them to me. Not love or kindness. Control. Entitlement for what they believe is theirs." Arina presses a motherly kiss to her forehead.

"The boy is not what you think," she says. "And you are not his."

But she's not Arina's either.

Later that night, the girl ventures to the boy's house. She plans to knock on his door, throw a lone pebble at his window, anything to catch his attention. But she hesitates. She's never approached him like this before. If she wants the truth, she has to act normal, pretending as though nothing is wrong.

She rushes home, pulling the covers over her head. But sleep doesn't come. It's too hard, too painful. The waves sound too much like Arina's laugh.

In the morning, the girl hurries to leave. Breakfast chewed and backpack zipped, she begs her mom to drive her to school early.

When she arrives, the boy isn't there. The girl scours the halls, the bleachers, storage closets, and empty classrooms. He's not here. He's not *here.*

The girl rides home with a vengeance. She forgoes the bus, disregarding the safety lecture her mother will give her later, and marches to the boy's house. His porch is empty, the book she dropped off for him lying untouched on the doormat. Rounding the house, the girl starts to panic. Until she spots him.

He stands on the shore, feet dug limply in the sand. The crest of the water hits his shins, rising higher and higher as the tide rolls in. He doesn't move, doesn't speak. He doesn't even look like he's breathing.

The girl walks to his side.

"Hey."

The boy doesn't respond.

"Why weren't you at school?"

Silence.

The boy looks out on the shoreline as if she isn't there. The girl isn't sure what to say. She reaches to touch his shoulder –

The boy grabs her wrist.

"I need to see her," he says.

"Who?"

"The one who sang." He whirls at the girl, nothing but feral desperation in his eyes. "You know her, don't you? You have to know her!"

"No!" The girl lies. "No, I don't!"

"You must've heard her, then. She was right here! I know it. I just know it."

The girl squirms in his grasp but can't break herself free. She expects the boy to let her go, sensing her fear. He only clamps harder.

"You're hurting me," she says.

The boy ignores her. He yanks on her arm, dragging her to the ground. The girl lets out a yelp of pain, but the boy doesn't care. "Take me to her."

The girl shakes her head.

"You have to."

"No. I don't."

"You don't understand!"

The boy drops her wrist and latches onto her shoulders. He shakes the girl violently until her vision blurs and all she can ground herself with is his voice. He sounds so broken.

So infuriating.

"I have to see her. I *have* to."

He repeats the words like an incantation until eventually he starts to whimper and he crumples right there on the sand. The girl doesn't kneel with him, doesn't rub his back, doesn't soothe him how she once imagined she would have. She simply turns to the sea, recognizing the boy at her feet as not a boy, but a soul trapped in a forbidden melody. He is no longer hers, no more is he his own.

"My house," she says. "Sundown. Don't be late."

She doesn't wait for the boy to reply. She merely turns away, the sand scalding her feet as she treks back home.

V – THE TRANSFORMATION

The girl leaves once she hears the song.

She doesn't wait as Arina told her to. She checks downstairs, ensuring her mom has gone to work, then hops the fence and runs for the sea.

Arina tilts her head to the sky. Eyes closed, she extends her arms, welcoming those her call draws near.

Before, the girl heard nothing but pained wails and screeches.

But up close, Arina's voice is beautiful.

Arina does not notice the girl until she reaches the chorus of her ballad. When she opens her eyes, she hisses. The song stops.

The song has never stopped.

Suddenly, Arina's hands are on the girl's shoulders, nails like knives in her collarbone.

"I told you not to come," she says.

The girl wriggles free of her grasp. "And *I* wanted to see."

Arina shakes her head. The girl gropes for another rebuttal when she realizes they aren't alone.

Bodies flood the beach, approaching from all angles. They range in height and build, age and race, but one thing remains the same.

The men encircle Arina in droves. It takes the girl a moment to hear Arina singing again. The group stares at her, dazed, their limbs lolling as though their bones were no more. Only wilted flesh held them together, rooting them to the beach.

Right at Arina's mercy.

The girl scans the crowd. Her chest tightens as she takes them in one by one. The barber. The crossing guard. The mailman who gave her kitten stamps when she was seven.

That inner child tells her they shouldn't be here. *They're good,* she says. *I know they are.*

But the girl thinks deeper, grappling for the truth. Every snide remark on the street. Every wandering gaze when her mother came near.

The bruises.

So many bruises.

They don't remember, but the girl does. She recalls every mark, every scratch, every "I'm okay" spoken through cracked lips and rolling tears. The nights her mother came home late. The nights she didn't come home at all. The last-minute trips.

The wobble in her step. The hollers on the bus. The landlord. That god-awful fucking landlord.

He's gone, the girl remembers. *They can all be gone.*

Arina keeps singing. The rocks around them serve as a chamber, echoing her call until it's all anyone can hear.

When it ends, Arina turns to the girl.

"Are you ready, my child?"

The girl nods and Arina smiles. Splaying out a hand, she beckons the first man forward.

The girl does not recognize him. She hopes that will make it easier.

It doesn't.

With an eerie calm, Arina slips her fingers in the man's hair and pulls. The man obeys. He tilts his head, exposing his neck to the light. The girl swears she can hear his heart beating. Arina must hear it, too. She ogles his vein, then licks her lips, revealing a sharp set of fangs. The girl does not gasp, does not look away. She merely watches as Arina kisses the man's temple, then sinks her teeth into his flesh.

The girl has read of vampires, the supernatural. Of creatures in books and TV. None of them tore as savagely through their prey as Arina. The girl watches her, fascinated. It's amazing the way the man bends to her will, the gracefulness in his destruction, how she wears his blood like a new gown. She tears her teeth from his throat and throws her head at the moon, laughing into the night. The men continue to sway, some falling to their knees at another clip of her voice. Meanwhile, the girl stays glued to the shore, haunted by her beauty.

Arina rips through the men one by one. None seem to notice the bleeding corpses at their feet. If they do, they choose to ignore it. The stacking bodies do not move them from Arina. Rather than be frightened, they look intrigued. Eager. When she points to the next man, and the one after that, and the one after that, they follow willingly. It was just as she said. They choose her. They choose this fate. They relish in her mouth on their necks, their blood in her throat. It's a ritual of the purest kind.

There is only one body left.

Arina lifts her hand, but the girl bounds in front, stopping her from touching the boy.

"What are you doing child?"

The girl digs her nails into her palms. The blood feels good on her skin. She lets herself imagine what it'll feel like to be coated in it.

"Let me," she says.

Arina backs away slowly. She licks the blood from her mouth before meeting the girl's eyes.

"Are you sure, child?"

"Will I be like you?"

Her question earns her a grin. "Yes."

"Then, yes."

The girl's chest swells with pride as Arina backs away, letting her approach the boy. He doesn't look at her, but at Arina, the same trance captivating him as it did the men before. Something about it makes the girl's blood boil. She doesn't squelch it. Rather, she lets it swelter beneath her skin, fueling her to do what she never thought possible.

She traces a finger over the boy's cheek. He shudders. Arina's voice fills in her ears.

"He will enjoy it," she says. "You will, too."

The girl doesn't think twice. Snaking her fingers into his hair, the girl yanks the boy's head and plunges her teeth into his neck.

She doesn't expect his skin to break so easily. Hot metal coats her tongue, her throat. She's tasted her own blood before, a quick lick of a paper cut here and there, but never has it tasted this sweet. The girl sucks what she can from the boy's veins, the flavor of him growing richer the more she drinks.

Something lands on her shoulder. Hands. Claws, trying to tear her away.

"Enough, child."

But it's not. How can it be? The moment her mouth latched onto the boy, something unearthed itself inside her, a deep, insatiable hunger not for flesh, but power. Control. Freedom greater than anything she'll find on land. The boy's blood won't fill the hole inside her, but it sure tastes good going down.

The girl grips harder. The boy's skin begins to pale. She feels his blood going cold, but she keeps drinking, drinking, drinking.

"Enough." Arina pulls on her again. The girl snarls, a sound she never imagined she'd make, and watches the boy collapse, the last remnants of his blood, so beautiful, so warm, soaking the sand in copper.

"I wasn't done!"

"I know, dearest," Arina says. "You never will be. But there is one more thing we have to do." She takes the girl's hand, her touch strangely soft compared to the strength she showed moments ago. "Come."

The girl follows her to the ocean's edge. She stops short, only for Arina to keep walking, straight into the blackened sea.

"What about the bodies?" the girl asks.

Arina gives her a lopsided smile. Her eyes flicker to the beach behind them. The girl turns, expecting to see the dozens of corpses piled behind her. But they're not there.

They're *moving*.

The bodies twist and scrunch, slinking towards the water as if pulled by strings. One by one, they bury themselves beneath the current. The blood vanishes soon after, washed by the waves hurtling onto shore. The beach is clean in a matter of seconds, as if they were never here.

The sheer fantasy of it all leaves the girl in a state of shock. She looks to Arina, then the moon shining above.

There's no reason to hesitate. She's made her decision. For the first time in her life, she doesn't feel like a coward.

She feels alive.

The girl bathes in the night sky before glancing at her house. The lights are off. No one's home. Then, with a final breath, she dives into the shallows.

VI - THE AFTERWORD

Winter rolls on the coast like a blanket of ice. The town feels empty, frozen, stuck in a permanent state of stillness.

The girl peeks up from the surface. She keeps her body below water, too fond of her fins to exchange them for the legs she once adorned. Her new form makes her feel secure. Her scales act as her shield, her tail as her weapon, and her teeth…

They make her a monster.

Sequestered behind the rocks, the girl catches a glance of the house ahead. She spots her mother in the kitchen window, sipping on her morning coffee. The counter is empty of food, the TV burbling low in the background of dawn. It has become her daily routine since the girl left, willowing in the living room, slunk in her plastic dining chair with nothing and no one to talk to.

The house around her is more extravagant than the last. Arina helped make sure of that, once they burned the other one to the ground. It's the last thing the girl remembers of that night. She can still smell the gasoline she doused over the patio, the stench of smoke and salt disrupting her senses as she devoured the bodies Arina collected for her.

She saved the boy for last.

If she thinks of it, she can still taste him, feel his presence deep within her bones. He's a part of her now, same with all the others. They served in her creation, and now, she gets to serve another.

The girl ignores the frown on her mother's face, the gleam in her hollow-set eyes, reminding herself of the good she's done. The men she's ridden. The endless jobs her mother was able to abandon. Thanks to her, her mother lives in comfort. She's warm, never hungry, always protected, whether she knows it or not.

It's better for her this way.

The girl – the *siren* – savors the sun's heat as it cascades along the sea. She feels another body swim next to hers.

"Have you found your meal tonight, Dove?" Arina asks.

Dove scans the surrounding streets. She spots a man approaching her mother's doorstep. She's seen him once before, slinking into bars, stuffing unknown bags in his pockets only to dispense them in others' drinks. The mother knows of him, too, though her knowledge stems as far as their first encounter in the grocery store parking lot. At the sight of him, Dove's smile turns feral.

"Yes," she says and Arina dips below the waves, leaving her to the hunt. Dove enjoys feeding with her, but this is different. This beach, this home, is hers, and the prey hers to kill.

The sun sets, the birds caw, and as the world starts to rest, Dove awakens.

The man knocks on the door right as Dove opens her mouth. And then she begins to sing.

3
SKIN AND BONES
IRELEIGH BENNER

You're not good enough. You can't do it at all. What if everything you do is the worst?

Abby gasped, interrupting her stream of thoughts and sitting up so fast the world around her collided into view in blurs of red and black. Attempting to focus, she stood and found herself at the edge of a cliff. She stumbled back in shock at the sight of jagged rocks lining a descent so deep, that she could barely make out the bottom.

Her wild hair whipped out behind her as the smell of sea salt burned her nose. Water sprayed her face, and she flinched, hugging her arms and burrowing deeper into her t-shirt, tied high like a crop top above her black jeans. Her hands were numb, the tinge of cold caressing her exposed skin.

"Where am I?" Her whispered words somehow rang loud and clear in the frigid night air.

"The Otherworld."

Abby jumped at the voice, turning as she sense a presence beside her. Her gaze remained on the cliff along with a lingering fear, that somehow, she might fall off it. She took several steps back, watching as the edge distorted between strikes of lightning and darkening shadows. Something wasn't right—The colors, the noises, all slightly off-kilter, slightly... unnatural.

She sensed the man beside her shift, and something about the way he moved kept Abby from wanting to see more. His figure was cast in black and white, stiff and stick-like. His clothes were several sizes too big as they shuddered against the wind, and his skin was so white, it was as if he spent his entire life in the shade.

"Otherworld..." she mused. "But—How did I get here?" She scanned the cliff's edge from a distance, as though the answer lay hidden there.

Out of the corner of her eye, she caught the man's pale face turning toward her hands. Following the movement, she glanced down.

Abby screamed. Her hands. She faltered back several steps, as though distance would be enough to make the sight unreal. Those hands had once been covered in perfectly smooth skin. Abby cradled them to her chest, convinced that, just like the world around her, they were still filtering through—still coming into focus. She blinked rapidly, hoping to clear the hazy lens affecting her vision.

But nothing changed.

Her hands were simply bones, the skin translucent—almost gone altogether now. She wiggled her fingers. They moved at her command, like thin, white spider legs. The small spaces between each bone showed so visibly, Abby worried for a horrifying moment that they would disassemble. Shivering, she tightened them into fists and pulled them back against her chest.

This isn't real. As Abby glanced around, hoping to find some comfort or reason for what was happening, she caught sight of others around her.

A long slab of elevated rock stood opposite the cliff, surrounded by groups of half-skeletal people. Abby clamped her mouth shut to stifle a cry. She did not want to be heard. Or seen. Thankfully, none seemed to notice her. She clutched her hands closer, watching the people.

Some had more on than others, not in terms of clothes— luckily they all had those— but in terms of skin. Several were only missing a few body parts, like herself. But each moved about without taking any notice of their surroundings or their missing skin. Their bones clacked together in stiff motions and awkward gestures.

Abby looked away, turning her attention finally to the man who had spoken to her. She jerked back so fast she fell onto the hard rock, and as she prepared for the hurt to ring out along her hands, looking down, she remembered they were only bones. And apparently, bone didn't feel pain.

This was getting ridiculous. Abby forced herself to address the man, the full skeleton staring back at her through twin holes as black as the suit and tie he wore. "I—I don't understand."

Silently, the man lowered himself to the ground beside her. His tie peeked out from his back pocket, which was covered slightly by the jacket tied around his waist. Various holes and scuff marks ran across the fabrics, all of which sagged over the hard edges of his frame.

He turned his gaze to the cliff, and Abby did the same, watching the zigzagging bolts of red cut through the harsh grays and blacks as a violent storm raged across the ocean. It sounded like white noise. Despite the chaos, everything felt hushed. Even the skeletons speaking behind her whispered.

"I— don't...understand," Abby said again. Her hands shook with every word. "Am...I dead?"

The skeleton huffed out a small laugh between the cracklings of his jaw.

"Am I?" Her voice trembled in anticipation of his answer, in fear of the things he did not say.

He turned his face to her, and she clenched her lips, unable to make out the expression on the face of pure bone.

"This world isn't for the dead." His dark voice filled the space between them and barreled over Abby with an intensity that made her fear this place even more.

"There are literal skeletons," she said.

The man looked back at the groups, then returned his attention to her. "Do you remember what happened before you got here?"

"I—" Abby frowned. She could remember being in her room at home, a decision growing in the back of her mind, but she couldn't remember what it was or what she decided to do. The weight of its importance had somehow melted into the weight of her hands, missing skin and laying on her lap.

"Listen," he said, his bones scraping against the rocky surface as he adjusted himself to face Abby. He held up two bone fingers. "You've got two choices. You can stay where you are and wait till you're just bone," he nodded at the group of skeletons, then cocked his head to the waves violently beating the cliff's face, "or you can go deeper. Somewhere different."

Abby considered the options, both of which she couldn't fully agree upon. Instead, she felt a strong urge to stay where she was. Stay with the growing skeletons. Stay with those who were like her. She shook her head and the urge dissolved into nothing. This wasn't her home. This wasn't a life to be lived.

"But what if I want to go back? Back to— Whatever was before this?"

The skeleton's jaw cackled loudly, and Abby could feel the sharp glares of the groups behind her angled on them.

"If you wanted to be where you were, then you wouldn't be here!"

"But I do!"Abby stood, forcing herself to remain steady. "I—"

The ground around her rumbled, the sudden loudness of everything finally breaking through the hushed silence around them. The booming thunder, the roaring waves, and the words of those around them. "I want to go back!"

What if this is as good as it gets? What if there is nothing better? What if you hit the only peak left?

Abby cringed at the intruding thoughts as she grabbed the man's bony arm, pulling him closer, anger seething through her. He flinched, and Abby could imagine him squinting his hallow eyes if he still had them. "Tell me how to get back."

"You can only get back," he sneered, "if you remember what brought you here." Mocking laughter rang out from all the skeletons at once. It echoed through the air, ringing loud in Abby's ears.

"But even if you do remember," his voice boomed as he took a step away from her, still laughing with the others, "you won't want to return."

"The fuck I won't," Abby said. She had a life and she wasn't going to waste it disappearing on some cliff.

She stomped away, strands of black hair whipping across her face with every wild turn of her head as she tried to get a better view of the land. Why couldn't she remember what brought her here? Could it all be a dream? But even dreams had a way out, a way of waking up. Why couldn't she figure this out now?

The skeletons mingled, laughing and cheering as they raced to join the man. The storm raged on and they sat along the edge.

Abby watched them for a moment. The growing skeletons spoke to each other, some pointed out flashes in the storm, a few threw small pebbles at the sea. All were content here, Abby noticed. All except for the complete skeleton.

He didn't speak to any of the others. He sat frozen like a block of ice. To the rest of the group, he probably looked calm, but something about his hunched shoulders and his stillness made Abby think he was contemplating something.

Several of the skeletons along the cliff grew more transparent, more of their skin fading away without them even noticing. Abby turned away.

The air stilled, and Abby caught sight of a tiny path she had somehow missed next to the slab where the skeletons had been earlier. The man hadn't mentioned it, and Abby hesitated to follow the dirt path leading to a place clearly no one cared to venture. Everyone sat content by the edge. Abby knew she couldn't stay and whither away with the others, but something about it felt comforting. She had to admit, there was a bond between them all, even if she couldn't understand what that bond was.

She had a life to get back to. She had had everything she needed: Good grades, somewhat friends, a life of her own.

Happiness, however, stood absent from her life, but Abby knew better than to blame all her problems on that. She survived life, she didn't need to enjoy it. Obviously, life would probably be better if she did - so, yeah, maybe she did need to enjoy it. But did anyone? Her whole life she'd watched people suffer. Unhappy marriages. Unhappy jobs. Unhappy futures of people who started out believing they were heading for something better, or remembered at one point having better. People always said there was more to life, and they meant happiness, but Abby wondered if there was more to life than just happiness. What if people were chasing the wrong thing? Or what if it was impossible for some people to have at all? And why chase something so fleeting? Besides, she had things to do and people to be there for. People depended on Abby. They weren't interested in her problems or dark thoughts when they had expectations and hopes of something better for her.

Abby started down the trail that led around the giant slab of rock. The storm roared behind her, yelling— *screaming*— at her with whistling winds and claps of thunder. Shades of deep crimson and dark beige covered the pointed rocks curving along the path. She quickened her pace as she caught sight of a small cottage nesting between two large boulders at the end of the trail. Two windows lined each of its wooden walls, and smoke piped out of its chimney, adding to the thick strands of fog that slithered abnormally around the house like small serpents.

Unsure if she should disturb the wisps of fog, Abby searched for any kind of entrance untouched by the creeping weather. Despite knowing that whatever lay in the house could be worse than everything else the Otherworld had shown her, the possibility of an answer drove Abby in.

Spotting a black wooden front door, Abby sighed and stepped forward, bracing herself for the cool of the fog. The closer she got, the more tiny hissing whispers tickled her ears. She shivered, unable to make out the words. The hair along her neck and arms stood up, and static charged around her just as lightning struck next to her, cracking against the side of the house. Abby screamed and the whispers around her grew. Fumbling with the brass nob, she managed to turn it and flee inside, away from the terrors.

In her haste, Abby swung the door wide. It banged against the outer wall, and she flinched at the sound. Abby jolted back, nearly falling back out into the storm at the sight of a woman with a full body, but with a skull instead of a face. Like the slow creeping snakes outside, her face angled towards Abby, jutting out and twisting to one side.

The woman wore a yellow sundress, her remaining skin shone clear and bright. She must be young, Abby thought.

The cottage layout spread before Abby in a simple manner. A long vintage red couch, a tiny kitchen with white cabinets, and a dark wood table with chairs.

The girl continued to stare at Abby.

"Choices, choices," she muttered. "You don't seem to be very good at them."

Abby narrowed her eyes and straightened herself before

entering further. She opened her mouth, ready to interrogate this girl on a way out but the girl started first.

"You're wasting your time."

Abby rolled her eyes, her mind set on getting answers. She wasn't going to waste another second. "Do you have memories from before here?" The girl nodded, and Abby took a few steps closer. "But then… do you remember what brought you here?"

"*I* brought myself here."

Abby stifled a gasp. "What? Why?"

"It wasn't on purpose," she snapped. "It just… slowly happened." The girl leaned casually against a marble counter, looking Abby up and down before meeting her eyes. "Are you afraid of death?"

"I—I guess." Caught off guard, Abby answered truthfully. It shocked her. She thought of death often but never made the jump toward it, no matter how much her pain begged her to.

"You don't want to die?"

"No," Abby scoffed. She crossed her arms, annoyed somewhat at the diversion, but curious as to where the girl was going.

"Why?"

"What do you mean why? So I can live. So I can be alive."

"And do what?"

"Would you stop!"Abby shouted. "No one really wants to die, that means it's the end. The end of everything. If I die then I wouldn't—" Abby stopped. She hoped that by continuing to speak, the answer would come to her. But it didn't. She didn't *want* to die. However, she also couldn't find a very good reason not to besides not wanting to be nothing, which in a sense, she'd already become. However, there was only so long that someone could be nothing, especially when no one else cared to notice.

"What if," the girl said, grinning between the words, "this place saved you from the very realization you just came to?"

"What?"

"This place. What if it saved you—"

"I heard what you said, but there's no way I'd want to die and then choose to come here—"

"You don't 'just come here,'" she mimicked with a talking hand in the air. "You're just fully aware of being here now. It's been happening for a while. Slowly."

"What exactly is here, the Otherworld?"

"It's like limbo. A place to wait."

"Wait for what?" Abby stared at the girl who shook her head with a thin smile.

Cold blew through the open door, sweeping over Abby and the girl. So intent to get answers, Abby hadn't realized she'd been leaning toward the girl until she shivered back. Something about her, it was off. Something about the girl wasn't like the others at the cliff.

"This place, it saves us," she continued, advancing toward Abby, who backed up so fervently, she hit the table behind her. She winced, pushing further against the wooden table, desperate to get as much distance from the girl as she could.

"From what?"Abby asked, lowering her voice.

"From death."

"So— I was going to die and came here?"

"Not exactly." She inched closer to Abby, who struggled to lean back and gain more distance. "We all have dark parts of ourselves. The ones who want to kill."

"Kill?"Abby's eyes widened. "Did I- you mean I was going to kill myself?"

The girl shrugged with a sigh. "Probably. But the dark parts, sometimes they save us too. That's why you're here."

"So...my anxiety and depression saved me? I mean that's why people commit suicide or hurt themselves, to begin with—"

"But haven't you ever had moments where it saved you too?"

Abby's eyes widened. Her anxiety had saved her. Lots of times. Anytime she contemplated killing herself, killing her pain, a voice would pop up and poke so many holes through the idea that suddenly it didn't exist at all anymore.

Say you did kill yourself, who would find you? Do you want to scar them for life? And what if you weren't successful? What if you failed to kill yourself and then *someone found you? How would you even kill yourself, to begin with? You're afraid of basically everything, Abby.*

In the end, she'd always continued living, but only because she couldn't find a comforting way to die. Or at least, that's what she told herself. Maybe a smaller part of herself didn't want to die at all, or maybe her anxiety feared death more than her depression wanted it. Either way, life became about surviving death.

It didn't make Abby feel any worse. She knew more people than not were doing the same thing, they just wouldn't admit it, or they had no idea. Sometimes Abby would pretend she was happy, that the whole life she created was enough. Society had taught her to be grateful, and grateful in a sense was happiness, right?

"So," Abby started, "you think this whole Otherworld is just saving us from..." She motioned with her hands, expecting the girl to fill in the blank. She didn't. Abby dropped her hands and rolled her eyes. "Okay, so I put myself here, *slowly,* to save myself from something—"

"No," she said. "Your dark self did."

"Okay cool, that clears it up."

"Being bitter won't get you answers."

"What else am I supposed to be?"Abby laughed. "I mean, I'm stuck in this Otherworld, *wanting* to leave and I'm surrounded by people-ish, who couldn't care less that we're all here! I want to leave, I want to live—"

"Why?" she yelled.

"I don't know!"Abby screamed, throwing out her hands. The girl didn't even jump at her movement. Shaking her head, Abby caught sight of her bony palms, and as her eyes trailed them, she saw the transparency had spread up to her elbow. Her voice started to crack as she spoke again. "If my other self brought me here then how do I leave?"

"You have to fight."

"What the fuck am I doing now?" Abby asked.

"Your dark self brought you here to fight the battle."

"What— What battle?"

"The one you have to fight."

Abby motioned theatrically out past the cottage with her spidery fingers. "There's no battle!"

"There is."

Abby dropped her hands with a groan. She could see the growing skeletons on the cliff, sitting at the edge through the window. The full skeleton man stood up, his arms drawn out at his side like swords.

"They're each fighting themselves." The girl's voice came out hoarse, as if she reminded herself daily of this fact. "Here we have a chance to return in a better way. But you have to fight for it. One part of you, it won't want to go back at all."

"Why haven't you done that then?"Abby asked.

"Because I know what I'll do if I return with my other self."

The battle, the Otherworld, it started to make sense. But Abby was different from the other people here. She *only* wanted to get back, when everyone else felt conflicted. This place had nothing to offer Abby. Home, however painful it was, held comfort in the fact that Abby knew what to expect. She understood it. If what the girl said was true, then part of Abby was lost down here. She'd need it to get back.

Glancing at the cliff, Abby wondered if, maybe, she could leave part of herself here. She could leave the part that always dragged behind her, reminding her, taunting her, with her mistakes, her failures, her embarrassments. Then again, that part of her also saved her.

Every time.

Abby still lived because that part of her convinced her to do so. She stood up, readying herself to leave, but turned to the girl one last time. Abby pitied her. Nothing to return to and nothing to do here. The woman had so little.

"Do the others live here too? The ones by the cliff."Abby watched her closely. The girl lowered her head, her fingers playing with the soft creases of her dress.

"We don't agree on things."

"I know you don't want to return…but have you ever tried?"

"No reason for me to."

"You're not as gone as some of the others, you still have most of your body." Abby leaned forward.

"I lost my face," the girl spat, "because I refused to show it before all of this. So it has no relevance here. I've made peace with that. And with this place."

Abby shuddered and rubbed her boney hands over the sides of her arms. What had she done before this to make it so her hands had no relevance?

"It's not the same," the girl said, seeing the contemplation across Abby's face. "Your hands and my face."

"Why not?"

The girl shook her head. Then shook it harder. Wails started vibrating against the thin bones of her skull. She began pounding her fist against the table next to Abby, who jumped to the side just in time to avoid impact from the girl's other fist, now pounding as well. She skidded toward the door, which still lay open, and fled.

The wind kicked up around her, and the sounds of the girl still flew from the house as Abby ran faster. Her hair danced wildly through the air, tearing at her eyes and cheeks. While trying to contain it, she felt her boney fingers begin to shake. She threw her arms down and instead let her hair fly free. Staring at her white palms, tears slid down her cheeks and flew off into the crazy growing wind. Lightning struck the sky in a glowing scarlet, and the thunder that followed rolled out so hard, the tiny island shuddered. Abby held her balance even though she had no reason to. There was simply nowhere else for her to go.

The girl had nothing more to say to Abby, and pushing away her feelings of loss and hopelessness, she started back towards the skeleton man. He knew things. Abby hadn't stayed long enough to find them out. Her heart beat against her chest, her breaths thick and heavy as she tried to draw in air. What if he had no more answers?

Her nostrils flared and she threw her hair back behind her shoulders. The air around her calmed, and for a moment, the island sat silently.

The skeleton man still stood at the edge. The people around him stopped speaking, apparently sensing that something was about to happen. The man stood, and all heads darted in his direction. He pulled his jacket off from around his waist, folded it, and placed it neatly on the ground. He turned to face the water, extended his long arms out once again—

Abby blinked as something moving towards the cliff collided with the man. A black figure jumped onto him, clinging to his back and sending them both off the edge in seconds. Abby sucked in a breath. She took a step back. The drop held so much silence, that Abby wondered if maybe, somehow, they hadn't fallen at all. The raging sea and thunders halted, as if to wish the man farewell. Then everything crescendoed into loud bangs and snaps and crashing waves. Abby raced to the edge, dirt, and pebbles scraping up behind her. None of the growing skeletons acknowledged her, their eyes stayed where the man had sat. Cold air rushed up the cliff, and Abby trembled. She picked up the man's jacket and gripped it tight before letting her eyes wander off toward the water. She couldn't see anything, but squinted between the darkness of the water and the storm, hoping to make something out. Waves pounded into the side, spraying salt water up at her as they made an impact against the jagged edge. Wherever the man was now, he was of no use to Abby anymore. Lightning ignited into a wave, illuminating it as it barreled toward the rocks with purpose. Abby stumbled back. The wave continued to grow, and more red lightning struck. Cold saltwater mist swept over her, clinging to her wild hair while pushing it back in a thick wind. The wave crashed against the side with a loud bang. More water spit at Abby, who wiped her eyes.

You've got two choices. You can stay where you are and wait till you're just bone. Or, you can go deeper.

But which was worse? Death, or staying here till she turned into nothing?

Abby knew that "deeper" could mean physically going somewhere else, another place. She took several steps back, fingers clinging to the jacket. What if deeper was worse? At least she knew what the Otherworld was now. Then again, what if there were more black figures waiting to push her into the water?

Home had terrors, but they were ones Abby could control, or deal with in her mind. This was getting too real.

She studied the skeletons. "What happened to him? What was that thing?"

The soft conversations had evaporated. The only sounds that Abby could hear were ones from the storm. Some still had their faces, and Abby noticed that more than one had tears in their eyes, as if they were mourning the lost man. But the longer she examined them, the more she couldn't help feeling that that's not what it was at all. They weren't sad for him. They weren't happy. They were frozen in a feeling Abby couldn't make out.

She glanced again at the stormy ocean. Between the lightning and the chaotic waves, she doubted she'd survive the jump. Even if she did, the ocean roared like a wild animal. It attacked the rocks with a vengeful force. It wouldn't stop just for her fall. And trying to swim in or through that would be a battle—

Abby gasped, dropped the jacket, and fell to her knees. Pebbles and small rocks scraped at her knees through the fall, but she barely noticed.

What— What battle?

The one you have to fight.

Tears stung her eyes, daring her to let them go, but like the others on the cliff, she held them back. She finally understood the pain they all held, the look on their faces as they stared down where the man was gone.

But you have to fight for it. One part of you, it won't want to go back at all.

Was this the part of her that didn't want to go back? The one telling her not to jump?

Abby leaned back onto her legs, her hands smacking against the sides of her head. She could feel the impact of it— barely— but her bones couldn't feel the individual threads of hair, they couldn't feel anything. It was spreading. Up her arm, down her elbow, up toward her shoulder. This thing, the thing that led her here, the one thing she should remember. What brought her here?

Abby screamed in frustration, her thin boney fingers dug deep into her hair, then pushed against her skull. She willed for the physical pain to be worse than her mental one, at least she could understand the latter. At least something would make sense. The tears finally fell, and all the pain caught up.

Through the agony, she'd shut her eyes, then opened them to see she was veering toward the edge of the cliff. Sucking in a breath, she pushed herself back. Her breath came in giant heaves, her heart thudded against her chest, tears burned against her reddened cheeks. She'd had enough. She didn't want pain, she didn't want the nothingness engulfing her. She wanted something else. Something away.

In one fluid motion, she stood. Her heaving breaths shushed those around her. She opened her hands like the man, closed her eyes, and leaned out towards the drop. That's what this place wanted. She was done fighting it.

But something held her back.

Her entire body tilted forward, toward the waves, while part of her was held back by the hem of her t-shirt till whatever held it yanked harder, pulling her so hard she fell against the rock.

She gasped. Above her, stood another growing skeleton. She spun around on her hands and knees and peered up at it. The skeleton wore the same t-shirt, and the same jeans, as Abby, but with no hair— no skin either— except its hands. She clenched her bone fingers as she registered the skeleton's. *Her* pale hands were worn by this— this *thing*. Shadows crept around the dark hollow parts of the skeleton, making Abby shudder.

Despite knowing exactly who the skeleton was, she had to ask.

"Who are you?"

The skeleton stared, frozen in place.

"Why did you stop me—" Abby's words halted.

Okay, so I put myself here, slowly, to save myself from something—

No. Your dark self did.

"You stopped me before— You made me come here."

The black in the skull's eyes thickened, but it did not respond.

"Why can't we just leave?"Abby whispered.

"I don't want to leave," it said. "Not yet."

Abby choked against a growing sob. Her dark self, here to finally finish her off. It had stopped Abby from hurting herself, so it could finally do the real damage. This place held everything dark, and Abby didn't relish the idea of dying at the hand of this skeletal version of herself. Jumping off the cliff held more peace than whatever ideas the skeleton had of disposing of Abby. However, if it did kill her, at least then, everything would be over. Everything would stop. Even if it wasn't peaceful, it would still be done.

"Go ahead," Abby said, standing to face her skeletal self. "Just push me off the edge. Just like what happened to the man."

"No," the skeleton said. "We can't go off the edge."

The skeleton clenched *her* hands and its jaw tightened.

"We can't go back, Abby."

Her eyebrows knit together. The skeleton's words shocked her, but the idea of getting back home nagged at her, it halted her wishful death for the moment.

"So down that ledge, it leads back?"

"Not directly."

"What do you mean 'not directly,'" Abby mimicked.

"You have to fight for it."

"Which we're doing right now—"

"You can't just run off a cliff and expect to survive—"

"But is this a real cliff? I don't know about you, clearly, you're... different— but I've never seen a storm like that." Abby pointed above them at the red and black storm, then toward the growing skeletons. "Or people like this. This could be fake—"

"Could's and if's don't matter here." The skeleton groaned, shaking its head. "This cliff is real— those rocks are real— those waves are *real.*"

Abby took this into consideration. "How real?"

"Just trust me."

"Trust the part of me that is why I'm here—"

"Why *you're* here?" It shouted. "Abby, we're here because *you* brought us."

"Why would I do that?"

The skeleton barked out a laugh. "The million-dollar question."

"Just like all the other questions I have! No one is giving me any real answers! Why are we here?"

"You brought us here..." its voice died out. It raised a hand to rub the back of its boney neck. "I mean— I guess it was both of us—"

"HA!"

"But you decided. I only pointed out that what we were about to do wasn't a good idea."

"As if you do anything else—"

"I do a lot!" it argued, arms stiffening at its side.

"Yeah," Abby scoffed, "you remind me why it would suck to socialize at parties, see people in general, do anything in life ever— Oh my god and you tell me things *all the time.* Don't forget that embarrassing moment in microbiology senior year when you were called on for an answer you didn't know but everyone else did, or don't forget at work when—"

"I don't remind you for fucking fun, Abby. You don't deal with things! I mean look at where we are, we are literally here not dealing with what you were about to do—"

"Only because you won't let me go back!"

"Because you still don't understand!"

"WHAT?" Silence rang out at the end of Abby's word. Her breath came out heavy from the argument, and sweat clung to her forehead and neck.

"You're not fighting to get back, you're fighting to keep running." Its jaw loosened and its stare intensified with what Abby could only assume was either an understanding or pity, but without the facial expression, Abby didn't have enough energy to decide which it was. "We can't go off that cliff till we are sure we want to fight. We don't have to right now, we can wait, we can acknowledge what's going on with us first—"

"You make us sound like a married couple."

"—And when we're strong enough, we can try to fight."

"*Try* to fight?"

"We can't just run off hoping. We have to acknowledge

everything inside ourselves. We have to jump and try for something better."

"Something better."

"It could be out there."

"Could it though?"

Abby reflected on her life. Her misery. Her survival. She couldn't lie, there had been good parts. But they were always tainted by thoughts and reminders of something bad. She overthought everything. She ruined all the good in her life. And she could never open up to those around her, those who saw her surviving and found pride in thinking that it meant she was happy.

"I-I'm scared to go back."

One part of you...won't want to go back at all. Abby was the part. She wanted to run. She wanted to run so far, so fast, that her thoughts and problems were out of sight by the time new ones arose. She didn't want a way back, she wanted a path away. A detour. However long. Even if it meant death.

"There are ways to get help."

Abby glared. "You mean like sending us here?"

"We can find help outside of here. But we have to leave to do that. We have to be ready to feel everything again. No more running." The skeleton extended a hand out to Abby. "You don't have to do this alone. We deserve something better than what we gave ourselves."

Abby took the offered hand, half expecting her skin to crawl back onto her bare bones. But they did not. The two stared off the cliff.

Abby knew there were ways of getting help. But talking about her feelings... was hard. Especially when she knew it made people sad. Their pride in her well-being, stripped away by the expression of her feelings. Thinking about it now, there were support systems that had people she'd never even met. But there was a possibility that it wouldn't work. Deep down, Abby wondered if *better* existed at all. If maybe she couldn't get better at all.

Could's and if's don't matter here. The skeleton's words echoed in her mind.

She took the skeleton's hand— *her* hand. They did deserve better than they gave themselves. There would always be possibilities, there would always be could's and if's. If Abby was willing to be nothing, to feel nothing, couldn't she be willing to risk it all for something better? If the alternative is *nothing,* what exactly did she have to lose?

Together, they edged nearer to the drop of the cliff. Still, the thought tugged in the back of Abby's mind, *What if there is something worse than nothing?*

The two faced each other.

"But what if there's not?" the skeleton rasped, its voice breaking through a pain they were both feeling. A faint smile played across Abby's lips.

Just as the two placed one foot each over the side, thoughts barreled into Abby's head. She fought each one. She wasn't alone, her dark self— It didn't want the worst. It wanted her to feel. It kept her going. Even if it went too far sometimes, she had a choice in whether or not to listen.

What if you're the worst? What if I'm not?

What if all there is, is pain? What if there's something better?

What if you never get something better? But what if I do? What if I get everything?

Air and wind pushed against her and the skeleton, so hard Abby feared they'd freeze mid-fall. But the ocean grew nearer, a giant wave kicking up over them. Abby trembled, the grip between her hand and the skeleton's tightening. She clenched her eyes shut with a tightly held breath.

She could sense the light shift as the wave continued to grow over them and felt the pressure of the air as it began to drop. Fearing the impact, Abby waited.

A loud crash and searing bang erupted.

Then nothing.

Abby squinted through one eye. Darkness surrounded her and as she opened both eyes, she could see several dim floating orbs high above wherever she was. They flickered over her in shades of white, illuminating one person floating in front of her with stiff limbs sprawled out in the air. The skeleton man. The harder she looked, the more she could make out the man's appearance. He was growing back. Skin crawled over his body and dark curly hair grew back across his head. His eyes were shut in a calm sort of sleep.

Taking another step forward, her skeleton let go of Abby. It lingered behind but made no attempt to stop her steps toward the man.

The man's eyes snapped open, halting Abby's advance as his eyes set on her and he floated back down now a full man.

"I waited for you," he said, crossing his *actual* arms. If it weren't for the same clothes he wore earlier, Abby wouldn't have recognized him at all. His suit fit him perfectly, the scuffs and tears no longer devouring the fabric.

"What happened to you—" Abby stopped. The black figure. It had been the man's skeleton moving fast beneath his black suit. He was ready to fight the battle and his dark self jumped on, ready to fight as well.

"We're all struggling. Even when you're alone, wanting to end it all, there are people just like you surviving so well it looks like they're happy. It looks like they're never in pain. It looks like we're the only ones. Remember all the bodies you saw here." He forced a grim smile. "When our pain makes others uncomfortable, we're taught not to seek comfort in them, for the pain we are bearing, but to instead push it so deep that the only way to get it out is to not be at all."

"Not be what?" she asked.

"Alive."

Abby shuddered but forced a nod. The man nodded back. He turned and walked further into the dark until Abby could no longer hear his soft footsteps or see his silhouette.

Looking back at her own skeleton, she reached out a shaking, bony hand. She'd fought through the water, she'd fought along the cliff, and now she was ready to fight one last battle. A flash of light ignited like a bursting star as the two touched, both ready to return, ready for one last fight.

A rush of wind swirled around Abby. It breathed through her black hair and nipped at her clothing before she rose from the ground, floating in mid-air. What looked like single threads embedded themselves in the wind in colors of deep cobalt blue.

Abby watched as the skeleton slowly dissolved part by part, the blue threads unraveling it bone by bone until all that was left were Abby's hands. Reaching out, Abby grabbed at them before they had a chance to disappear. The threads encircled around her before turning bright red and yellow, and diving at her, ready to sew her hands back on.

Every memory that Abby had ever run away from came back. Pins and needles pricked at her mind until the pain was all she could think about.

The time she'd said no to hanging out with a friend and spent the rest of the night feeling guilty and obsessing over it.

The time she'd walked into target alone and swore everyone critiqued which aisle she lingered too long in while trying to make a decision.

The time she spent the whole night laying on the floor wondering and contemplating life.

And the time when— when she almost— when she—

Tears tore down her cheeks like knives splitting through paper.

The time when she almost took all the pills but ended up in the Otherworld.

Abby took it all, forcing her eyes shut. She withstood the

pain of each stitch of the thread. She clung to her real hands, focusing on what she was fighting for.

Something better. Something whole.

Abby gasped, opening her eyes. She was in her room. *Her* unmade bed sat in the corner. Light streamed in from the setting sun of *her* window. Taking a deep breath, she looked down at *her* fists, her fingers uncurling. In the palms of her hands were dozens of pills. Between the two, sat a glass of water. Her hands started to shake, realizing what she'd almost done.

Carefully placing the pills back in the bottle, Abby stood. Her body still shook, the knowledge of everything finally kicking in. Her time in the Otherworld. Her time before the Otherworld. Her time right now.

We're taught not to seek comfort in them, for the pain we are bearing, but to instead push it so deep that the only way to get it out is to not be at all.

Not be what?

Alive.

Biting her lip, tears sprouting in the corners of her eyes, Abby reached for her phone and googled the suicide hotline number, knowing that she deserved something better than what she'd spent her whole life giving herself. But to do that, she had to acknowledge the pain buried deep inside her, and she'd need help doing that.

4
THE PUMPKINHEADS
FELICITY DEVORIA

They waited until a month after I'd come to town.

The inn had become something of a home. The owner, Lassie, was something of a mother to me. She fed me porridge for breakfast, lunch, and dinner, and she didn't talk much. But she was smiles, smiles, smiles, and we got along alright. The day I'd turned up in Woodbridge, she'd been full of questions. Where did I come from? Was that my family's name? What sort of business was I in? I quickly learned that in Woodbridge, anyone who wasn't open about themselves had a reason not to be. No answers were as damning as bad ones.

It took a while to find work. In those days, women weren't sought after for jobs. There were only a few acceptable roles. When the Gates family put out an advertisement for a new governess, I jumped at the chance. There was a certain hush-hush about the situation, of course. When I told Lassie I'd got the job, she'd given me a sad smile. "It'll be alright," she whispered. "When you meet the right man, he'll overlook this little hiccup."

You see, in order to work, a woman was supposed to have

already exhausted her options for marriage. An unmarried working woman was a harsh statement that had to be softened by a dreary disposition. But I was not some pitiful governess looking for a job because I'd had no luck at the marriage market–I was an actress, a façade. I was used to not fitting in. My entire childhood had been a primer in being the odd one out. Here was a chance to blend in. I put on a sad face and Woodbridge believed me.

Mr. Gates was a dejected man of nearly fifty. He came from impressive means made dreary by his circumstance. He'd been widowed twice by women who were described as vitality itself. His wives had birthed five children apiece, but only one of them had stuck: Marcie. I knew Mr. Gates was lonely, despondent, even. But I hadn't guessed he'd be so stony. As he described the role to me, his face never wavered from that slight frown. It was as if he'd been chiseled from a hunk of marble.

The day I came to work, he started off with a speech. "The quality I'm most looking for in a governess is love," he concluded.

"Love?"

We were in his office, and he'd positioned himself at the window. He took a long look out. In the distance, Marcie and her keeper were running through a field of wildflowers. A large dog bounded along with them. The keeper was yelling something I couldn't make out through the glass.

"Marcie's keeper, Nancy, hasn't taken to the girl. Says she's too wild."

"Some children are," I countered.

He looked at me then, gray eyes piercing. "My Marcie has lost her mother. If it takes her being a little wild to be happy, so be it. I'd prefer her wild to somber."

I nodded. "I'm always happy to acquiesce to a parent's requests."

This didn't seem to agree with Mr. Gates. "Love doesn't come by request." He and his hardened frown swept from the room, leaving me to meet my charge.

MARCIE and I took to each other quickly. She had a freckled face, fierce eyes, and a grin that stretched on for days. We learned mathematics by counting flowers, and English by writing haikus and limericks. I conducted our lessons under a big birch tree at the edge of the property, and whatever Marcie learned, her dog, Pickle, had to learn too. Pickle didn't mind his lessons. He was always lying around, his tongue stuck out in a perpetual loll.

One Friday evening, as Mr. Gates paid me my salary and dismissed me, his gray eyes got a bit misty. "Marcie just adores you."

"She's a good girl. She would adore anyone who taught her."

"No." Mr. Gates shook his head. "No, Marcie didn't like Nancy. Nancy wasn't like us–Nancy was cut from a different cloth."

I took a deep breath, trying to understand this sudden change. "Well, I like Marcie too."

Mr. Gates finished up my paycheck and I took it, smiling at him on my way out. He stopped me before I could get through the door, grabbing my wrist.

"Please stay," Mr. Gates whispered.

"I … I have a perfectly fine room at the inn, and you pay me so generously–really, it's no trouble."

"Stay," Mr. Gates repeated. His grip was like a shackle. "Stay, for Marcie's sake."

Just then, Marcie ran by the room, the hardwood thundering under her feet. "Papa, help!" she shrieked. Pickle yapped ferociously behind her. "There's a beast chasing us. He's big and hairy!"

Mr. Gates came back to his senses. He let go of my hand and straightened his suit. "Please think about it. And now, if you'll excuse me, I have to go and save my daughter from a fit of her imagination."

Mr. Gates strode from the room. I realized only after he left that his face hadn't budged one bit from that familiar frown. A couple of servants rushed in with my coat and hat, and I thought of it no more that night.

THE NEXT MORNING, I studied Lassie's face over a breakfast of porridge. As always, she wore a smile of the genuine sort that couldn't be faked. It never wavered, not even when another patron spilled a glass of grape juice on the pure white tablecloth. No, Lassie simply wiped it up, smiling. She smiled at regular guests and new visitors. She smiled as she patted my shoulder and called me 'munchkin.' She smiled at me as I left, though I thought I heard a faint sigh as she cleared the dishes.

On my walk to work, Bill the butcher came out on the front stoop to give me a grim wave. His apron was discolored by years of dried blood. His eyes scrunched, sizing me up. "Need a chop?" he asked, raising his cleaver.

"No need!" I called back. "Lassie is making an excellent stew!"

Bill hummed at this. His wife stumbled out onto the stoop. A little thing, she was a woman prone to annoyance, and even eight months pregnant, she seemed to hold no excitement for the baby. She leaned down, placing something orange on the ground. *A jack o' lantern!* I giggled at the sight–what a harsh face for a pumpkin. I stared at it for a moment; its stiff face was carved into the same hard line as her husband's.

THE WEEK'S conclusion marked All Hallows Eve. I'd officially been in Woodbridge for a month. Mr. Gates's estate had taken on a spooky theme in light of the holiday. The smell of fire carried through the breeze, and Jack o' lanterns lined the front walk, each carved with great attention. Some of them had begun to rot though– two great big ones with beaming smiles sagged towards the ground. Even the little gourds looked to be suffering. The unseasonable heat must have gotten to them.

That evening, Mr. Gates announced they would be holding a holiday feast. Marcie's nanny took her to freshen up for dinner, and Mr. Gates decided to escort me. As he offered me his arm, he regarded me with that familiar frown.

"Have you considered my offer?" he asked.

I stared at his face. It was as still as death. Something about it shook me ... stumbling, I took his arm and steadied myself.

"Lassie has been good to me." The words fell out of me as I put on a cheery grin. Mr. Gates just kept on frowning. "I can't bear to part with her lovely little inn. I'll be lonely without her."

"Very well," Mr. Gates said.

The feast was excellent– roast turkey, potatoes of many varieties, and an excellent cranberry purée. When we finished, plates were cleared and a great cake was brought out on a tray. It was placed in front of Mr. Gates, who studied it solemnly. Along with the pretty pink cake was an assortment of large butcher knives. I supposed this was some kind of cake-cutting ritual for the holiday.

Marcie clapped her hands together. "Is it finally time?" Her voice was high-pitched and always delighted.

Mr. Gates stood abruptly from the table, his chair dragging against the wood in a drawn-out moan. He picked up the longest of the knives. It glinted in the candlelight, a sinister little hook at the end. He turned towards me. Unsmiling, solemn, a mysterious sadness to him. But his eyes were warm, inviting, frenzied. He stepped closer. His hand reached out and caressed my face.

He cleared his throat. "Ms. Carrol, over the last month I have found myself terribly, painfully infatuated with you, and the only way I can think to ease my pain is by asking you to be my wife."

The servant assigned to stand in the corner gasped. I looked about wildly then. How many dinners had I survived at Gates Hall with nary an excitement?

"What, me?"

"You," Mr. Gates agreed. He didn't smile once–he couldn't even spare it for a proposal? "Then you shall never be lonely again. But take heed–if you agree to marry me, Beatrice, you will be agreeing to Woodbridge and its rules as well." He took his hand from my chin, tracing a finger along the edge of the knife. "You see, Woodbridge has its traditions, and it would be terribly unfit to not hold you to its standards."

Across the table, Marcie wore a gap-toothed smile. Her crooked teeth were showing. A toll of terror went through me.

"Please," Mr. Gates begged.

Marcie smiled. Marcie smiled wide.

"Alright, Alright. I will."

I'd never before heard Marcie cheer so loudly.

Mr. Gates approached me, knife in hand. The burning began before I could even protest.

OUT IN THE YARD, just beside the gates to the hall, a jack o' lantern grew a new face. It was a face previously unknown to Woodbridge. It smiled quaintly, demurely, and a small patch of yellow on its orange flesh seemed to fall like a tear.

High in the sky above Woodbridge, the moon rose to its apex. All Hallows Eve had never known such a glow. The little town called Woodbridge blinked out candle by candle. Under the cover of darkness, the Pumpkinheads lay in wait.

5
THE OXBLOOD DOOR
ALEXANDRA FASZEWSKI

The manor rose from the cobbled street before him, its turrets reaching into the night-dark sky like the spires of a crown. Anton dragged his bags behind him to the front steps, the straps of the painter's easel tight on his back. All in all, it was not the most dignified arrival for the new master of the house, but the staff had not arranged for a valet to accompany him.

He wondered how Oliver had felt, arriving at this very same spot only a month before. The man had been the former master of this place after he'd married its rich young mistress, but it wasn't long before he had disappeared without a trace. Now Anton was here, taking his place.

Everyone in town had known of Oliver and Margarida's union. Gossip travels fast, after all. There were whispers that Oliver had never even made it to his wife's bed that first night, that he had been taken to some strange dark part of the manor and left there to rot. Others said he was tortured, and that his ghost roamed the grounds. They said that the servants at the manor had concealed his disappearance from his relatives for weeks, that the manor was cursed.

Some hissed that the woman he'd married was a witch.

But Anton was here because he had no choice. He had married the young mistress of the manor because nobody else in their town would, not after she began cycling through husbands like day dresses. Rumors and reputation aside, however, she was perfectly lovely, and wealthy to boot. As long as he didn't see any tortured ghosts, he could find himself at home among the opulence of the manor.

He shivered and tried to pull himself from his swirling thoughts.

A servant in black stood in the doorway, hands clasped in front of her. It had been almost impossible to see her in the shadows. "Master Anton."

Anton recoiled, bumping his knee against one of his bags in his haste.

She looked about as old as the manor itself, coarse white hair scraped into a low bun at her nape. "Mistress Margarida and I welcome you to Lyon House. If you would follow me, please, I will show you to your rooms." The housekeeper stepped forward to grudgingly take one of the bags by the handle.

Anton's eyes rose to the windows. His new bride was not here to welcome him to their home herself? He supposed he should not be surprised. The action did not befit someone of her status.

A dark flash of movement caught his eye, drawing his gaze to one of the windows in particular. Was that a figure he'd seen silhouetted in the glass?

Anton tipped his chin up toward the windows. "Seems one of your ghosts is already curious about me," he said lightly. He made a joke of it because the rumors were too ridiculous to be believed– but when he was standing out here in the dark, he still didn't like the crawling feeling of being watched.

The woman didn't crack a smile. In fact, her mouth seemed to only deepen into a frown as she looked at him stonily. It was plain that she disapproved of him, or maybe of their match in general.

"Please, lead the way."

As they entered the manor, the heavy oak door slammed shut behind them. Anton jumped, his heart stopping for one painful moment. The hallway was scarcely lit, feeling more akin to a dark tunnel than the imposing entryway he imagined it to be by day. Perhaps they needed to install more sconces, or, perhaps it was unusual to receive visitors at such a late hour. Though, in this case, the guest was Margarida's new husband himself, and not a visitor at all.

The housekeeper glided down the hall, her old eyes uninhibited by the gloom. She had obviously walked this path many times before, maybe even guiding Margarida's past husbands on their first night here.

They traveled into the bowels of the house; Anton would need a candle to find his way at night.

The housekeeper stopped so suddenly in front of him that he almost stepped on her heel. "You will not, under any circumstances, open that door." She gestured down the hall to a single, arched wooden door. Unlike the rest of the house, it was well-lit. The door's rich oxblood paint gleamed in the light of the wall sconces that framed it on either side. Brass handles and hinges stood out against the red in sharp contrast.

His painter's hands itched. What could be behind that door? A treasury? A dungeon?

The housekeeper's mouth pinched. "This is an order from Margarida. You must not enter that room," she repeated. Something flashed in her eyes, which had been hard and expressionless until now.

It had been too quick to catch in the gloom, but– had that emotion been fear?

Anton nodded, concealing his anger. "Of course. I would not dare disrespect my wife." He turned away from the door. It should not matter what was behind it. He had the rest of Lyon House at his disposal now, as well as the coffers of his beautiful young wife.

"Your rooms will be this way."

He followed her black-clad form up the stairs, watching her shining white hair in the darkness to find his way.

Anton's room was the first door at the top of the stairs. He considered where his wife slept at night, for the housekeeper had clearly set up this room to be his and his alone. Amused, he thought of the separate bedchambers of the kings and queens of old. He was now the king of Lyon House, he supposed.

The housekeeper hesitated by the door once he stepped into the room. "Mistress Margarida's rooms are farther up the hall." She gestured vaguely with a hand. "She is not to be disturbed."

Surely he was going to be permitted to spend time with his wife? If that was not the case, his whole purpose for accepting this match was moot. Before he could find his voice, the housekeeper shut the door curtly behind her.

And he was alone.

Anton ran his trained artist's gaze across the room. It was much nicer than any accommodations he'd had before. There was a plush braided rug and a canopy bed that dripped with brocade linens. Those were real threads of gold and silver shooting through the comforter.

He ran his hand over the textured surface, a bit in awe that this was his.

A glossy mahogany desk and side table both sat against the wall underneath the window, a candelabra on the side table lit in anticipation of his arrival. In the corner sat an easel, made from the same rich mahogany. Unnecessarily expensive, but Anton was heartened that Margarida had even personalized the room for him. Painting was his livelihood– though he did not need a livelihood anymore, now that he was the master of Lyon

House. In the face of the kind gesture, a pang struck him at the thought of what he was here to do.

He moved to the window to peer outside, pushing aside the cream and gold drapes. Someone could have watched his arrival from this very window if they had been so inclined, situated as it was, overlooking the street.

He thought of the figure in the upstairs window that he'd glimpsed. Had it been from this window the person had been looking? Had someone even been there at all? He couldn't be certain– it had looked like a smudge of a thing, barely substantial, and it'd been dark out. But he had felt eyes on him then, and not just those of the housekeeper. He remembered the crawling feeling of not being alone.

Anton went to the door to retrieve the bag the housekeeper had deposited there. He might as well begin to settle into his mysterious new home, and hopefully, it would be time for dinner shortly– a late dinner nonetheless, given the hour, but he'd only just arrived, after all. The housekeeper's hard stare appeared in his mind. She *was* going to feed him, wasn't she? Maybe that was how the husbands kept disappearing.

Carefully, he unrolled a length of leather hide from his bag on the desk. Glass vials of liquids and powders stared up at him, and he ran his fingers along the daggers that interspersed the hide. There was one needle-thin knife that he could slip into his boot, another with a short, curved blade that the blacksmith assured would butcher a pig. Satisfied, he rolled the weapons back up and locked them out of sight in the desk drawer. He was prepared with the necessary tools to make Margarida's fortune truly his own, and they would also save his skin from whatever fate had awaited the other husbands at Lyon House.

He was not the first husband to walk through these doors, but he would be the last.

As Anton began to unpack his few belongings, his thoughts strayed to the exquisite oxblood door again. What secrets could

Margarida be hiding behind it? If he did not enter the room, he could hardly be reprimanded for that– just a tiny peek. His feet seemed to carry him on their own, down the stairs and past the door again.

He paused in the hallway to stare at it. It remained unchanged from how it had appeared just an hour or so prior. It was a lovely door, but he had other things– more important things– to focus on. Anton thought again of the drawer full of weapons upstairs, and of his beautiful, absent bride.

A throat cleared behind him, and his heart nearly stopped.

The housekeeper was standing there. She watched him with unreadable eyes. *How long had she been there?* "Dinner is ready, Master Anton." She walked away without another word, obviously expecting him to follow.

He wondered if she would say anything about the door.

Anton was seated in the dining room across from Margarida's empty seat. It was all very mysterious, and frustrating. His bride clearly had a flair for dramatics and intended to make him wait.

The housekeeper stepped forward to fill his glass with wine, though he noticed it was a different bottle that she poured from to fill her mistress' vessel.

He fiddled with the stem of his glass and gazed across the table, stomach faint from hunger. The room was silent as they waited.

Moments later, there was a rustling at the doorway as Margarida swept into the room and seated herself at the table. She was as elegant as he remembered, dressed in an eggplant-colored gown that slipped off her shoulders, and a thick collar of diamonds. Just one of those diamonds could have made him a wealthy man. "I hope I haven't kept you waiting, dear husband," she said with a decidedly coy smile, lifting her glass to him.

Under her arresting gaze, Anton couldn't help but blush. Any man would have done the same. This was why men continued to tie their fate to hers, even after each husband disappeared not a month after their wedding day.

He was saved from answering by a smattering of servants, who entered with platters of food. Clearly, they had just been waiting in the wings for Margarida to make her grand entrance.

Anton accepted the plates set before him– piles of meats, hard cheeses, and crusty bread for sopping up the juices of the meat. It was a veritable feast– so unlike the meals he'd scraped together as an enterprising young portraitist. He could certainly get used to this decadence. Did Margarida eat like this every night, or was this a welcome dinner, put on for his benefit? Looking again at the stack of diamonds around her throat, he thought that it was likely to be the former.

Once he had killed her, all of his bride's wealth would be his, and his alone.

The housekeeper stood at Margarida's shoulder. "Have you made my orders clear to our Anton, about that room at the far end of the hall?" Margarida speared a cube of meat on her plate, but she was not looking at the housekeeper for a response– she was staring straight across the table at Anton.

Anton's eyes flicked to the housekeeper. Would she tell her mistress she had already caught him prowling around by the door before dinner?

But the housekeeper said nothing. She seemed to deliberately avoid his gaze. "Yes, I let him know upon his arrival," she said stoutly.

Margarida broke into a smile. "Good. Welcome to Lyon House, Anton. If there is anything you ever need, Blanca will be happy to help."

The housekeeper – Blanca – nodded sourly.

As they began to eat, Blanca melted from the room, only appearing periodically throughout the meal to stiffly refill Anton's and Margarida's wine glasses. After the second pour of wine,

Anton gestured across the table with his own glass. "What is it that you are drinking?" Blanca had continued to pour Margarida her drinks from a different bottle than his own. Whether that was an indication of Blanca's personal opinion of him, he did not know.

Margarida smiled secretively, and her tongue darted out to draw in a bead of red that had clung to her bottom lip. His eyes followed the movement hungrily. "It's a special blend," she responded vaguely.

The dinner passed by in a blur as Anton drank freely and chatted leisurely to Margarida. Throughout, she seemed to regard him with an indulgent smile. Almost as if he were a child. He'd eaten more varieties of cheese and fruit than he had ever been able to afford on his artist's commission, and certainly not in one meal. He was contemplating this fact, twirling his wine glass around by the stem, when his wife drained her glass and stood.

"Good night, Anton," she said serenely, and floated from the room before he could respond.

At that, the servants returned and began to carry away the platters and glasses. One took his plate right out from in front of him with a hushed, "Master Anton."

Dinner was over, then. Anton dabbed his mouth with the silk napkin from his lap and set it on the tabletop. If nothing had been achieved here tonight, he at least had a sense of how Margarida expected him to behave. As if it were *he* who was the wife.

Margarida was still the master of this house, but that would change once she was dead.

Anton headed back toward his room, and for the first time since walking down this hallway, he noticed the paintings that lined the walls. All of them featured a beautiful, dark-haired woman throughout the ages. They could not all be Margarida– some of the portraits were ancient– but there was something akin to her in each figure. The curve of her lips, the knowing gleam in her eyes.

The eyes... Now that he was looking, it seemed that the gaze of each painting was tracking his every movement. His skin crawled, and he avoided eye contact with the painted women.

Anton's attention was caught, though, by the closest painting. This one was certainly a portrait of Margarida. Her flowing dark waves cascaded over her shoulders, and she watched him from the canvas with a beguiling smile. Her eyes flickered with his movements, following him. It certainly seemed as if she was watching. Laughing at him.

It had to be the wine, making him imagine things. Right?

BLANCA CAME to fetch him again for breakfast in the morning, but when Anton sat down at the table, the food came out before Margarida had arrived. It was a quieter affair, with only Blanca bringing out platters of fruit and flaky biscuits drizzled in butter and honey.

He realized that the table was only set for one. "When will I see my wife?" he asked as Blanca re-entered the dining room, a pitcher of grapefruit juice in her hands.

It frustrated him how it seemed Margarida had all of the power still, even though as her husband, he should be the master of the house. He was expected to accept her terms here, handed down by Blanca. How was he supposed to get close to her?

"Mistress Margarida is busy." She set the pitcher down and wiped her hands on the pristine apron tied to her front. "Too busy for you, husband or not. You'll have to otherwise entertain yourself during the day."

Anton paused with a biscuit halfway to his mouth. The honey trickled down the sides, onto his thumb and forefinger.

Surely he could ask a question– Blanca was not his superior. "Busy doing what?" It wasn't like Margarida had an occupation, besides being wealthy.

Blanca noted his surprise, and her eyes darted away. "You have an easel, don't you?" She said brusquely, waving her hand.

He swallowed the biscuit and licked his fingers. "I suppose so…"

"Well, then." The housekeeper bustled away quicker than was necessary. He couldn't help but think that it was to avoid any more of his questions.

How strange. He was being left to fend for himself– though perhaps he would enjoy it, being able to do as he pleased, when he pleased. After all, he would never have to want for money again. Yet, he couldn't help feeling there was something odd about Lyon House. The figure he had seen in the window, the woman in the portraits, the silent staff, and the rumors of ghosts– he felt in his bones that this was no ordinary manor.

After he sated himself with melon and berries and biscuits, he returned to his rooms for his paints. He strapped the new easel to his back and tucked the lacquered box of paints and brushes under his arm. As he left, he tossed one last look at the desk drawer where his knives waited. He would be putting them to use soon, once he finalized his plan.

The portraits on the walls seemed less foreboding by daylight with the drapes pulled back from the windows, washing the space in warm golden light. Dust motes sparked slowly through the air, on their downward trajectory.

Lyon House should have a garden where he could try his hand at *plein air* painting, but Anton was accustomed to painting portraits. He hardly thought Blanca would humor the request to sit for him. The easel was beginning to grow cumbersome on his back as he prowled the hallways aimlessly.

A flash of sunlight caught Anton's eye, and his gaze was

drawn to a gilt mirror on the wall. So it was to be a self-portrait, then.

He pulled his arms through the straps and began to set up his easel, peering around the corner of the canvas to frame his reflection in a more interesting composition. When he painted commissions, the model was always staring at him head on. It was the same thing, painting after painting. Anton was hardly able to provide any sort of artistic direction. That was not what his patrons paid him for. *This* would be more challenging.

Quickly, he fleshed out the shape of his face, the placement of the one eye that he could see looking out from behind the canvas. His expression in the mirror looked stricken. Not at peace. Gooseflesh crept across his arms as he stared at his reflection. Why did he look that way?

Anton dabbed burnt umber onto the canvas to define his curls and sighed in frustration.

He'd somehow lucked into a marriage with the most stunning woman in town, and wealthy too, because of the rumors and of Margarida's string of disappearing husbands. The opportunity for the match wouldn't have arisen otherwise– not for a man of his decidedly plain lineage. He was poised to act soon, with his vials of poisons and his knives locked away safely in his room. But he couldn't shake the conviction that something was not quite right here.

"This isn't working." He set down his brush and ran a hand across his eyes.

Anton let his feet lead him in pursuit of a new subject, a new distraction– anything. Was this what boredom felt like? He'd never had the luxury of being bored before he'd become wealthy. Before, every moment of his day was filled by some task or other, and he found now that he did not know what to do without that structure.

No. He had hit a creative wall.

When his feet dragged to a stop, he was only half surprised

to find that he had come to the oxblood door yet again. There was something about it that stimulated a response in him. Perhaps it was because it was forbidden. But his creative spark jumped in him when he looked at the spot, and he hastened to set up his canvas again.

He must paint it.

Without a twinge of regret, he loaded white paint onto the canvas, covering his half-finished portrait with broad, quick strokes of his palette knife. Anton toned the canvas and took his India Red and Perylene Red paints– mixed them on his palette. No, the color wasn't quite right. The door was the color of blood. The color of garnet. The color of Margarida's wine at their dinner table.

Was that what she kept behind this door? Was it a wine-making space, for her special blend?

Focus on the work.

Anton's fervor subsided as he sketched out the scene with his paints, and he fell into that peaceful, almost catatonic state he reached when he was immersed in his art. It consumed him until it was time to prepare for dinnertime.

That evening with Margarida was more of the same– they exchanged pleasantries and sipped their wine, and Anton refrained from asking her how she spent her day. As did she. The less he spoke with Margarida, the less guilt he was going to feel when he plunged his dagger into her smooth skin. Though he still needed to get closer to her. Maybe he should make a visit to her chambers soon. He *was* her husband, after all…

After dinner, Anton lay restlessly in bed. He couldn't sleep– perhaps he should have drunk more of the wine to dull his troublesome thoughts. His gaze searched out the desk drawer in the dark. Maybe he should take out one of his knives and creep down to his wife's room, where she surely laid asleep in bed. This would be the perfect time to end this farce, but he would have to be subtle about how he did it.

As if in response to his treacherous thoughts, a low moan sounded down the hall.

Anton clutched the sheets in one fist and stilled.

As he listened, soft footfalls began to reverberate, accompanied by the sound of something being dragged across the floorboards. Another disembodied cry came, sounding closer this time.

Anton closed his eyes, as if that could stop the noises he was hearing. No, he would not go out there tonight, he decided. Perhaps he was just imagining the sounds– a possible side effect of the dark manor and the wine at dinner.

There was a thud and a whimper at what sounded like the staircase.

No, he was not imagining this.

If he hadn't been an artist, his fingers would have been trembling as he lit the candelabra and held it aloft. Instead, his steady hand cast the chambers in a warm yellow glow. He crept to the door as the horrible dragging sound tapered off into the distance.

"Hello?" He threw the door open and peered outwards, candelabra at the ready.

But the hallway was still and silent, empty save for a portrait of Margarida smirking down at him.

"BLANCA." Anton hadn't slept a wink the previous night, but that hadn't stopped Blanca from rousing him for breakfast bright and early– as if tardiness were a federal crime. Once he'd blown out the candles and returned to bed, the noises had started up again at the end of the house. He didn't know what to make of it, and he couldn't help but wonder if the rumors *were* true– that Margarida's missing husbands haunted the manor house.

Before, he had brushed it off as silly superstition. Now, he resolved that he would not let himself become the next ghost.

The housekeeper stopped and turned, almost unwillingly. She waited for him to speak.

"I heard noises last night," he started self-consciously. "It sounded as if someone was out in the hallway– hurt, maybe. Do you know what it was?"

Blanca's expression betrayed nothing, but an almost imperceptible twitch passed across her face. She turned on her heel to leave and spoke over her shoulder. "I will be back in later to clear the dishes. Please enjoy."

Anton would not be able to get a word out of Blanca. He didn't know why he thought that he would. He clenched his fist in his lap as he watched her leave.

In the daylight, thoughts of the strange noises from the previous night seemed less frightening. Instead, his mind turned to the mystery door and his painting as he drank his grapefruit juice. The paints should be set enough on the canvas that he could begin to layer on the details, like the shine of the metal hinges and the wood grain texture that peeked from beneath the finish. A burble of excitement rose in his chest. He could not wait to finish his breakfast and get back to painting.

When he set up his easel again in the hall, the brass handle on the door winked in the light, as if welcoming him back. He'd brought a second canvas, too, so that he could paint the door as he remembered it that first night, glowing in the light from the sconces, a beacon in the murky dark of the hallway. The image was beginning to haunt him.

A few hours later, Anton paused in his work and leaned back from the easel to regard the door, arms crossed. He wanted to convey the curiosity he felt about the door clearly on the canvas. What was it that needed to be guarded behind this door?

It was then that a shadow fell across the canvas, and he startled. His first thought was of the noises from last night, that one of the ghosts had come to harm him.

But it was only Margarida standing over his shoulder and frowning at the painting. How had she crept up on him so silently?

"You shouldn't be here," she admonished. Her eyes were dark as she met his gaze. "You know that this door is forbidden, Anton. You should stay away."

He faltered under her gaze. "I wasn't going to enter. I'm just painting it."

"You shouldn't be so curious about it." Her expression changed, softened. "If it's a subject you want, how about I sit for another one of your portraits?"

The offer surprised him, as did seeing Margarida here, during the daytime. Hadn't Blanca said that Margarida would be too busy during the day? "I would be honored."

As Anton replaced his canvas on the easel with the extra that he had brought, he noticed that Margarida looked pale. She was still impeccably put together, but her skin was waxy and her eyes were ringed with dark circles. It looked like she had not slept, either.

Regardless, he would make her beauty shine through in this painting.

The best thing about portrait painting was that you had a captive audience, and he was going to use this opportunity the best he could to ingratiate himself to her. Anton busied himself by squeezing new paints onto his palette. Truthfully, this would have been the perfect opportunity to murder her, if he had only had his knives with him. "Did you sleep well last night? I know I didn't– I heard the strangest noises in the house. Did you hear them, too?"

He chanced a look at Margarida.

His wife smiled, cat-like. "I'm afraid I don't know what

you're talking about. It must be the wild animals outside that you're hearing."

He knew he hadn't imagined it, and it had sounded like it was something inside the house. Anton could feel that his brow was furrowed as he thought. He continued to blend the paints to achieve Margarida's rich, tawny complexion.

"Well. I'm sure it will be quieter tonight," she said. She must be humoring him. As though he were a child. The thought irked him. "Are you enjoying Lyon House so far, my husband?"

It had only been a day or so, and Anton didn't really know what to think of the manor. He had to admit that he hadn't quite known what he was walking into. "I expected that we would spend more time together," he answered honestly. After all, his plan hinged on getting close to her, as a husband should surely be able to do with his wife.

How was he to kill her otherwise?

Truthfully, Margarida was an enigmatic and pleasant enough woman. She was bewitching. It wasn't that he hated her– everything would just be easier with her dead. After all, he wasn't a fool. The woman surely had something to do with her husband's disappearances, and if he sat back and did nothing, it would be him who was next. But if *she* was the one who disappeared, he would be able to live the life of luxury a simple man like him could never dream of otherwise.

Margarida tilted her head thoughtfully. "I suppose dinnertime is hardly enough." She pulled her wrap closer around her body. "I'll come back and sit for you tomorrow, if you like, too. You can hardly be expected to finish a portrait in one day."

Perfect. It was a start. The sooner Margarida was dead, the better, he thought, ignoring the twinge in his chest. He needed to do it before he got too attached.

A HIGH, keening wail and a thud woke Anton that night, and he scrabbled for the candelabra in the darkness. The same dragging noise from before started up again, punctuated with a grunt, as if one of the ghosts– or whatever it was– was dragging something particularly heavy.

How could Margarida not hear this?

Anton lit the candelabra and armed himself with one of the wickedly sharp knives from the desk drawer.

He was going to end this before he went insane.

"Who's there?" He hissed, swinging open the bedroom door, but again, nobody was there.

A moan echoed in the darkness of the house, and he followed the noise, creeping towards the kitchen. Could the ghosts hear his heart, thudding too fast in his chest? Anton was sick with nerves.

The house was still, and dark as night, the only sounds coming from Anton's own feet and his short, labored breaths. Every once in a while, as he crept down the hall, the moan would come again, from deeper in the house. Taunting him.

Or luring him in.

Anton clutched the knife tighter in his hand, the handle pressing uncomfortably into his palm.

A candle, lit in the kitchen, gave him pause.

There was something bubbling on the stove. The scent was heavy and sharp, almost metallic. It blanketed the air so that he could smell its particular tang even from where he stood in the doorway.

He crept closer. And recoiled.

The pot was filled with blood, black in the darkness.

Anton wheeled back and pressed a hand over his nose and mouth.

When he peered over the edge of the metal pot again, though, it was only a thick tomato sauce bubbling cheerily away that met his gaze. It charred at the edges, as if it had been forgotten in the rush of the earlier dinner preparations.

Had that truly just been his imagination? If so, he couldn't even trust his mind in Lyon House.

Anton shuddered and backed away, out of the kitchen.

A creak sounded, and he turned in that direction, knife poised at the ready. But nobody emerged out of the gloom– no ghosts, not Blanca, and not wild animals, either.

If he was going to get to the bottom of this, he would have to follow the noises.

He stalked the creaks and groans until he reached the oxblood door.

Why was it that he was always drawn back here?

This time, though, there was something different about the vignette. The sconces were still lit, and there was nobody in sight, but the door stood ajar, just a crack.

Something, or someone, was on the other side.

Anton moved as if in a trance. He stowed his knife away to free his hand, and slowly reached out towards the door handle.

He had to know.

A cold hand fell on his shoulder, and he cried out.

Blanca's sharp gaze cut into him. The candelabra cast shadows across the wrinkles in her face. "Let's take you to bed, Master Anton. You're sleepwalking."

Was he dreaming this? Anton shook the sleep– and the wine– from his head. He followed Blanca back towards the stairs, but cast one last glance over his shoulder at the door.

It was still cracked open.

ANTON DREAMT VIVIDLY for the rest of the night.

He found himself standing outside the door, and it glowed,

taunting him. The crack beneath shone golden, as if there was a pile of treasure gleaming inside, just beyond his reach. Every time he stepped closer, though, the entryway seemed farther away.

Anton began to hurry forward, afraid that the door would retreat from his vision entirely, and his sight narrowed until it was all that he saw in the dark void. The more that he tried to rush forward, the slower he seemed to move. It felt as if he was up to his ankles in the honey he had eaten for breakfast.

As the door faded away, a thin wail arose and his blood ran cold.

Then he realized the person crying out had been him.

MARGARIDA CAME to sit for her portrait the next morning, as promised, but this time it was Anton who was waxen and pale.

His bride looked radiant. She brought a stool to sit upon while he painted her, arranging her skirts coyly as she sat down. A flash of ankle peeped out at him. "You don't look like you slept well, my husband."

Was that a knowing glint in her eye?

It took Anton a moment to respond. "I heard noises again last night," he said. He picked up the Black Spinel paint with his brush and started to define her hair on the canvas. "I don't know how they don't bother you."

Margarida's smile was tight. "Perhaps I've gotten used to them. Let's talk about something else, my dear." They were silent for several minutes as Anton painted and let his mind wander. He was sure her mind was doing the same, though he couldn't imagine what she was thinking behind her mask. After his restless night, his thoughts were sluggish and unfocused.

But he kept seeing red. First, it was the pot of blood– or was it tomato sauce?-- that he had seen in the kitchen. And then, his introspection moved, predictably, to the oxblood door. It permeated his thoughts, and now it even invaded his dreams. Anton cursed the door.

He wished he had been able to open it last night, before Blanca interrupted him. At least then he would know what his wife was hiding there, and possibly even uncover the true secret of Lyon House.

Perhaps it was treasure inside, like his dream had suggested. Perhaps it was a workshop of sorts, and that was where Margarida spent her days. Though, what she could have been doing in there, he had no idea. His wife was only known for her charisma and incredible beauty, as well as her money.

Well. And her missing husbands.

"Yes, let's talk about something else," he said at last.

Margarida startled out of her reverie and turned cool eyes upon him.

"The oxblood door– what is inside?" He gestured behind her.

His wife's hands clenched in her lap. "This house has *one* rule," she hissed. Before he realized what was happening, she stood up, knocking over the stool in her haste. She stormed off, her strides long and fast.

Anton wasn't sure what sort of reaction he had expected. His gaze lifted, slowly, from the canvas to the door. He considered it.

If there wasn't something valuable inside, it wouldn't be forbidden– would it? And maybe– if there was something valuable inside, he wouldn't have to carry out his sordid plan. He could lift it and be gone before anyone even realized a thing.

His stomach turned at the thought of his wife's blood, spattered across the hardwood floor. He had never actually killed before, but he couldn't allow himself to back down this late into the scheme.

Tonight. He would open the door tonight.

ANTON WAITED for the noises to begin before he flung himself out of bed and hurried down the staircase, peering into the shadows for the telltale gleam of Blanca's head. She was not going to stop him this time.

There was a creak and a whimper from down the hall. He was getting closer.

Anton held the candelabra aloft to keep the shadows away, as if it would keep the specters away, too– whatever it was that he was hearing.

As he approached the door, he saw again that it was standing ajar. The same thuds and moans that he heard night after night were coming from the other side.

What could be going on in there? Had ghosts made their way beyond the door, too?

Anton hesitated in front of the door. His hand hovered above the handle. If he did this, he broke Lyon House's most cardinal rule. There may be no turning back afterward. He didn't know what sort of penalty would be carried out if he was caught.

But he had to know. He feared the door was driving him mad.

The scent of copper filled his nostrils as he stepped inside.

The room was bare and dark. If he'd had to paint it, he'd have used shades of brown or blue to capture the inky shadows. A rope creaked from the ceiling, and Anton looked up to see a body swinging from the beams, suspended by a disjointed arm.

His strangled gasp echoed in the darkness, and his heartbeat thundered, as if it were trying to escape his chest.

The man's corpse was stiff, a wound at the base of his throat. The body glowed bone white in the moonlight. Not a single drop of blood oozed from the wound, and Anton glanced to the floor– it must have splattered or dripped.

But the floor was clean. The corpse had been completely drained of ichor.

Anton didn't want to look any closer, but a sick sort of fascination urged him to look at the man's face, partially obscured by his long brown hair.

An electric spark of recognition ran through his veins.

It was Oliver, Margarida's last husband. He had disappeared not long before Anton and Margarida had wed.

Anton clapped his hand over his nose to block the stench of rot. He was choking on it. Oliver's body couldn't create such a smell on its own.

Anton staggered forward and swept the candelabra across his line of vision, and there in the shadows, he saw them. The bodies swung silently on ropes of their own. All men. All bloodless. All of Margarida's husbands.

There was Alec, the blond foreigner. And Elijah, who used to frequent the printing press with his political pamphlets. The older names and faces began to blur together, and some of the corpses were in such a state that they were no longer recognizable.

Terror narrowed his vision. He had to leave here, *now*.

There was a monster in Lyon House.

He fumbled backward, a cry trapped in his throat. And bumped into something.

Sick with the thought of touching one of the bodies, he turned slowly, almost afraid of what he would find.

Margarida stood behind him. Her eyes glittered in the low light, and she *tsked*. "You've been bad, my darling."

Anton's thoughts whirled as he tried to put the disjointed pieces together. His pulse sped like a frightened rabbit, even as he stood frozen in fear. *Margarida did this?*

Her fangs came down and indented her lower lip, and she stalked forward.

6

HEART OF THORNS

KIMBERLEY FORD

They say that the wood used to be safe, once. Even on the deepest, darkest nights. But that was before the curse - and the girl who cast it.

Now, we dare not set foot beyond the wall after the sun sinks below the horizon. For, after nightfall, the trees drip with thorns as long as your forearm, their trunks shifting from their usual daylight brown to deeper shades of midnight. Vines rise from the ground, snaking through the undergrowth, ready and waiting to drag you into the hollows. And that's if the voices don't get to you first.

If you dare to wander too close, the wood calls to you with a voice only you can hear, begging you to stay, to leave the paths far behind. Sometimes it might sound like a brother, a lover, a child; other times like voices you long to hear again. Luring you straight into the mouths of the hungry things that lurk in the shadows.

But you would do well not to listen. To close the shutters and lock the doors. We villagers all know this well. Scarred hearts make for strong minds, never to be scarred by the same thing twice.

So, tonight, I hurry back to our cabin, my lantern raised high against the encroaching dark. It's almost winter, here in Vale, and night is falling too fast, the last of the leaves crunching beneath my feet as I follow the path along the wall. It's the only physical protection we have from the wood and the beasts, and it is crumbling where the villagers don't care to mend it. Not much of a protection anymore, for our home on the very edge of the village.

Now, only my grandmother's wards can truly keep the wood's monsters out. But not for too much longer. As each year goes by, the wards weaken around our cabin and the beasts prowl ever closer.

I keep my steps light, fast, until the cabin comes into view, the windows glowing buttercup yellow in the light of the candles within. I am halfway up the steps, almost within reach of the front door, when I hear it. The unmistakable crack of a branch underfoot. But when I whirl, eyes scanning the dark beyond the reach of my lantern, there is nothing there. I pause, listening, but nothing moves. So I shake off the feeling and reach for the door. Probably it's just another of the wood's tricks.

But then I hear it again.

This time, all I see is a set of huge green eyes, blinking in the light of my lantern, before the shadowy thing turns tail and scrambles back across the wall. I don't want to think about how long it might have been following me.

So much for thinking the wards were holding.

I say as much as I rush through the door, the warmth of the fire in the hearth enveloping me as I shut the door tight behind me, sliding the bolt across more firmly than I usually do.

"They should hold for at least another year," my grandmother replies absently, her back to me as she grinds some herbs into a thick paste. No doubt for another of her tonics. Perhaps another of the Blaise kids is ill again.

"But I just saw something outside," I say as I shrug out of my cloak. "Something from the wood."

That gets her full attention. "You saw what?"

"Something. Huge eyes. Not sure what, but it was just outside. Gone now though."

"Are you sure it wasn't just the Blaise's barn cat again, Immy?"

I sigh. "Are cats usually this big?" I stretch out my hands wide to illustrate the massive size. Far bigger than a dog, but not quite as big as a horse.

Now she lays down her pestle. Grips the countertop with both hands. "No. No, they're not," she admits, weariness curving her shoulders as if I've just dropped a large weight on them. And I guess I have. Only my grandmother's magic is strong enough to set the wards now. And, as the years pass, even her magic wanes. The last of the Greenlakes, except for me.

"So, what do we do?"

"We go into the wood. I'll lay some wards from inside. If one creature broke through, there will be more."

"Into the wood?"

She nods. "First light will be best."

That only makes me feel slightly better. Though the curse weakens in daylight hours, the wood is always a formidable place. A place where you can never drop your guard.

Before...

It began a long time ago, but not so long ago as you'd expect.

And it started with a girl. A Greenlake girl. Her family passed the name down through the maternal line. Mother to daughter, daughter to granddaughter. A single name through the ages. A single line. Unbroken.

Back then, the Greenlakes lived by a great forest. A forest alive with all manner of furry, friendly creatures - tame as anything - and plants that shone green as jewels in the morning sun. A good forest, rich and plentiful. At least, for a time.

The girl grew up strong, her feet bare. Knowing the paths in the forest as well as she knew the lifelines snaking across her palm. Knowing that the forest was a place of safety, a haven she could go to when the raised voices in her parents' room grew too loud for her to sleep through. On nights like those, she would slip outside like a ghost and plunge into the waiting arms of the trees. Curl into a hollow just like a squirrel. A safe place where she wouldn't cry, wouldn't cry. Until she'd fall asleep, wrapped in a blanket of leaves.

Until one night, when everything changed.

That night, after the harsh words turned into harsh lines down her face, she'd run from the house, barely sixteen now, with blood seeping down her forehead. She hadn't started the fire that burned there later, reducing the house to ash, but the fury burning in her blood very well could have.

That night, her fury, her grief, her sheer frustration, it burned beneath her skin like a living thing. Hotter than any candle. Hotter than the fires in the village hearths. Because she knew she could not go back. Not to that house.

And as she ran, she fell, tripping on a tangled old tree root. In that rush of shock, as the ground rose to meet her, she stretched out her hands to save herself. Hands which burned so hot they glowed as they made contact with the mossy ground beneath. The resulting flare of light blinding in the near-dark.

As the glow died, fading away like a miniature sunset between her fingers, suddenly she could feel it. The forest.

She could feel it breathing, the sensation coming from all around. Like its very pulse thrummed beneath her fingers. And then: more. She felt the tiny, fluttering fear of mice darting between the leaves. The bold confidence of foxes, trotting between clearings. The melancholy of wolves, roaming under the moon. The peaceful slumbering of song-

birds, dreaming the dark away. The brightness and the thrill of new life, nestled in the soil right beneath her hands.

As she sat up slowly, she realised it wasn't just a feeling. Realised it was real as she lifted her hands and saw, beneath them, in the leaf mould that was bare moments before, two new saplings unfurl.

She concluded later that it must be magic. A type of magic not seen for hundreds of years, flowing from her to the forest. Allowing her to grow new life, to heal what was broken. To start fresh in the tiny house she built herself under the trees she loved more than her own family.

But, the girl was not quite right.

The magic didn't just flow from her that night. It flowed from the forest. As she took on the forest's energy, it in turn absorbed her hurt and her pure, burning fury. The fury raged like wildfire in her blood. The forest absorbed it all, drawing it from her hands down into the soil, down into its roots, into its heart.

After that moment, both she and the forest were never the same.

I TOSS and turn all night, my dreams haunted by green eyes glowing in the dark. By the thought of walking in the wood beneath the towering, hungry trees. Knowing that chances are the voice that will call to me there will be my mother's.

It is still not yet light when I give up on sleep altogether. I push back the blankets and slip into the kitchen. The fire has banked so I stoke it again, feeding it more logs until it flickers merrily in the grate. Once it's hot enough I set the kettle over the flames to boil, making sure to catch it just before it can scream the house down and wake my grandmother. Then, steaming berry tea in hand, I pace in front of the window.

Outside, the darkness is gradually leaching away, the day dawning grey and cold. Mist slowly rises from the trees, shrouding the distant mountains. Usually, I love the promise of morning, of a new day, chasing the dark away. But today, all I feel is nervous, the churning anxiety like claws tracing across my insides. The mist doesn't help. I don't like days like this, where you can't see clearly what's in front of you.

It's also the reason I don't see him to start with. The man struggles over a low gap in the distant wall, clutching his arm. I don't see him until he topples and falls, the movement catching my attention as he lands in a crumpled, dark heap at the base of the wall.

My internal debate lasts only a few seconds as I watch him. To stay, or to help? But my feet are already moving for the door before I make a conscious decision. I run down the cabin steps, the cold biting through the thin sleeves of my nightdress, my spilled tea lying abandoned on the kitchen table.

The man groans as I reach him, and, as I kneel beside him, I see in the murky dawn light that he is young, probably about my age. But he's unfamiliar. The sharp lines of his face belong to no one I know in Vale. He's also only wearing trousers. No shirt. No shoes. Dirt covers the bare skin across his chest in broad swathes.

But as I lean closer, into the shard of light spilling through the cabin door, I realize it's not dirt at all. It's blood.

That's when I call for my grandmother.

TOGETHER, we somehow drag him into the cabin. Immediately, I get to work on boiling the kettle again and soaking rags to sterilise them, while my grandmother inspects the wound. In the light of the fire in the hearth, I can see the source of the blood is a deep wound to the stranger's shoulder. Something sharp seems to be sticking out of it.

"That's an arrow. Well, part of one," my grandmother explains as I hand her the first of the rags. Now that she says it, I can see it for what it is, the broken shaft sticking right out of the wound. Perhaps he snapped it in two trying to free himself.

The sight of it, going straight through his shoulder, is rather nauseating and so, instead, I turn my attention to his face. He looks more peaceful now since my grandmother gave him something to help with the pain, the lines of his forehead smoothing out.

As if sensing my gaze, or the swift strokes of the rag as my grandmother starts wiping the blood from his chest, his eyes open. As they meet mine, I'm struck by the colour. A bright, clear hazel, more green than brown in the light of the fire. I reach out to squeeze his hand, to reassure him that he is safe. That this safety is real. But he tangles his fingers with mine first, his fingers long, strong.

As his skin touches mine, the contact sends a strange shock up my arm that I can feel all the way down to my toes. He must feel it too as his eyes widen. "Don't leave me," he says, his voice low, soft, pleading, his grip on my hand almost bruising. Then he falls back against the pillows, unconscious.

"I won't," I tell him, even though he can no longer hear me.

My grandmother straightens then, the rag in her hand soaked scarlet with blood. "We should probably get that arrow gone before he wakes."

I nod, mirroring my grandmother as she presses him down against the mattress with one hand, using my free hand to press on his uninjured shoulder. I can't watch, though, as she slides the arrow free. I can only grip his hand tighter as he lurches back to consciousness with a roar of pain. Can only keep pressure on his chest. Forcing him to lay flat.

"It's okay, it's okay," I repeat as his muscles slowly relax beneath my hand. He lies back again with a groan and I trace his hand with my thumb, moving in slow, soothing circles until, at last, deep sleep claims him.

When my grandmother moves to start the healing, to knit

his skin back together, I peel his fingers from mine. My hands already know what's coming next, itching with magic in answer to my grandmother's as she summons it forth. Greenlake magic. It longs to escape, to reach for the man's skin. To join with my grandmother's energy. To help. To heal. But I squash the sensation down, down, down, refusing to set it loose. Doing so has never turned out well.

She tries to keep me there, to show me how the process works. Just like she always does. So that I can be better, be stronger. But I shake my head and retreat to the safety of my room. I close the door tight behind me and lean my back against it, eyes closed. Waiting for the magic thrumming inside me to slip away.

I only re-emerge when she knocks to tell me it's done. When my magic has coiled back so far inside me again that I can no longer feel it.

My grandmother says nothing as I pass her. But I read it in her eyes. Her regret, her guilt, her sadness. It shines there before she turns away, back to the sink.

I will not use it again. Never. No matter how much it battles with me. It's a fight I must win. Always. Even if she can't understand it. Even if it was so easy for her to move on. To live as if the space between us - the empty chair at dinner, the empty room between ours - doesn't exist. To ignore the stares we get in the village now. The whispers.

For me, it's not so straightforward.

Before...

Ivy Greenlake was always used to being the outcast. The girl who vanished into the forest, forgotten. Alone.

The girl with thorns around her heart. Thick and cruel as bram-

bles. But in her little house under the ancient, twisted oaks, she finally feels the thorns loosen.

For a time she is so happy, spending the days tending her little house and her little garden, that she doesn't notice the change in the trees. Sleeps so deeply at night that she doesn't hear the howls and the screams rising in the shadows. Doesn't see the eyes glowing in the dark.

By the time she does, it is far, far too late.

WHEN THE STRANGER WAKES, it is almost evening again. The mist has cleared and the moon rises in the east, a silver sickle in the sky.

He wakes unsure of where he is, his hands searching the blankets, until his gaze finds me, sitting in the chair by the fire. He relaxes then. Lies back against the pillows. But his eyes stay on me, tracking me as I rise from the rocking chair and set aside the sock I was mending. I might not be able to assist my grandmother with magic, but I can use my hands for other things.

I pour him some water and go to sit on the edge of the mattress beside him. "Thought you could use this," I say, offering him the cup.

"Thank you." He takes it gratefully and, like before, there's that strange shock as his fingers brush mine. He pauses, our hands still touching, his eyes searching mine. More brown than green in the firelight, the rich colours of the earth and the trees. It's like I can see a whole forest contained in them.

"Imogen!" I jump at the sound of my grandmother's voice as she peers around the back door, causing the water to slosh between us. Some of it drips down my wrist as I turn towards her. Of course, she chooses now to ask for my help in fetching something.

But she seems to change her mind about whatever it is

directly she sees her patient is awake. Instead, her focus leaves me and alights on his face. "Ah, I see you're up, Silas," she says. The smile she gives him practically glows.

Of *course*, she's somehow already got his name. Probably before she sent him into sleep after the healing. There is never anything she doesn't know and I still don't know quite how she does it.

I match the name to the stranger's face. *Silas*. He looks back at me, still, with those bright eyes of his, his tawny hair falling across his forehead in messy waves. For some reason I find myself wanting to push the strands back, out of his eyes. But instead, I drop my hand from where I'm still partly holding the cup, severing the contact between us.

"I have to go out - there's another fever at the Blaise's," my grandmother continues. "Imogen will be here though if you need anything." She smiles again at Silas and reaches for her cloak. "A few more hours and you'll probably feel right as rain-apart from the bruising. That will have to heal on its own."

"Thank you, Ms. Greenlake. For everything," Silas says.

"Don't thank me yet," she replies with a laugh, then ducks out the back door, her cloak rippling behind her.

When she's gone, Silas turns to me. "She did it with magic didn't she?"

"The healing? Yes," I say warily, watching for his face to close up. For the hatred and the suspicion to bloom. But rather than being frightened by it, Silas leans forward, eager. "How does it work?"

I try to hide that I'm taken aback. "You really want to know?"

"I wouldn't ask if I didn't."

"It's kind of a long story."

He smiles. "I have time."

And so, slowly, I tell him. About Ivy Greenlake. The first of us. I tell him how she changed the wood with the simple touch of her hands to the cool, hard earth. How she cursed it. Cursed us, to live with the same magic coursing through our veins. I tell him, just as my grandmother told me, and her mother before her.

"Generations of Greenlake women before us worked to be accepted. They worked as healers, like my grandmother. They worked hard so that we could at least be respected here. So we wouldn't be cast out because of our magic."

"What changed?" Silas asks softly, his face cradled in his hands. He's drawn up his knees to his chin to listen.

Something about the clear, honest way he looks at me gives me the courage to say it aloud. "My father. He fell ill and my mother couldn't save him - nearly drove herself mad trying to. And eventually, she used too much power. Too much for her body to take. Now, because of her, people are afraid. Our magic, it's a curse, Silas, running through our veins. That power to heal - sometimes it's too strong. Sometimes it does things you can never take back. And some of us —" I pause as my voice trembles; swallow hard. "Some of us can't control it."

He lays a hand on my arm. His fingers are warm. Almost too warm. "Your family's magic. It is a gift," he says softly.

"It's a curse, Silas."

"And yet here I am, alive with barely a mark on me."

"You don't know what it's like. To feel the magic rise in you and not know for certain if—" My eyes sting and I look away.

He moves then, to cup my face in his hands. To turn me to face him. That same shock passes through me again at the touch, making my skin feel alive, alive, alive. But he doesn't acknowledge it. He just looks directly into my eyes, his expression serious.

"I know what it is to live apart, truly apart, from others," he says. "I know what it is to have others fear you. To see the hate in their eyes. No matter that you can't change what you are, even if you wanted to. I know curses. And, trust me, your magic,

Imogen? The magic that flows through your family? In your veins? It is not one of them."

We talk until we are both yawning, mostly about the village, the wood, and the fairy tales surrounding it, the warmth of the fire making us drowsy. My grandmother still doesn't return, even as the night deepens.

Eventually, I fall asleep leaning across the mattress, my head pillowed by Silas's legs. I must not fall truly asleep straight away, though, as I swear I feel his fingers in my hair, smoothing the strands gently. His touch light as a feather. Light as a lover's.

I don't remember anything else until morning.

The next day brings with it the first snow. At some point in the night, my grandmother must have finally crept in, as I wake to find her making tea. I can tell by the light behind her that the snow outside is settling - and it's still falling. I can see flurries sweeping past the window as she stands at the sink, gazing out at the wood, a full cup steaming in her hands.

"I see you two made friends," she says when she notices I'm awake. She looks pointedly at where Silas's hand is tangled with mine, resting on top of the blankets. I immediately move to withdraw mine but his hand doesn't budge, his fingers still tight around mine. Even in sleep. My grandmother chuckles. "He's a nice boy, Immy," she says. "You should take him out for some air later, it will help with his healing."

"Where were you last night?" I manage to get out between yawning.

"After dealing with the fever - it was Tomas this time, poor mite - I went to check the wards."

"In the dark?" I raise a brow.

"Well, first light would have been better," she admits as she passes me a cup.

"Are you crazy! What if something—"

"I took a lantern and a knife." *Because that will help against a monster as big as a horse.* Like the one I saw by the wall only the night before. "And I could feel the snow in the air. It had to be done."

The tea is chamomile, but it does nothing to calm me. "You could have been killed!" At the shrill note in my voice, Silas stirs, his fingers flexing and tightening on mine. I soften my tone. "Please tell me you won't do that again."

"I can't, the snow will probably be here for a while now." It's not what I meant and she knows it, but before I can challenge her, Silas sits up.

"It snowed?" he says, rubbing bleary eyes with the back of his hand.

"Rather a lot, it would seem," my grandmother says, craning her neck to look down at the ground. "Perfect weather for juniper berries."

I groan, catching her hint. "You're not seriously going to send me out in this?"

"Both of you. As I said, Silas will need some air."

And so, that's how I find myself leading him down the cabin steps and into the snow an hour later. My breath rises in clouds as I turn back to help him with his borrowed cloak. He still hasn't managed to secure it, probably because of the bruising in his shoulder. I take the pin from him and stab it into the fabric, catching the two sides together before fastening it tight so the wind can't get to the shirt he wears underneath. Likely one of my father's, pulled out from a dusty cupboard.

"There," I pronounce, flicking the now-secured pin with my gloved fingers. It's silver, formed in the shape of a wolf, while the one holding my own cloak together is of a little, pudgy wren. He glances down at the pin, expression carefully neutral before he breaks into a grin at the sight of the snow all around us.

I can't help but smile, too, watching him turn in a circle to absorb it all as fresh snowflakes collect in his hair. He raises his good arm so he can catch some of the flakes in his palm.

While he's distracted, I bend and scoop up my own pile of snow. When I throw it, the snowball explodes by his feet. He jumps as the snow spatters his boots, then he laughs. Prepares his own ball to throw at me.

Laughing until we're breathless, we chase each other past my neighbours' houses, firing snow at each other. All the way to the place the juniper berries grow.

By the time we're there, my cheeks hurt both from laughing and the cold. I lie back in the snow, catching my breath, and Silas flops down beside me, lying on his good side. Together, we watch as the snow falls in seemingly infinite swirls above our heads. Gradually my heart rate slows.

I can't remember the last time I felt like this. Laughed like this so freely. I feel Silas's eyes on me and I turn my head. His eyes, more brown than green now, almost glow against the blanket of white beneath us. And I find myself caught in them. In the mossy depths of his irises. The girl reflected in them stares back, eyes wide, her curtain of brown hair spread on the snow. A smile lingers in the corner of her mouth. But then he sits up and the spell breaks.

I also rise, shaking the snow from my hair, my cloak. I feel damp all over, but I don't care. I'd rather live this moment a hundred times over than do this alone.

It turns out my grandmother was right, it is the right time for juniper berries. Just as she's right about most things. The trees around us are full of them, their evergreen branches laden both with berries and snow. We quickly fill the bag she gave us, the berries a grey-blue of storm-kissed skies. Then we head for home, Silas's arm looped through mine.

This time we walk slower, content to breathe the clear air. The snow is lighter now, only a few flakes drifting through the air as Silas matches his long steps to my shorter ones. I didn't notice before how tall he is. But now that he's directly beside me, he stands easily a head taller, the top of my head just about level with his shoulders.

"What?" he says, puzzled, as he catches me looking up at him.

I shake my head. Smile. "Nothing."

But really, it is everything. Today is everything.

THE CABIN IS empty when we let ourselves inside, brushing the snow from our boots. It is dark, cold, and the fire in the grate has sunk to embers. I build it up again with a few new logs, placing our sodden cloaks beside it so they can dry in the warmth of the flames. Silas puts the bag of berries on my grandmother's workbench and helps to light the candles in the windows. The candles that will draw my grandmother home like a beacon against the winter dark.

Hopefully, she will be home soon. She knows better than to risk the dark again so soon. To risk the gaps in the wall. In the wards.

While we wait, Silas and I munch on a dinner of bread and cheese, play a game of truth or lies, and curl up by the fire with a mug of tea in our hands. I sit in the old rocking chair, Silas stretched out on the floor beside me, his head resting against my knee. I use the blanket normally slung over the back of the chair to cover us both as the temperature drops outside. As night takes over; its raven wings unfolding across the sky.

Eventually, I shift from the chair to join Silas on the rug, to better share the blanket, my head drooping to rest on his shoulder.

We are asleep long before my grandmother returns, he and I, bathed in the warmth of the fire.

I WAKE in pitch darkness to find that, beside me, Silas is shivering. Uncontrollably. Shudders wracking his whole body.

When I light the candle beside me, I see the fire has burned low again. I rise to mend it but Silas grabs for my hand before I can go any further. "Leave it," he says between gritted teeth. "You need to get away from me. *Now*."

"What?"

"Imogen, listen to me. If you don't, I could hurt you."

"What? What do you mean?"

His grip on my hand is so tight it hurts. "Trust me, Immy," he pleads as another shudder wracks him. This time the pain of it sends him onto all fours. He drops my hand.

"Silas, what's going on?" I demand. But he's past talking. Has no more words to give as the shudders worsen. As his spine bends unnaturally with an awful crack. He lets out a howl, a guttural, wild sound filled with pure agony as his body contracts and elongates, rearranging itself. As it becomes something new.

In just a few moments, Silas is gone and a wolf stands, panting in the place he had been, claws digging into the rug. Bigger than any wolf I've ever seen. But as it raises its head, its eyes lock with mine, the colour of them more green than brown.

My hands fly to my mouth as I fight back a scream.

But the wolf makes no move towards me. To hurt me. It simply stares back at me, those familiar hazel eyes filled with immeasurable, unspeakable sadness.

Then there comes a sound at the door and our heads both whip towards it as my grandmother spills through, bringing a wave of frigid air with her.

The wolf glances from her to me, its gaze lingering for just a fraction longer on my face, before it turns tail and bounds past my grandmother and out into the night.

WHEN I WAKE the next morning, feeling like the rug has been pulled out from under my feet, the only traces that remain of Silas are the paw prints he left in the snow. But even those are disappearing as my grandmother comes to stand beside me on the front step, placing my cloak around my shoulders.

Now we know the truth of it. Of him.

Silas is a monster. A monster from the wood. It explains both so much and so little. My mind spins with question after question that I want to ask. Until the weight of them all is overwhelming.

"Don't you go looking for him, Immy," my grandmother warns as she presses a kiss to my cold cheek, as if she senses my turmoil. "The wood is where he belongs."

But even though I know this, seeing him there on that rug - man turned to wolf, bare skin to fur, hands to claws - it changed everything.

Because a little thought sprouts in my mind. Starts to grow. To take root. The thought that perhaps, maybe, possibly, some of the monsters in the wood aren't so monstrous after all…

Before...

It is midwinter when Ivy finds the wolf on her doorstep. The night is full dark, the new moon rising, blocking out the stars.

At first, she is not exactly sure what wakes her. But she finds herself unable to get back to sleep. Unable to grasp at her dreams and draw them in closer again. Giving up the struggle, she casts her blankets aside and finds herself at the window, gazing out at the shadowy trees and their reaching limbs, the branches bare and skeletal.

It is then that she hears the scratching of claws on wood.

Begging to be let in.

A WEEK PASSES and Silas's absence feels like a gaping wound. Like a missing puzzle piece that I didn't realise was lost until I found it and lost it again.

Before, I was content, if not happy, to live life exactly the way we were. Walls up. Doors locked. Familiar. Comfortable. But, now, I wonder if there is more. More to this lonely life we've led, my grandmother and I, these past few years. More to it than curses and forests and nights spent in fear.

Every morning, I lose a little bit of hope when I open the cabin door to check and Silas isn't there. But I still open the door.

Before...

AT FIRST, Ivy doesn't let the wolf in. Why would she? All the stories she'd ever read as a child told her that wolves were not to be trusted. They were beasts, after all, creatures of tooth and claw and nothing more.

But this wolf was different. As the morning broke above the trees and the sun climbed sluggishly into the slate-grey sky, the wolf changed. Its body stretched out, unfolded, and twisted, its fur falling away. Until a young man lay in its place on her doorstep, exhausted and bleeding.

She opened the door then. Healed his wounds. Fed him soup and bread and the vegetables and herbs from her little garden.

At nightfall, he changed again. Man to wolf. Hand to claw. Vanishing back into the darkness as if he'd never been a man at all.

But by morning he returned, on two feet rather than four.

Slowly, it started to dawn on her that he changed like the forest. That the rhythms of the change were the same. At night, he grew thorns, just as the forest did; great claws that could rend and tear and score. But the wolf in him was always gone by morning, when the trees returned to their usual friendly green. Like the light chased the beast in him away.

But Ivy knew better. Knew it in her bones. Knew it in the way her hands trembled at the thought of what she'd done all that time ago.

And when he'd found the voice to tell her, the wolf that was also a man told her that he hadn't always been a wolf. He'd been just a man. A simple, honest woodcutter, happy with his simple, honest life at the edge of the forest. But all of that had changed one night when he was making his way home after hunting beneath the trees, back in that time when the shadows were safe even on the darkest, deepest nights. When the beasts in the forest were just beasts and nothing else, nothing more.

But that night, he remembered that a strange power had lit up the forest in a flash of light. Brighter than any he'd seen before.

THE WINTER GROWS DARKER, deeper, and colder in the month that slips by without me noticing. It's like I am as frozen as the ground. Stuck in the moment I lost Silas and the unspoken, warm thing that was budding between us. I go about our usual routines, smile when I know I should smile. But my eyes are always drifting to the trees.

Then one day, one murky hour before dawn, my grandmother bursts into my room, shaking me awake. "The guard watch has caught a wolf," she says, breathless and wind-ravaged.

At the mention of a wolf, I'm already out of bed and shrugging on my cloak over my nightdress, stuffing my feet into my boots. The watch is kept by some of the village men around the centre of the village, where they've bothered to maintain the wall. And I know all too well what they do to anything they find wandering too close to the wrong side of it.

Together, we leave the cabin behind and sprint through the dark, our lanterns raised high, my grandmother only a half step behind. My heart is like a caged bird beneath my ribs, straining to break free. I pass our neighbours' houses without seeing them, running all the way to the other side of the village, to where a small crowd has gathered at the wall.

It's as bad as I suspected. Some of the villagers brandish torches. Others, scythes or pokers or great, carving knives. And in the middle of the crowd lies the wolf, tangled in netting. It yelps as we draw near, as a villager prods it. The rest of the villagers cheer, clapping them on the back for their bravery.

But there is nothing here to celebrate.

Before my grandmother can stop me, or remind me that this would be a very bad idea - that we should solve this rationally with the village leaders - I stalk into the crowd, deliberately pushing back my hood so they can see my face. Power surges through me, crackling at the tips of my fingers. Barely leashed, it thrums beneath my skin. But I hold it there, my head held high.

At once, they draw back, murmuring. Recognising my face. The family to which I belong. I'm too focused on the wolf ahead of me to gather much, but I hear my name whispered, along with that of my mother's.

I shoot a glare at the woman who dares to say the words *Irena Greenlake.* She shrinks back from the look in my eyes. The sparks at my fingertips.

And then I fall to my knees beside the wolf. I already know what I will see as I crouch beside its head. As its hazel eyes roll up to meet mine, the colour in them far more green than brown.

"Silas," I breathe.

THE VILLAGERS WON'T LISTEN. Won't let him go without a fight. He's a wolf, they insist. As monstrous as anything in the wood. Even as he lies there, wrapped in their ropes, defenceless and hurting, his bonds cutting into his skin.

Instead, they try to drag me away. But their grip is too cautious, like I'm a wild thing who could bite and claw as much as any wolf, and I break free, throwing my body over his.

"Get out of the way, *witch,*" the men jeer at me. But I'm already sawing at the ropes that hold Silas with the knife I always keep in my cloak pocket.

My grandmother steps forward too, placing herself between the villagers and me. "You're fools, the lot of you," she says as she stares them down. Shouts a retort for every insult they throw at us. Buying me - buying us - time. Time for me to release him. Time for my magic to find its way through his fur, deep into the gashes in his skin, knitting them together as I use one hand to saw at the ropes and the other to brace against his side. It pours from me to him like an unstoppable flood. A river containing all of my hopes, dreams and deepest fears.

But then finally Silas is free, struggling to his feet beside me. And the magic in me fades, settling back beneath my skin. But I still feel it thrumming with my pulse, ready and waiting if I call.

Run, my grandmother mouths to me between her arguing.

We don't need telling twice. I surge forward with Silas at my side, his head nearly level with my shoulders in his wolf form. Villagers shriek as they dive out of our way. Out of the way of the witch and her wolf.

And then all that remains ahead of us is the wall. Silas leads the way alongside it, his great paws pummeling the bare earth of the path beside it until we reach a break in the crumbling stone. I don't think twice about following him through.

I can hear the rising shouts of the villagers behind us, claiming injustice. Demanding blood. I can see the flames of their torches when I dare a glance back over my shoulder.

But we are already halfway across the narrow, grassy field that stretches between the wall and the wood when Silas falls to the ground with a shout of pain. As the weak winter sun starts to rise in the cloud-shrouded eastern sky.

My heart lurches as I think immediately of the arrow my grandmother dug out of his skin before. Thinking he's been struck again.

But his body contorts, just as it did that night on the rug by the fire. This time his fur retracts and becomes smooth, sun-freckled skin as his limbs shrink, warp, and extend. Into arms. Legs. Hands.

When the change finishes shuddering through him, Silas the man looks up at me, clad in only a shredded pair of trousers. Just like the night I found him. I want to throw my arms around him. To hold onto his hand and never let go. To keep him always this way. With the tousled brown waves in his hair and his bright, curious eyes.

But, instead, we have to keep running. Running towards the wood.

Before...

Ivy isn't sure when she fell in love with her wolf. It happened gradually. Like a flower slowly opening to feel the warmth of the sun.

It did not matter to her that he disappeared at night, to roam the shadows. His howls the most mournful. The most true.

As long as he came back, it did not matter. Even though the guilt of what she'd done ate at her during the nights she spent tossing and turning alone under the bedsheets. She only held him all the tighter at dawn, when he'd slip into the bed beside her, hers and human once more.

She clutched him selfishly, without trying to right her wrong. For, without the curse she had unknowingly cast that night long ago, she wouldn't have had him at all.

We are almost at the first of the trees when my shoulder explodes with pain. My vision blurs with it, like a million snowflakes blinding me, and I stumble. But before I can fall, Silas's arms envelop me, steady and strong.

I blink, my eyes on his mouth, but I can't read what he's saying as a ringing sound fills my ears. My shoulder burns.

But then the ringing clears and I can hear him. Repeating my name over and over. Almost like a prayer.

Immy. Immy. Immy. Immy.

I dream in flashes.

Silas lying next to me. Staring up at the snow as it falls around us, coating the trees.

Silas whispering my name against my skin, over and over.

Silas standing beside my mother at the edge of the dark wood. Their voices calling to me. Pleading. Asking me to stay, stay, stay.

Then I wake up.

THE PAIN IS SO EXCRUCIATING that at first, I don't realise where I am. The first thing I see is Silas, leaning over me with shining eyes. Then I see the window behind him, my grandmother standing by the sink, the sky darkening behind her. And I know then that I am safe in our cabin.

"Don't," Silas says as I touch my shoulder and my hand comes away sticky. "Don't move."

I don't like to tell him that my body feels like lead. That my head feels stuffed with wool. That my shoulder is screaming.

He takes my non-sticky hand in his and brings it to his face. I'm so out of it that I think I imagine him pressing his lips to my palm.

"We almost lost you, Imogen," my grandmother says over her shoulder. She says it almost flippantly, but I hear the undercurrent of hurt in her voice. I hear what she's not saying. *I almost lost you, too.* Just like we lost my mother.

"What happened?"

"The arrow was meant for me," Silas says. Oh. *Oh*. That explains the agony. And the stickiness. Now that I think about it, I can smell the herby poultice my grandmother must have placed on my skin.

"Don't ever do that again," Silas murmurs, low enough for only me to hear. "You're needed here, Immy."

I want to yell *so are you*. But he squeezes my hand one last time and gets up, heading for the door. "I'll be back by morning," he says as he peels off his shirt and drops it into a heap on the floorboards.

I want to protest. To keep him here now that I only just got him back. But he is gone into the night before I can say a word, the door latching closed behind him.

My grandmother must've healed me with magic, as I wake the next morning feeling only bruised and battered; the pain a dull throb rather than a never-ending roar. She sits beside my bed, her head pillowed on her arms as she leans part way across the mattress. Keeping watch over me. Well, until sleep claimed her anyway.

It makes it all the more difficult for me to slide my legs free of the blankets. For me to bite back on a groan as the movement disturbs my arm. But somehow I leave the room without waking her, butterflies churning in my stomach.

I don't care that I'm in my nightdress. I sling my cloak across my shoulders anyway and slip out the front door. It must be only an hour past dawn. As I step outside, there's no Silas waiting for me at the door. Not on the steps either. So I trudge down them and head for the wall. Back to where it all began.

There is only a little snow left now and the uncovered grass crunches beneath my boots. Every few feet, fresh green shoots pierce the ground. Crocuses emerging from their winter slumber.

"You couldn't just wait, could you?" A familiar voice calls to me. And there is Silas, leaning casually against the wall. He steps away from it, a grin spreading across his face.

And then I am running the rest of the way to him.

When I reach him, I throw my arms around him, colliding with him so hard that I knock us both to the ground. He laughs breathlessly, rolling us so that he hovers above me. My shoulder twinges as I lie back on the cold ground, my palms flat against the grass, but I don't care. Because he came back. He came back.

As I gaze up at him, he leans in so that our noses brush. Just like before, there's that shock of energy between us. That spark. It travels through my whole body. And in response, I feel it. I feel everything. Rising up where my fingers touch the ground. I feel the wood, just over the wall. I feel the wind, sighing through the trees. I feel the birds, flitting from branch to branch. I feel the buds, turning their faces to the morning sun. My magic thrums beneath my skin. It feels glorious. Strong, steady. Like it never has before.

And as Silas' mouth finds mine, I feel the thorns around my heart - around the wood - loosen.

Later…

SILAS ONCE TOLD me that our magic is a gift, but I like to think of it as balance. When Ivy Greenlake stole from the wood, she didn't intend to. But where she spread darkness, born of anger, despair, and fear, the people I love show me that I can spread light. If I open myself to it.

For even after the darkest nights, morning still dawns bright, fresh, and clear over the wood. Keeping the shadows at bay.

7
CEMETERY BY THE BAY

LAURA GULBRANSON

Maeve Nova peered at her broken watch. She was never good at keeping track of time, and that hadn't changed now that she was dead.

Staring at her non-functioning watch was a more conducive alternative to staring into blinding mist and fog. Twelve hours ago, Maeve's weightless body made impact with the gritty tarmac.

Maeve didn't remember much about the events between her death and getting here, wherever "here" was. One moment she couldn't breathe, and the next she was floating in the air, the earthly world shrouded in an opaque cast. She was free falling. Skydiving into a yawning chasm.

But where was she?

Looking up from her watch with a wary gaze, Maeve eyed the bone-shaped gates. The constant buzzing of the question "Where am I?" kept better time than her inoperable watch. The question she ruminated on morphed into, *What will happen to me?*

Wait...

Maeve blinked. Why was she even thinking about keeping time? How had she forgotten so easily?

She knew exactly where she was supposed to be.

Vague memories flooded her mind of a conclave, the walls glistening moonstone, the floors paved in quartz. Her body vacillated in the air before being flung back into an invisible chair. Maeve's eyes were blinded by an orb of spectral light. It shone from where the stalactites bundled atop the conclave's cavern ceiling

The susurration of *what ifs* were cut short when Maeve's gaze met the nine hooded figures seated on their glittering thrones of sapphire, diamond, and gold.

A pulpit stretched across the cavern, shielding the bottom half of the hooded figures'

billowing forms. Maeve's eyes adjusted as she read what looked like Latin letters transforming into English across the pulpit.

Limbus Conclave.

Conclave— she had heard that word before, used in institutions to denote a council of some sort.

The Council's onyx garments shielded their faces, the contrast blinding in the prismatic light of moonstone. The stones glutted the cavern walls like barnacles attached to shells and coral.

Maeve had waited *forever* just to get through one line to meet with the Council for the first time. To think she was back in the same line as before, to meet them once more? Maeve didn't realize that the afterlife would constitute her waiting in line for eternity *again.*

Those gates! They were the same!

The bones comprising Death's Gates curled into themselves, the skeletal remains taking on the form of a ravenous mouth with fanged incisors, rather than the shimmering golden-laced gateway Maeve had imagined in her mind.

Standing in line, Maeve would have much preferred to be back floating in the void. It was cataleptic, at best. Half-conscious, as if waking from a deep slumber. She could not see her body, and any remnant of her physical being had been shrouded by the clouds she floated through twelve hours before. It was only upon landing on rocky terrain that Maeve could feel her legs, wobbly on the cratered surface of the unsteady ground. She bent her knees, her finger swiveling through pebbly black sand that loosened from the craters with each unmeasured step she took.

Even in the throes of Life and Death, the two extremes now blurred, no longer existing as a binary. Maeve only wished that, in the furor of her fate being hung on an already teetering balance, Life *or* Death would rid her of mortal fear. But she felt it here. It never left her, even when she came face-to-face with her demise.

The fog dissipated in whorls of mist, revealing the queue of wavering silhouettes. The dead souls she was among resembled a murder of crows on an endless cascade of asphalt. She didn't even bother to make eye contact with any soul in line, but the more that the air cleared, the more she was able to take in the sight of the rusting red cords suspended in the air, metal joining the bridge together on either side of the asphalt pathway.

Above, a brewing storm materialized. Angry clouds conjoined and dismantled in fervor, creating colossal splotches of gray that swallowed whatever trace of sky there once had been.

Maeve mustered whatever courage she could salvage from within to turn around. She asked a man dressed as a clown behind her the question she had contemplated now that she could see her surroundings and the bloodcurdling gates a thousand paces ahead. Could she be wrong? Maybe she had dreamed up the last time she had met the Council? Maybe whatever she had imagined before was just a long-winding dream while her soul had been escorted to this queue.

"Where are we?" Her voice was tinny, a floating plume in the air.

"We died, didn't we?" The clown said in a gruff tone, the annoyance multiplied by the frown lines melting on his forehead, where blood mixed in with fading paint.

It didn't answer her question, but at least he responded.

"What happened to you?" Maeve asked the clown.

The clown grumbled, "After a hard day of 'entertaining' bratty children at a birthday party, I hit the bar. Little did I know that the Serial Killer Clowner was out and about in the city."

"The Serial Killer *Clowner?*" Maeve looked at the man's corroding makeup. The unevenness of his face and even the tattered state of his jester costume, the bells on his multicolored cap jingling and jangling with every erratic movement and violent shake of the head.

"I never saw the eyes of the killer," the clown continued, "just knew that after being beaten to a pulp and forced to drink chemical acid, I was a goner. Never again. When I get through those gates–" The man pointed to Death's Gates, waving a fist in the air as if he himself could beat the gates to a pulp. "Never again, I tell ya!"

"Wait—" Maeve paused. "You know what happens when we get through those gates?"

The man let out a clownish laugh. "Of course not! I'm a clown!"

Maeve furrowed her eyebrows, not sure how that connection was relevant, but getting the answer she needed.

"I can't believe it," Maeve murmured.

The clown moved closer to her, his eyes inquisitive and intrusive.

"Really?" The clown looked at Maeve incredulously. "You

can't believe it?" You must be twenty? Twenty-five? Thirty? How old are ya'?"

"Eighteen," Maeve said, feeling old and young at the same time. But she could care less about her age now that she was dead.

"Ehh... kids are looking older these days and getting stupid," muttered the clown under his breath before continuing. "Just as it's common knowledge for every kid to hate clowns, it's common knowledge that whatever is behind those gates has somethin' to do with the next life. And in the next life, I want a promotion! No more clown business for me! No more! I need a raise!"

Maeve ignored the theatrics of the clown. She could see it – one kernel of truth– that didn't take a netherworld genius to figure out. Of course, it made plenty of sense. She knew it all along.

This was a repeat. These were the gates she had dreaded...

"I'm in the wrong place!" Maeve exclaimed, her eyes scanning the crowd again. These were new faces, but the place was the same.

A cackle echoed behind her. Maeve looked over her shoulder to see a wan face and sunken eyes the color of ice. "Keep on telling yourself that. I'm in the wrong place, too!" The ghoul smiled, revealing teeth as sharp as icicles. She wailed her arms in the air, pointing to random souls in the crowd. "He is! They are! We are all in the wrong place!" The ghoul howled hysterically.

Maeve turned back to the clown. "No. I'm *actually* in the wrong place. I've met the Limbus Conclave already!"

"The Limbus who?"

Maeve cursed. "Look! Believe me! When you get inside those gates, you're going to meet a group of hooded guys called the Limbus Conclave. They are going to give you a survey that asks you questions about your last life and the next. They will put you on an improvement plan and make you sign a–"

"An improvement plan? Like a promotion, ain't it?" The clown's eyes grew in alertness.

"That's beside the point, clown!"

"Don't talk to me if you're going to be snappy with me! Kids these days! No respect!" The clown readjusted his cap then quipped, "If you are telling the truth, what were the questions on the survey? How many questions were there?"

"999."

"999?" The clown went off, but Maeve was too preoccupied with one question she remembered the Council asking her. She had known the answer to their question right away.

What are the top three destinations you would like to be placed in when you are reborn again?

Maeve had named idyllic islands and warm, sandy beaches.

Not this— an entrenched line of souls atop a dismal bridge.

"Give me a hint. What questions they asked ya? You might've screwed them up, but that won't be me!" The clown cackled. "Jeez, you gotta get back in the line again?" He wheezed in between words, "What did you do wrong on the questionnaire? You flunked it?" His stomach jiggled with every sinister guffaw, the blood on his face melding deeper into his frown lines.

Maeve glared at the clown. He wasn't helping the situation at all. She wasn't going to humor him any longer. Maeve turned around, walking in the opposite direction of the line. She fought through the crowd, ignoring the clown's lauding shouts to come back and tell him the contents of Death's 999-question survey.

Maeve's mind replayed the questions she had answered so carefully… all 999 of them.

THE WHIRLWIND of being lost in the Council's questions distracted Maeve. She paused at the railing of the bridge, the fog thickening again until the wisps dissipated, unveiling the shoreline not too far ahead.

Maeve laughed sardonically. If there was one thing that the Limbus Conclave granted her, it was the view of the beach. Maeve looked down below at the jutting rocks and to the opposite side where the view parted to reveal bleary hills.

Something else caught her eye.

She scanned the horizon, the wisps of mist ebbing and flowing and sporadically giving way to a dusting mist that had uncovered the shoreline.

A tugboat fighting the tide.

Her gaze darted back to the shoreline where two small boats were dragged to shore. Three, or perhaps, four figures in raincoats and boots hoisted the boats to land, the chilling waves sweeping across the sand like a shark's gaping mouth preying on the shoreline.

Should she just stay and wait for who knows how long to meet the Council again?

Maeve didn't even know if it was possible to make it to shore if she walked to the end of the bridge and down to the beach.

One step in the opposite direction of Death's Gates turned into two. Her pace quickened until she found herself at the bottom of the bridge's stairs, enveloped by fog. She kept her eyes planted on the shore. The waves roared, and her legs staggered from the combative winds. Maeve hugged her arms and propelled herself forward. She stumbled over seaweed and kelp that washed ashore, the sea plants tangling with her feet. Her nails dug into the sand in an attempt to fight the wind from tearing her away from land and into the turbulent sea.

Her eyes fixed on the group of individuals and their tugboat still fighting the tide, but they made it to shore. They were alive. It was the motivation she needed.

Maeve dug her nails deeper into the sand until the wind died. She took advantage of the moment to prop her knees up and make for a run. Out of breath, Maeve nearly stumbled into the silhouettes. The individuals had their backs faced to her, but Maeve could see their callused hands tying the boat to a stump.

"Hey!" She yelled over the wind. The figures turned toward Maeve, a moment that Maeve was unprepared for. "Who are you?"

"We're the rescue team," said a woman in a yellow raincoat, her voice husky and rough like the crashing waves.

"The rescue team for what?"

The woman glanced at Maeve briefly before her eyes returned to the rope she was knotting.

"What's your name?"

"Maeve."

"I'm Brielle. You see that fog coming along the shore and across the bridge, Maeve?"

"It's everywhere," said Maeve, peering down the shore and back at the bridge, the vapor curdling and dispelling. "It would be hard to miss."

"That fog is the result of all our fears encapsulated by the lost souls of the bay. And below it, is Fear itself. Me and my crew- we are the Cadre."

Maeve's imagination spiraled into oblivion. "What do you mean by Fear itself? Like sirens? Sirens below the bridge leading to Death's Gates would make a lot of sense."

"Why do you think sirens drag sailors to sea?" asked Brielle, but Maeve could read in her eyes that she already knew the answer.

"Just for sport? For the kill?" Maeve didn't know. She just knew in legends they were known for their entrancing voices that led sailors to their death.

"Oh no. Not at all. Sirens are lonely creatures, craving company, just like the Creatures of the Bay. The only difference is the Creatures of the Bay feed on one's fears. Sirens feed on one's lust and heart. Our job is to rescue those whose hearts and souls are in despair. Why else would anyone jump?" Brielle finished knotting the set of boats and finally looked at Maeve face-to-face. "You've come down here from the line that leads towards Death's Gates. Are you here to save a life?"

Maeve shook her head. She had not come down here to be anyone's savior. How could she, if she couldn't even save herself?

Brielle started knotting another set of boats together. "There's a handful of us out here." She nodded her head in the direction of the bridge. "When you are on the bridge, you only see the dead. But below the bridge, when my crew and I go out in the eye of the storm, we see something else. From below, the fog parts momentarily, and we can see the living. Those at the cusp of life and death." The woman paused from knotting the ropes. "We try to convince the living to turn back. To step away from the edge of the bridge. Sometimes it works. Sometimes it doesn't. But we try. Me, Haven, Lennard, and Ewa are the main crew. It's a risky job."

"Then why do you do it?" asked Maeve, incredulous of the crew.

"Maybe we're trying to make up for what we didn't do in our old lives." Brielle looked off to the distance, at the waves that lapped the shore before churning into its violent form.

"It's not like it's always rewarding," said Brielle. "We've buried so many dead souls on the shore. Thousands more are lost at sea..." Brielle's eyes hardened. "We're not the only ones out there. Beyond the fog— the creatures of the bay live there. The sea is their territory. Those at the top of the bridge: they either see us, or they see the creatures. But to save at least one life, maybe it's worth it. If not, we still bury them. Whatever their reasons were for forgoing life, we give the forgotten a burial. At least those we can get to first before the creatures get them."

Maeve's mouth parted, incredulous of Brielle's crew. They rescued the living *and* the dead?

"Are you in?"

Maeve shook her head, still in disbelief. "I haven't agreed to anything."

"You haven't, but you've also walked out of the line from the bridge to come to shore. You wouldn't be here if you weren't even at least slightly interested." Brielle pointed to a slab of stone that separated the beach from the looming fog that grew beyond it. Maeve's eyes narrowed on the tally marks. She didn't count all of them, but it was clear these markings signified the passing of time. "That's how long I've been part of the Cadre. I never went back to join the line."

"Brielle!" A hooded man shouted over the waves, a new boat being pulled to shore. "This one made it! He was almost taken, but we got to him before the sea could. I think someone else climbed up the bridge when we left our post."

Brielle nodded at the hooded man, waving in acknowledgment. "I'm heading out to sea. You can either stay in line or be of some help. You're not going anywhere for the next five-hundred years anyway."

"You've been on this shore for five-hundred years?" Maeve asked. Had she been in line for that long the last time she met Death's Council?

Brielle shook her head, an ostentatious but curt laugh ringing out.

"I've been out here longer. I've just been keeping track of how long it takes each soul on the bridge from the end to make it to the front of the gate. It takes five-hundred years, sometimes more, sometimes less, depending on how many souls depart from the living to the dead." Brielle pivoted and kneeled by the body that collapsed out of the boat. Maeve shook as the shrunken form of the body convulsed. She watched the soul cough out the water and seaweed lodged in his lungs.

Brielle raised her eyebrows as an invitation to Maeve to join her; she pushed the boat to sea and hopped into the vessel.

Maeve had no time to react. She jumped into the boat with Brielle, the waves carrying her away from the shore, and into the gurgling maelstrom.

A Hundred Years later

MAEVE DEVELOPED an eye for spotting movement from the living who climbed up the bridge. She knew that waiting for high tide was how she'd get to the bridge at a faster rate, despite the peril of which it also consisted. Brielle cautioned Maeve that there was only so much that the Cadre could do when the tide was too high, the enveloping water like tsunami waves that could swallow the whole shore.

Maeve had never imagined she'd be part of the Cadre for this long, but the adrenaline that came from entering the water was nearly intoxicating. But it wasn't just the water; Maeve went into those waters for similar reasons as the rest of the Cadre.

Even if they had made no impact or difference whatsoever alive, they would make one now, on the shores of Death's Gates. The ocean and sand were its cemetery, the bridge was its vessel.

Maeve had been out patrolling for so long that she disregarded Brielle's warning about the calm before the storm. The full moon shone brightly in the eternal darkened sky. The fog hung on the horizon as the moon kissed the waters in the distance.

The calm before the storm.

Maeve pushed a boat to sea, taking in the tranquility of the night, and for once, she could feel the peace of a night at sea wash over her.

Gradually, the bridge of the dead she was accustomed to, transformed into the bridge of the living.

The Cadre patrolled in pairs, but tonight, Maeve was alone.

There were some nights that there was no movement on the bridge. All that could be heard was the occasional rumble of cars. Maeve couldn't see the cars, or what she presumed to be pedestrians and bicyclists on the bridge. But then again, it made sense that if she could see anything at all, it would be those at the edges of Life and Death. Maeve had grown used to seeing these souls once in a blue moon. It almost felt like going fishing and returning home with nothing caught.

She wasn't here fishing for souls. She wasn't here to be someone's savior. That mindset had never changed, ever since stepping off the bridge and joining the Cadre.

And maybe that was the reason why she never seemed to find a soul on the bridge herself. For the first decade since joining the Cadre, Maeve would just help the crew make rope. She was in charge of studying the ebbs and flows of the sea and picking out patterns of fog as signals of when it was safe to enter the sea.

She didn't think tonight was the night she would have misgauged the calm waters.

Maeve lingered under the bridge in the boat, her eyes drooping when she heard sudden movement above.

Maeve saw him. A soul wandering upon the bridge. His hair blew erratically in what looked to be a windy day among the living, despite the waters being calm from where she lay in her boat.

There was a wildness in his eyes, and her body froze when his eyes met hers. Her chance to help would only dwindle if she didn't latch onto the connection right away.

"Hello." Maeve greeted the man, being wary and measured, making sure that her voice was level so that it didn't frighten the person from losing his footing and falling into the chilled waters of the bay.

"You can't save me!" the man yelled out to her.

"I'm not here to save you," Maeve responded, now even more unsure of what to say. "But is it worth it?"

The man stared at Maeve incredulously.

"I don't remember much about the time when I was alive, but I think I spent most of my life waiting for the moment of death instead of living. To think that even now in Death, I'm still waiting. It never ends."

Maeve didn't have a chance to hear the man's response, for the water trembled below her. The calmness of the depths picked up speed and transformed before her eyes.

Maeve gripped the boat's sides, witnessing a whirlpool form in open water. She paddled with all her might, but it was of little use. This was the calm before the storm that Brielle had warned her of.

It wasn't the storm she feared.

The boat capsized, and her body chilled on impact with the glacial water. She could not keep her body afloat, the monstrous waves tugging her deeper into the depths of the bay.

For a moment, she opened her eyes in the water, but immediately closed them at the sight of spiraling tentacles that multiplied as if she were seeing the spawning of snakes from the source of the whirlpool. Here underneath the storm, she was in the clutches of the Creatures of the Bay.

"Maeve..." they called her name as if they were sirens beckoning her to her death. Their snake-like tentacles wrapped around her body, each faceted with beaded eyes that glowed like moonstone. Maeve couldn't breathe, but she remembered Brielle's words:

They feed off one's fears.

Is that the reason why the creatures had not devoured her already?

Up until this point, Maeve thought it was fear, but all she had ever felt was a coldness. *Unfeeling.*

It ebbed and flowed. Indifference.

But the moments where she did feel something were on the shore among the Cadre, bringing back a rescued soul, or burying them beneath the sand.

The image of what Maeve wanted became clear, now that she was in the clutches of not Death, not Fear, but Apathy. The apathy within her melted away the more that the tentacles constricted her body in a strangulating hold.

This was her time.

Before one serpent tentacle could tighten further on her throat, Maeve found her words– her voice– and although it felt like her body was being snapped in half, she spoke to one of the tentacles, the numerous moonstone eyes staring at her.

Water entered her lungs, but she said the words that crystallized in her mind out loud.

"I want to live."

A bright light seared Maeve's eyes through the stormy sea. She still had fight in her. Her legs and arms lunged forward. Maeve swam toward the light.

She felt the deluge of the waves pull her back, her body landed with a thump.

Maeve opened her eyes, no longer seeing the endless night sea, but red steel.

Calluses ruptured from where her hands bled. Her fingers gripped the edges of the bridge. Maeve pulled herself up and fell back on the bicyclist route, crying from the pang of pain that shot up her back. She lay there, remembering that she had lived the past 100 years on the brink of life and death.

Here, on the Golden Gate Bridge, she was alive again.

MAEVE SAT on the beach where she had first met Brielle and the Cadre. The sun shone, the glimmering rays warming her cheeks as her toes dug into the sand.

She basked in the sun and embraced the sound of the waves, a melody of new beginnings. *Of living.*

Maeve's phone buzzed. She peered at the caller ID and took the call.

"Hello, is this Maeve Nova?"

"Yes, this is she. Thank you for your time," Maeve spoke through the phone.

"No, we thank *you* for applying to volunteer for the San Francisco Suicide Prevention. We reviewed your application, and we want you to be part of the team. We think you'll be a great fit! When can you start?"

Maeve Nova sat up straight and pressed the speaker button so she could type in notes and important dates for training on her phone.

"I look forward to volunteering," Maeve said before placing her phone back in her jeans pocket.

Maeve looked to the bridge, and the mist and fog evaporating from the sun.

Here, where she lay on the beach, was where she first met the Cadre. And even though the Cemetery by the Bay was invisible to the living world, she knew it was still there.

"I don't know if you can hear me, Brielle, I'm here among the living."

Maeve didn't know if her friend could hear her, but at that moment, the waves roared, sea foam collecting around her feet and legs. When the tide fell, Maeve smiled at the bundle of shells that were left at her feet. It was all the sign she needed.

8

ONE LAST TALE

HASFARIZA HASSAN

This was a tale like no other, filled with complexity and depth. One to always be remembered. Wasn't that how life was? Filled with moments that surprise you, and moments that you forever wish that you never encountered. Some may even say that it's human nature to live and die with an infinite number of regrets. The never-ending cycle called the circle of life has many connotations and elements associated with it, but nobody could try to capture its true essence. Except for *them*. They defined it and conquered it all.

"IT'S NOT FAIR," the girl said, folding her arms across her chest, already irritated that the orange-brown stain on her pinafore stood out like a sore thumb. Her irritation grew even more, as she knew that she was going to be late for school again. She defiantly glared at the rearview mirror, watching her little sister in the backseat, pretending to be innocent as she widened her big doe eyes and mouthed "What?"

The girl shook her head angrily and glanced at her dad. "*Appa*, why does she get to go first?"

She glanced at her watch again and saw that it was almost 7:15 AM. She didn't want her name to be written down again. It was embarrassing and she absolutely hated it.

"*Appa*." She tried again. "The bell is going to ring in 5 minutes."

She sighed. "This will go on my permanent record. This would be my sixth time that I'm late."

"Bumi *ma*," He started slowly. Ma was an endearment that Bumi knew he used just for her. It made her feel special and one-of-a-kind. One that *Appa* didn't use, even for Anjali. But Bumi knew better than to fall for *Appa*'s charms. He was trying to gloss her with sweet, syrupy honey before the wild bees came raging in and destroyed her completely, wasn't he?

"No *lah*... we can still make it. We'll send Anjali first. She has *pengawas* duty today."

See, that was where the raging bees came in and stung her.

"*Appa*!" She exclaimed. "Anjali doesn't even do her duty. They don't even take it seriously at her—"

Anjali cut her off abruptly, raising her voice. "They do." She shook her head violently, hinting at her frustration. "You're not in primary school anymore. What do you know?"

"Stop being so rude! Why are you raising your voice at me? I'm the one who is always late, and your school only starts at 7:45 AM. Why do you have to be there so early? You're already in standard six."

"Because I'm a prefect! They're watching me, and if I'm late, they'll remove my position, *even* if I'm in standard six. You don't understand because you never had a position before."

"Girls, we're nearby already. You can both make it." *Appa* tried to diffuse the fire that was about to flame.

But it was too late. It was blazing.

"What do you mean?" Bumi asked Anjali harshly.

No response came.

"Bumi..." *Appa* said gently, but Bumi didn't want to budge.

"I asked you a question, so answer me!" Bumi's face blazed red with anger, which was a rare sight. She was always calm and composed, because wasn't that what was expected of her? *Amma* and *Appa* expected her to always give in to Anjali just because she was the *akka*. So what if she was older? They always took Anjali's side. All she wanted was to be understood. They said that they didn't have a favourite, but she knew better than to believe her parents' lies.

"I said, answer me!"

"Bumi *ma,* enough!" *Appa* raised his voice, his patience waning. Bumi knew how much *Appa* hated it when they fought, but she couldn't understand why she had to stop. She wasn't the one who was insinuating something. Bumi was tired and angry. Angry that she had to keep silent. Angry that Anjali always got her way. But most of all, she was angry because she couldn't do anything about it. Because this was her life. *Fine,* she told herself. She'll stop for now.

But, Anjali had her own plans, because *Appa* telling Bumi to stop meant that he was on her side. To ensure that Anjali had won this battle, she knew what she had to say. Anjali hated that *Appa* was on Bumi's side. It was clear that his favourite was Bumi. Bumi *Ma.* That's what *Appa* always called her. Why, because she was the eldest? She knew that the youngest meant nothing, it weighed a worthless title. Despite being a prefect and making sure she always came first in class, she was set aside like a rag. She wanted to feel victorious for once.

"You want an answer. Fine, I'll tell you." Anjali's voice came out steady.

"Because you *never* get the grades. That's why you didn't become the *pengerusi.*" She smirked maliciously. "You're the last number in class. You really thought that they would pick you."

Anjali cackled. "It's not like *Appa* and *Amma* had any expectations for you anyway."

"ENOUGH, BOTH OF YOU!" *Appa*'s face hardened. "Stop being like this! Some people don't even have siblings, and both of you are fighting like mad dogs. I'm tired of this."

"*Appa*, she's the one—" Bumi started again.

"I SAID ENOUGH! Whoever speaks one more time can leave the car." *Appa* unlocked the door to show how serious he was.

Anjali saw Bumi's facial expression change into something she had never seen before. Victory was hers, but she wondered why it wasn't as sweet as she thought it would be. Anjali reverted her eyes to the window, where the day had already come alive with the ongoing traffic, and the cars honked as if it was their own melody.

Bumi felt like she was stabbed in the heart several times. Wiping her tear-stained face, she wondered if that was what her family thought of her.

A failure.

A nobody that cannot accomplish anything.

Finally, *Appa* reached the grey-chipped front gate of Anjali's school after being stuck in a traffic jam. Anjali skipped out of the car and hollered out, "Bye, *Appa!*" as she disappeared into the school grounds. Bumi turned away, when all of a sudden she heard a thud on her window, and yelped. Anjali was about to knock on the window once more as Bumi slowly opened the window.

Anjali fidgeted with her hands slowly and muttered, "I'm sorry, *Akka*." Grabbing Bumi's hand, she repeated, "I'm sorry." There was a glint in her eyes. Perhaps it was hope that filled them. Who knew if it was genuine?

"I hate you," Bumi snarled, shutting the window with a bang. People said that family would always be on your side, but *she knew better*.

Appa pulled up to her school and as Bumi opened the door, he said, "What Anjali said isn't true." He combed the crown of his head with his hand, making it messier than before.

"You do not have to study so hard *lah*. *Amma* and I want you to be healthy."

Slowly unclenching her fists, Bumi forced a smile. "Love you, *Appa*." She slammed the door and didn't look back when he reciprocated the statement.

Because even *Appa* didn't believe in her.

PUTERI LISTENED to Puan Liu mindlessly, wondering why they didn't have *perhimpunan* this morning. It was bad enough that today was a Monday. What was worse about Mondays was not having assembly. Assembly didn't need concentration or any real brain power. All Puteri had to do was be on duty and make sure the rest of the prefects did their job. Now, she was stuck listening to Puan Liu.

Puan Liu's nose flared up. "How many times do I have to tell you ah?" She smacked the table. *Thump.* "SPM is coming and none of you are taking this seriously. No class today, then."

"No, Cher."

"Sorry, Teacher."

"*Aiyah*, Cher," the class chorused.

Puan Liu curved her lips with satisfaction. "Good, then, *lah*." She continued to write some mathematical equations for differentiation on the whiteboard. "You know how important SPM is. Make sure you do well." The brand new marker squeaked as she pressed harder. "Some more for Add Maths, because you're in the science stream."

Rat-a-tat-tat.

"Good Morning, Puan Liu," Bumi squeaked, clutching onto the side of her pinafore. Puteri glanced at the clock that hung above the whiteboard. It was nearly 8:15 AM. Bumi had never been this late before.

"Sorry, Teacher. I had to write a *karangan* because I was late for school." Bumi bowed her head.

"Why were you late?" Puan Liu frowned at Bumi. "You're always late."

"My father's car broke down," Bumi lied. Shaking her head, Puan Liu continued writing on the whiteboard. Bumi hesitated for a moment before entering the class, hoping that meant she was excused. She pursed her lips and tried to be as quiet as possible as she slid into her chair. When she slid her plastic desk closer to her, *squeak.*

Bumi's full cheeks tinged red. She slowly moved her desk closer once more. *Sigh.*

"What are we doing now?"

Without looking up from her notes, Puteri answered, "Copy what she's writing on the board." Rolling her eyes, "She spent 30 minutes yelling at us. Lucky you missed that."

"So... Anjali again?"

Bumi nodded. "She's annoying. This was the sixth time I was late today... ugh. They took my name down and said it was going to be on my permanent record." Bumi took out her stationary and clumsily started copying Puan Liu's notes.

"It was your first time writing an essay in the pengawas room, right?"

Bumi nodded, then rubbed her hand gently. "My hands hurt so much, *lah*. I rushed so I wouldn't be late."

"I warned you," Puteri said pointedly, tucking the loose strands of hair back into her blue hijab. Her intricate golden name tag shone in the sun, making the engravings stand out.

Puteri was the assistant head prefect and emitted the ambiance of the main character in every movie who was always number one in class. Well, number two. Meanwhile, Bumi was the exact opposite. Where Puteri got the grades, she had always been last in class. Number 34 was hers forever, without a doubt.

People always wondered how they worked, since they were basically *bagai langit dengan bumi.* Puteri was the bright, appealing sky, while Bumi was the taken for granted earth that was thought to stay constant. The proverb complemented them since they had never been alike.

"Why didn't you try jumping the fence?" She grinned mischievously.

Bumi let out a soft chuckle. "You're the head girl and you're planting all these ideas in my head?"

Puteri winked. "Rules are meant to be broken, *kan*."

Another difference between them. Bumi thrived on rules. The world only worked with them.

Rat-a-tat-tat.

"Sorry, Cher," a voice mumbled roughly.

Puan Liu nodded and went back to explaining the equation on the whiteboard. Ethan sauntered into the classroom with his *Pengerusi* badge pinned to the top of his white crisp-clean uniform, holding the attendance book in his hands. His spectacles brought some gravitas to his face that fit perfectly with his personality. His aura exuded a sense of confidence that even teachers admired. Teachers tend to only see what they want. Truths have a way of being disclosed. His classmates saw beneath that glossy overachieving facade. *Arrogance and pride.*

"Who does he think he is?" Puteri frowned with disapproval. "Walking in here and acting like he did nothing wrong. Did you see him at the front gate?"

"I did," Bumi muttered, wondering if he had to write a *karangan*, too. Earlier, when *Appa* had sent her, she ran as fast as her feet could and passed Ethan, who was taking his sweet time with his long strides, as if the bell hadn't rung at all. For someone who was the class monitor, he sure didn't care much about his record.

He *never* deserved it in the first place.

"Any questions?" Puan Liu asked aloud as a formality.

A boy groggily lifted his head from his tattered desk, pushed his tousled jet-black hair back, and perched his long slender fingers on his chin. He cleared his voice, catching Puan Liu's attention. "Teacher, why is that the answer to question five?" He scratched his head. "If that is supposed to be differentiated using the formula..."

Puan Liu scrunched her face momentarily and erased her answer. "*Aiyah,* my bad."

She corrected it as her marker screeched on the whiteboard. "Thanks, Chuan Zhe."

As Chuan Zhe nodded, Bumi caught him peeking at Puteri before laying his head back on his desk.

"Bumi," Puan Liu called out. Bumi prayed to the Gods that she wouldn't ask her to solve an equation.

She pointed with the tip of her marker. "Solve question six."

But luck was never on her side.

Bumi stared at the question. Puan Liu said to use the same concept from last week's lesson. But how could she when it was completely different? Bumi slowly copied the formula and tried to insert the values into it. Clicking her calculator, she wondered why her digits were way off. She flicked her gaze to Puteri, and Puteri was mouthing something that she couldn't comprehend. Shuffling her feet, she hesitantly said, "Teacher, I don't know."

Puan Liu's bloodshot eyes stared back at her with disappointment. "Bumi. I don't know how you're going to sit for SPM." She aggressively tapped the marker on the whiteboard, making Bumi flinch. "Everything you don't know."

Puan Liu sighed with frustration.

"*Cher,* can I try?" Ethan stood up, taking the marker from Bumi, and perfectly answered the question while she stood there awkwardly.

"Correct." Puan Liu nodded with approval. "Bumi, sit down."

Bumi touched the back of her flushed neck.

Static.

Bumi winced slightly.

PARA GURU ADALAH DIMAKLUMKAN BAHAWA MESYUARAT AKAN DIADAKAN SEKARANG. Murid-murid diminta untuk berada di dalam kelas. Sekian, terima kasih.

"All teachers, please be informed that there is a meeting now. Students are asked to remain in class. Thank you."

Bumi and Puteri exchanged glances. Bumi thought it was weird that they were having a teacher meeting now. *Did they find vape in someone's bag again? Or was there another vandalism case?*

Even when it was time for recess, Puan Liu didn't come back.

THE TEACHERS SHUFFLED CLOSER, wondering why they were having a meeting this early. Wasn't their next meeting on Thursday afternoon? It was natural that the Monday blues were affecting them. Encik Ranjit fiddled with his bushy moustache and tapped lightly on his desk.

He smiled cautiously. "Thank you everyone for coming to this meeting on short notice."

His smile faltered. "Puan Khadijah, please take the lead."

"Yes, Sir. At 8 AM, I found two boys behind the Biology and Chemistry lab, where the old classes were situated. There was a *pengakap* camp over the weekend."

The teachers nodded in understanding because the scouts were known for their annual camp.

"The students seemed…" Puan Khadijah hesitated. "Strange," she finally said.

"Define strange," Encik Singh said with a creased forehead.

"There was this eerie expression on their faces." Puan Khadijah rubbed her arms up and down. "It gave me the chills."

"Where are they now, *ah*?" Puan Liu asked.

Encik Ranjit answered instead. "They're being observed in the St. John's room."

Puan Khadijah's face became pale as a ghost. "But that's not the worst part. When I went into the St. John's room, *tahu tak apa I nampak*? They took the gold fishes from the aquarium with their bare hands and plopped them into their mouths."

"Maybe they were hungry?" Cik Anis placed her hand on her chin.

"No *lah*," Puan Khadijah disagreed. "It was *memang pelik*. Not normal at all."

"We have to keep them under observation and investigate what happened. Under no circumstances is anyone to go in there, understand?" Encik Ranjit's tone grew urgent.

"Yes, sir," Everyone chorused in unison.

"Good, because we don't know what we're dealing with," he said.

UNCLE LI WAS SMK Mujarab's version of Handy Mandy. Whether it was a ball on the roof or even a pipe leakage, everyone knew they could count on him. Uncle Li had worked here for 20 years and was nearing his retirement. It felt like it was yesterday that he was freshly appointed on the roster to clean the boys' toilet in Block A. Looking back, cleaning that toilet gave him the strength and push he needed.

Uncle Li hummed to the rhythm of *Petang*, moving his body to the motion of the swinging metal toolbox. His daughter was coming to pay him a visit from Seremban, and the thrill of meeting his newborn granddaughter formed goosebumps all over his arms. His son was cooking *manuk pansuh* for the special occasion, and his mouth watered thinking about it. Jingling his keys, he wondered whether he brought enough light bulbs to change in the St. John's room. He twisted the door handle open and saw two boys sitting up straight, side-by-side on a bed. Uncle Li dropped his keys in surprise.

He spoke as he bent over to pick them up. "Boys, what are you doing here? Did you accidentally get locked in here?"

A boy with a scar on his lips was suddenly face-to-face with him, staring at Uncle Li without flinching.

"*Terkejutnya*." Uncle Li touched his chest instinctively. "Boy, *ah*, how did you get here so fast?"

The boy didn't answer, and his dark, lifeless eyes kept staring at him.

"Boy, are you okay?"

The boy started muttering something repeatedly like it was a mantra.

"Hey, boy."

The mantra kept getting louder. It was a mixture of a lullaby and a strange rich sound that sounded so familiar, yet so unfamiliar. It was beauty and sadness formed together with a single utterance of the mantra. Uncle Li could feel something pulling at him, making him lose touch with himself. He slowly moved backwards, and *bang*, he hit something blocking the door. He slowly turned around to find the other boy. He grinned wickedly at Uncle Li, blood oozing from his white pearled teeth. The boy lunged forward and thrashed him without effort. Uncle Li's lifeless body lay on the ground in a puddle of blood.

"That was far too easy," he cackled.

The boy with the scar muttered, "Keep your end of the bargain, Master."

"Of course. A promise is a promise." He squatted on the

ground and touched the forehead of the old man sprawled on the ground. He licked his lips. "This is an interesting one."

He simpered, looking pleased with himself. "All of you will be rewarded."

AARON HELD out a bouquet of blood-red hibiscus. "Oh, hi. Your name is Puteri? Can you put three babies in my life?"

Puteri cringed internally. *What kind of pick-up line was that?*

"Uh… what?"

Aaron flashed a crooked smile, kneeling on one knee. "I like you so much. Puteri, will you go out with me?"

Not this again, she thought. "Aaron, I can't go out with you."

He smiled kindly. "It's okay, Puteri. I'll wait for you. I understand-"

Puteri cut him off. "No, Aaron. I can't date you, now or later."

"Why not?"He pouted.

Puteri massaged her head with her right hand. "Because of the *same reason* I've been telling you for the past few weeks. I'm not interested in you."

"I'm in it for the long game." He smirked.

Puteri grabbed the bouquet from his hands and flung it into the nearest rubbish bin.

"I said no!" she snapped and walked away from the tunnel that intersected with the canteen.

Bumi slung her arms around Puteri. "You okay?"

Anger engulfed her as she snorted, "Stupid *lah,* what was he thinking?"

"I would've snapped every limb in his body, but you said you'd handle it." Bumi gave Puteri a thumbs-up and giggled, "*Padan muka dia.* I bet he never saw that coming."

"I'm so tired of all these guys pressuring me to accept their confessions. If you want to confess, confess, *lah*. But no need to go to that extent."

"Right." Bumi thought for a moment and winked mischievously. "I know you don't date. But, is there not even a person who interests you?"

Puteri hesitated before answering. "No."

Puteri told Bumi that she had to continue her rounds, if not, Puan Nur would scold her for slacking off, and they parted ways. Puteri shrugged her dark-blue prefect blazer off after eyeing that there were no teachers around. She caught a glimpse of a guy with tousled jet-black hair arguing with the Canteen Aunty, and noticed the slump on his shoulders as she walked away. Chuan Zhe turned around and their eyes met. He darted his eyes away and started trailing away. But it was too late, Puteri was already on his heels.

"Chuan Zhe!" She called out. "You can't pretend that you didn't hear me." She called out again, "Chuan Zhe!"

"What?" He turned around abruptly, making Puteri lose her balance momentarily.

Regaining her balance, she asked, "What was that?"

"What was what?" He feigned ignorance, shrugging his shoulders.

"Why were you fighting with the Canteen Aunty?"

"We weren't fighting." His hands flung to his hair and rested there in irritation.

Puteri took a step towards him but maintained a halal distance between them. "What's wrong? You can tell me."

Chuan Zhe looked at the ground, not meeting her eye. "Zhe…" she trailed.

He shut his eyes. "It's not your problem, Puteri."

"Not my problem?" She placed her hands on her hips. "How can you say that when you've been avoiding me for weeks ?"

"I haven't." He denied.

"Don't lie," Puteri scowled. "We've been friends since standard three. You were there for me when my dad ab- abandoned us."

"Puteri..."

Wiping a tear away, she continued, "I don't want you to struggle alone. Let's share the burden together." She gestured towards Chuan Zhe's shoulders, taking his burden for herself. "There."

With a twinkle in his eyes, he grinned. "Puteri Alisya, you're *memang*, one of a kind."

Puteri grinned back and urged him to continue.

Chuan Zhe's shoulders slumped again. "My dad is ill and business has been slow. I've been taking all the night shifts, but nothing's helping."

"And that's why you asked the Canteen Aunty if you could work part-time?"

He nodded.

Puteri immediately asked, "How about I help?"

"No, you help out so much during the school holidays." Puteri opened her mouth to protest, but he shook his head. "I have a plan, but you won't like it. I'm taking a break from school."

"No," Puteri interjected. "We'll find a different way."

Chuan Zhe made a face that seemed to say *I told you so*. "I'm not quitting. I just need time to figure this out."

Puteri looked away. "How long?"

"I don't know," he answered honestly.

"Whatever happens, we're in this together."

And he believed her.

BUMI SIPPED her Milo while queuing up. She sighed, it was taking forever. She wondered if she would be able to get her *rumah sukan* shirt at the *Koperasi*. Glancing at her watch. Recess was going to end soon. As she threw away her Milo box, a scream pierced the air. Bumi's eyes widened in disbelief. Students scampered on their hands and legs, using them as their forefeet, chasing other students with speed and precision. They growled and thrashed them to the ground as if they were predators hunting their prey.

Cries of help and hysteria filled the air, like an echo effect foreshadowing impending doom. Students bolted away, but amid the chaos, nobody knew where they were going. The animal-like human pounced on Bumi, tugging her across the cracked ground. Clamping its jaw open, it bared its sharp teeth and sank them into her arm. Jerking away, she slammed its head and pinned it to the ground. Hoisting herself up, she raised her foot and kicked it. Bumi sprinted to Block C's staircase, knowing she had to escape. Another creature appeared on the staircase, blocking her way. She backed away slowly, turned left, and took the route to the canteen. Students fought off the creatures as they stood on the canteen tables, struggling to keep their balance and eventually plunging to the ground. More and more students were becoming them. Bumi flicked her eyes, searching for an escape. The Bougainvillea room and *Surau* were locked. A hand grabbed her, she shrugged it off and raised her leg when she heard, "It's us, Bumi."

"Don't kick," Puteri panted and Chuan Zhe was beside her.

Bumi wrapped her arms around Puteri in relief. "What's happening?"

"We don't know." Puteri hugged her back.

Chuan Zhe muttered, "Not wanting to spoil this moment, but we have to get out of here, now."

Puteri let go and nodded. "Can we make it to the main gate? If we can get out of here first."

Bumi and Chuan Zhe nodded in agreement.

Puteri grabbed onto Bumi's hand while Chuan Zhe held the sleeve of her blue *baju kurung*. Sliding across the seats of the gazebo and jumping down, they darted in the direction of the school's main gate. The chipped rocks from the road rustled as their shoes made across the parking lot. Bumi dragged Puteri to hurry up their pace, and Chuan Zhe tightened his hold on Puteri's sleeve. Craning her neck, she caught a glimpse of the creatures at the gate and turned in the direction of the classrooms downstairs. They tried pushing past the classroom doors, but the doors wouldn't budge and the window panels were shut completely.

"Help!" They called out, but it was no use. Shifting towards Block A, they rushed up the stairs and turned to level 1.

Puteri shrieked, "Go upstairs!"

A creature trotted, inching its face behind them. Chuan Zhe pushed it forcibly down the stairs. Puteri pulled onto the edge of Chuan Zhe's shirt that stuck out as Bumi led the way.

"Go to two *Permata*, it's always open!" Puteri yelled.

They knocked on the door repeatedly. "Open the door! Help us!"

The door swung open and they were pulled in.

"*Cepat lah*, lock the door," Kadam growled, making a face at the boy dressed in the school's grey PJ shirt and long track pants. The boy hurriedly kneeled on the ground and pushed the lock into the slot.

Bumi asked what everyone was wondering. "What was that?"

Fear struck a cord through them because they didn't have an answer.

Were they really possessed?

Static.

All students are informed to take refuge somewhere safe. The school authorities are taking action to overcome the situation at hand. This is an emergency situation.

Static.

But who knew if they were ever coming?

THE CLOCK TICKED and hours passed. Another announcement wasn't made. 999 hadn't picked up. If they weren't coming, who was?

Ethan stuck out his tongue as he scribbled the correct answer he previously got wrong for question seven.

"How can he be studying right now?" Chuan Zhe whispered to Puteri, opening one eye whilst resting his head on a desk.

Puteri shrugged, wondering if this was how he beat her in class.

"It's not normal." Bumi rolled her eyes.

"I think it's ambitious." The boy who wore PJ clothes and whose name was Amarpreet beamed with admiration. He got left behind by his classmates from two *Permata* while he was changing his clothes.

"Come on, kid." Ismail stopped rolling the unlit cigarette in his hands. "You should have greater dreams in life."

"Cigarettes aren't allowed at school."

Ismail snapped the cigarette into two.

"*Abang,*" Amarpreet added quickly as a form of respect.

"And *some more* the *penolong ketua pengawas* is here." Kadam sneered.

Amarpreet glanced at Puteri, waiting for her to confiscate it from Ismail.

Puteri ignored the jab and turned to Amarpreet. "He stopped smoking 6 months ago."

Puteri pointed at the snapped cigarette. "That helps him not relapse. Satisfied, Kadam?"

"Stop acting like you're all that, Puteri." Kadam stood up abruptly.

Puteri was unfazed and kept examining her nails. "You're pissed, I get that. But are my notes that great?"

Kadam's face turned red. "You're the one who ripped your notes when I asked you for them."

Waggling her fingers, she smiled innocently. "I'm not the one who borrowed my notes before and decided to lose them. And why would you need my notes when you go for ten tuitions?"

Kadam didn't answer, and instead barged up to Ethan and snatched his Biology workbook out of his hands. "You're the *pengerusi*. Do something, *lah!*"

Ethan's expression grew cold. "Why should I do anything?"

Ethan moved closer to Kadam and glared at her. "I never wanted to be *pengerusi*."

He stepped away from her as she regained her composure.

Bumi shook away the chills down her spine and stood up. "We can't keep waiting. We have to get out of here."

Bumi looked at Ethan. "Our robotics' club made a drone, right?"

Ethan nodded.

"We'll use it to survey the premises."

"What about looking for teachers?" Puteri suggested.

"We can split up into groups. That would be faster," Chuan Zhe suggested.

Ismail interjected. "I'm not leaving."

Amarpreet agreed. "Same."

Bumi flashed an irritated look, scratching her arm. "Fine, we'll pick lots. Whoever gets picked has to go."

"Who put you in charge, number thirty-four?" Kadam jeered.

"Do you have a better plan?" Bumi cocked her head. Kadam cursed in an unfamiliar language, perhaps in the Aslian language.

Bumi tore a leaf of paper from a notebook and ripped it into smaller pieces. Handing them the pieces, she asked them to write their names on them. Each of them placed their names into a small jar. Bumi shook the jar and handed it to Kadam. "Pick one."

Kadam picked up a piece of paper and unfolded it. Smiling smugly, she said, "Puteri."

Puteri took the paper out of Kadam's hand and found herself staring at it in disbelief.

Ismail snatched the jar from Kadam's hands and took out another crisp of paper and murmured apologetically, "Bumi."

BUMI COULDN'T BELIEVE she got stuck with Ethan. She couldn't understand why he even volunteered to go with her. *So what if he knew where the drones were kept?* Bumi couldn't understand why he was so persistent in coming.

Swiveling her head, she motioned Ethan to come closer. "Which ICT room are we going to?" she whispered in his ear.

Feeling the heat from her breath, he whispered back, "The first one."

Creatures were swarming around them, their speed was inhuman. She called them creatures, but it was odd, because earlier today, they were her teachers and schoolmates. *How fast things change,* Bumi thought.

Bumi pulled Ethan along and increased their pace. The creatures were catching up and were nearly behind them. It didn't help that they were using their hands as feet. It gave them leverage that Bumi and Ethan didn't have. They were supposed to turn right, but Ethan turned left. Noticing that he wasn't behind her, she tried the opposite direction. Wherever they went, more creatures scurried towards them. Sooner or later, they were going to meet a dead end. Stopping to fight the creatures would be no use, they were outnumbered. Catching up with Ethan, he beckoned her to follow a path that she didn't recognise.

He pointed to the fence and uttered, "We need to climb the fence. Careful."

Ethan extended his hand out, but Bumi dismissed it and hurriedly crawled up the fence, placing her foot delicately on the wooden gaps. *Almost there,* she whispered to herself as she worked her shaky legs up the fence. With a slide, she slipped backwards, instinctively shutting her eyes tight.

Feeling a strong pair of arms around her, Ethan whispered in a raspy voice, "I got you. Didn't I tell you to be careful?"

Ignoring the thuds of her heart, she made it across the fence. With Ethan's lanky frame, he swiftly leaped over the fence with no problem. Charging towards the ICT room, Ethan fumbled with the lock of the newly-painted door.

"Faster, *lah*!" Bumi cried out frantically. She scratched her arm harder and pulled at her nails, the anxiety and unease filling her up similarly to a faucet rushing into an intricate vase fitted with broken shards. The leakage of the water contained would be inevitable, just like the ticking time bomb in her.

Ethan twisted the key into the slot, opening the door. Bumi was suddenly thankful that he was the president of the Robotics club and couldn't bear to wonder if they hadn't had a key.

Bang, the door rattled. *Bang.* Their eyes locked, the nervous tension brewing between them. They craned their ears, but silence filled the air and solace became their refuge.

Bumi burst out laughing and Ethan peered at her warily. That made her laugh some more.

"I never expected anything like this."

"Who would? We're practically in a horror movie." Ethan's eyes darted around, searching for the drone.

"No, it's just..." Bumi struggled to find the right words. Ethan raised his eyebrows and she continued, "I never thought to be in an impossible situation, especially with you."

Bumi babbled on, "Because we hate each other."

"I never hated you," Ethan mumbled, warmth filling his eyes. This was the first time Bumi noticed his caramel chocolate eyes with hints of buttered toffee swirls, trapped by a black, hazy limbal ring that embodied the darkness within him.

"Wha..." Bumi's eyes lit with confusion. "Why did you come with me? I could have come alone."

Bumi's head whirled up as it struck her. "You pitied me and thought I couldn't do a simple task?"

"Wait," Ethan shot out, but Bumi interrupted and shot back.

"It makes sense now. No wonder, you were acting so nice." Tears welled up in her eyes. "Everyone thinks I'm stupid, I get it. The teachers chose you over me to become *pengerusi* when you didn't even want it, fine."

Her eyes blazed with anger as she exclaimed, "But I won't stand you looking down on me!"

"You're wrong. I didn't come here to help you. I came here for purely selfish reasons." Ethan avoided her gaze.

"Explain to me why," she knotted her eyebrows.

"I like you." He gazed into her eyes.

"What?" she stammered, not believing what she heard.

Red tints formed on his cheeks, making him look shy, and Bumi never thought that was possible. "You're positive, kind, loud, and... a rule-follower. Everything I'm not."

Bumi didn't know what to say.

Ethan pulled his hair gently. "You've always hated me, so I pretended to hate you more."

Sighing, he said, "I'm not asking you to accept my confession. I'm telling you because I don't want to see the person I like hurt."

Bumi felt hot all of a sudden. "We have to get back."

Ethan nodded, not meeting her eyes.

AWKWARDNESS WAS A CONSTANT FOR THEM, but now there was room for them to breathe. Misunderstandings and miscommunications were no longer a hurdle for them. Ethan clutched the drone closer to him as he dashed behind Bumi. Thrusting the wooden stick in his hand, the creature fell backwards, groaning in pain. Shuffling through the grass, Ethan put his index finger on his lips and pointed to the back of the car. This creature was a little different than the rest; it embodied its former human form rather than its animalistic nature. It was standing on its two feet. He stepped closer to the creature and was ready to strike, when a fake red Polo shirt caught his eye, making him hesitate.

It looked weirdly familiar.

The creature turned, and Ethan's heart stopped. His fingers shook and his lips quivered.

He couldn't understand why this was happening.

"*Abak*," Ethan cried out in Iban. "*Abak*, it's me, Kinua."

The creature didn't respond, it kept swaying and peered at Ethan with its gouged eyes.

Wiping his tears away, he gulped, "I was supposed to make your favourite *manuk pansuh* tonight."

There was no response.

Ethan stepped closer to him and trembled. "*Abak*, let's go home."

He cried louder, "Let's go!"

Ethan crouched on the ground and wept. He wished he never told *Abak* that he was embarrassed by him. He was a terrible son and didn't deserve forgiveness. He punched his chest over and over again. He didn't want anyone to know he was Ethan Kinua Anak William. He told *Abak* to go by Uncle Li and not William. *How could he be so cold-hearted?*

Tears kept falling and he couldn't make them stop. He no longer had a dad.

Bumi wrapped her arms around Ethan and gently brushed his hair, trying to soothe his pain as tears drenched her face. She cooed softly and took his hand in hers.

"Ethan, let's go, okay? We'll be back for Uncle Li."

Ethan gulped, his Adam's apple bobbed violently, and he wondered whether he would ever be able to breathe again.

SWEAT TRICKLED on Chuan Zhe's forehead as he tried to steady his ragged breathing. Clenching onto the desk, he staggered a little and didn't realise he bit his tongue until he tasted the metallic taste of blood in his mouth.

"Did you find any teachers?" Amarpreet worried.

Puteri glumly replied, "All of them are possessed. They couldn't recognise us."

"What about the drones?" Kadam's voice edged with fear. "What did they show?"

"That's the thing, I don't see anything," Ethan croaked, different from his usual cool and indifferent tone.

"What do you mean?" Kadam grabbed the drone controller out of his hands. "Why don't I see anything?"

Sighing, he murmured, "I told you."

"Hey, Chuan Zhe," Ismail approached him. "You okay? Man, your nose is bleeding," his eyes flashed with concern before turning to face Puteri.

Wiping his nose with the end of his sleeve, a voice bellowed in Chuan Zhe's mind. *Snap his neck.*

Stepping closer to Ismail, he could feel the blood rushing in his body. Licking his lips, he extended his arm slowly and wrapped his hands around Ismail's neck. *Squeeze his neck. Crush his bones.*

Ismail yelped, "What the hell are you doing?" Ismail struggled out of his grip, but his grip was iron steel.

Everyone frantically rushed forward, trying to persuade him to let go. A lullaby coursed through his ears; something about it was enchanting and made him want to drift away. He was fading away into the darkness. His younger brothers welcomed him as they chimed, "*Dage*, come play with us."

It looked so peaceful. He wanted to go. He wanted to be happy. *Go with them.* He took a step forward when he heard the voice. It was the only ease he had ever known.

"Zhe, let him go." Puteri's voice was gentle. "Fight it."

Loosening his grip as he recognised the long eyelashes that peeked out from her rustic-rimmed spectacles. "Puteri…"

"Stop." Puteri stood in front of him, stopping Ismail.

"Move!" he barked, but Puteri didn't move. "He almost killed me."

"But he stopped himself," Puteri retaliated.

"That doesn't change things," Ismail uttered with fury.

Chuan Zhe side-stepped her. "He's right."

Puteri's forehead creased with worry.

"There was this voice, it told me to kill him."

THE CLOCK STRUCK SEVEN, and they no longer wondered who would save them. Day was shifting to night, but they were constant.

Hunger and fatigue overtook them. Silence echoed the walls except for Chuan Zhe's constant struggle against the ropes that caged him. Puteri wondered which version he was now as he bared his teeth, munching on the side of his hand one moment and smiling with his eyes another moment. Puteri's thoughts went back to the creature that pinned him to the ground and stared into his eyes as if it was sucking his soul, with drool dripping from its mouth.

Puteri covered her mouth with astonishment. W*hat if that was what happened?* Reciting *Ayat Al-Kursi* under her breath, she glanced at the rest who were nodding off. She was about to nudge Bumi when her eyes caught on the red patches on her arm. The nails on her index fingers were missing. Puteri furrowed her eyebrows. Bumi had self-control when it came to picking her nails and scratching.

A cackle erupted in the air, waking everyone.

"Let's play a game, shall we?" Mischief glinted in Chuan Zhe's eyes.

"Don't listen to him," Chuan Zhe interjected.

"The harder you reject me, the more you lose control, and eventually, you'll be gone."

He clapped his hands and tilted his head. "That's why I have a proposal. Ask him to willingly let me reside in him, and I'll give you three hints to any questions. "

"And why would we agree to that?" Ethan scoffed.

"Because if you don't, his soul will be gone. I'll be all that's left," he sneered.

"What's in it for you?" Bumi eyed him warily.

He smirked. "We'll never know who'll win. "

"Take me instead," Puteri pleaded. "Leave him alone!"

"I don't want you, girl," he said, ignoring her pleas. "Do we have a deal or not?"

"Let me talk to him." Puteri stepped closer to him.

"Make it quick," he said smugly.

Puteri didn't recognise that expression.

That wasn't the Chuan Zhe she knew.

"Puteri, it's going to be okay." He raised his hand for their secret air handshake.

"Promise, you'll come back to me?"

"I will," he promised.

His face distorted into an expression that Puteri had never seen before. "So…"

"We have a deal," she choked out.

"Good," he munched on his pinky. "Choose your questions wisely."

Kadam blurted, "What's happening to us?"

"Kadam!" everyone exclaimed with disapproval.

"Possession is the key to your problems."

Ismail rolled his eyes. "Why'd you ask that?"

"How did this start?" Bumi questioned.

"A ritual," he teased with a wink.

"What do you mean?" Ethan asked.

"A ritual," he repeated. "I cannot say more."

Ethan sighed defeatedly. "What about the last hint?"

"Not everything is what it seems and perhaps someone is extending their powers."

"What do you mean by that?" Puteri inquired further.

He shook his index finger. "No can do."

"What did he mean by a ritual?" Bumi scratched her arm harder, the red marks becoming more apparent, as if they were one with her skin.

"During the annual scouts' camp, they do one," he muttered nervously. "Which was yesterday..."

"Because of the tale?" Ismail quipped.

Amarpreet nodded shakily.

"What tale?" Puteri asked.

Kadam answered instead, "The tale where our school was an old factory and one of the worker's sons got hurt in an accident. The worker made a doll out of his son's bones. Apparently, his spirit still lingers here. *Tu melampaulah.*"

"Even if it's extreme, what are the chances that it could be true?" Bumi picked on her nail beds.

Nobody responded, perhaps because they didn't want to jinx it, or deep down, they knew the truth that they couldn't run from.

"WHERE ARE WE GOING?" Kadam whined.

"A bit further," Amarpreet told her.

They edged to the back of the Biology and Chemistry labs and slid down the hill, reaching the unused classrooms from when there were afternoon sessions. Amarpreet strained his eyes as he directed their way in the dark and stayed on the lookout for any creatures. The grass blades were alive, like waves rustling in the sea that seemed to complement their heavy breathing. Shifting to their left, he muttered uneasily, "We're here."

The field was wide and empty apart from a couple of tents that blended with the green, lushness of the field.

"Now what?" Ismail gestured to their surroundings.

"We have to do the ritual." Amarpreet pointed at the middle of the field.

"Is that safe?" Ethan shifted slightly on the balls of his feet.

"I don't know," Amarpreet whispered sheepishly. "Nothing happened before this year. They always played it as a joke, that's what my brother told me."

"We have to call out to the spirit." He inhaled sharply.

Puteri and Ismail looked at each other. "We can't take part in the ritual. It's not permissible in Islam."

"The rest of us are more than enough."

At the centre of the field, a circle was drawn, and a porcelain doll and a sharp-edged knife lay there. They stepped into the circle, passing the knife around, and slit the tip of their index fingers, blood oozing out. The doll was placed upright in the middle of the circle. As they joined their hands, they chanted in unison, "Spirit of the underworld, we beg of you to return back to your rightful place. We offer you our blood as our sacrifice."

They waited, but nothing happened.

They chanted again, "Please take our sacrifice and let them go."

All they heard was the moaning of the wind.

"Why is nothing happening?" Kadam turned to Amarpreet.

He shrugged. "I reversed the chant of the calling upon spirits."

Kadam glanced at Chuan Zhe. "Spirit, tell us what went wrong!"

"Time will tell," He answered cryptically.

"Tell us, now!" Kadam grabbed him by the collar and his body shook with laughter.

"Let go of him!" Puteri yelled.

Ethan noticed the scratches on Bumi's arm and asked her, "You okay?"

Bumi scratched her arms harder and felt blood dripping from her nose. Sounds of whispers and rattles filled her ears.

Clapping her hands over her ears, she groaned, but the voices became louder. *We're coming to you, Master.*

A harsher voice took over her. "*Child, you've done your part. Now, it's mine.*"

She dropped her arms and grinned. "I feel perfect."

Bumi levitated into the air as hundreds of creatures appeared, surrounding them. She cackled and looked down at Chuan Zhe. "I told you I would win."

Chuan Zhe kneeled on one leg. "My apologies, Master."

"Bumi, what's happening?" Puteri shrieked.

"You still don't understand. What a pity."

"We have to get out of here," Ismail said.

"No one's going anywhere," Bumi replied.

"Bumi! This isn't you." Ethan rumpled his hair.

"I always keep my promises," Bumi flashed a wrathful grimace.

The creatures scuttled closer, and before they could escape, the creatures ripped their bodies. Sinking their teeth into their meaty skin and crunching on their bones until there was nothing left of them.

They had lost.

EPILOGUE

The crowd had a life of its own, dressed in both vibrant and dull colours. One can know a lot about people this way. People say don't judge a book by its cover, but their clothes allow us to get a glimpse of their lives, whether they crave attention or yearn to live in solitude. All of that could be known. People watching was a favourite of hers, especially with the guide who wouldn't stop chattering about every piece in the exhibition.

He moved on to the next piece and announced, "This is our newest piece. It's a painting of an incident that happened years ago, of a school that was burnt down. Until today, nobody knows what happened. There were no survivors."

She scrutinised the painting, taking in the different shades and hues used for the painting. Beneath the painting was a golden plaque that read: *"In loving memory of"* with names listed underneath, and her gaze caught on one. *Bumi.*

She smirked and still couldn't believe the charm worked. All she had to do was grab Bumi's hand and it did the trick. She didn't think it would affect the entire school, but it didn't matter. Because Bumi *deserved* it.

"Anjali *ma,* there you are." *Appa* wrapped his arms around her.

"I was just here, *Appa.*" she inhaled the strong scent of coconut that surrounded him.

"I was so worried about you," He said, touching her head gently.

He noticed the painting behind her. He paused and took a step forward.

Anjali slung her arm in his and slightly touched him with her hand. "*Appa,* let's go."

Breaking away from his daze, he nodded.

Victory was hers once again.

9
ENCHANTING EMILIA
JULIA JACKSON

We live in a world of secrets and deceptions. Each day no better than the last, being tricked by even those we trust the most. And I live it. Breathe it here on stage, the grandest lie of all— *magic.*

Peeking out from behind the crimson velvet curtain, I smile to myself. The audience sits silently in the dark. They're ready for us, and I'm ready for them. Adrenaline rushes through my veins, heart thrashing in my chest in response. The thrill of the show—the deception—is my everything. It has been since Father first pulled that copper coin from behind my ear, flipping it in his fingers and looking at me expectantly. It had shocked me then, just as I shock others now.

Mother's life ended as mine began, but father managed to raise me on his own for sixteen years. He saw the joy in every moment and was determined to instill a sense of wonderment into our otherwise desolate world. I wish the scarlet fever hadn't taken him before he had the chance to see me up on stage.

"Ready, my pet?" Max whispers too closely to my ear, sending a shiver down my spine to the place where his hand meets the small of my bare back.

I turn my entire body toward him, breaking the physical touch. But I smile, cautious to let him know how his closeness causes my stomach to turn. "Always." My saccharine smile wide and beaming to hide the bile rising to my tongue.

"Let's give them what they want then, shall we?" He walks through the small opening of the curtain, answered by loud applause from the full theatre. His arms raise, unnecessarily ensuring that all the focus is on him. "Thank you, thank you. I am The Mystical Maximillian and I promise you an evening of shock and awe. In fact, I guarantee a night you will never forget."

The applause turns to cheers. He takes it all in, walking slowly across the stage. Left. Right. Bowing a few times in between. The bastard hasn't even performed a single act, yet they eat up every step he takes across the wooden floorboards.

"And I have a special treat for all you fine gentlemen this evening— my assistant, the beautiful Emilia. Emilia, come join us, won't you?"

I take a few seconds to roll my eyes, breathe in and exhale before I push aside the heavy curtain. The crowd cheers, but it's different than they did for Max—full of hollering from the sweaty men that fill the seats. Yet, I beam from ear to ear. Shake my hips. Even do a spin. Not because I want to, but because I have to. I can still feel the imprint of his hand across my cheek from the last time I didn't "put on a tantalizing show."

"My dear Emilia, could you please bring the trolley out?"

"For you, Mystical Maximillian, of course." I wink and walk to side stage, where a dark-stained wooden cart sits in wait. The large planter pot atop it vibrates slightly as I roll the trolley to Max. Over the scuffed floor and the outline of the trap door that only Max and I can see.

"What if I told you I could speed up time?" Max asks the audience.

I walk around the cart, dragging my fingers across each

surface in a delicate motion, showing the spectators that this is, in fact, a regular cart. My hands grip the side of the cold pot and I lift it into the air, high above my head. Peering at the bottom, I widen my eyes and shake my head from side to side. "Nothing under here." Laughter rises and I place the pot back down gingerly.

"Let me prove to you that indeed, I can manipulate time. Though, I don't think that will help your wives cook your dinner any quicker," he says. I grind down on my teeth. These comments. His view on women.

We are nothing but servants and whores.

"I need complete silence." Max closes his eyes and rubs his temples. A wonderful actor, I must admit.

The flames of the lanterns lining the stage cast a strange glow upon the many faces behind them, the only light in the black as night theatre. Row upon row of wide eyes stare Max and me down. Waiting. Watching.

And then, a tiny bud pops out of the dirt in the pot, rising up, up, up, into a stem, multiplying. Bright green leaves appear from the new branches of the suddenly formed tree. The crowd tilts their heads in unison, mouths dropping as they stare in awe at the oranges that emerge from the tree, growing to their full size in the blink of an eye.

It is no wonder the audience is so taken aback. They would never have seen these things in their dull, dreary days. They may be the richest of society, with their silk dresses and handkerchiefs, sitting in a place of such opulence, but they lie to themselves, really. Commending each other for being the masters of the city when, in reality, they hide behind their extravagance, avoiding those like me that live among the rats.

They are the real rats. Horrible and despicable, just like The Mystical Maximilian.

The rats stand to applaud the showman. I feel their eyes follow my behind as I walk away with the time-defying orange tree. The velvet curtain is soft on my skin as I brush past it to retrieve the next prop.

"I have proven that I can move time. Now let me illustrate my ability to make a living, breathing thing disappear." Max's deep voice carries like a tune, introducing his next masterful piece.

In the darkness, behind stage, I find the brass cage. "Hi little birdie. I'm so sorry," I whisper to the tiny bird held prisoner. It's soft blue, so pretty even in the absence of bright light. I hate being part of this trick. A poor animal should not have to die for Max to look like some hero.

He's no hero. He's a chauvinistic, murdering, monster of a man.

I try to focus on the sound my too-high heels make against the wood as I return to Max. The smell of the kerosene in the lamps. The chill that lingers on my exposed skin in this teeny gold costume I wear. Anything to distract myself from what is about to happen—the guilt that slices through my soul every single time we perform this part of the show.

The bird's wings flap violently against the bars of the cage, as though it knows the fate that lies in wait for him. *Death.*

"Here, I have a simple bird," he laughs, holding the cage out in front of him. "He's a feisty fellow as you can see. And here is a simple cloth." Max pulls a red cloth from inside his shiny black suit jacket, snapping it in the air a few times. "Would you please hold this for me, Emilia?"

My hands reach out toward him, a finger wrapping into the loop at the top of the cage, and the opposite hand laying flat below it. Max waves the fabric in the air again, exchanging it from hand to hand. Walking to the edge of the stage, closer to his fans. He leans over, doing a delicate dance to mesmerize them into a trance as they follow the red cloth. I hope the flames of the lamps flicker high enough to catch his pant leg. To turn into a blazing fire that not even God himself could put out.

The crowd is in absolute silence once he returns to me and the bird. My blue friend makes one final *chirp*, and I hold back the tears that fight so desperately to fall from my eyes. As Max drapes the fabric over the cage, our eyes meet. His brown eyes almost as dark as his soul. Then he nods.

I must keep this smile and pretend like I am not about to kill this innocent creature. But it *is* me. Forced to kill the bird with a pull of the loop at the top of the cage and one at the base at the same time. Triggering the contraption that collapses a false top to the bottom, crushing the bird. Pressed to death before the cage returns to normal. I have to be quick. Can't make a mistake. My breathing stops altogether as my hands move just enough to pull the cage up and back together, but not enough that anyone would question what is happening behind the veil of this cloth.

The Mystic Maximilian's grand disappearing act.

The red fabric—the same color as the bird's blood that I know is hidden in the metal of this damn metallic prison—floats away revealing the now empty cage. The audience explodes into cheers. Max laughs and stuffs the fabric back into his coat, bowing slowly.

I sneak behind the curtain again, placing the cage on the trolley next to the orange tree. "I'm so, so sorry sweet birdie," I whisper to its corpse.

The death of another bird opens the raw scab of grief in my heart from losing Father. Those with power make no efforts to assist those in need, especially the sickly—left to rot and die on the cobblestones.

And then it hits me. What I have to do. He so easily ends a poor bird's life. So effortlessly strikes me across the face. Over and over and over again. Night after night. Show after show.

But not anymore. There's no reason his life is more significant than this bird's.

I am the real magic behind the show. Not just some assistant handing over the tools the skilled master needs. *I'm* the one that builds the contraptions. Understands the way the mechanics work. There would be no orange tree without my gears. No disappearing bird without my springs.

Rabbits from hats, apparitions appearing from fog, mirrors reflecting false images... all rudimentary. I could do so much better than him.

A female magician.

The absolute unthinkable in this deplorable society, yet something I hold close to my heart and see in my dreams.

The Enchanting Emilia.

Max scoffed when I mentioned it to him originally, telling me that I should know my place. An assistant. A treat to the eyes of his fans, only good for my body and my pretty face.

Since he said that, I have kept my aspirations quiet. I bide my time, absorbing all the lies he tells his adoring fans. Listen to him read all the headlines in the papers about our illusions that have not once made mention of my name. The only attention I get is that of the men's eyes that easily follow me at showtime.

I am a woman with a brain. With talent. And maybe if there is no more Max, I will have the chance to take center stage. To return the true awe to magic that he has sucked clean from me between the abuse and monotony of it all.

I will be the greatest conjurer of all time. Not a charlatan willing to spill the blood of the innocent.

"I think we should bring out the box next, don't you, Emilia?"

This has all become so boring. The same routine. So predictable it is difficult for me to remember that this is all new for those watching. They don't know about the hidden compartments in the box that I curl into, making myself tiny and contorting in the places Max knows not to drive the sword down into.

"While Emilia gets into the box, could someone please come

inspect this sword for me?" Every male hand shoots up from the audience, some even standing and hopping up and down to be chosen. *Fools.*

I spin on my heel, walking fast to get the box big enough to be a coffin onto the stage. The wheels under it squeak as they turn, as I roll the black box center stage and push down their locks with the tip of my toes.

There's a plump man with rosy cheeks furrowing his brow on stage when I arrive, carefully running his hand along the flat side of the steel blade, inspecting it very closely. "It's real," he grumbles, gazing out at the audience, proud of himself.

"Of course it is!" Max exclaims, retrieving his sword and motioning for the man to return to his seat. "I am not here to bamboozle you fine people!" They laugh. I gag.

I'll have to spill his blood first. The Mystical Maximilian will die by my hand. I'm not sure when or how, but surely, I can figure it out. Perhaps an accident during one of his tricks. It's not like he truly understands anything that we do anyways. It should be easy.

Max removes the large lid, nearly as tall as him, and places it on the ground. "Come, Emilia, I will help you into the box." Max extends a hand and I take it. His fingers and palms are clammy and smooth from not working a day in his life. I wonder what it must have been like to grow up with such privilege, and how he is so cruel despite never having to struggle. "There you go," he says as he gives a gentle push behind my thigh and I make my way over the edge and inside.

The space around me darkens as the lid lowers over me. Black. Cold. Dark. Just before he closes it completely, he looks down upon me. "Ready for the grand finale?" His mouth moves into a side grin. I smile back, thinking about how glorious it will be to see his smile fall and fade into nothingness one day soon. My heart gallops in delight.

My arms squeeze toward each other, crossing over my chest.

Ever so slowly, my heels inch towards my bottom until my knees touch the lid of the box. I tilt my head to the right until my ear kisses my shoulder. Finally, I rotate completely to my side. We've performed this act a hundred times. It's like clockwork to us, but to them—to them the magic is real.

Between two slats of wood, through a sliver of an opening, I am able to take in the beautiful theatre. The large white columns leading up to the balcony. The ladies leaning over the edge, chests heaving in their too-tight corsets.

"I must warn you lovely ladies to not fear." He must have noticed their bosoms too. "For this next trick, I will be driving my sword through the slats in this box repeatedly. There will be blood. But I shall put Miss Emilia back together again. No need to panic. Just sit back and enjoy how I am far better than any street magician you may have seen before."

Blood?

There shouldn't *be* blood.

"Max?" I yell.

"Ah, yes, you don't need to worry either dear Emilia. This will all be done soon." He laughs, reassuring the crowd. But I am not reassured.

What in God's name is he doing? This isn't in the script. This isn't what we have done time and time again.

"Let's give her some applause." I hear those weak hands of his clap together, leading the rest of the room to a volume where they can't hear me.

"Max!" I scream. "Max, what are you doing?"

The blade skims my nose, so close to breaking the skin that my breath catches in my throat. He scares the life from me, and I know he did it on purpose. He knows the exact spots to pierce for the illusion. It only appears that he would hit me from the audience's point of view...but he never does.

No. No, no, no. This is all wrong.

"Ah, no blood this time. I shall try again." Cackles fill the room louder than before.

Do I move? Do I push the lid open and escape? If I rotate, even an inch, he could slice through me, missing our usual mark.

But in the end, it doesn't matter.

The sword plunges through my thigh. The scream burns as it leaves my throat. Tears running hot down my cheeks.

He's—he's doing this on purpose.

"Oh, don't be so dramatic, Emilia." The blade pulls out of my flesh, up through the slats. I can't believe he is doing this in front of a live audience.

They gasp when they see the blood. Then silence. Deafening silence in the hallowed theatre.

I spin around quickly and push up against the lid, but the bastard is pressing down firmly on it. "Max! Let me out! God damn it!" I want to sound strong and brave, but it comes out as desperate and scared pleas muffled by my tears and mucus.

The glint on the steel falls through the center of the box, but before I have a chance to move away, it plunges into my stomach, pinning me down in place.

I scream. I scream in so much pain that the imbeciles watching me die realize that this isn't a trick. That Max will never be able to make me whole again.

"Help! Please!" They know this is wrong. They have to. They must.

"Is she okay?" A man's voice calls from somewhere. My vision goes blurry, my mind a fog.

"That looks like real blood!" A shrill cry.

"One more time should do the trick!" Max yells above them.

The death blow. Straight through my chest. I choke and sputter on the blood. The taste of tin as sharp as the blade in my lungs. My cry is nothing but a gurgle, the warm blood falling from my mouth.

Chaos percolates in the theatre, bubbling and boiling with each new cry of disbelief and drop of blood from the sword onto the stage. The ladies scream against the bone in their corsets.

They'll save me. They'll end this.

But the lid doesn't open. The pain doesn't cease. And the sounds of the theatre fade into the same darkness as the enclosure of my new coffin.

I failed Father. I was too slow. Too slow to realize that Max would put an end to someone that was better than him. Someone that could possibly pose a threat.

As my world turns silent and dark, I know that my dreams now die along with my body. That I will never be The Enchanting Emilia.

Instead, I am The Mystical Maximilian's greatest disappearing act.

10
THE NIGHT GAME
GABRIELA LAVARELLO

I

Jack Renolds looked over the New York City skyline with a frown. It was his city, and he could take everything from it with the snap of a finger. But it didn't matter since he was going to die next week.

Condensation dripped from a tumbler of whiskey, pooling on the glass table in a semicircle. It was the only disruption in his perfect office, the only thing that wasn't set exactly right.

That, and the IV drip anchoring him to his brand new wheelchair.

Jack used to be perfect, but now he was a dark stain on the perfect lines and clean-cut corners of his skyline office. He'd built himself up to be the most successful man in the city, and had done everything it took to get there. People asked if he regretted the blackmail and risky business in order to get to the top, and that, *"maybe you should retire and live out the rest you've got on a private island. You can afford that much."*

But Jack only laughed when they said those things. If there

was anything he learned about being close to death, it was that he didn't regret his past actions.

Not even close.

A knock at the door made Jack jump, and the IV needle reminded him of its presence. He winced and cursed under his breath before calling in the only person who was allowed to knock on his door.

"Jonnie, it's my thinking time," Jack said in greeting as his pretty blonde secretary opened the door.

"There's a miss at the door for you, Sir," Jonnie said with a blank, yet polite smile plastered on her red-painted lips.

Jack frowned. "A miss who?"

Jonnie shrugged. "She won't say, just tells me she wants to talk to you about your... condition."

Fury and fear reared in his stomach, and Jack bit back another curse. He hadn't told anyone about the cancer slowly eating away at his body, not even his own mother. Not that he talked to his mother very much anymore, but the point still stood. He'd want the public to think that his death was an accident when it happened, not that he was beaten by something in his own body. How could this mysterious woman know a single thing about his sickness?

"Bring her in," Jack said with a wave of his free hand.

Jonnie glanced at the IV drip before nodding and closing the door, giving him a moment to compose himself before the door reopened and a woman stepped inside.

She was tall and intimidating, and Jack fought a strange shiver at the sense of *wrongness* that rolled from her and permeated the air. A black trench coat covered her body, and the tips of her high-heeled boots peaked from under the duster as she took another step forward. Long platinum hair was coiled into a tight bun at the back of her head, and equally light eyelashes framed eyes so dark they seemed black.

"Hello, Jack," She said, her voice low and measured as it

slipped from thin lips.

"Who are you?" Jack replied, and he wished for the hundredth time that morning that he could rip the IV out of his arm.

"My name is of no importance," She answered. "But if it's easier for you, just call me Doctor D."

"Dee? As in the letter D?" Jack asked, and the woman nodded.

"You're going to die soon, Mister Renolds. Is that correct?"

It was hard not to jerk back, as if she'd just shot him in the chest.

"How do you know?"

"I know many things, Jack," Doctor D paused. "Can I call you Jack?"

"Knock yourself out, Doctor D," Jack grumbled.

"Wonderful."

The woman named D strode to the long glass table before which Jack sat, pulling out a manila envelope from the depths of her coat.

"What is this?" Jack asked, eyeing the envelope as her long fingers pushed it across the table.

"A cure to your sickness, Mister Renolds."

The world shattered before molding itself back into place, though all Jack did was blink.

"Bullshit. The doctors told me that not even their treatments can save me," Jack retorted, the envelope crunching under his fingers.

Doctor D didn't blink, didn't smile, nothing. Her gaze was blank as she nodded.

"That might be so, but my scientists have created more than just a treatment. It's a cure that can wipe the disease straight from your body in less than forty-eight hours."

Jack couldn't help it. He laughed.

"Okay, cut the crap, Doctor D," Jack chuckled. "This has to

be one of the more creative ways someone's tried to blackmail me."

The woman only gave him a bland, close-lipped smile and rose from her chair.

"I have other appointments to make, Jack. Please feel free to look through the offer, though I'll need you to call this number by ten o'clock tonight if you wish to proceed. If I don't hear from you, consider my offer withdrawn."

And then she was gone, high-heeled boots clicking mercilessly across the room before she disappeared, leaving nothing but the manila envelope and a cream-colored business card behind, upon which a simple phone number and name were printed.

999-606-6699

The Night Game

Jack thumbed the business card with one hand, envelope in the other. What kind of medical organization was called The Night Game? Maybe it was a play on words, but he thought it was stupid. Besides, he'd never heard anything about a Doctor D as the head of a medical institution in the first place.

Was it all a lie?

The offer of a cure made him almost hungry, but the woman gave him the creeps. However, who was he to judge someone's character when he knew he wasn't a good person either? Besides, the government made money from people dying, so maybe this was his ticket to screw the system and laugh in their faces.

Besides, he wasn't ready to die. Not quite yet.

"Damnit," Jack sighed, and with one swift movement, ripped the seal on the envelope.

Doctor D invites you to play The Night Game.

The rules are simple, but don't assume it's easy.

Only true winners can beat the game, and the reward isn't for the faint of heart.

Beat the maze.

Get out alive.

Eternity awaits.

Jack leaned back in his chair, the IV dripping its poison into his body. *Beat the maze, fuck, I can barely stand by myself,* Jack thought. But why would Doctor D offer him the chance of a cure if she didn't think he could play the game? The business card yelled at him, and the numbers beckoned him closer.

The phone was in his hand and the numbers were being dialed before he could think twice.

Silence answered him on the other end of the receiver.

"I want to play the Night Game," Jack said, forcing the desperation back from his tone.

Crackle.

"An address is on the back of the business card before you. Be there at midnight tonight. The maze awaits."

Jack flipped the card over, finding an address typed on the back. He frowned, not remembering it being there before.

"I'll be there," he said gruffly.

Call ended.

He tried to ignore the faint feeling of dread that anchored his stomach to the ground for the rest of the day.

II

Midnight couldn't come fast enough.

But now that his limo pulled in front of the windowless skyscraper, Jack suddenly wanted to go home.

Two men dressed in black waited in the empty street, their faces blank as they waited for Jack to exit the car. He grasped the sleek black cane at his feet like a life raft as the driver opened his door and waited for him to exit. The cane *click click clicked* on the sidewalk as he approached the men, the business card held in his hand like a knife.

"Is this Doctor D's office?" Jack asked the bodyguard on the left; a man built like a brick and whose face looked like one too.

As he spoke, the double glass doors slid open and Doctor D stepped out. She was still dressed in the same coat and boots as before, and the same sense of wrongness made him fight the urge to run back into his car, but the driver was already pulling away.

"Good evening, Jack," Doctor D said. "Please, follow me."

D turned and walked through the doors, leaving Jack no choice but to follow. Fluorescent lights greeted him as he entered, and the soft footfalls of the two men ambled behind him in harmony with the *click click click* of his cane.

Windowless hallways of sleet grey and artificial light wrapped around them like a glove, and Jack's already weak heart began to patter frantically in his chest. He hadn't walked this much in months, and the sense of wrongness trailed behind him just like the two blank men.

"Is this your medical facility?" Jack asked, peering through the window of a metal door.

A leather patient chair sat in the center, facing a screen with hundreds of wires spilling out of it.

"This is the game control center," Doctor D replied, and Jack tore his gaze away from the window, hastening after her. "The research and medical facility is on the lower floors."

The lower floors? Jack wondered, looking down at the floor as if it would open up and show him.

"Please, follow me," Doctor D said, opening another metal door.

They entered a room nearly identical to the one before, with the leather chair and screen. Two women and one man wearing white coats milled about the room, preparing long wires that trailed from the screen and other medical tools.

"What is this?" Jack asked, though he eyed the chair hungrily.

His heart begged for rest, and sweat paved salty trails down his spine. He needed to catch his breath.

"This is the game room," Doctor D said calmly. "You will be connected to the game via electrical microbes, and my team will track your progress through the screen before you."

Jack frowned as he sank down into the chair, which wasn't as comfortable as it looked.

"You're going to see the inside of my brain?"

"Not your brain, Jack. Your mind," Doctor D replied. "It's a fully immersive game, and I will see if you win or not."

"And what are the rules of this game?" Jack asked.

Doctor D met his gaze, her black eyes flashing with something that Jack didn't like as she replied, "Survive."

Before he could speak, before he could even blink, the lab-coated people surged forward and grabbed him, gently pushing him against the chair so that he was laying fully. A strange sense of both excitement and dread lurched in his throat, and he held back his complaints as they pressed the wires to his forehead and neck using small sticky white pads. The sense of wrongness flew through the air again, and Jack took a steadying breath.

Then, they bound his wrists.

"What the hell are you doing?" Jack demanded as thick leather restraints tightened around his wrists and ankles.

He stared at one of the lab-coated women, whose hair was the color of sand. She didn't acknowledge him, didn't so much as glance in his direction as she secured the restraint almost painfully over his right wrist.

"It's a safety procedure," Doctor D's voice cut through his alarm. "The game can get quite intense, and one's body can be led into a state of panic. I wouldn't want you to fall in your fragile state."

Something told him that she wasn't quite telling the truth, but he bit his tongue and nodded. It wasn't like he had much of a choice anyway.

"This better be worth it," Jack muttered, and the whisper of a smile crossed the sandy-haired woman's lips.

"I'm offering you a cure, Jack," Doctor D replied. "I find that worth more than anything you've ever accomplished."

Jack only glanced at her from the corner of his eye, though all he could see was the toe of a black boot. Once the wires and straps were secured, the women and man set to work on small tablets that they withdrew from their coats.

"The game will begin shortly," Doctor D announced, and the wide screen began flickering.

A sense of unease ran through him, so strong he almost gagged. Perhaps it was simply the sickness continuing to spread through his body.

"What do I do?" Jack asked.

"The rules of the Night Game are very simple. Beat the maze and don't get killed."

Her voice was cold and merciless, and Jack didn't really like the sound of that.

"And if I lose?"

"Just as I said, Jack," Doctor D replied. "You die."

What kind of hellscape have I gotten into?

But it was too late to back out now. He was quite literally stuck here, and he would beat this damned maze and get that cure. He had more life to live, more money to make, and more power to gain. He felt weak and scared, and Jack Renolds wasn't the kind of man to have those two adjectives attached to his name.

"Let's get this over with," Jack huffed.

"Very well," Doctor D replied. "Put him in."

The woman with sand-colored hair tapped a few times on her screen, and a strange dizziness swept over Jack. The world swayed and his vision broke into a thousand tiny pieces, making the world look like a TV gone static.

And then it went black.

III

"Welcome to the Night Game. Follow the red light through the maze. Don't lose it, or else the demons will find you. Once you've beaten the maze, simply walk through the door and you will receive your reward. If you lose... well. Just don't lose. Eternity awaits."

The robotic voice permeated the dark, and Jack could hardly feel his own body.

Dim blue lights suddenly lit the air, and a gasp tore through his lungs. He blinked a few times, letting his eyes adjust to the game. Towering walls of black stone rose on either side, revealing a narrow path before him. The path split in opposite directions a few steps ahead, each spilling into darkness.

He looked down, finding that he was still in the clothes that he came to Doctor D's office wearing; black track pants and t-shirt to match.

"The countdown will begin momentarily. Get in position."

The voice lit through the air again, and suddenly a red glowing light the size of his fist appeared ahead. Jack scrambled to his feet and found that his muscles felt strong and steady, and he wasn't out of breath from the simple movement.

"Three."

Jack jumped up and down a few times, getting used to the new power in his virtual body. If only he could feel like this again in real life.

This was exactly why he was playing the game.

"Two."

The red light pulsed as if inviting him to move.

Something growled behind him.

"One."

A loud blaring horn made him jump, and Jack was off in a steady jog, heading toward the red light. It shot to the right-most tunnel immediately, and he turned to follow it when he reached the split in the maze. The black walls were threatening in their presence, and Jack hated the way they seemed to close in.

That growl behind him wasn't any help either.

He tried to glance behind himself but found that he couldn't. It was as though his neck and body were forced to look ahead, leaving his back exposed to a void of mystery. Jack swallowed his nerves and focused on the light again, which seemed to get bigger as it pulsed, now the size of a dinner plate.

A growl sounded again as Jack jogged, *left, right, straight, right, right, left.* Growl. *Left, right, straight.*

The wrongness followed Jack as he jogged. The game was too quiet, too normal, save for the constant growling behind him. Minutes dragged by, the light now the size of a large dog and moving faster, making him push forward even more. The nice thing about being in a game was that he wasn't out of breath, though a thin layer of sweat trickled down his brow. He could do this, as long as the red light didn't get too big and the maze ended soon.

And then something stabbed him, and the world turned red.

Jack slammed into the ground, and the curling fist of a bloodied hand shot across his peripheral. *The demons,* Jack thought with a curse. He scrambled to his feet, daring to glance at the hand coming ever closer. It was sinewy and dark, as though the life had been sucked out of it. Blood dripped from bony fingers, and Jack realized that the blood was his. He glanced at his side and was greeted with the sight of blood sticking his shirt to his skin.

"Fuck," He cursed, scrambling to his feet.

Move move move.

The lights flashed, and now the whole world was red, no longer just an orb guiding him. He was on his own now. Jack knew nothing but fear and red as he ran and ran, the growling and bloodied hand following him all the way there.

Left, straight, straight, right, left, left, right.

Two growls now followed him, and another slash of burning pain echoed across his back. It wasn't exactly pain, not really. Because it wasn't real, and this was all a game.

But why did his side hurt so bad?

A bloodied finger clawed his neck, and he caught a glimpse of a cracked fingernail before pushing himself faster.

There had to be some way out. The maze couldn't last forever. It had to end.

A yell tore through Jack's throat as the ground began sinking, the substance beneath his feet changing from hard rock to sand.

I must be getting closer, Jack thought as he ran. *Right, straight, right, left.*

A shadow passed across the red path, molding across the floor before sticking to the black walls to his left.

And then the shadow moved again, but so did his surroundings. A door glinted in the red light, just ahead. Jack pushed, pushed, pushed, but the demons followed and so did the shadow.

And then it was before him, ten feet tall and swathed in darkness. Doctor D, or at least a rendition of her. Cracked, bleeding antlers protruded from the platinum tresses of her hair, and she smiled at him as she stepped in front of the door. He slowed down, unsure how to proceed. Was she going to guide him through the door, or was she trying to stop him?

Hands grabbed at Jack's ankles, and he stumbled as one of them yanked back. He fell forward, face cracking against sand. He once believed that sand was painless to fall onto, but he was proven wrong.

"No!" Jack cried out, kicking out.

His foot met something hard, and the sound of cracking bone answered. The thing behind him screamed, and Jack clawed back to his feet. The door was hidden behind Doctor D's enormous body, and hunger welled behind her black eyes. She held out a hand, and the tips of her fingers were shaded darker, though it was hard to tell with what, in the ever-red light.

The growling breaths were now wet and ragged, and Jack walked forward.

Doctor Dee simply shook her head, hand still outstretched.

"Eternity awaits, Jack."

Jack knew what he had to do.

It was just a game after all.

"No," Jack spat. "I don't think it does."

And then he ran.

Ran into the red light and Doctor D's darkness. He closed his eyes, readying himself for impact with the woman's cloaked body. But instead, he went *through* her, and the metal door handle was biting into his skin and he was wrenching it open, jumping into the darkness that awaited.

IIII

The room was empty when Jack woke up.

Sweat coated his entire body, and the screen before him was static. Fluorescent lights stabbed into his eyes, and Jack looked down at his hands and ankles.

The leather straps were gone.

Jack scrambled up, but instantly, his sick body said its greetings. He glanced to the left, where a metal table with a glass of water, a pill, and a note, were waiting. He picked up the note with a shaking hand.

Congratulations on making it through the door, Jack.
Take the cure.
-D.

He looked down at the pill, small and white and unassuming, though it could possibly save his life. He better not have gone through that for nothing. His muscles still shook and his heart pattered like a jackhammer.

He brought the pill to his mouth with shaking fingers, and then it was in his system, swallowed with a glass of lukewarm water. Jack drank the rest of the glass, his throat feeling like a desert.

Life flowed back into his body almost instantly, and a laugh fell out of his mouth before he could stop it. Jack didn't care that he was alone, didn't care about the sense of wrongness that nearly strangulated the air. He didn't care that the scientists and Doctor D had left the room. In a way, he was glad of it.

"Time to get out of this place," Jack said, swinging his legs over the seat and straightening.

The electrode pads came off his skin easily, and he dropped the wires carelessly before standing. He took his cane, which was propped against the chair, but he was so relieved to be done with the game and to have taken the cure, that he almost didn't need the support.

The wrongness was still there as he moved for the door.

The doorknob was cold under his fingers, and he thought of the game. Why did it feel like he never left the maze? There was a chill in the air, and something like metal clung to his nostrils. Jack shook his head and opened the door.

Red light spilled over his shoes.

He looked out, and dread dropped in his stomach like a cement block. It was silent, but the red light was there. Jack walked through the door and turned in the direction of freedom, but it still felt wrong wrong wrong.

And then the breathing started.

Jack turned around, and what was an empty hall before wasn't so empty now. Jack's muscles seized up the way they did whenever he used them past their limits. He wasn't cured yet, but he needed to run. The demons had followed him out here.

It was supposed to be a game.

11

A CROW'S CALL AT NIGHT

ANAÏS MILO

The night of the incident was cold and wet. Winds from the north had blown in, sending ice through the mountains and whipping up a storm. Trees bent and creaked, howling with the thunder as rain came down hard and fast. Alison Shaw was at home in her cottage, droplets of water pounding the roof as she caught up on paperwork. The house had been given to her after her grandmother passed; it had been the location of many childhood memories and she remembered it quite fondly.

She considered herself lucky that it had come into her possession. It should have gone to her mother or sisters, but they had already settled in their own houses. Her eldest sister had moved out into the southeastern portion of the state, a good drive away from the mountains, and her mother had followed. Her other sister, Marie, had moved out West, to live in the fast lane and a house with a white picket fence. Alison had just graduated with her master's degree and hadn't quite settled, so when the time came for the cottage's fate to be decided, her mother had surrendered it to her.

Whenever they would visit, her sisters made a point out of

asking about the isolation. Alison always brushed off their remarks and snide comments about how lonely it must be. They were right, in a sense. There were neighbors, but it was quite a walk to reach them, and so most of the time Alison spent at her home was spent alone. She had never minded the solitude as her sisters so did, though.

The incident occurred two weeks before the women were next set to visit. The day passed by quietly, rain pattering gently on the roof and windows. Clouds painted the sky a lovely grey and for a time, Alison sat on her porch watching the storm. It was cold, but she wrapped herself in a blanket and sipped on a warm cup of hot chocolate. Not a single thing seemed out of the ordinary.

As the sun began to set, she had gone inside to do her paperwork. She hadn't yet begun preparations for her mother and sisters' visit—she had a tendency to put that off until a few days before they arrived—but she knew that if her work was not completed well before they came, it would likely not get done at all. She couldn't afford not to have it finished, so she took her blanket with her to the desk and began filling out forms.

Hours passed by quickly. The rain created a sort of white noise and the inky sky outside allowed for time to melt into nothingness. The cottage was still and quiet, aside from the gentle rolling of thunder and pattering rain. Other than the light of a small desk lamp, the house was dark.

When the first call came, it came as quite a shock. It was a guttural, piercing cry that struck the silence like a bolt of lightning. Alison's back straightened and she turned to face the kitchen window. A second cry came, wrenching her heart from her chest. Carefully, she stood up and crept to the window.

She looked outside, but there was nothing to see. The storm clouds darkened every bit of light from the moon, covering the ground in black. Her face and fingers pressed against the cold glass, sending shocks of ice through her skin. She paused, waiting for any movement or noise, a sign of life. There was nothing.

The floorboards creaked as she stepped backward, darkness eating at everything around her. She sturdied herself against the kitchen counter and took a deep breath in. She had never in her life been afraid of the night, and she certainly did not intend to start. She filled a cup with cold water and took a sip.

Wind chimes rang out, accompanied by a terrible dragging noise and then a crash. Alison spun, dropping her cup in the process. It fell to the floor and shattered. There was a biting pain as some of the glass shards cut her bare feet, but her eyes were glued to the door. A crash of thunder shook the house, causing her desk lamp to flicker. In the momentary darkness, she felt sickness in her stomach. The rhythm of her heart was matched by a dull thumping from outside the house.

Shakily, she hoisted herself onto the counter. Her arms trembled and threatened to give out, but she forced them still long enough to stand. Again, the lights flickered, and she almost lost her balance. She tried to see onto the porch, but there was no movement other than the beating rain. The other noise continued, low and steady. *Thump, thump, thump.*

A knot twisted about in her stomach, wriggling like a pile of worms, as she stepped off of the counter. The floorboards felt cool on her feet, reminding her of the biting pain of multiple tiny cuts. She ignored it and started forward, creeping towards the door inch by inch. She reached the glass and peered out.

Rain distorted the window. The moon fought for its right to shine, painting everything in a deep blue. Still, there was no movement, but the thumping continued. Hands trembling, Alison drew back the sliding glass door and stepped into the night.

Water coated the porch, making it slick and hard to balance

on. Rain soaked her clothes, chilling her to the bone and plastering her hair to her face and neck. It calmed her burning feet, though, and allowed her to step around the corner. Without the glare of her desk lamp, she could see much better.

One of the deck chairs had been knocked over, its pillow flapping against the porch. *Thump, thump, thump.* The wind blew the cushion against the wall, before allowing it to fall and throwing it back up again. She exhaled, her breath burning her throat. It was then that she remembered her floodlights, which were set to turn on with any real movement. The pillow was too low to activate it. Nothing was on her porch, aside from wind. She was relieved, but yet the sick feeling in her stomach remained. She carefully walked back towards the door.

Upon arriving, she idly glanced up at her floodlights; the guardians, with their big eyes and pale frame, waiting dutifully by her door. Except, she heard a scratching noise behind them. She noticed the wires gently scraping the walls of her house. The lights were sitting crooked, pushed away from the wall. They should have come on when she went out.

A piercing shriek from the woods behind forced her inside. She slid the door closed with a smack and locked it just as fast. Blood pounded in her veins, a quick, thick beat. Her body fell to the ground and she crawled away from the door. The worms in her stomach had turned into snakes.

The cry came again and again, each time from a different spot. It seemed almost as if they were all around her. She pulled her legs against her chest and covered her ears, counting under her breath. Her hands were wildly shaking and cold as ice. Her eyes squeezed shut, blocking out any sight of what was out there.

At the count of twenty, she opened her eyes. There was nothing to see but the atrous sky and rain on glass. Slowly, she lowered her hands and stood, legs wobbling like a newborn fawn. The sound had ceased. Relieved, she fell against her rocking chair, where she sat for quite a while, idly picking at the skin around her nails. Somewhere in the house, a clock ticked by.

It was uncomfortable to sit. As much as she tried, Alison couldn't quite seem to put her mind at ease. Her eyes felt tired and sore, her body ached, but she could not get rid of the sickening snakes writhing about. Her mind felt foggy, yet very clear. She pictured what her sisters would say if they saw her now. All the taunts and snide comments about how this is what happens to people who live in the woods. In the woods and those mountains. Strange things happened there, bearing stories that would live for generations. She'd been told many growing up, but had forgotten them as she'd grown older. Eventually, bills and classes claimed the spaces made by childhood legends, until there was nowhere left for them to go and they faded from memory.

It was with that thought that she finally rose from her chair. There was something nagging at her mind. It made her put on her socks, her shoes, her coat. It drove her to find a flashlight and go toward that door, which slid open with ease. It forced her into the cold, damp night.

If she could have, Alison would have wondered what her sisters thought when they learned about the incident. Whether they would have laughed in their casual way and said it was what she deserved for living out there all alone, or whether they would have felt pity and tried to take her home. Of course, though, she'd never get the chance.

Freezing rain bit her skin as she walked into the darkness. She had always been a curious child. When her grandmother would tell stories of creatures that lurked in the woods, she would not feel afraid, but rather interested. While her sisters wished for the stories to end, Alison wished to meet the beings that the elders spoke about. She wanted to see them for herself and maybe tell a story of her own. That same curiosity is what drove her forward, into the night.

She did not have an umbrella to shelter her from the storm. Her fingers grew stiff and cold, her breath fogging in front of her. Her flashlight led the way, ripping at shadows clinging to the trees. The ground was uneven and damp. Her feet sunk into the mud, but she paid it no mind. Something was still nagging her and she could not turn back.

It wasn't until she was completely surrounded by trees that the crying call sounded again. It was far ahead, beckoning her further. She hesitated, breath heavy in her chest. The snakes felt like a ball of lead now, no longer moving but weighing her down. Exhaustion pulled at her eyes and senses. The adrenaline which drove her outside was beginning to wane. Still, she heard the call and could not resist.

She followed its direction as it took her deeper into the woods. She was no longer afraid of it because she was not afraid of anything. The cold rain had slowed her down and made her tired, movements becoming more lethargic by the second. She almost felt as if she could fall asleep then and there, surrounded by the forest. It was not will, but the calls, that kept her feet moving.

And then, they stopped. Alison stood there, quiet, as she waited for another noise. The rain was light, now, no longer pouring. Clouds were starting to disperse, allowing beams of moonlight to flood the ground. Her flashlight flickered and went out.

She tried in vain to tap it back on, but it wouldn't go. Her head felt light and her eyes were drifting shut. She stood, swaying back and forth, trying to keep from passing out. A broken call directly in front of her woke her up.

Her eyes flew open, adjusting to the dark. For a few moments, she could see nothing but an inky blur. Slowly, it began to take shape, and her breath caught in her throat. An invisible hand grasped her heart and the snakes began moving. Her legs threatened to give out.

A figure cloaked in a white dress, muddied and torn from being left in the woods, stood in front of her. Its hair was long and dark, stuck against its pale, paper-thin skin. Black veins stood out like diamonds, crawling across its flesh. It staggered towards Alison, milky eyes focused on her. Her legs crumbled beneath its gaze.

She tried to push herself backward, but the mud gave her no traction. A sharp, ringing noise flooded her ears as paralysis began setting in. Her body was in fight or flight, but she couldn't seem to move. Instead, she froze. Unbridled horror shook her body, her chest compacting, rib cage crushing her lungs. She wanted to run, but her muscles would not obey.

The creature bent down to her level and grabbed her throat. Its hands were like a corpse's, colder than the dead of winter. She fought as best she could, nails scraping at its freezing skin. She tried to kick and squirm, but it did not flinch and did not hesitate.

A bright, hammering pain exploded in Alison's throat, as it pushed its fingers hard against her voice box. She wanted to scream, but she didn't have the air. She slammed her fists against its arms, face, body—anything she could reach—but it was not enough. Her voice box was crushed by the time it released her.

Every breath felt sharp and hoarse. Alison watched as the figure crawled backward and away from her. Its eyes shone in the light, but they were no longer milky. They had started to become dark, taking color as the eyes of a person should. Its veins retreated beneath its skin, which was regaining warmth and color. Its body was no longer contorted and when it moved, no longer disjointed. It began to look more human.

When Alison was a child, her grandmother told her about

crows that would call at night. It was said that hearing a crow's call after dark meant you would be the next to disappear. Alison had always believed it was a local story to keep children away from the dangers of a dark forest. Yet, when she opened her mouth to scream, all that returned was the caw of a crow.

12

LUCK RUN OUT

MADDI NEUENSWANDER

The rain streaks down my back in tiny, icy trails, trickling into the space at the back of my Doc Martens. My eyes pin onto the blurry image of a headstone. (A tiny reminder of my sins.)

I know the man buried there. (Although I wish more than anything I didn't.) His name is Woody Costa, and I killed him. I killed him for a foolish thing called love.

(Well, I guess it wasn't love just yet.)

Let me tell you my story. It's long, a little boring, and by the end of it, you will undoubtedly hate me. (But I don't blame you. I hate myself a little too. Not that I used to, it's just–well–you'll see.)

My story starts in a crowded university auditorium. Freshman English–I mean English 101. (If anyone can tell me why English is even a rational part of the kind of coursework a young witch needs, I'll give them a million dollars.) Anywho, I'm minding my own business, things spread out across my desk and the empty one next to me. But then some random (and entirely too symmetrical) guy shoves his hands in his pockets and smacks his gum at me. (Why is he late? Is he even in this class? If he is, there isn't much use coming to this one; it's half over.)

"If that seat's empty, I'd very much like to sit there." He gestures to the desk holding half my things with his foot. He's wearing tightly laced Converse Chuck Taylors–green. (My favorite color.)

I roll my eyes, scoop up my things, and press myself as closely to the side of my desk as I can, the skirt of my dress riding up a tiny bit as I do so. (Why do I hope he's looking?)

He taps me on the shoulder. "I don't bite, you know."

"I don't know you or your oral tendencies." I cross my legs to distance myself even further from him. (His biceps ripple out of his shirt, and his messy hair tells me he just woke up.)

"Maybe you want to know about my oral tendencies." My pulse throbs against my skin at his words. (Why is he so deliriously sexy?)

"Please be quiet. I'm trying to listen."

I can almost hear him roll his eyes as he snaps his gum at me again. "No, you're not. You're doodling little cats all over your notebook."

I meet his eyes for the first time, my ears burning with embarrassment. They're blue and green and gold all at the same time and set above a chin scattered with stubble. (I like that a little too much.)

"How do you know this isn't how I take notes? For all you know, the little cats mean something entirely different than the big ones. Then there's the tails and the ears and the eyes."

"For someone who wants nothing to do with me, you sure are a bit rambly."

I turn my eyes to my notebook and draw a big, ugly cat. Two lopsided ears, a squished nose, paws the tiniest bit too small for its body, and one impossibly long, skinny tail. (Why won't he leave me alone?)

When I look up, he's standing. There is only me and him left in the auditorium.

"If I didn't make it clear enough during class, I don't want to talk to you."

He shifts uncomfortably from foot to foot. "Look I need a favor, and you look like you can help me."

I roll my eyes and prepare to mock him. "Look, if you're looking for a hookup, I'm not your girl. But I do know a few who might be–"

He puts his foot on the chair next to me and ties his shoe. "Not that kind of favor. I heard there's a witch on this campus who can do me a solid."

I brush past him. "Not for you I won't."

"You're really going to turn down a paying customer?"

I stop at the door. "How much?"

"Whatever you want."

Squishing my tongue between my teeth, I swivel around to face him and those annoyingly intense (and sexy) eyes. "What's the favor?"

He sighs. "I need you to give someone a Brackish Rose."

A heavy curtain crowds my eyes as I narrow them. "I thought those were fairy tales."

"Oh," he says, sitting back down. "They are very real. Just hard to come by."

I rub the tattoo on my wrist and breathe in the feeling of the cat purring and curling into my veins. I rub until the skin burns, and the cat nips at my finger.

"Nice ink."

"I'll think about it. Not because I like you. Only because college is expensive." I gather my things. "If I decide to do it, you can't give me a deadline. I don't know how long it'll take me."

He readjusts the bag on his shoulder. "Name's Ian, by the way."

"Violet. Pleasure doing business with you."

A smirk sneaks onto his face. "Pleasure, indeed."

I roll my eyes but blush anyway. "Don't be crass. Give me your pen."

"Here," he digs his hand into his left pocket and pulls out a cheap, plastic ballpoint pen. "Now you have to give me one of your pens."

I roll the pen between my fingers. "*This* is your pen?"

"One of them, yeah."

"A cheap, plastic pen?"

He shrugs. "I'm a college student. It's a cheap pen. You do the math."

I roll my eyes. "The Council gave you this junk to use for your Intinn Pen? The very pen you can lend out to the one person you can trust to write over your thoughts?"

"Oh, that pen."

I press my lips into a tight line. "Stop wasting my time."

He swallows quickly. (Why does his bobbing Adam's Apple make my knees go weak?) Shifts his eyes to my shoes. To the window. Back to me. "Um," he says, licking his lips and stretching the tiger in the skin on his neck. "I don't have one,"

"Your ink is obviously charmed. Did you misplace your pen or something? Give it to an ex-girlfriend who never gave it back?"

He licks his lips, casting a glimmer over his partially parted pout. "I didn't lose it. I just don't have one. Well, I used to have one. But it's complicated."

I pull a breath in through my nose. "I see."

(He broke the law. And had his magic revoked.)

Now I feel like a jerk. I don't know him. (And I certainly want to, despite my denial and his rude interruption to my solitude.) But I can't help how my heart drops into my shoes as my mind turns to what it would mean to lose everything.

The glint on his lips keeps my eyes. No matter how hard I try, I can't pull them away.

"But I don't need a pen to know what you're thinking." He licks his lips again, and my knees go weak. "You want my pen."

"You just said you don't have an Intinn Pen."

He waggles his eyebrows at me. (Why do I like that so much?) "Not that pen."

"Would you cut that out?" I snap, sliding a scrap of paper over to him and trying to keep the blush from my cheeks. "Scribble down your digits so I can get a hold of you."

"I can't cut it out. At least not when you're so obviously attracted to me." He tucks the paper into the pocket of my dress.

Cheeks now the temperature of black asphalt under the sun, my fingers fumble with the strap on my bag, the end of my braid, and finally the slick metal of the doorknob as I hurry away from him. Outside, the inky sky sobs fat tears. I squeeze my books to my chest and run as fast as I can to the Fulcrum. (It's like a Normie bus station, I guess. Makes sense. Since that's basically what it is.)

The doors whoosh open into the Fulcrum, and warm air assaults my features. It's packed inside, shoulder-to-shoulder people with bags and umbrellas. And the smell. Like a sweaty gym bag or laundry that's been sitting in the washer for four days.

A gag catches in my throat. I press my jacket sleeve to my nose. Stepping carefully around a couple sucking each other's saliva, I slip closer to the index wall. My eyes scan past the golden labels on the tiny, boxed key holders. Center Circle (I never liked that one much, the key is a giant, translucent joke), Merilbury Lane (that one's my favorite, a long, curly one), Scissly Loop (I like that one, it's thick and sturdy), Branlin Cross (that one's a bit boring, almost flat). And finally, Nettleton Avenue. I grip the key, a tiny, wooden thing with carved hatch marks, and join the line to get to the door. (It's about five miles long.)

As I wait, I pull a book out of my bag—Ethical Magic Volume 2. The index tells me what I'm looking for is on page 272. My eyes swim across the page until they catch on the words:

Brackish Rose

Formed from omens, a Brackish Rose settles a debt.

"THAT'S IT?" I slam the book closed.

The person behind me elbows me in the back, the key dangling off his finger brushing up against my back. (Rude!) "Are you going or not?"

"Yeah," I mutter, shoving my book into my bag.

The key nestles perfectly into the lock on the door. A tingle ripples up my spine. A beam of light flashes under the door. It's ready.

A breath of wind rustles against my ankles as I open the door and step through into Nettleton Avenue. The breeze gathers up the fraying edge of my braid, licks up the hem of my dress, and tickles my ears. Cinnamon and honeysuckle fill my nose. I strip my jacket off my arms and let the stars drink them in. The light lifts from my eyes, and the street comes into focus. It's empty.

My feet patter over the pavement and the night air kisses my skin. The sidewalk stretches endlessly as I make my way to Pipp's. Her house stretches up, up, up as I draw closer. The house was built all wrong, with all the rooms stacked one on top of the other instead of side by side like it should have been. (Which I adore.)

I let myself in, slip off my shoes, set down my things, and climb the tall, twisty staircase. My head draws large loop d-loops by the time I get to the top floor, and I have to steady myself against the curly railing.

The door at the crown of the steps is just barely ajar.

"Pipp?" My voice shakes with unbridled excitement mingled with nervousness. (The idea of making Ian happy thrills me, but the cost fills me with dread.)

"Just a minute," she says, but her voice is far away.

Paper wings whisper in the distance. A door slams. Pipes creak with the influx of rushing water. I nestle myself into the space between the door and its frame and squeeze my bones through. This room is familiar. Books stacked so high they snuggle the ceiling; worn wood floors; moonlight glittering in through giant windows. (All the ingredients for my all-time favorite room.)

"What can I do for you, Sugar?" Her familiar form rounds a tall bookcase, and I drink her in: her short frame, her colorful attire, and (my favorite), all the gold and glittering chains around her ankles, wrists, and neck.

A smile flickers on my lips. "I have a question about something I came across in a textbook."

"Lay it on me, and I'll see what I can do." Her voice is chicken soup to my nerves.

I gulp down gasps of air. "Have you ever heard of a Brackish Rose?"

Pipp slides her glasses (they're so uniquely her–sparkly little things shaped like bird wings) up her nose. Lowering herself onto the window seat, she pats the space next to her. "Where on earth did you hear about a Brackish Rose?"

"Just one of my textbooks. Why? Is it bad or something?"

Pipp tucks in her lips and takes three short breaths in her nose. (She's trying to decide how to say this nicely.) "They used to be popular, back when I was in college. But the council banned them after one caused something really terrible."

My voice wobbles on my words. "What happened?"

She places her hand on my knee. "Don't worry about it, Sugarplum."

"Pipp." Her eyes match mine at that one word. "Please, I need to know more about it. It's for my Creed class." (This is definitely a lie. But just a little one, so it's okay right?)

Pipp shakes her head but moves over to a bookshelf against the wall. She crouches down to the bottom shelf, pulls out the three books on the end, and shoves her hand into the subsequent hole. Her eyebrows shoot into her silver hairline, and she pulls her hand out. And with it a thick book.

"I can't tell you about it. This book should tell you what you need, though."

The book slides into my hands, the anchor to drag my hands to the floor. "Thanks, Pipp."

"Take your time."

I rifle through the pages (back to front, because I'm a psychopath) to find the index. My finger strokes the parchment to find the words I'm looking for. My lips curl around the words, 'Brackish Rose' over and over and over again until my finger pauses just above the text. Page 721.

The pages whisper hushed warnings as I flip them over. (A pit gnaws into my stomach.) Page 1101. 1000. 983. 845. 799. 730. 729. 721.

Brackish Rose

Are your debts too great to bear? A brackish Rose will take care of everything. A type of dark, ancient magic, the twelve steps to creating a Brackish Rose make it nearly untraceable. The following process will create one.

What you'll need:

Thirteen cats

Thirteen mirrors

Saltwater

One white rabbit

A bat

An Unmarked grave
What You'll Do:
Find thirteen black cats.
Kill the cats.
From twelve cats, take the ears.
From the thirteenth, take the tail.
Set aside.
Find thirteen hand mirrors.
Break the mirrors by smashing them with your left fist.
Collect the pieces and grind the fragments into sand.
Collect salt water from thirteen beaches.
Separate the water from the salt using heat, sieves, and air tubules.
(This process will take several days.)
Mix the sand, salt, ears, and tail together to create a putty (it should be thin enough to mold but thick enough to hold its shape.)
Feed the putty to the rabbit and wait for it to pass a salt stone.
While you're waiting, kill the bat.
Remove the wings, and wrap the salt stone in the bat's wings to create a seed.
Plant the seed in the unmarked grave and water for thirteen consecutive hours.
Pluck the rose.
Give to your debtor.

"I can see why it was banned, Pipp."

"Pretty dark stuff, huh?"

I worry a hole in my cheek. (The iron makes me queasy.) "Not so much dark as heavy. But I guess it's dark too. Just a lot of death. How could someone do that to so many innocent animals?"

Pipp scrunches her thin shoulders together and relaxes them open again. "Guess you've got to be pretty desperate."

"And what happens if you make one?"

A heavy sigh contracts her chest. "Assuming you get caught,

you'll have your magic taken away, and live the rest of your life in regret. Bottom line is don't do it. It's not worth it."

"Life might be a little simpler without magic. I mean, thousands of people live every day without it, so it can't be that bad. Right?"

Pipp presses her lips together until they turn white. "You're not thinking of making one, are you?"

I shake my head, my curls tickling my nose and poking me in the eyes. "No, just trying to see all the angles."

"Good." She folds her hands in her lap. "As I said, it's not worth it. Not worth it at all."

The pads of my fingers ghost over my wrist when worry strikes me, and I rip out the page. "Thanks, Pipp. I've gotta go."

She pinches my cheek. "Anytime, Love. Grab a snack on your way out."

Gliding over the blue and green tile, a broom stands straight in the center of the kitchen. The stand mixer on the counter chatters away about nothing. Water drips from the sink. A light on the fridge blinks on and off, and its fuchsia pink door flaps wildly open and closed, open and closed.

"Hey, Estella," I say through a smirk. "What do you have for me today? Pipp said I can't leave unless I take food with me."

(That's a lie–but I'm a starving college student. So it's justifiable?)

The fridge burps loudly. A pie appears in my hand. It smells like garlic and Cornish hen. When I bite into it, the sweet savor of roasted carrots and parsnips explodes over my tongue.

I snap and point a loose finger gun back at the fridge. "Thanks 'Stell."

The floor inches forward beneath me until I'm at the front door. It creaks open, and I step outside into the muggy air. (Don't ask me how the weather changed from delightful to misery in the space of twenty minutes—I have no freaking clue.)

Abrasive sidewalk scrapes my thighs as I sit down. I cross

my ankles (I don't want to flash anyone.) and pull the page out of my pocket. My eyes glide over the instructions a second time, but my brain doesn't process them. A breath huffs past my lips.

"Am I really that desperate?" (I shouldn't be. I'm only attracted to the guy. Not in love with him!)

The wind replies by ruffling my hair into teeny tiny knots.

I nibble my bottom lip until it's as raw and bleeding as fresh roadkill. (And hurts like hell.) The word desperate repeats in my mind over and over and over again. Desperate. Desperate. Desperate. Am I desperate enough to risk this? (I must be. Or maybe just crazy. I'm thinking about it a little too much either way.)

My mind turns to the dark cloud covering the conversation I had with Pipp. Gut-wrenching terror fills my veins at the consequence. But then it's gone. I see myself, money in one hand, Ian's fingers in the other. A warm smile adorns my face. (Would I be happier without my serendipity?)

Maybe I would be happier without the burden of speciality. Maybe I could finally be someone new. (I'd give anything to be someone else, someone interesting. Even a slightly less lonely version of myself might be nice.)

(I'll think about it.) It's my own voice. Spoken a bit too harshly to a stranger in a university auditorium not even two hours ago. And I am thinking about it. Maybe a little too much for my own good. Too much for a girl with a good future.

My face falls into a neutral grimace as I push off the concrete and rock back and forth on the soles of my sneakers.

"Where am I going to get thirteen black cats?" My words surprise me.

When did I decide I didn't care if I lost everything I've known my whole life? When did I decide I didn't want to be special anymore? When did I decide that everything I've ever stood for doesn't matter? (Do you know? I sure don't. And, to be honest, I don't even care.)

I turn in a small circle to clear my mind and focus. Another turn. Two more turns. Three more turns—don't do the trick. So I switch to kicking rocks. Two rocks—A teeny tiny half rock and a medium-sized flat rock. Four more rocks—A red one, a shiny one, a dull, gray, boring one, and a heart-shaped one. By the time I've kicked all the rocks on the street, my head is no clearer than when I started.

I dig the scrap of paper out of my pocket. The numbers 271-885-5555 are neatly scribbled over it. His image comes to mind: cool and casual, slouching and sexy. My breath keeps time to a fast-paced song in my head. After quickly typing and sending a text to him, I pace back and forth on the sidewalk.

The stars have dimmed, the very beginning of a sunrise peeking over the horizon, before he shows up, snapping his gum (as usual) as he swings his body off his Harley. "What's up? Decided you're too chicken to do it?"

My mouth runs dry. "I just—I just—What's it like?"

"What's what like?"

I rub the ink on my wrist, the cat purring gently. "What's it like—having had magic and then not having it anymore?"

He pauses, flicking his beautiful eyes to mine. He holds my gaze for a minute too long. Then looks away again. "It was hard at first," he says, dropping to sit on the sidewalk. "But it gets easier. The worst bit is, it's kinda lonely. Not a lot of Magi risk as much as I have. Or at least get caught doing it."

The top of his hand is warm, like the sun sitting so low on the horizon, and that warmth flies to my cheeks when I realize that I've just held it. I rub the cat on my wrist again and send my eyes to the concrete. "Sorry, I just—I wish–I'm sorry you feel so alone."

Ian shrugs, snaps his gum and stares at the same, dark spot on the sidewalk. "It's not all bad. Normies have a lot fewer rules than Magi. Plus, you get cool Normie toys."

I nudge my head toward the bike leaning against the curb. "Like that? I much prefer using the Fulcrum."

"Motorcycles aren't bad. I'll give you a ride sometime if you want."

(I'd like that.)

I press my lips into an awkward little line and scuff the front of my shoe. "You can go ahead and give me a deadline now. If you want."

He shrugs. "Just get it done. Don't care too much when you do."

He's met my eyes, his complex hazel holding my green. "I–I'll do my best to get it done by the weekend." (Might be a tall order, given it's Wednesday evening now.)

"You haven't told me how you want to be paid yet." He winks at me, and my insides go all mushy. (I'm also pretty sure I'm blushing even harder now–if that's even possible.)

I shrug. "I don't know what I want yet."

He arches an eyebrow at me. "I think you do. You just haven't admitted it to yourself yet."

"And how would you know that?"

"Your cheeks always seem to be bright and red when I'm around." He snaps his gum one more time. "Maybe it means something. Maybe it doesn't."

I roll my eyes. "Whatever. There's something else I need to talk to you about."

"Shoot," he says through a lopsided smirk.

I fish through my bag for it. My fingers filter past my English textbook, three spiral notebooks, a metal water bottle, and a little baggy of granola bars to find the tiny, golden pen at the bottom of my bag.

Rolling it between my fingers, I hold it out to him. "Here, use this if you need to get a hold of me. I want to try my best not to get caught."

"And if you need to get a hold of me?" His mouth loses its teasing tilt.

The cat on my wrist is getting a little too much love tonight. "I haven't figured that part out yet."

He shrugs, and the cute lopsided grin jumps back to his face. "Alright. Is that all you need from me?"

All the moisture drains from my lips. My desert tongue flicks out to fix it. It hangs there, half poking out, just a little too long. "Uh, yeah. I think."

(Why can't I stop thinking about how his lips would taste against mine?)

He takes a step toward me, and his breath mixes with mine. "You think, or you know?"

(I know I want him.)

His finger brushes a loose curl off my cheekbone, and it's lightning to my senses. "I—I—I—"

"Do I make you nervous?"

I try to roll my eyes, but they don't make it all the way around. (Ian's gaze is penetrating in all the wrong ways, and my eyes get stuck on them.) "Of course not."

"So it's not nervousness tying your tongue." He winks, and my insides go all mushy again. (I really wish they'd stop doing that.)

My curls bounce side to side "As if."

He shrugs (in a halfway, lopsided kind of way that's all too cute) and stuffs his hands into the front pockets of his jeans.

My desire swallows me as he walks away. (Are jeans meant to mold to the body so perfectly? And if so, why am I just now noticing?)

I pace back and forth, training a neat little ditch into the unruly grass against the sidewalk until I can clear the weeds in my head and forge a clear path to my next steps.

(Cats. Thirteen cats. Thirteen.)

I'll spare you the nitty-gritty details, but I get thirteen cats.

Stole some. Bought a few. And worst of all borrowed one from a friend. (Doubt she thinks of me as a friend now.)

Don't be like me. I'm a monster.

I think you know what happens next too. But I'll tell you anyway. I kill a bat. And not just any bat. My bat. My good buddy, Tiddlywinks. (He's been my companion for as long as I can remember.) But, apparently, I don't care. (The only thing I care about–the only thing I can even think about–is that darn lopsided smirk and those glittering gold and green and blue eyes.)

That's when it happens. Words prick into my mind like ice (cold and penetrating and unfamiliar).

Meet me at the Fulcrum.

The words whisper away as quickly as they came, and I find myself sprinting down the street to Pipp's house. I burst through the door and almost knock her over.

"Someone's put a scorpion in your cauldron. What's your hurry?"

I swallow past my racing breath. "Fulcrum. Now. Meeting someone."

The creases in the corners of her eyes wink at me as a knowing smile smooths over her lips. "A boy."

I'm panting so hard that talking is out of the question. So I just nod.

Her knowing smile sinks deeper into her skin as she ushers me onto the sidewalk. "Let me just get ready. Then you'll be on your way."

I squish her in a hug. "Thanks, Pipp."

She's gone for (probably) half a second.

My mind spins on him. (His green and blue and gold eyes and his sexy, slouching form.)

I'm coming. Don't worry.

I know it's useless talking to him. But I can't help it. It makes me feel a tiny bit better at least.

When she returns, her hair flows over her shoulders in loose curls (the curlers have done a perfect job at transforming her naturally stick straight hair into flawless waves.) A light dusting of pale violet powder sits on her eyelids, and pale lipstick coats her pout. She's gorgeous. And way too cool to be a grandma. (That's why I call her Pipp.)

"Let's go." She offers me her elbow.

I take it, and we step out onto the curb. She holds up her arm, counts to three under her breath, and spins us both a quarter turn to the left. My stomach whirls into a somersault as we flip into the coach.

My fingers run over the seat's fabric, velvet as dark blue as the night sky, and my stomach settles again. I move my eyes to Pipp.

Her smile splits her face in half.

"You must have done this a hundred times, and it still amazes you." Her laugh is tickling chimes dancing in the wind.

I shrug. "It's amazing. Isn't it? I mean, who would have thought stage coaches would still be a thing in the twenty-first century?"

Her smile falters a little and my stomach sinks into my toes. "Well, who would have thought witches would be a thing in the twenty-first century? The Normies tried really hard to make us disappear on and off from the fifteenth through eighteenth century."

I roll my eyes as the coach screeches to a stop, and the door flies open. "I find we're a bit like weeds; try as you might, you can't get rid of us."

The smile returns to Pipp's face as she steps out of the coach. "What kind of weed do you think I am?"

"Uhm," I follow her onto the curb. "I don't know that I want to compare my grandmother to a weed. Doesn't feel overly respectful."

I can almost hear her roll her eyes. "Don't call me your

grandmother."

"That's what you are, isn't it?"

She shrugs. "Well, yes, but grandmother makes me sound old. I much prefer Pipp."

I tousle her hair with my fingers. "Don't worry, Pipp, the name grandmother can't make you seem older than you really are."

She nudges my arm away. "Here you are. I'm off now. Tell me all about this boy over dinner tonight?"

"Do you actually care, or are you just being nosy?"

She winks. "Maybe both. You didn't think I'd bring you all this way for nothing, did you?"

I shrug, give a halfhearted little wave, and head into the Fulcrum. He's there–swallowed by a sea of strangers and slouching against the wall. Our eyes meet around elbows, over shoulders, and in the space left between faces. There's something empty in his green and gold and blue eyes.

Like a wave rising slowly onto the shore, he wades through the crowd to reach me. He tips his head to the side, and I follow him out one of the doors.

"I'm sorry." He looks down at his toes and nudges an acorn on the sidewalk with the white edge of his Chuck Taylor. "I never should have had you do this."

I shrug. "I didn't have to do it. I wanted to."

He sucks a breath in through his nose. "But I know the consequences. And they're not good."

"I don't care." I bump his elbow with mine. "I wanted to do this–I want to do this. And I know all about the consequences."

He grabs my hand and the warmth from his spreads to my cheeks. "You may know about the consequences, but do you understand them?"

His fingers slip past mine to weave our hands together. It's quiet between us, and the wind gathers my hair into a snarl. I can feel his heartbeat in my hand.

"Ian," I say (even though my mouth feels like cotton). "Don't worry about me. I'll be fine."

"Just stop, and you will be."

My mouth settles into a thin line. (Almost like it's got its own brain.) "No. I need to finish what I started, then I never have to see you again."

"Never knew you were so stubborn." He rolls his eyes with a smirk and squeezes my hand. (My heart jumps out of my chest.)

I brush his hand away. (Even though I don't want to.) "How would you? You hardly know me at all."

"Yes, but I'd like to." His eyes pin into me, the pupils dilated to massive black holes in the middle of his mesmerizing eyes as he rakes them up and down my body. (Is he attracted to me? Why do I like that he might be?)

I set my eyes into a firm stare. (Even though my stomach has thrown a dance party.) "Let me get this straight. You've known me for just a few days, yet you want to help me evade the law. And for what? The chance to fulfill some fantasy based on attraction?"

"I know a few relationships based on much, much less."

"No thanks. Besides, I'm not even attracted to you." My insides twist at my lie. "I'll just finish up. And then I'll be out of your hair."

His lips part. Then close. Brush up against mine. (They taste just like I thought they would. Why do I like that so much?) "Violet, I don't want you out of my hair. I want you in it. All in it."

"Gross." My tongue goes dry. "Leave me alone."

I pivot on my heel and stalk away from him. But every time I close my eyes, I see him. A playful smirk twisting his lips. The slight curl of his shoulders. And those eyes. Green and blue and golden. And twinkling with teasing.

My insides go all mushy and I take deep breaths to stabilize them. (It doesn't help.) I keep walking. (Even though the only thing I want to do is run back to him.) So I'll finish what I started, and come back to him. (If he doesn't hate me like I'm sure he will.)

The rose takes forever to make. (This favor is turning out to be a much bigger time commitment than I signed up for.) But when it's done, a weight lifts off me

Ten pounds lighter, I whip out my phone and text him. Not three seconds after it's been sent, he reads it.

And then nothing.

Nothing for six long minutes.

(Ian, please. Talk to me. Do you want the rose? Do you want me to deliver it?)

The pinging of my phone jolts my heart awake like a pair of defibrillators pressed against the cold chest of someone just flatlining. I answer it, palms dripping with nervousness.

"What do you want?" His voice is empty of teasing.

My mouth runs dry. "It—it's finished. Is that all you wanted from me?"

The other line goes quiet. Two breaths.

"Obviously, that isn't all I want from you.."

I huff a breath out my nose. "Ian, just tell me what you want me to do with the darn thing."

"I want to see it." (He's getting emotional, the gravel in his voice says so.)

I roll my eyes. "Don't start crying on me or anything. Meet me at the corner of Nettleton Avenue, and I'll show it to you. Then we can part ways for good."

I pace in Pipp's driveway until I hear his motorcycle and break into a sloppy run to the corner. He's just dismounting from that crazy thing.

"Do you have it?" His voice is still just as cold as it was on the phone.

Nodding, I pull it out. I unfold its crushed petals to avoid his eyes. The brush of his fingers against mine brings my eyes to his. His pupils dilate as our fingers slip past each other beneath the rose.

It's silent as he turns it over in his hands. "This is immaculate."

A blush creeps across my nose. (Why am I so happy he likes my work?) "Thanks."

"It's even better than the one I made."

His words knock me off balance. "If you made one, why on earth would you need me to make you one?"

He scuffs his sneakers on the sidewalk. "It was a long time ago."

"Why did you do it?"

His shoulders cinch up to his ears and dip back down again. "It was a favor. I thought he was a friend."

"I see." My voice is muffled against my sleeve as I wipe my nose. "What do you want me to do with it, then?"

The concrete kisses his legs as he sits down, resting the rose in the seam between the grass and the sidewalk. "His name is Woody Costa. I need you to give it to him. He has a show at Pindling Theater tonight."

"Why him?"

Ian pulls blades from the dirt. "He killed my sister."

I sit across from him, our knees brushing, and pull three pieces of grass out of the crack in the sidewalk. "What happens when I give it to him?"

He stands up, scuffs his shoe again, and swings across his motorcycle. "It's better for you if I don't tell you."

The bike roars to life. I look at the blades of grass in my hand. When I look back up, he's gone. The blades filter through my fingers (like the love we almost had) and I scoop up the rose.

Shoving it in my pocket, I shuffle back to Pipp's house and let myself in. Estella waves hello to me with one of her doors.

I take the stairs three at a time. "Pipp!"

"Yeah, Hon?"

I wipe my palms against the skirt of my dress. "Can I get a ride?"

"Where to, Sugar?"

"Pindling Theater."

We take the carriage again, but this time it feels tighter. (Like we're stuffed inside a tin can.) Pipp's emerald eyes pin into mine, questioning. "You don't like the theater, so why are we going to one?"

I pull the rose out of my pocket without thinking. "I have to give one of the actors this."

Pipp's face hardens into an emotionless slate. "This is serious stuff. Why?"

"I think I'm in love."

Pipp cups my knees with her palms. "If you're in love with him, I think we ought to turn around."

"It's not him, It's Ian. The guy who asked me to do it."

"If this guy loves you back, he wouldn't ask such a life-altering favor." She takes a breath in through her nose and lets it out slowly. "Have you thought about this?"

"So much my brain hurts. Plus, I've already gotten this far, why not finish strong?"

The air is growing warmer as daylight approaches, and I hurry inside. I wait in the last row of dingy theater number three. Ian's words stab into my thoughts as I scan the program for the fifth time. His name is there, in solid black letters: Woody Costa.

I doodle in my notebook as I wait for the show to be finished. (I think it's about the plague or something. All I know is it's way too boring to pay attention to.) The thunder of a thousand clapping hands pulls my eyes from my page (I've filled it with all shapes and sizes of cats) to see the cast taking their final bows. I stuff my notebook in my bag, sling it over my shoulder, and creep up the rows to lurk by the stage.

"Woody," I squeak. "I have something for you."

He clears his throat. "For me? What is it?"

I fish the rose out of my bag and hold it out to him. "A rose. For a stunning performance."

"Thank you." His thumb and forefinger turn gray as they grip the rose.

I don't stick around to watch. I don't need to know what happens. I don't need anything. (Except Ian.)

I wander back to Pipp's and collapse on her sofa, suffocating on my own guilt. Delirious with worry, I roll onto my side to watch her come in. She sets down her bag, her clothes wrinkling over her frame. Hair sticking out at all sorts of angles, she smooths out her clothes and sits on my feet.

I wriggle out from under her and scowl at her a little. "Pipp, I'm lying here!"

"Not anymore, you're not." Her words carry a wink. "What's got you down, Sugar?"

The room fills with the metallic peal of wind chimes, and Pipp wheels around to look at the toaster sitting in the windowsill. A letter with a golden seal sticks out of one side of it.

"Violet," Pipp says slowly. She gathers her hair into her hand and twists it into a neat knot. Her wrinkled fingers clutch the letter from the toaster and rip it open. "The council wants to see you."

Fear fills me like water pooling in an ice cube tray.

Pipp wraps me in a tight hug. "Just tell them the truth."

So here I am, standing in total darkness, total solitude. The skirt fluttering around my knees shakes with my hands. Tears burn in my eyes. My pulse pounds in my throat. I suck in an unsteady breath, wipe my hands on my skirt, and reach out into the shadows. (Why am I so afraid? It can't be that bad. Right?)

I step into light as blinding as the highest sun reflected off of snow. I squish my eyes closed (to block out the light and the shame all in one.)

"Miss Samson." the voice is familiar. (And eerie and unsettling and hollow.)

I peel my eyes open just enough to see three ancient women (pretty much the living embodiment of time with all their wrinkles and sags) all sitting at a table on a hovering stage.

"Stand up straight, girl."

My back goes rigid (without my willing it to.) and the words, "Yes, Ma'am," spill off my tongue.

Then something strange happens. My mouth sticks together, and I am unable to say anything. (I am trapped. I am stuck. I am afraid.)

The smallest of the three ancients, the middle one, leaps from the stage to stand in front of me, poking at my skin and tugging at my hair. She circles me, her eyes stabbing into my itching skin.

"Why on earth would you sacrifice so much for a stranger?" Her voice is creaky and thin.

My mouth peels apart like thighs on a summer day. "Um." Rain pours from my palms. "I, um,"

"Spit it out, young lady." The ancient on the end sounds as if she should have died ten years ago, her voice raspy and almost snakelike.

A yearning fills me when I think of him. His lopsided smile. The infuriating sound of his snapping gum. The teasing in his smile.

"Neloise, she doesn't need to say a word. Her stained cheeks spell it out as clearly as the moon. It was love." The first one coughs on her words.

"I care little for why; in the end, it's still deplorable."

Tears spring to my eyes. (I'm horribly embarrassed.)

"Shall we begin?" The smallest ancient says, sweeping a glance between the two others.

They nod. And my stomach falls out from under me.

The raspy one (Neloise?) snaps her fingers and unfurls a

long, time-stained piece of parchment. (It looks about a million years old and has lines and lines of scribbly somethings on it.) She runs a skinny, crooked finger down the lines of curly script.

I don't know what she's looking for exactly, but I'm not about to ask.

"State your name."

(The words leave little room for negotiation.)

"Violet."

Neloise peers over the parchment and her wobbly glasses at me. (Her nose is scrunched up like I just farted in her face.) "Your full name."

I swallow past the lump in my throat. "Violet Xandrinah Samson."

Neloise takes a long, feather-like pen from the sleeve of her robes and draws six long scratches. (Probably right through my name.)

A cold burning zaps through my veins. Bells roll against the pulse in my temples.

"Whinnestah, search the elemental registry."

"I—I—I don't have elemental magic."

Neloise glares down. "Did I address you?"

I shake my head and squeeze my eyes shut. To block out the anxiety filling my bones.

Whinnestah clears her throat, a smile twisting at her lips. "There is no need to be cruel, Neloise. She was being truthful. She does not have elemental magic."

Neloise's grimace deepens. "Xarlitte, search the next registry. I sense incredible power within her."

Time creaks onward, the seconds stretching into minutes before the third Ancient speaks. "Aura magic is free from her."

A snarl pulls at Neloise's lips. "Search it again. I am certain she has an aura."

Xarlitte's brow curls into itself. "I am certain her name is not here."

"Fine. Let us begin the removal then."

She snaps. The lights go out. Creaking floorboards. Cold hands over my skin. Bruising flesh. Bleeding pores.

Then the lights go on again. Out again. On. Off. Blinding and piercing into my green eyes over and over again. A horrible pulling in my navel. Tension in my shoulders. Ringing in my ears. A chill spreads. I'm falling. (I hope the floor never catches me.)

The falling stops. Concrete hits me. Pain up and down. Nausea. More ringing. Fear. My eyes hold my pulse. My migraine is too intense to open my eyes. My insides twist and wrench until they're tied into a pretzel. And then the emptiness hits me. (I am a fraction.)

I'm outside again (and things don't feel quite normal). I dial his number as quickly as my thoughts fly through my brain.

"Hello?" He's just woken. (I can tell by the thickness in his voice.)

I breathe a sigh. (His voice feels comfortable, like my favorite pair of jeans.) "Why do I feel naked?"

He coughs on the other line. "Excuse me?"

"It's gone, Ian." There's static on the other line for four heartbeats. "So I risked everything for you, and I don't even get a thank you?"

The line goes dead. I was hoping for some sympathy, maybe, or at the very least a sarcastic comment or a joke.

An empty ache fills me as the sun fills the horizon, fully peaking into daybreak. The solitude sinks into my skin, deeper and deeper until it sits at the center of the hole inside me. A voice in my head screams out in agony for my magic, my loneliness, and my ego. The scream bounces around my skull for twelve heartbeats.

Then it's replaced with the roaring of a motorcycle and footsteps pounding down the sidewalk.

"Violet!" Ian folds down next to me and squishes all my broken pieces back together.

I swallow and speak into his elbow. "I can't believe I killed a man."

He squishes me tighter and drops a kiss into my hair. "I'm sorry."

"I thought you hated me?"

"I wanted to," he says. "But after I heard you screaming like that, I just couldn't."

My eyebrows wrinkle over my eyes. "You heard me?"

He scuffs his shoes (those same Chuck Taylors he wore when we met) on the pavement. "Well, um, I don't know if you could say I heard you, exactly, but yeah."

Our eyes meet. His eyes hold none of the teasing I've come to love.

(Can you hear me?)

His eyes twitch. He grabs my hand, a gesture that is no longer strange, but welcome and comfortable. "Yes, Violet, I can hear you."

Can you hear me? He winks at me.

My heart pounds in my chest, like some kind of wild animal, I grip his hand and nod.

(Do you hate me?)

Never.

He swings his body over his bike and reaches his hand back to me. *Coming?*

I toss my head back with a laugh. "I've never been on one of these stupid looking things."

"There's no time like the present, Vi."

Rolling my eyes, I press my body against his on the bike. "Let's go then."

The bike roars to life, and we're off to find our next adventure in the daylight. Pipp was right, witches are like weeds. And it turns out I'm a bit more like a weed than I thought.

13
TALES OF THE KARSHA
XYVAH M. OKOYE

Morpheus tipped the contents of his pipe out the window, watching the rain of ash fall like the fine sands of his eulclear, probably to settle on some unsuspecting passer-by. Hopefully, that passer-by would be Mortimer. And hopefully, the vexatious reaper would not—for once—be wearing his ridiculous bowler hat.

A smile tugged up a corner of his mouth. Bracing a hand on the smooth wood of the sill, Morpheus leaned out the large window to glance down at the street. His eulclear dangled before him, the small sandglass restrained only by the silver chain about his neck as it bobbed and shone in the late afternoon sunlight, reaching anxiously for the deserted cobblestones five floors below.

It had been a fool's hope to expect some form of levity today. Even the usually-boisterous winds were still and silent, already in mourning. Morpheus shrugged away his disappointment and stuck his tongue out, not caring that he was in full view of anyone coming by the courthouse. They could all go to hell. Seeing as he might be getting a head start today, he leaned further out, wagged his tongue, and threw in an obscene gesture —for good measure.

"I could push you if you'd like."

Morpheus clutched the windowsill, the grating sound of amusement in Mortimer's voice stirring bile in his gut. "Come to gloat, have you?" he asked, a forced note of glee underlining each word. He would not break. Not before the end. Not in front of Mortimer.

"Now, why would I do that?" Mortimer chuckled. "Finding joy in my little brother's misfortune is a bit low, even for me, don't you think?"

Morpheus spun to face Mortimer, his eulclear swinging in a wide arc. "They've decided?" He clutched the cold crystal sand-glass to his chest, glancing down the empty corridor behind the black-clad reaper he was unfortunate enough to call his brother. The shadowy path betrayed no secrets.

"You could still run, you know," Mortimer said with a smirk. "Though I would not suggest jumping out the window. Not with your eulclear in the black, anyway. Broken bones might make escape a little difficult."

Morpheus glanced down at the small rectangular prism in his palm. Within it, black sands ran smoothly from the top bulb of the sandglass to the bottom one through the thin neck between them, only to be emptied into the prism itself to rise like a swirling mist and return to the top bulb as particles of sand once more.

"You should not wear your heart for all to see, Morpheus. It is unbecoming of a Son of Somnus."

Morpheus growled, tucking his eulclear beneath his shirt. "The Sons of Somnus can all burn in hell, along with those farts you call Elders."

Sighing, Mortimer pinched the bridge of his nose. "Just be grateful a eulclear cannot be taken, or someone would have snagged yours decades ago." The reaper turned, black cloak bustling with the movement. "And those *farts* have reached a verdict." Mortimer started down the corridor, leaving Morpheus no option but to follow.

It was not his first time walking this hallway. But, somewhere deep within him, Morpheus knew this time would be his last. This time, he had gone too far, and even his status as a Son of Somnus would do little for him. That is, if it wasn't the very thing that condemned him to a fiery eternity.

His honorary membership to the Sons of Somnus had come with considerable benefits, Morpheus had to admit. But, as is the nature of power and prestige, the price for the privilege to walk among the living was a steep one. Morpheus had earned his eulclear in less than half the time it took other Karsha males, but instead of joining the reapers, Morpheus had chosen to become a sandman: for the travel benefits. And because he only had to work nights. *And* because he did not want to compete with his siblings.

Being Mor's and Mort's reckless little brother was bad enough.

With each step, each heartbeat, each carved wooden door they passed, anxiety swelled in Morpheus's chest. He would lose it all: his privileges, his *job*... He glanced up at the reaper before him. He would lose their respect. Being a sandman, if nothing else, had earned him their respect.

The reaper stopped before a large gilded door and turned to face Morpheus, and the disappointment in his brother's gaze weighed Morpheus's chin down. His eyes searched the ground, watched the thick shadow circling around his brother's polished boots, a shadow that had loomed heavy over him for all of his existence.

"Don't do anything stupid," Mortimer said, then pushed the door open.

Orange light flooded the center of the pentagon-shaped chamber from the circular skylight, spotlighting the single red-cushioned chair that awaited him. Straightening his shoulders and tipping his head back, Morpheus marched up to it. He would receive his verdict with pride—something the seven enthroned cowards encircling him in the shadows could not afford.

Mortimer stood guard by the door.

"The Elders have reached a verdict," a shrill voice sliced through the silent chamber, shrewd and unpleasant as the Elder it belonged to.

Morpheus had often indulged himself in pleasant thoughts of dousing the female with enough sleeping sand to knock her out for a century or two, but the fact that Karsha females did not need eulclears to walk among the living made it almost impossible to know the precise moment to strike.

That, and because Elder Raidne was his sister's best friend. Morana would never forgive him for hurting her.

"With little deliberation," Raidne continued, "the Council of Karsha Elders has decided—unanimously—that you are to be stripped of your post and all privileges." She paused, hesitant, before adding, "And you are to be relieved of your eulclear."

The world grew cold. Morpheus placed a hand over his chest, over the sandglass that was, in many ways, his heart and soul. His eulclear? They would take his eulclear? He could not imagine an existence without the ability to walk among the living.

Never again would he feel the warm sun on his face, or the gentle breeze kiss his cheeks, or the pleasant burn of tobacco in his throat. Never again would he feel the earth beneath his bare feet, or dance with the lovely girl behind her father's market stall. The lovely girl was the reason he was in this mess in the first place.

"Not my eulclear." His whispered plea was met with silence. "You cannot take my—"

"You are a sandman, Morpheus," Raidne hissed. "A Son of

Somnus. One of our finest Karsha. Yet you recklessly exposed our world to the living. To a child! A child who can no longer sleep! A child who now thinks monsters lurk in his trunk because you shadow-walked right in front of him!"

Morpheus swallowed his retort. The charges were not entirely true. Yes, he had indeed exposed their world to a child, and yes, the child now suffered from insomnia after watching a sandman step into a shadow and disappear. But he hadn't shadow-walked recklessly. In truth, he hadn't shadow-walked at all.

After more than a few drinks (and a little too much tobacco), Morpheus had forgotten to switch his eulclear back from the black. As a result, he had lost control of his shadow, leading to a wild chase that had ended in the child's bedroom, where he had promptly fallen through his shadow—almost dragging the child completely through with him before having the good sense to let go—and landed back home.

But Morpheus couldn't tell them that, because that would mean admitting he had left his shadow in the land of the living. And Morpheus could never admit that. Losing a doorway to the Afters earned Karsha clipped wings and a one-way trip to the fifth level of hell.

Morpheus had planned to return to the child's bedroom in the little town of Tire, but without his eulclear… "You cannot take my eulclear," he said, desperation raising the timbre of his voice.

"The Elders have decided—"

"No!" Morpheus clutched the sandglass to his chest.

From beside the door, Mortimer clicked his tongue. At this, Morpheus bowed his head in shame. Had his brother not warned him against doing exactly this?

Taking a steadying breath, the sandman fought to comport himself. Keeping his head was key to keeping his eulclear. "There must be some other solution to this," he said, "Some way to fix this, to undo the damage done—to set things right..." He floundered for ideas in the ensuing silence. "I mean, you said it yourself, I'm one of the best. Why hurt the Sons of Somnus by putting me out of commission when we could find a way to fix this?"

Fabric whispered from the shadows as more than one of the Elders shifted in their seats.

Morpheus plowed on, clutching desperately to his beloved eulclear, praying silently to The One Who Claims All that he did not damn himself in the process. "What if I reverse the damage done?"

"You cannot make him forget," Raidne said.

"But what if I can undo his insomnia? Make him sleep again?"

"He has been into the Afters, Morpheus. Sleeping sands will no longer work on him."

"So what do you plan to do? Send Mort to drag his soul back here?"

Mortimer sighed from his post. Morpheus half-expected Raidne to have him chained and thrown in a pit. Instead, she said, "We are considering other alternatives."

"Such as?"

"That is not your concern, Morpheus." Raidne's tone lost any sliver of warmth it might have held.

Morpheus knew he was treading dangerously, any leniency their shared history had afforded him was all but spent. He lowered his voice and his gaze, the portrait of humility, and said, "I am a sandman, Elder Raidne. For over twelve decades, I have dealt in sleep. I made this mess. Please, give me a chance to fix it." He squeezed his eulclear and closed his eyes, offering one last plea. "Give me ten days. If I cannot cure the child's insomnia in ten days, then I am not worth my sand."

Ten days would never be enough. Without his shadow, it would take him seven days to get to the Western Gates. Then it would take three more to get to the land of the living—that is, if he could get a Ferryman to ferry him across the Lemosyne—before he even began the journey east, to Tire. It was a bold, desperate request, but Morpheus was all out of options. "If, after ten days, I cannot make the boy sleep soundly through even one night, then I deserve to be stripped of my post and privileges... And my eulclear."

The moments rolled painfully by. Morpheus felt his hopes being dashed against the hard rocks of pride and obstinacy and prejudice that kept most of the Elders quiet. Today, he would lose his eulclear. Today, he would lose everything.

"I must admit, Raidne," a rasping voice broke the tense silence, "it is an appealing alternative."

Morpheus did not recognise the voice. Raidne was the only Karsha on the council he actually knew.

The male said, "Perhaps we should consider his proposal, Raidne."

Morpheus held his breath, the flickering flame of hope blazing bright once more.

"I do not think it wise..." She paused, everyone in the room waiting expectantly for her decision. Finally, Raidne moaned, a sound Morpheus knew meant she was about to cede, albeit reluctantly. "Fine. Ten days, Morpheus." She groaned, and fabric whispered once more, informing him that the svelte female had risen from her seat. "Don't make me regret this."

Even after the footfalls had died out and only his brother remained with him, Morpheus sat clutching his eulclear in both hands.

"Ten days." Mortimer chuckled. Morpheus looked up to see his brother approaching. "Not bad. I must confess, I am looking forward to seeing how you pull this one off." The reaper stopped before him. "Your eulclear is still in the black, Morpheus."

Sighing, Morpheus loosed his grip. He pinched the eulclear

between his thumb and forefinger, its black contents filtering between mist and sand. It was beautiful, even Mortimer had admitted that. His brother had once told him it was one of the finest eulclear seen in centuries. For a moment, Morpheus wondered if his mother had been right in professing that a Karsha's eulclear reflected the true heart of the male.

With the eulclear steady in one hand, Morpheus snaked his index finger down the length of it, whispering the simple words in ancient Karsha to reverse the black. Almost instantly, the sands and mist faded from the deepest black to the purest gold.

"Good," his brother said. "Now, I believe you'll be needing this." Mortimer waved a hand, and Morpheus watched, wide-eyed, as his shadow—*his* shadow—slid across the floor to settle comfortably beneath him. "Ten days, Morpheus," Mortimer said, sinking into the shadow pooled at his feet and disappearing to only the Mother knew where.

THE BRICK WALLS of the manor seemed greyer than Morpheus remembered. He gazed up at the mammoth building looming above him with the melancholy of a reaper waiting on a soul. He supposed having one's child inflicted with an incurable illness would rob any great house of its splendor. Even the halls of Black Mountain had lost their luster for a time after the blood blight struck young Leah.

Morpheus squeezed the handle of his briefcase so tight that his leather gloves protested audibly.

That had been the first time he had seen the Prince of Light weep. It had also been the time he had first understood why mortals feared the great divider called death, and why Karsha males would lose their immortality if they ever gave their heart to a mortal—not that he ever planned to give his eulclear away to the fickle creatures. He placed a hand over the sandglass, tucked safely beneath his shirt. A mortal could never care for it the way he did. The blundering creatures were more likely to shatter it in the blink of an eye.

With a sigh, the sandman rolled his shoulders back, tipped his chin up, and started for the front door.

The hollow sound of his knocks echoed eerily through the halls within, and Morpheus was half-tempted to turn back down the pathway and up to the village. This house had little to do with the living now.

Well, what had he expected after dragging their only child to hell and back, literally? Footfalls sounded within, sluggish and unsteady as a newly awakened drunk, then the large doors groaned open to reveal the scowling face of a gnarled old man whose towering, crooked frame suggested he must have been intimidating in his youth.

"Another physician?" The old man's twitching green eyes scanned him from his fine—foolish-looking—hat to his polished black boots before settling on his briefcase.

Morpheus clutched it with both hands, positioning it before him, as though it were enough to answer the question. Affirming the man's suspicions would be a lie, and Karsha could not lie.

So Morpheus simply presented him with the facts and let him draw his own conclusions. "I'm here to see the boy."

The old man made a guttural sound, like a wad of phlegm was stuck in his throat. "Where from?"

"The West," he said, another technical truth.

Again, the man made that unpleasant sound. "Name?"

"Mo—" He hesitated, then decided there was no harm in giving his full name. "Morpheus."

"Morpheus," the man tested the name on his tongue. His eyes grew distant for a moment. "Morpheus," he muttered, as though trying to recall where he had heard the name before. Then the man's eyes focused once more. "What house do you serve?"

The sandman raised a brow. "Is that important?" he stalled as his mind raced to come up with an answer that would conceal his lack of understanding of the question itself.

But the man chuckled, making that guttural sound once more. "I suppose not. At this point, the Master will take whatever help he can get." Glee and malice shone in those green eyes as the man stepped aside and pulled the door wide open. "Follow me."

Inside, the house was more lugubrious than Morpheus had expected. It stirred up the same eerie feeling he got when following his sister through the catacombs that hid the entrance to her home. And the old man's unrequested narration of goings-on as he limped ahead did not help improve matters. The man sounded too gleeful, too happy with the misfortune of his master's house—a house clearly falling to ruin from an unsettling level of neglect.

But what unsettled Morpheus most was not the white cloths he noticed draped over all the furniture as they passed by open doors on their way to the bifurcated staircase. Neither was it the thick layer of dust that marked his presence when he dragged a finger over the wooden banister, mentally blocking out his guide's incessant droning. Nor was it the darkness pulsing against the flickering flame of the lantern in the old man's hand as he led them up the stairs and down a large hallway.

What unsettled him most was the cobwebs, hanging like garlands from the walls and ceiling, hiding in corners and lurking in places far beyond the borders of his vision. There were cobwebs everywhere. And cobwebs meant spiders.

Shuddering, Morpheus pulled his briefcase to his chest. It was empty and useless as the hat he wore—both to disguise him as a mortal physician. He supposed coming in the front door would serve his purpose of healing the boy better than shadow-walking right into the child's bedroom.

The child had been in the Afters, which meant the child could see him even with his eulclear in the gold. And it would do no one any favors to have his *patient* raving about a man only he could see. Presenting himself this way gave him direct access to the child, the treatment records, and the surplus amount of tobacco he planned to request from the Lord of the house.

"Here." The man stopped before an inconspicuous door and knocked. "Perhaps this is where I should wish you good fortune, Morpheus," the man offered him a crooked smile before turning back to the door, "but the only gods watching over this house now are Morana and Azrael. And I pray each day for their swift arrival."

Before Morpheus could fully process the man's words, the lock clinked loudly and the door swung open.

"Ah, Tidus," a stout man greeted in a tired voice. "Another one?" Tidus nodded as the man waved for them to enter. "What is the fee this time?"

Like the rest of the house, most of the bedroom was shrouded in darkness, but Morpheus knew from memory where everything stood: the vanity between the two large windows, the reading desk against the far wall, the armchair in the corner, and the thick rug he had tripped over at the center of the room, lying just before the large trunk at the foot of the bed.

His gaze lifted to the bed, sweeping over the woman asleep in a chair beside it, and his heart sank at the sight of the pallid, emaciated child lying in it, covered to the neck with white sheets; at the despair in the boy's eyes as he lay there awaiting the time his sheets would be pulled up over him completely.

A frown settled on Morpheus's face. Something wasn't right. He moved to the side of the bed opposite the sleeping woman, and leaned in to examine the child in the dull glow of the lone candle on the bedside stool. "Light!" He gestured to the two men. "I need light!"

Tidus stumbled forward, lantern outstretched, the stout man following a step behind. "What is it?" The man asked, peeking around Tidus's frame. Morpheus could not help but note the hope in the man's voice as he asked, "Did you find something?"

It was unclear what he was staring at. Blue veins bulged at the child's temple, webbing their way past his hairline. His bloodshot eyes stared blankly ahead, rimmed by dark circles that, on closer inspection, Morpheus recognised as the same pulsing blue veins about to spring forth. The sandman clicked his tongue and straightened. He had dealt in sleep long enough to know that *this* was not insomnia.

Morpheus fought back a grin. He was not responsible for the boy's situation after all. He could go home, tell Raidne what he had discovered, and they could all put his misbehavior behind them. He'd get to keep his eulclear, and maybe even his job if he—

"Well?" The stout man's voice cut through his thoughts. "What is it?"

"It is not insomnia," he announced proudly, picking up his briefcase.

Even in the dim light, Morpheus could clearly make out the man's puzzled expression. "Well?" the man asked finally, nose twitching with impatience. "What is it?"

"I cannot say for certain what it is, but I know for a fact that it is not insomnia." He tipped his hat in farewell and started for the door.

"So that's it?" The man stepped in his path. "You're—you're just—" He flapped his hands helplessly. "Just—leaving? What about my son?"

"I am a sleep specialist." Morpheus tried hard to keep his elation from his voice. "And *this*," he gestured to the boy, "has nothing to do with sleep."

The boy's mother drew in a sharp breath, the first sign that she had stirred.

"Nothing?" The man's nose wrinkled and his voice rose with each word—to Tidus's obvious delight. *"Nothing?* My son has not slept in days! You are a physician! Sleep specialist or not, you took an oath to care for the sick!"

Morpheus had taken no such oath. He had no interest in the sick, or in caring for anyone but himself. But he supposed he could indulge the grieving parents a few moments before leaving and giving up his ruse. And perhaps he could request a reasonable amount of tobacco as a small consultation fee.

With a sigh, Morpheus put down his briefcase. "Let me see his records."

Only slightly pacified, the man snapped his fingers, and Tidus hobbled towards the desk, the lantern light revealing the mess of papers littering it. The old man fumbled through them, gathering up a bunch and returning with them.

Taking the stack, Morpheus thumbed through the records. There were far too many sheets for any regular patient.

In the five days since Morpheus had been there, the child had been seen by more than thirty physicians, each testing and treating for different things from incontinence to the blood plague. One record even claimed the child was cursed by a flyflok: the dark soul of an undead that fed on the souls of the living in order to maintain their facade as regular mortals. As suspected, some were written by quacks, out to profit from the family's misfortune—not much unlike himself. But a great number of them were genuine. And all of them, inconclusive.

"Well?" The Lord of the house grunted his impatience.

Morpheus glanced up at the man from below the rim of his hat and was about to spout something foul and hurtful when there was a gentle knock on the door. Tidus made that guttural noise of his and made to get it, but then it opened and *she* walked in.

The room melted away as Morpheus stared at the lovely girl in her tattered clothes, with a basin of steaming water wedged in the crook of her arm, and a washcloth slung over her shoulder. She paused on seeing him, recognition flickering in her large brown eyes—those eyes he had stared into on so many nights before. He could stare into them for the rest of her mortal life, and then some.

"Avora," Tidus greeted, breaking their trance.

The girl bowed her head towards the Master of the house, then to Tidus. "My apologies." Her voice was a timid thing, a sharp contrast to the hearty laughter that plagued his memories from the nights they had danced together to the soft sounds of music filtering out from the town's square. "I did not realize we had company."

She was different here. Her clothes had never been so tattered. And her dark sea of curls were now a dull, tangled nest on her head. What had happened to her?

As though in response, she started for the bed, bowing her head to the mistress of the house before settling herself beside the woman and giving her focus to the boy in the bed.

"Do you care for him often?" Morpheus asked before he could stop himself.

"Avora?" the Mistress rasped, her voice still lost somewhere between sleep and waking. "Since the night he got sick. She worries for him like he were her own." The woman stared at the girl peeling back the covers to wipe down her son. "In a way, I suppose he is. I have no idea what we would do without her." She brushed a knuckle across Avora's cheek, and the girl smiled, sad and small.

Morpheus turned his gaze to the master of the house and bile rose to his throat at the hungry look in the man's eyes. A look that was fixed on Avora. Morpheus wanted to punch him, and he was glad when he noticed Tidus clearly felt the same way.

Morpheus cleared his throat, drawing the Master's attention. "Perhaps I could be of some assistance after all."

"You... can?" Avora whispered, hope reverberating in each note. Morpheus met her gaze and smiled when he saw the same emotion moisten her eyes.

"I not only can," he announced, "but will. I *will* fix this." *For you*, he wanted to add. *I'll fix this, for you.*

The girl whimpered, clasping the washcloth with both hands in an attempt to hold back her tears. The child's mother showed no such restraint. She wept openly, throwing herself over her dying son.

But the Lord of the house remained unimpressed. "Am I to believe you can achieve what many others have failed to?" He wrinkled his nose. "A moment ago, you had no idea what afflicts the child!"

"Looking at these records," Morpheus started, measuring his words as he fanned the papers in the man's face, "it should not be too hard to figure out."

The man threw his head back and laughed. "And what will this cost me?"

SMOKE BILLOWED out the bedroom window. Against the backdrop of an inky sky, Morpheus sat on the window ledge, pipe in hand, the rustling of his papers the only sound to intermittently break the silence as he thumbed through record after record.

It had been three days since he had been put up here by the Lord and Lady of the house. Three days since he had agreed to find a cure for their son. Three days, and nothing to show for it, save the many cups of tobacco he had puffed through.

Morpheus did not worry about his habit. The Karsha were undead. And even after his eulclear had been in the black for days on end and his body began to adjust to the feel of mortality—like it had begun to do—he only needed to slip into the Afters a few moments, and all strength and vitality would be restored.

Groaning against the tiredness now plaguing his being, Morpheus stretched his sore limbs and clambered clumsily down. There was no use fooling himself. It wasn't as though the records would somehow change overnight. Morpheus knew most of them verbatim at this point.

It troubled him that the boy's detailed accounts of seeing him shadowwalk remained—*curiously*—omitted from each record.

He tossed the pipe and papers onto the work table nearby and headed for his bed. It was a comfortable piece of furniture. As comfortable as every other in the little room. He supposed, to a mortal, it was large and extravagant, supposed he should be grateful for it. But Morpheus had tasted the finer things of many worlds and this paled in comparison to most of them. Perhaps his nitpicking was due to sleep-deprivation. He flopped onto the bed, sighing gently as the soft sheets enveloped him. Perhaps his eulclear had been too long in the black.

The sandman rolled onto his back and retrieved the small sandglass from beneath the collar of his shirt. Taking the time to admire it before switching had become his usual manner. Morpheus was about to utter the words to switch to the gold when a soft knock sounded at his door.

He sat up, a curious sort of hope and excitement flooding his chest as he bade them enter, curious feelings that only grew when Avora waltzed in with a tray of food and a smile that would bring kings to their knees.

She headed for the desk, keeping her eyes fixed on the tray she carried, ignoring him as she had done each time she had brought him supper or treats. They had not spoken since the night he had arrived and, at first, Morpheus had considered it normal, seeing as they had never really spoken prior to that anyway.

Since the first night he had stumbled upon her behind her father's stall, dancing to the fading music from the market square, all they had ever done was dance. Night after night after night, he had visited, and each time, she had been there, in her simple dresses and warm smiles, awaiting his arrival with open arms and readied feet that carried her over the grass with an elegance akin to that of a Karsha female.

Even Raidne had never made his heart skip the way it did when watching Avora dance.

"Thank you, Avora." Her name tasted sweet on his tongue, a sweetness he hoped reflected in his voice. But Avora only nodded, focusing now on the records he had deposited so carelessly onto the desk.

Morpheus had been content with watching, lifting her, twirling her, holding her beneath the stars as he gazed into her eyes. But seeing her again, learning her name, discovering the things she cared about... contentment was no longer good enough.

"Avora—" Morpheus slid off the bed, and started for the desk. He wanted her to speak to him—to look at him—but he had no idea what to say or do to make it happen. Stopping beside the girl, he uncovered the tray and pretended to examine its contents when really, all he wanted was to be near her. "Soup?" He raised a brow, smirking as he glanced sideways at her. "I'm sure it tastes delightful."

He had never had to try this hard for anyone's attention before. It had only been three days, and Morpheus had already exhausted all his ideas and methods for getting her to notice him. Now, he had taken to repeating his lines and smirks and gestures. It was almost pathetic how badly he wanted her to smile at him.

Avora reached for the papers.

Morpheus watched her delicate hands gather them into a neat pile, and a knot tightened in his chest when she placed a palm gently on the stack with an audible swallow that told him she was fighting back tears. Morpheus turned to her. Her lovely eyes shimmered wet as they stared at the papers beneath her fingers. It was breaking her, he realized. The child's condition was wearing her out in more ways than one.

Resting a hand tentatively on her shoulder, he said gently, "The child will be alright."

Avora's gaze grew hard as it slowly shifted to him. "It's been three days." The words came out strangled. "Three days, and all you've done is eat, and smoke, and examine him to no end." Tears slid down her cheeks as she whispered, jaw tense with the effort it was taking to hold back her frustration. "Tell me the truth, Morpheus. Can he be helped? Or are you just here to profit from our pain?"

Morpheus's hand fell limply to his side. He had no answer to give. None she would want to hear, anyway. He had tallied the child's symptoms, and they all pointed to one thing. He cleared his throat. "I would not have promised to fix this if I could not." It was true. If it were a lie, he could not have uttered the words.

"Then what is taking so long?" Her words came clipped as she balled her hands into fists. "Is it money? Because I can get you the money." A shadow passed briefly over her face. Morpheus did not want to imagine what she would need to do in order to get money from the miserly Master of the house. The whole town knew what the disgusting little man wanted. Both Tidus and the Mistress had said as much, volunteering more and more information with each of his visits to examine the child.

Avora had never caved, never indulged the Master, never even been interested, despite what many gifts and favors the man had thrown her way. She had turned them all down, accepting nothing more than what she was owed for her services.

And now, that she would take up the Master's offer—that

she was even considering it—all so he would help the child… Morpheus felt sick.

"I promised," he ground out through gritted teeth. "I promised you I would fix this."

Avora leaned forward, tiptoeing to get her face close enough for them to share breath. "Then what is taking so long?"

Morpheus held his ground. He was a Son of Somnus, and he would not be intimidated by this petulant little woman. He scowled. The sheer audacity. The impudence. That she would even dare to get so close. So close. His breathing grew labored as he fought to steady his quickening pulse. *Too close.* She was too close.

Avora drew back, a flash of embarrassment flushing her cheeks as she blinked rapidly. Then her sights fell on his eulclear. Time stopped as she dragged her eyes back to his, and the rawness of the terror in them was enough to have shattered his eulclear. No word could have been more damning than the one she spat next: *You.*

The girl backed away.

"Avora." Quickly tucking his eulclear away, Morpheus raised both hands before him. "I can explain." But the girl shook her head, retreating towards the door, yet unable to break their gaze. "Avora, please—"

"You did this to him!" Moisture glistened on her cheeks as her words choked and died to a whisper. "You—*you* did this." Morpheus watched helplessly as her emotions shifted from terror, to anger, to… hurt. "You—" She clasped both hands over her mouth to hold back a sob.

Panic rose within him at the sound.

Morpheus swept across the room, closing the growing distance between them so fast that she jumped and squealed when he gripped her arms. "Avora, please, let me explain. Avora—"

The girl shook her head violently, her tangled locks flying

wildly about her. But even as her chest heaved and her body trembled, she did not struggle to break free. And she did not look away.

Morpheus gazed into those lovely eyes, those eyes shining wet with the manifestation of her hurt, of the betrayal she felt, of the dying ember of hope she clung to as tightly as her clasped hands covered her mouth. Morpheus focussed on that hope. She was giving him a chance to prove he was not the devil she thought he was; to prove that the male before her was not a monster.

But how could he, without exposing his world to her? Without becoming guilty of the very crime he was working to avoid being punished for.

The girl's eyes welled with fresh tears as she watched him, deducing what she would from his silence. And a small, broken sound escaped her.

Morpheus could not stand it. The Elders be damned, he could not take seeing her like this, knowing he was the cause of this. So Morpheus closed his eyes, took a deep breath, and fetched his eulclear from beneath his shirt. "My name is Morpheus," he began softly. "And I am a sandman."

AVORA STARED at him like he was insane.

Morpheus sat beside her on the bed. He had told her the truth. The whole truth: about who he was—*what* he was—and why he was there. She had laughed when he had told her about the Afters, and gone weak in the knees when he mentioned Mortimer and Morana. He had helped her to the bed at that point. But Avora had fallen silent when he had talked about his eulclear, and she had remained that way even after he had finished his tale.

"Say something, Avora." Morpheus struggled to keep the

worry from his voice. Perhaps he had been a fool to bet on her trustworthiness. She was, after all, a mortal. "Avora? Say something. Anything."

Avora angled her head, her large eyes narrowing slightly as she studied his face. "You expect me," she whispered, choosing each word carefully, "to believe… to *believe…*" The girl shut her eyes and shook her head.

"I am a Karsha, Avora. I cannot tell a lie."

The girl folded her arms. "You lied about being a physician. You pretended to help—"

"I did not pretend to help. I *am* helping." Morpheus scowled at her before adding, "And I never said I was a physician."

"*Not* telling the truth *is* lying."

"Well, what do you think would have happened if I had told the truth?" The sandman raised a brow, watching her lips purse tightly as she tried to think up a response. "Would you have welcomed me if you had known who I was—what I am? Would you have let me anywhere near the child if you had?"

Avora looked away.

"I am not the enemy, Avora," Morpheus whispered. "I am only trying to help."

Morpheus watched as her gaze shifted back and forth between the door and the desk; as her jaw tensed and relaxed repeatedly. Why was she angry? He had told her the truth, so why did she seem so angry?

Huffing loudly, the girl stood. Morpheus rose with her, waiting patiently as she tapped her foot frantically until her frustration grew too much to contain. Avora stepped up to him and jabbed a finger in his chest. "You should have told me sooner," she hissed.

He blinked at the girl. "What?"

"You should've. Told me. Sooner." She punctuated her words with a jab, each one harder than the last.

Morpheus frowned in his confusion. "Avora, this is the first conversation we have had. *Ever*!" His flattened palm swiped the air for emphasis.

"Exactly! I've known you for... how long? And this is our first real conversation." The girl stormed towards the desk. Morpheus followed, even more confused now. But before he could speak, Avora asked dryly, "What makes you believe it is a flyflok?"

"The symptoms add up." Morpheus peeked over her shoulder as she rifled through the papers. "A flyflok is the only —" Avora's elbow slammed into his middle and he reeled back, winded. "Wha—"

"You were in my space!" She tossed the words over her shoulder with a quick glare before muttering, "You were breathing on my neck."

But even as her lips pinched into a frown, Morpheus caught the slight hue of red tinge her cheek just before she turned away. He cleared his throat and, despite the sudden warmth welling up in his core, pulled himself together.

"If it really is a flyflok," Avora said, examining one of the reports, "then why didn't the Muradora cast it out?"

"Even your magic healers are not trained to deal with a flyflok." The girl shot him a look, but he ignored her. "That is not what worries me, though." Taking the reports from her, Morpheus stacked them neatly at the center of the table.

What worried Morpheus enough to repeatedly draw him back to those reports was that the healer had not identified the flyflok in their report or—try as the sandman might to find one —left any clues as to their identity. Which, perhaps, was the greatest clue of all. Because it meant only one thing: the flyflok had been in the room with them when the healer had made the diagnosis.

Morpheus took a deep breath, then turned to Avora. "Avora, I—" His words clogged in his throat, and he swallowed down the lump forming in it. "I am sorry."

The girl watched him, curiously at first. But then her eyes widened and her hands fell to her side. Avora shook her head slowly as the tears returned to her eyes. "You promised," she whispered, backing away slowly. "You said…" her chest heaved as she whimpered. "You said you would help him. You—you gave me your word."

"I—" Morpheus frowned. "Wait. What are you talking about?" His tone snapped her out of her fit.

"You said you were sorry. I thought that meant you couldn't help Borin." She frowned too and placed both hands on her hips, angling her head as she asked, "What *were* you talking about?"

"Erm…" The sandman scratched his head.

He could tell her he thought she might be the flyflok. She was the most obvious suspect: young, beautiful, and with unrestricted access to the boy. If he was right, he could bind her, save the boy, and be gone by morning. But if he was wrong…

"Avora, I—"

"You do know how to banish a flyflok, don't you?"

"Erm…" He would have scowled at her for constantly interrupting him. He had plagued even Karsha with sleep sickness for less. But something about her audacity intrigued him. That she would still treat him like a regular mortal even after knowing what he was made him feel… different. "Maleficent spirits are not exactly my area of expertise." When she scowled, he raised a finger and added, "But I do know a way to trap one."

The girl's lips twitched towards a smile. "And you're sure it will save Borin?"

If all went to plan, then yes, it *would* save Borin. Banishing a flyflok—or any maleficent spirit—was the reapers' domain. He couldn't win if he went head to head with the creature, but if he could trap it, that would sever its link to the child, then he could dump it somewhere else in the town. Or perhaps, if he was feeling generous, leave the creature on his good-for-nothing brother's doorstep. "Yes," he said finally. "I'm sure."

"A FLYFLOK?" the Mistress asked from her seat at the side of Borin's bed. "You think my son is possessed by a flyflok?"

"Afflicted," Morpheus corrected.

"Nonsense!" The Master gauffered. "That's preposterous! You expect me to give credence to the mad ramblings of religious fanatics?" He looked about for support.

Tidus and Avora remained silent. Both stood before the bed, staring solemnly at the dying child. For the first time, Morpheus thought he saw sorrow and regret shimmering in the caretaker's green eyes. But then the Master resumed his bellowing, and it took all of Morpheus's conscious effort not to shut the man up with sleeping sands.

The manor's remaining occupants had gathered in the boy's bedroom at the sandman's request. Being the only ones present when the Muradora had given the diagnosis, the four now standing—or sitting, in the mistress's case—around the bed were the only suspects. Morpheus divulged that piece of information too.

"One of us?" the Master laughed, a sound that was starting to grate on Morpheus's nerves. "You think it's one of us?" The stout man gestured vaguely.

Avora stared at the boy, unperturbed. But Tidus made that guttural sound of his and stepped away from the bed, visibly shaken by the news.

The Mistress sobbed, brushing her son's hair back from off his clammy, gray forehead. "A flyflok," she whispered repeatedly, as though trying to convince herself, as though finding relief in the fact they now had a confirmed diagnosis. Suddenly, the woman turned her face to Morpheus. "But how? How would a flyflok..."

"It would have needed access to his food," Morpheus said calmly.

At that, all eyes turned to Avora.

Tidus muttered both prayers and curses as his trembling hands searched within the folds of his tattered robes.

"Avora?" The Mistress hiccupped a sob. "Avora, tell me this isn't true."

But the girl kept her sights fixed on the boy. Morpheus watched the girl's jaw tense and her eyes well up, and something deep in his chest cracked. "Avora?" he whispered.

Slowly, those lovely eyes found his, and there were tears in them once more. "I..." she started, but was cut off by the old caretaker.

"Devil!" The man hissed, uncorking a large black vial. "I bind you, devil. With this sacred water, I bind you. " He flicked his wrist, sending a small spray of water at the girl. She flinched and cowered from it. The caretaker advanced. "I bind you!"

"Stop!" Avora's brows twitched, and Morpheus could tell this was irritating the girl more than anything.

But the caretaker, convinced by her initial reaction, raised his voice and hands. "With these sacred waters from the Gingerdale River, I—"

Avora charged for him, punching him in the gut before snatching the vial from him. "You fool!" She turned on Morpheus. "Really? You think *I'm* the flyflok?" Hurt and accusation underlined her words. "Perhaps *you're* the flyflok!" She flicked the vial, sending droplets splattering onto his face. "Or you," she seethed at the caretaker, sending a splash at the now-cowering old man.

Morpheus watched the girl, wanting to reach for her, to promise her he believed her, to promise he trusted her. But that would have been a lie. In truth, she was the most likely of the bunch to be guilty. And water from the magic-infused river would do nothing to bind a flyflok, despite the foolish old caretaker's beliefs.

The Master of the house reeled with laughter. This only served to frustrate Avora some more. She marched right up to the stout little man and jerked the vial in his face. "Perhaps *you're* the flyflok!"

The man wiped his eyes, trying hard to rein in his laughter. But Avora wasn't done. She turned on her Mistress. "You think I'm the flyflok? After all this time?" Morpheus grabbed Avora's arm, but the girl shrugged off his grip and started for the bed. "After all I've done for you and your wretched little family, you think *I'm* the flyflok?"

"Avora... please..." the Mistress whimpered, eyes wide with terror as she watched the approaching girl. "Avora, I—"

"You what?" the girl growled. "You think I'm capable of hurting your son?"

The woman shook her head violently.

"Well, perhaps you're the flyflok," Avora mocked, spraying the woman as she had done the rest of them.

A loud, inhumane screech filled the room, followed by the sound of snapping bones and tearing flesh. And Morpheus stared in horror as the beautiful Mistress morphed into a creature too gruesome to belong in any world.

It towered over them, a giant with the head of a spider and the wings of a moth. It smelt like death. Six hands jutted out at random and unnatural places from its humanoid torso. Rotting skin hung off it in strips like gray rags, revealing the black blood and inflamed sinews beneath.

The creature hissed, sending a spray of thick, luminescent saliva onto the floor and bed. The substance sizzled on landing, eating away at the wood and the fabrics. And Morpheus had not felt such dread and despair as he did when the creature's refracted sights locked on Avora.

14
IN DARK CORRIDORS
MIREYA G. PARRA

I: Secrets

It's coming for me. It's coming for me. It's coming for me.

It all looks the same at this moment. Sample after sample, naming and cataloging them for Ms. Sharma. It's exhausting and my eyes are getting as tired as I am.

I take my glasses off and put them on the table. A long sigh leaves my lips as the door behind me opens. I don't need to turn to see who's there.

Minerva comes to my table and puts down a container with more samples to look at and catalog. I love my job but it can become quite monotonous sometimes.

"I don't think we're finishing tonight at this rate, Jules," says Sonna, with a little, playful laugh, at her working post in front of me.

"Me neither."

I recover my glasses and get up to distribute the new samples between Sonna and me while Minerva ends the paper-work. Have to make sure everything has been delivered to us in case any of the project leaders want to look at the records later on.

"Sorry friends—" says Minerva with a low, sleepy voice and shrugging. She moves in front of me while I separate the samples into two symmetrical columns. "—But it is what it is. They're making a lot of work down there tonight, so we have to get this done as soon as possible."

Sonna rolls her eyes behind Minerva, composing a silly face and making me snort. She thinks that *we* is actually just her and me, because Minerva is more of a delivery girl than anything else, though she actually works with Ms. Sharma more directly than us. To this day, neither Sonna nor I know exactly what is going on behind those closed doors.

Not like we're not curious about it, but we'd be fired if we ever tried to find out. So, cataloging samples and, from time to time, running some experiments it is.

In the distance, almost imperceptible, a soft voice says my name, like coming out of a dream and reaching for someone. I ignore It. I don't have time for It now.

Minerva rips off a copy for us to sign and turns to me with concern. There's sweat all over her face and she's chewing on her pen cap, already covered with lots of teeth marks.

She looks paler than usual, even under the artificial light, as if life had been drained from her. There's a haunted look in her dark eyes and her gaze doesn't dare to meet mine. Should I wait until she decides to speak or should I ask right away?

Do I want to know what's going on in her mind?

Sonna shares a quizzical look with me and, not breaking the silence or making any sudden move, I signal to Minerva with my eyes. Sonna nods in understanding and comes closer, putting a hand on the supervisor's shoulder. Minerva visibly relaxes and her eyes change. Seriousness. There's no place for doubt. That's the Minerva we've known for the past months. But the worry is still written on her face.

"Can I ask you a favor, Jules?" Voice low, almost trembling. She doesn't want to be heard. By who?

The walls listen. They listen. Shhh.

Sonna arches an eyebrow, curious as usual, and gets her column of samples without a word. Instead, she gives her back to Minerva and smiles in my direction.

"What is it?" I inquired, gaining Minerva's attention again.

She breathes deeply before taking one last sample out of the container. It's a microscope slide with a black spot on top of it, a single drop, secured inside of a petri dish. The sample is already processed, so I don't know what Minerva wants me to do with it.

"Can you… I want…" Minerva's struggling with her words, so I take the sample from her cold hands and place it on the microscope.

Back in front of me, Sonna has everything prepared to look at the new samples, but she's looking directly at me. Waiting. She gives me a little, encouraging smile.

Minerva takes a position on my right.

"Just, tell me what you see, Jules."

"Sure."

Under the vigilance of a pair of eyes, I work with the microscope until I'm looking at the sample with maximum capacity. There are some cells. Nothing else that clues me into what I'm looking for.

The weird thing is, there's no movement.

Most of the samples we are sent are kept alive so we can look at their mobility or run some tests, but a few are processed and the sample is killed so we can look at other characteristics.

But, the one that Minerva has brought…

It's supposed to be alive. Even the most simple organisms have some movement.

"…Don't think they're listening, Min," Sonna's voice is faded.

I step away from the microscope, rubbing my temples and

addressing the girls, but mostly Minerva, the interested party here. Sonna alternates between us, eager.

Too many eyes on me. *I hate being observed.*

Minerva's clever even if she doesn't give that impression, so I go directly to the point.

"Where did you get this? It's not one of ours."

You see ghosts everywhere.

They're not ghosts if people really act suspicious.

Minerva looks at Sonna, then at the door, and back to me. She whispers, so low, that Sonna and I have to inch closer to her.

"From the secret… project."

The silence that follows is unsettling. Sonna looks at me and back to Minerva. I eye the room.

I've always suspected the walls have ears. But I've never had secrets.

Until now.

A cool sensation travels down my spine taking all the warmth with it. Nothingness settles within my ribs, my lungs, my throat.

Someone's watching me. Watching us.

"How did you get this?" asks Sonna, putting a hand on my arm and looking Minerva in the eye.

There are some rooms in the facilities that not even Minerva can get in. And yet, she did. Why?

"Not important. We shouldn't talk about it."

Minerva keeps looking around, expecting something. Maybe, expecting someone to tear down that door and take us to Ms. Sharma's office. But there's something else. An abnormal fear when the maximum punishment is being fired.

She knows things. Keeps secrets. Don't trust.

"You know what?" I try a nicer approach. "Once I'm done with today's work, I'll take a deeper look at it, maybe even do some tests."

Minerva agrees, a bit more relaxed than moments ago, and goes for the door. Sonna comes from my right side.

"But first, dinner."

WITH SOME SANDWICHES and water in our hands, I can't stop thinking about that sample. I wish Minerva had given us more details about where she got it. What kind of being would produce that?

They're watching.

The cafeteria TV is off. I can see myself on its surface, like a gray and distorted mirror. I look worse than expected. I need a haircut, on the sides and the nape. And I need to get more sleep; the dark circles under my eyes prominent on my pale skin.

But, that sample...

Can they listen to your thoughts too?

I ignore the TV and its unnerving buzz as best as I can and turn all my attention back to Sonna. She's quietly chewing her last bite, leaving half of the food at the table, checking the glass of water as if it is the most interesting thing in the room.

A robotic voice comes from the little device on her forearm. Equal to mine.

"It is recommended that you finish eating. Those proteins and carbohydrates are always welcome into the organism."

Organism. My AI says the same about me. As if Sonna or I are only our cells and all the chemical reactions happening instead of whole persons with a lot more. But, for the eternal, joyful teasing between us:

"I agree."

Sonna stares at me. I divert my eyes to the floor.

"Of course you do."

She sounds serious, but, as she picks the sandwich up again, she can't help the smile that forms on her face. She looks at the water again.

"Weird sample back there," she whispers, though only the waiter could hear us and he's not really paying any attention.

She gives me no time to answer.

"Forget that. Remind me: what was it that your brother would always say? About movies."

Her voice is low but steady. She looks at me directly, forgetting the water right away.

"You only remember the "movies" part?"

"Humor me, will you?"

Sonna smirks and motions me to answer before she becomes bored and changes topics again. I wouldn't mind her going back to the sample, I'd like to know her opinion.

"Madoc's famous phrase." I try to do my best impression of him. "Enjoy, but make sure you don't turn your job into one of those old sci-fi movies you like so much, Jules."

I'm not even finished showing off my acting skills and we're already laughing. If Madoc was here he would laugh too, probably so loud that we would be told to get out.

I miss him a lot. Hopefully, Ms. Sharma will let families visit us again next month. Sonna's sister will come with her kid too. Sometimes, when we're all together, I feel like we've made our own family. A chaotic one, but a family nonetheless.

Sonna has definitely been family to me since those first weeks we started working together. And she will always be.

I look at her, trying to memorize every detail, while she keeps laughing at Madoc's eccentricities, some wrinkles appearing at her lip's corners. She thinks him a walking joke. I agree.

They're. Always. Watching.

A headache is making its way through my brain.

"Sonna."

We're both done with our food by now.

"Right. Your mysterious sample awaits you, sir." She giggles her eyebrows and I snort.

Out, on our way to the lab, Sonna repeats something my sister Sheila always tells me when she calls.

"Jules, don't obsess with this and overwork yourself to exhaustion. There are a lot of days in our future. And I don't think a single sample deserves so much of you"

II: The Nightmare Begins

I remember falling asleep, but I don't remember waking up. And, yet, I find myself walking down a corridor of the facility, darkness surrounding me. Cold making a home out of my body.

Cold?

I look down, at my bare feet, at my white trousers and gray shirt. I frown. The colors are wrong. It's disturbing.

"Julesss."

A soft voice, a whisper of my name fills the place from every possible direction and echoes through all my pores, hurting. I put my hands over my ears to shut It up, to no avail.

It's coming from far away. From the darkness in front of me. It's in my ear, even though I know there's no one there.

I hit the wall with my shoulder. The physical pain grounds me, but it doesn't help. I fall to my knees and, finally, the whispering stops.

It leaves a warm sensation. It's strange because I can still feel the cold biting at my ankles, trying to climb my legs and failing to do so.

I need to get out of here.

Putting a hand on the wall, I get myself up and check my pockets. My phone is in one of them. I don't have a lot of battery, so I'll leave it for later. For now, I can use the walls to guide myself around. Destiny? My room.

The other pocket is empty.

Orientation has never been my forte, but I've walked these corridors enough times to know where I'm going. Turning right at the next corner. Then two times to the left. Next,

A noise. Behind me. Scraping, on the floor. It develops into scratching; chalk against a board. The sensation travels all over my spine to my teeth.

I sigh. Why do my dreams have to feel so real?

Not a dream. It's coming. Run.

A wicked laugh, muffled.

Whatever that thing is, is getting closer. Running seems like the best option.

My feet and heart fall into a rhythm in mere seconds while I try to get away from my pursuer. But its heavy breathing and low growl are exactly behind me. On my side. At my neck. Its claws almost grabbing my ankles.

I take a hard turn to the left; that thing isn't fast enough and slips on the floor in the other direction, away from me. I've gained a few seconds of advantage, but they won't be enough.

There's a window in the middle of the corridor and moonlight shines through it, illuminating a door at the not-so-far end. A room.

The silence is heavy, weighing on my shoulders. And that breathing is at my neck again. Something rips at the lower part of my shirt while I sprint to the door, throwing myself at it when I reach it.

That creature, because I'm pretty sure that's what it is, doesn't follow me here. To this…room.

No way.

It's not a room.

My lungs are burning and my heart could explode from the effort. I bend slightly and put my hands on my knees.

It's an open field.

How can I be outside?

I'm definitely dreaming.

I turn around, expecting some enormous creature to be preying upon me, but there's nothing except hollow nothingness. A black hole.

The door's the same, but not the facilities. It's a wooden house now. Creaking, hovering over me, breathing on me. A growl. I stumble back but don't fall down. At least, it looks like I'm safe out here. And, I can see better.

Darkness has engulfed the sky, but I can make out the sun up there and, with its warming light, almost everything that accompanies me.

It reminds me of a storm with no rain. I love storms.

There are some trees in the distance, scattered throughout the grass. I move my toes, but I'm met with a close space instead of the caress of nature. Looking down I see I have my shoes back. A pair of nice, white sneakers.

I breathe deeply, letting my head fall backward while I close my eyes. My legs, my fists at my sides, my whole body trembling, both because of fear and relief. I could have died.

"My dear."

Not even the fear rushing through my veins can prevent me from breaking peace and turning to the source. A few paces away from me. It stands tall, walking among a never-ending fog. It looks human. I don't think It is.

Stay. Away.

I take a few steps back, towards the door. The creature or this humanoid figure? At least, inside, I can go look for help.

"Jules."

It's not moving, but It is calling me. Quietly, not wanting to be heard. Like Minerva.

Even after months of working here, I've never been able to shake off the idea that something's wrong. Those secret projects Ms. Sharma is always involved in. Things not adding up. And the disappearances.

A snap behind me. I'm too slow. Large and grayish claws

grasp my shoulders and force me back inside. I struggle against it, kicking with all I have: my elbows, my feet… I always hit hard rock and the pain travels all over me.

Finally, I hit it in the face and break free, returning outside. The humanoid figure is gone. Only the trees will be witnesses to my death.

Sweat runs down my body. Both my hair and shirt stick to me like an insect stuck in a spider's web. I wish the storm above me would explode with rain at this very moment. Cool the air. Help me relax. Maybe, even wake me up from this nightmare.

A heavy grip on my ankle, scratching, opening skin as if tearing paper. Warm and sickening blood falls free down my leg, soaking my trousers, my sneakers, and the ground under me, turning the grass into a deep red that the sky matches in mere seconds. Nature is mocking me.

The creature pulls and I fall to the ground, using my hands to reduce the harm my face receives. Its claw is still deep within my leg, opening the skin more and more with each tugging until I'm back inside. Surrounded by darkness. At the monster's complete mercy.

I kick it with my free leg and hear a clank against the floor. My phone. I touch all around me with trembling fingers, looking for it, while half crawling half pushing myself around the ground to avoid my attacker.

I can't find it. The throbbing pain of my ankle, adrenaline rushing through my system, all the different noises the creature is making. And the fact that I can't even see my fingers.

It's too much. I can't think properly.

"Left," says that familiar voice, so low that, at first, I think I imagine It. A product of my overstimulated brain. It repeats itself until I listen and do as It tells me.

My fingers make contact with a rectangular object: my phone.

The creature is on top of me, turning me around with one of its strong claws, which lightly pierce my arm skin.

You're dead. Poor Jules. A cruel laugh coming from the depths of my mind.

I struggle with my phone for a moment before turning on the flash and directing it towards the creature to see what I'm fighting against. But the second the light brushes its skin, the monster retreats as if it had been burned.

"Clever." The voice praises me. Warmth spreads across my cheeks. I'm glad nobody can see me right now. Reacting like this to a voice I don't even know where It's coming from.

Maybe, that humanoid figure. A line of thought to follow later.

With my free arm and leg, I put some distance between those lethal claws and me, until I hit a wall. That way it can't come from behind. Now, I just have to find a way to get out of here before my phone dies. Or I die.

The creature advances, getting near me but stops before the light touches its body again. That's why it didn't follow me out. This thing doesn't like light or maybe is even weak against it.

The creature launches for me, but I hit it in the eyes with the flashlight at its maximum brightness, trying to blind it. It works and, while I step aside at the best of my current ability, that thing hits the concrete wall. A low whimper escapes its lips and a shiver travels through my body.

"Neck," says the voice with an unusual raspiness that sounds threatening enough to make me wonder if it's actually trying to help me or commanding the creature.

Then, in a more softer and urgent tone, It says my name, followed by more words that I can't discern. Until It becomes a murmur in the background.

My focus goes back to the creature that has recovered and it's circling me, taunting, waiting to find a hole in my defenses.

Neck, It has said. Should I…try….breaking…

I can't help shriveling down as I imagine the motion and sound it would make. A crack, like a tree branch. And the possible blood falling down my hands. I'm going to be sick. But, if that's the only way of escaping.

Don't trust. Don't trust. Don't trust.

I get up with a hand on the wall while the other directs my weapon to the creature, making it withdraw a few paces, though I can still make out its form. It's disturbing, generated from my most troubled thoughts: four big silver eyes and large face, grayish skin, large claws whose strength I have already checked.

I don't move, but make sure to keep the light always in front of me and my breathing steady and silent. It's observing me but, if I don't make any sudden move, it won't probably try to attack me.

Of course, I'm wrong.

It gets on its hind legs, towering immensely over me while opening its mouth, full of fangs. Some saliva falls as its tongue passes over its teeth and the creature looks me up and down.

Fucking hell.

I didn't sign up for this.

A step to the left and pain fires my nerves, makes me grind my teeth and scream. Unapologetically. My fingers fail and my phone drops to the ground, the flash still illuminating us. The creature laughs; a guttural cackling from deep within its throat.

Amusing.

I try to ignore the pain as I dodge to the side and pick up my phone. I direct the light towards it, but the monster sweeps me off my feet and I fall hard on the floor, face first. I don't need more pain.

I need a plan. I need to be as aggressive as the creature.

Make a plan. Make a plan.

Get. Out.

I get up and, without stopping to think, I throw myself at the creature. Full force, like a bulldozer, though this thing is twice my size. But, I don't want to die without taking my chances.

I force my way around its body like a snake, hit it in the face with my phone, and bring it down with me. We fall, the creature on top of me, while I'm hugging it from behind. It struggles against me, growling, scratching the floor. I tighten my grip, adrenaline pumping and that voice circling me with words I can't decipher.

Can I actually break its neck? It's almost free. I should just do it. At once. Without thinking.

I position my hands around the head, left and right, and take a deep breath. A rough and loud howl echoes through the corridors making all my hairs stand on edge.

A quick move. A reverberating crack. No blood except for the one where I've hit it before. A sickening silence.

I take the body off myself and stay there for ages. Breathing. Thinking about everything that has happened in the last hours. Trying to make sense of it.

But it's impossible.

No matter whether dream or reality, the pain is probably going to kill me. If the blood loss doesn't do it. If I'm not dead already and this is the desperate last plea of my brain, attempting to understand it.

There's a buzzing, a stirring sound at my wrist. I've forgotten about my little assistant. Though creepy supervisor suits it more.

"Would you like some morphine, Jules?" I'd give anything to never listen to that voice again. "Your vitals are skyrocketing. Pain is getting near intolerable levels."

Don't. Trust.

Something pierces my arm.

"Morphine injected."

"Whatever," I say as I lay down, eyes closed, processing the fact that I just killed a beast three times my size and that it may be as real as me.

Is that the secret project? I don't want to know anymore.

A warming sensation spreads all over me, my muscles relaxing and my thoughts slowing down. The pain fades to a throbbing sensation that will let me walk, but not forget that I almost died tonight.

Everything fades. I'm almost floating. No gravity.

It's freeing.

I'll stay like this forever.

"Jules!" Sonna's voice, produced by my brain, makes me come back to my senses.

With a deep groan, all my joints echoing within me, I get up. First, sitting. Then, on my knees. And, finally, I stand. I lean against the wall and close my eyes so the floor stops spinning.

That voice around me increases Its volume so I can make out some of what It's saying, though I can't filter It out from the ringing and my palpitating heart and my heavy breathing.

I recover my phone and, limping, I approach the corpse. The head is at a weird angle, while the rest of the body just lays there. A threat. I killed it, but I can't help thinking it's going to get up and try to retaliate.

There's a viscous liquid falling from where I hit it earlier.

I rub my eyes, but it's still there.

It's like the sample that Minerva brought us.

What's going on in these facilities? Do they know these creatures are free and roaming the place?

It's a dream, Jules. Stop the nonsense.

Right.

I pay attention to the whisper and what It's saying. Because It's exactly what I want, doing what I need.

Talking about answers.

I decide to follow that soft voice, maybe after the promise of knowledge, maybe after the promise of something else.

Later, I find myself in front of a door. The voice has stopped and there's dark energy coming from behind it. I open it and enter.

Faint, blue light illuminates the room.

A heavy presence, the one that has been following my every step, sits at the center. Around It, one of the walls is filled with handwriting in a language unknown to me.

I get closer to make sure my eyes are not deceiving me. They're not.

There's a bunch of people in front of the wall, on their knees, eyes white and staring at the ceiling. I glance at it. Nothing.

Those people don't see me. I take the four steps that separate me from them. I want to see who they are.

I stop in front of the closer one. Doctor Mendoza, my therapist.

Strange.

I don't recognize the others.

The high is warming off, my body getting tired. I yawn.

Someone approaches me from my left side. I turn to look at them.

"Jules, you came".

I know that voice. Soft, welcoming, like getting home after a long day and being greeted with a hug.

Home.

Don't trust.

Listen to It.

It's a walking shadow. A humanoid figure that I can't discern from the darkness enveloping It.

"You're real." I can barely manage a broken whisper.

"Of course," It says while opening Its arms to the sides, as if that was something obvious.

All my hairs stand on edge. I must leave. It's not safe.

"Leave, if that's what you want. But you could know everything, dear. Stay".

It's coming for me.

It would be so easy to say yes, to agree to that voice that has been with me for a long time. Intoxicating, accelerating, like the adrenaline of before. A rush that I don't really get in this job. And all the answers I could have, to share them with Sonna.

But my eyes go back to all those people. Puppets in Its game, with whoever purpose the figure wants them to have. It's a major warning.

I cannot accept...

"Join me, Jules." It extends a hand in my direction. "Infinite knowledge."

III: No Matter Dream or Reality

Yeah, no. I get out and walk in long steps, getting as far away from that room as possible.

My feet take me to a corridor, dimly illuminated by the light getting through the large windows on one of its sides. I stop and stare out, even though I can't see anything. That storm from the field is here too, spreading the dark in all directions.

Scratching. A deep howl. I should have kept my guard up, but the Presence really knew how to get inside me and distract me.

A cruel laugh.

I turn and one of those creatures is on me before I can register it, throwing me out the window with its sheer force.

A scream that I don't locate as mine is the soundtrack of my death.

MY BODY never hits the ground. But I'm still screaming for my life as I wake up curled on a metallic chair.

I'm hugging one of my knees to my chest while the other

rests on the floor. My breathing is ragged and I can't stop swallowing saliva, adrenaline, and morphine rushing through me, getting me high and euphoric. Exactly what I don't need right now.

I have to ground myself.

I stop screaming and take deep breaths to calm myself. Then, slowly, dreading the moment, I open my eyes and stick my head out to look around.

I'm in a white room whose color hurts my eyes after spending so much time in the dark. There're diplomas on the walls and some shelves with books and fake plants.

And there's a hand on my shoulder; a rich brown with golden subtones, with a ring on its annular finger. I look up. Doctor Mendoza, frowning, sweat all over his brow, looking at me like I'm some lost child.

Maybe I am.

"Everything is fine now, Jules. Do you want to tell me what happened after I asked you why you're here at this late hour?"

While I find my voice, he goes back to his chair, on the other side of the table.

"Dream. It was a dream. It was..."

A nightmare.

I gulp loudly, diverting my eyes from Doctor Mendoza to the papers on his desk.

"You can talk about it, Jules, you're safe now. Here. With me."

I stop listening and look at those papers. They bear my name and a psychological study. I remember when I did that, a few days before I started working here. And another one a couple of weeks before today. But I've never seen any results.

Time to develop the skill of reading upside down while trying not to get caught.

Why do I make my life so complicated?

There's a carnet-sized photo of me with basic data at its side: DOB, address, blood type, etc. Below is the important stuff. A lot of questions they asked me, handwritten notes, and the results.

"Paranoid. Delusional. They should cease every activity".

What?

Paranoid?

Doctor's lying. Play the game.

I'm being observed. Mendoza follows my line of sight as I go from the papers to his face.

"They suggested firing you. Said you have become too... Unpredictable".

"They?"

Doctor Mendoza puts his hands in his chair arms.

"La Junta, Jules. The Board. They want you out. Or wanted. We interceded".

I hum, prompting him to continue.

"Sonna, Ms. Sharma, myself. Even some other coworkers".

I shrugged. He massages one of his knees. I remember now: he was one of those people, with the Presence.

"It has you," I whisper.

"Excuse me?" Doctor Mendoza cocks his head, one eyebrow raised.

"Did something else happen, Jules?"

He knows. Shhh.

A ghost-touch lingers on the side of my neck, warming the space in all directions, almost bringing a smile to my lips and a flush to my face.

"No. Nada".

I've spoken too fast. Doctor Mendoza eyes me with suspicion. I raise a hand as if I'm swearing an oath and offer him an open smile.

"Promise".

There's a shift in the air before I hear the Presence's voice right in my ear.

"Keeping me a secret?" It hums. "Cute."

I ignore It and pay attention to Mendoza, who now has his hands intertwined on the table, on top of my record.

"Well, you're probably right and I'm just seeing signs where there are none. I apologize".

"No need".

A jarring silence settles between us. Mendoza fixes his ambar eyes on me, but I'm not able to retaliate and stare at his hands.

The clock marks the seconds in the distance. Only our even breaths accompany it.

With a smile, Doctor Mendoza breaks contact and closes my record.

"So, can I go now? There's a lot of work to do, reports to fill out. That stuff."

Mendoza makes a gesture towards the door.

I make a beeline to it, but the thought still lingers. How did I survive that fall? Maybe it's all been a dream after all.

"No, dear Jules," says the Presence.

I step out, into the darkness, and almost trip over my own feet. I'm back at the window. I can see the outside again.

That's it. I'm losing it.

I recline against the window, just breathing.

Why? How?

"Those meds were something else".

Speaking of *else*.

That warming sensation lingers on my neck, making me remember my lie to Mendoza and what really happened in that room.

"INFINITE KNOWLEDGE."

This should be good.

"Let's start, then. You know my name but I don't know yours."

It chuckles.

"Some people here call me the Presence. My real one is unpronounceable for your kind."

It's walking towards me.

"I see." I cross my arms over my chest. "So, what are you? I'm presuming not human."

Before I can think of anything, the Presence's running a hand through my hair. I lean into it. It's grounding, calming.

"Clever. I'm not. Some have called me deity, others, an alien, a few, the name of some catholic demon."

The touch is so relaxing that, for a moment, I think of just focusing on that and ending the conversation here. But I want the answers, as confusing as they are.

"But you're not any of that."

"No."

It moves Its fingers slightly, fiddling with the ends of my hair.

"What're you then?"

It whispers in my ear, giving me shivers.

"Whatever you want me to be, dear Jules."

I gulp. The possibilities of that statement…

No. I can't follow that line of thought. I have to put some distance between us.

"Leave my hair alone."

The Presence does so and there's a hollow feeling when the contact is lost, as if my body misses it. I don't. It's too much, and I need to think clearly. I can't fall into Its trap.

That doesn't mean the touching has stopped. Instead, It tugs at my trousers, getting them up enough to show my wound. It's not bleeding anymore, but it still looks gross, fresh, and painful, though the morphine is doing a good job. I have almost forgotten about it.

"I apologize for that. I'll take care of it".

I should be creeped out. It just admitted that those creatures served It.

"How is it possible that something like you exists?"

"How is it possible that humans exist?"

It's getting near me, but not touching me again. For now.

"We evolved".

"So did I".

Fascinating.

The Presence circles me, settling behind me with Its hands on my shoulders.

"I control this place, Jules. Is a matter of time before I introduce myself to those humans you call friends." One of the hands moves to my neck, slowly, caressing it, with a touch as soft as Its voice. "You could be by my side when that happens".

Promises of knowledge, as much as I want. Of power. Of salvation when Its creatures invade the facilities.

"Sonna too," I demand in the same low voice, not to disturb the atmosphere created.

The Presence makes a noise of agreement as Its other hand starts traveling down my chest.

I throw my head back, enough to rest it on the Presence's shoulder. I could stay like this forever. Lost in Its touch. Enjoying the undivided attention.

It wants to kill you!

True. I snap back to reality and slap Its arms to get them off me, getting away from It.

Silence. I feel bad for how I treated It. No need to be so aggressive.

No. Manipulation 101.

"I'm not joining you," I declare as I limp to the door.

The Presence doesn't follow me or say anything else. It lets me go. Its eyes fixed on my back.

Seduced by an alien entity is not how I want to end my days.

BURYING the memory deep within my mind, I start walking in some direction so I can get back to my room. That's my goal now. Get to my room, lay down in bed, and sleep until I forget.

Though, I'm gonna need a compass to get me through this place.

A hysterical laugh escapes my lips as I get further and further into the darkness, letting it swallow me whole.

LOST. You're getting lost.

Yes…

No. I know where I'm going: back to Sonna. She'll know what to do.

Or maybe not. But, at least, I'll have a friendly face with me.

I keep walking, turning, helping myself with a hand on the wall. Can I trust my memory anymore? In the dark, all these corridors feel the same. Wide, deadly, cold, full of dangers.

I groan loudly. Where am I going?

Lost. You're lost. My mind is mocking me.

I'm not. I'm close, I can feel it in my guts. Round the next corner and

Dead end. Nowhere to go except back.

Lost. I'm lost.

I fall to my knees, defeated. There's a lump in my throat and I close my eyes, retaining the tears.

I just want to get out of here.

A spark. A thought, morphing into an idea that could make perfect sense. That makes perfect sense. The Presence has told me very clearly.

It wants me. To add me to Its collection of people.

Hell no.

I slap myself with all the strength I'm capable of. It stings, but I repeat the action.

"Wake up, Jules!"

My shouts reverberate in all directions, probably alerting more of those creatures of my position. I don't care. I'm getting out of here no matter what.

I keep hitting myself and screaming. Hopefully, that'll startle my brain out of this dream.

Wake. Up.

One final hard slap.

Bright, white light behind my closed eyes indicates to me that I'm not in the corridor anymore.

"Jules, stop it. Jules!" Doctor Mendoza's voice reaches me through my stupor and the ringing in my ears.

He grabs my hands, forcing me to stop and open my eyes to look at him. The light is too much, so I regret the action immediately.

I blink to alleviate my eyes. Burning touch on my wrists. The feeling of being observed.

We're watching. Help us.

Don't trust. It's a lie.

For once, I look directly into Mendoza's eyes. They're a deep amber tone. A shadow crosses them.

Mendoza kindly backs away, smiling, calm, but he's still holding my hands.

Sweat. Heat. Disturbing.

"Don't touch me!"

I snap while getting away from him as far as this chair allows me.

He eyes me with concern but does as I've asked him while walking a few steps backward to give me my very needed space.

The scene changes.

Doctor Mendoza is sitting, one leg crossed over the other, on the patient's chair, wearing regular clothes.

I find myself on his chair, plastic creaking under me with my quick movement as I get up. The meticulously organized desk is in front of me, its things, for once, facing me.

My psychological report is there, too. Empty.

I direct all my attention back to Mendoza and put my hands on the table, feeling the wood with my stretched fingers. When I speak, it's not only me doing it.

"We're getting rid of you".

There's a chorus of sounds, voices high and low, soft and rough. It's me. It's The Board. It's the Presence.

It's Us.

"You can't do that," he exclaims, getting up and putting his hands on the table too. "After all these years working for you."

He loses his strength as he speaks.

Two creatures appear at his sides, on their hind legs, looking at both of us. But they're here for Mendoza. I'm not the enemy. Not at this moment.

They each grab one of his arms.

"Do not make us repeat ourselves."

Doctor Mendoza plants his feet on the floor, making a case of not following the orders given. Resisting.

Don't listen to them. Listen to me. To you.

Wake. Up!

My own shouts reach me, turning all the white in the night for a second.

When I can see again, one of the creatures is moving its claw. I can only watch as it pierces Mendoza from behind and goes out through his chest. Skin, spine, lungs, ribs, more skin, muscles, tendons. And blood, getting everywhere. The desk, the floor, my face. It's warm and fills the air with a metallic taste. It falls off my hair drop by drop, exploding against the white tiles. It falls down my arm with a steady stream, like a river of death.

I do not scream.

The scene changes again and I'm back on my chair, in front

of Doctor Mendoza, who gives no sign of knowing whatever just happened and is, also, very much alive. My eyes travel to his chest, clothed in a blue jersey under a white coat.

He's in one piece, there's no blood, and my voice is just mine.

What…?

A slap echoes through my bones.

Back to the dark corridor.

"Wake up, Jules! It's not real."

Another slap.

I'm not on my knees anymore.

"Jul?" Sonna always sounds like home. "Hey!"

I wake up exalted, almost hitting her with my elbow. She backs up but keeps a hand on me. Warmth spreads all over and I know I'm safe with her. I'll always be.

She's still wearing day-to-day clothes, but there's no coat, and her brown curls are loose; it looks like a halo, encircling her head. For a moment, it could be, because this really feels like a miracle.

The nightmare has ended. I close my eyes for a second as relief overflows me.

Sonna's hands move to cup my cheeks. I open my eyes and share a deep breath with her.

"You almost woke up the entire facility with your screams. Bad dream?"

She gets a stool and sits right beside me.

"More like a nightmare," I try to joke, but it's not funny.

Sonna looks at me with fondness, almost smiling, her hair accompanying every slight movement of her head. Then, she points at my microscope with her chin. My glasses are on the right side. The mysterious sample is on the platen.

A headache sits on my brain, palpitating to a rhythm of its own.

"I need to ask. Is it still Friday?"

Sonna alternates between the microscope and me before laughing, briefly and quietly.

"Technically, Saturday, given that it is almost five in the morning. But you can say so if you want to".

"Right".

Don't trust. Don't trust. Don't trust.

I know. Shut up. It's Sonna. I trust her with my life.

"You've always been a deep sleeper, Jul, but damn."

I snort. If she only knew.

"So, did you find something?"

I put my glasses on.

"About what?"

"The sample, obviously," she says while flicking me in the head.

"Obviously."

I turn to the microscope, not knowing what to answer her. I can't even remember if I saw something before all of that.

One of her hands finds my knee.

"Are you sure you're fine, Jules? If that nightmare rattled you so much, we can leave it here and go to sleep, or talk to someone. I'm sure Doctor Mendoza wouldn't mind talking to us at this hour".

Doctor Mendoza. The memory of blood fills my nostrils, the crack of bones fills my ear.

"Is he okay?

I can't help wondering, even if that makes me look suspicious to Sonna.

"Yes. Why wouldn't he?" Sonna straightens and gives me a look.

"It's a long story."

"I'm dying to hear it."

Hilarious.

I nod. She gets closer to me and wiggles her eyebrows.

"So." She gestures to the microscope.

Right, the sample. With the same characteristics as the creature's blood.

They don't like light. They can move on it, but it has to be pitch black. They tolerate artificial light, but not sunlight.

"Like vampires," says Sonna matter of fact.

I was thinking out loud. But she's correct, even though I don't believe that's what we're dealing with. Whatever they are experimenting with down there, it's not vampires.

"They're nocturnal. What they're keeping behind that door. They live in the night."

If we take a look at the sample before night bleeds into day again, there's going to be movement, unlike when Minerva brought it.

Only, we don't need to. It's quite obvious.

Sonna frowns, wondering.

How can I explain everything to her?

A few seconds pass, her hand doing little circles over my clothed knee. But, in the end, she doesn't comment on it. Instead:

"We should go to sleep. And we'll talk with Minerva first thing in the morning."

"Agree."

I get up from my stool, the leather complaining, whining under me. But I don't go very far from it. I hit the floor with my left ankle and pain erupts, burning my nerves until there are no thoughts and only screaming through all my body.

My teeth grind as a yelp escapes my lips and I fall down, to Sonna's arms.

She knows I just didn't trip with my own feet.

"You okay?"

I nod and put my hands on her shoulders to stabilize myself. Without another word, I move a hand to my trousers, to the leg that's killing me.

"No matter dream or reality", I have thought once. Now I'm sure everything that happened was both.

I crumpled the fabric between my legs, getting a strong grasp around it, though my fingers won't stop trembling. Sonna notices and puts a hand over mine, the other on my side, stabilizing me, rubbing the spot for comfort. Not really working, but I appreciate it.

Painfully slow, I put my trouser up until we can both see what's under it.

A scar. Red, closed, with dry blood all over it.

It's been real.

I see Sonna's lips moving, but I can't hear her. My ears ring, my brain's silenced.

What about the Presence? What about what happened to Doctor Mendoza? And the creatures.

All real.

Sonna shakes me and I focus on her. Her dark face, her freckles, her panicked eyes, and her voice.

"What happened, Jules? You haven't moved from here, have you?"

"No." My voice is too weak. I don't like how I sound. I clear my throat and try again. "I'll explain everything, I swear."

Sonna accepts that answer for now.

Little smiles, mirroring each other, formed on our faces. We've only known one another for some months, but it feels like a whole time. It feels like forever.

Sonna puts my arm over her shoulders to take some weight off my injured ankle.

"I'm taking you to see someone and, meanwhile, you'll explain yourself, sir."

"Yes, my captain," I say while saluting her.

Step by step, we leave behind my discovery and get closer to the door.

A dark energy presses against my shoulder blades and surrounds me, breaking the comfortable silence.

"Jules. You can't escape me, dear." I know the speaker. That softness.

The Presence's voice is coming from every direction, directly to me. Its words are only for my ears; just like that relaxing touch was only for my body.

Cold blood rushing alongside fear and excitement. Intoxicating.

Sonna carries us out of the room, towards the infirmary. But my thoughts go in a very different direction.

It's coming for me.

Coming for me.

Me.

Or, maybe, It already has me.

15
THEM
TIFFANY PAIGE

Every night, I grew fearful when the moon replaced the sun. When the songs of the air were no longer in the breasts of birds but on the legs of crickets. And when the air was still, heavy fear smothered me during the cloak of darkness. As the knowledge of the evil of the world burdened my body, I laid awake with shallow breath and a pit in my stomach. For it was night when *they* would come and leave *their* mark.

On Sundays, Ma would rise early and get started in the kitchen to prepare for our big Sunday dinner. She rose after the moon hid but the sun had not yet shown.

"It's the best hours of the day." Ma would say. "It's just you and God in the still of the morning."

In our small kitchen, she would prepare pies, create the dough for her legendary butter biscuits, and fill the glass pitcher to brew sweet tea in the afternoon sun. She'd set out our church outfits and keep herself busy until it was time to return to the house of the Lord.

Our community piled into the doors of Beaworthy Baptist, squeezing into the hard pews. Paper fans waved up and down the aisle as friendly voices danced through the heated church. The children, sweaty in our Sunday best, bobbed our heads as we were unable to see over the fancy church hats of the mothers who sat in front of us. The white gloves of the ushers were a costume of helpfulness and a symbol of purity as they handed us tambourines and more fans. Although Miss Betty, the lead usheress, was a force to be reckoned with, I still felt safe when I saw those gloves. The gloves were the opposite of *those* who wore a white costume of hate.

Every Sunday, Reverend Sam would shout until his voice was hoarse with his biblical message, and sweat pooled at his temples. He was a heavy-set man with reading glasses on a golden chain that rested on his big belly. He had a powerful presence. He would spend an ample amount of time preaching about how to keep ourselves out of hell. That the mere thought of devils and demons for all of eternity should set us straight. I felt, however, that Reverend Sam didn't spend nearly enough time on the devils and demons in the world around us. What did we do wrong to suffer in the way we had?

I could also tell if *they* came Saturday night when I was at church Sunday morning. Even if I didn't see them, *they* always left *their* mark. I could tell by the hushed conversation of the adults before church started. Pastor Sam would say a prayer over the family of the body that was found. I never needed to know the details to know what happened. I didn't need details to know it was gruesome, unwarranted, and evil. That's what *they* brought when *they* came.

My parents' interactions were also a dead giveaway. No matter how often *they* would come, it always brought a cold cloud over our town. As a community, we grieved every time. My father, a serious man, grew even more serious than usual. I could see the rage bubble beneath his skin. Where my mother would weep or busy herself to keep from weeping, my father would grow stoic and seething. He would leave our house before Sunday service and sometimes not return until after service, alongside the other men in our community, like Mr. Waters.

Mr. Gerald Waters was a tall man. Tall and skinny. He owned a small convenience store and a few shoe-shining stands in town. He was friendly to us kids, but his reputation betrayed him. Some kids from school said Mr. Waters was the reason *they* came in the night. That *they* didn't like him and the things he was up to. Mr. Waters was considered a troublemaker to *them* despite Mr. Waters being praised in our community. He used his money to contribute to our causes and lend to his neighbors. He was able to keep us afloat and *they* despised that. He was actively working on bringing us further and *they* would not allow it.

I always liked Mr. Waters. He lived across the road from us and would slip Ella and me hard candies anytime we passed by his store.

"Staying on the straight and narrow, Elvin?" He'd ask me before letting me choose a sweet treat from the palm of his hand. I would nod eagerly every time. Grateful for the special attention he showed us kids in the neighborhood.

"Don't tell anyone I gave this to you for free now. You'll run me out of business."

I'd heed his warning, laugh, and scurry on my way. I knew he sang the same song and dance for all the kids in the neighborhood. Mr. Waters knew a small gesture of kindness was always needed and he wanted us to be taken care of.

But when I woke up that Sunday morning, everything was quiet. Everything felt normal. Just like many of the mornings before. It had been too long. The whispers of late-night meetings would spread to *them* like wildfire. Deep down I knew *they* would be back that night.

After the service and after the fellowship, Ella and I walked home behind Ma and Pa. The heat of the afternoon sun was almost unbearable in our scratchy Sunday best. But I welcomed the sun. She could grow as hot as she needed. Her bright light is what kept me feeling safe.

Ella and I changed out of our church clothes and into our play clothes. And without hesitation, we were out the door.

"Gerald said tonight." I heard my father's deep voice float out of our window.

Mr. Waters.

Mr. Waters wasn't only a target for *them* because he was wealthy and gave back to his community. It wasn't that simple. Mr. Waters brought us together. He held progressive thoughts. He talked about voting, equal rights, and ownership. He knew as a race we were more than the color of our skin. Mr. Waters wanted more for us. And for *them,* that was not okay.

I tried to hang around the window to listen while Ella was already in the backyard among the fruit trees but my father's hushed tones with my mother were not clearly audible.

IT WAS the time before dinner when your stomach was ready but the cooking wasn't. I helped Ella pick a plum from the tree, and we quickly devoured the juicy fruit and threw the pit behind us. Ella asked to play and I did my best but I was distracted. Ella was still immune to the world around her. My parents and I made sure of it. Ma would discreetly tell me to avoid Main Street and I almost certainly knew that meant Mr. Water's store was targeted. Or it could have meant that the police in town were hanging around and handing out beatings for fun. Mr. Waters' store was often a target of *theirs*. Broken glass. Stolen items. Unsuccessful arson. *They* always left their mark.

"C'mon and play!"

I heard the voice of Freddy Andrews. He lived further up our dirt road, his house pushed back closer to the woods. I used to go there often to play, to escape the day's heat. To get my feet wet in the creek that snaked between the trees. This was before I knew what happened in those trees and in that water. Before I knew the sun was my friend.

I instructed Ella to knock on the Waters' front door and ask for their daughter, Anna Mae, while I made my way up the street to Freddy. Anna Mae was the same age as Ella and Mrs. Waters watched Anna Mae like a hawk. She didn't trust a soul when it came to her daughter and I couldn't blame her. I liked when Ella went over there because I knew she too would be watched like a hawk.

"Tag, you're it!"

Freddy gave me no opportunity to greet him. He was already on the go. I knew I could use a game to distract my mind from my hungry belly and the last words I just heard my father say about tonight. Once Freddy and I tired ourselves out, we laid in the tall grasses next to his house.

"It's almost been a year. Since Peter." Freddy's voice was solemn; it took a completely different tone than just the few minutes before when we were laughing and running and hiding behind bushes and homes.

Peter.

Peter Andrews, Freddy's older brother, was a lot older than Freddy and me. He was one of those cool older brothers that all the kids in the neighborhood wanted to be around. That was until *they* got involved.

I shuddered. Forcing the trauma of that day out of my mind. It was when I realized that Mr. Waters wasn't *their* only target. It was truly all of us.

"You alright now, Freddy?"

Freddy was quiet. He then responded without answering my question.

"My pops has been on a rampage for a year now in wanting justice for Peter. In the station every Monday, asking for updates on Peter's case. Even when they spit in his direction or laugh in his face, he never backs down. That's the ultimate sign of bravery, I think. Never backing down."

It is me who was quiet then. I thought I held all the suffering but Freddy lost his older brother. Mr. Andrews lost a child. It was no wonder the Waters' were so over-protective of Anna Mae. I lost my innocence and the neighborhood lost a trusted face. We were all in pain.

I stood up and a slight breeze tickled my skin. The sun began to bid her farewell and it was time to head home to eat and prepare for the night.

"You know they're coming. Tonight. Pops and the others, they talk about it all the time."

I swallow hard. Dramatically even.

"Why?" I asked a question no one knew the answer to. Why did *they* come?

"A bunch of devils. But we're ready. And they're going to pay for what they did to Peter."

The vengeance in his voice gave me goosebumps. I ran home.

Inside, the house was warm and filled with the scents of a homemade meal made with love. I hugged Ma and she shooed me off and told me to wash up.

"Where's Ella?"

"The Waters," I responded.

The slam of the front door felt strange.

My father stood, watching my mom move across the dirt road and knock on the Water's door, from the window. He smoked his pipe, with cherry-flavored tobacco; I loved the smell.

"Everything alright, Elvin. Wash up. We starved now."

I wash the dirt and stress of the day off and change into my bedclothes. When I was done, Ma was hugging Ella in the main room and Pa was back to reading a newspaper in his chair. I heard Ma give Ella the same wash up instructions.

"Something going on?" I asked and Ma shook her head. Her favorite dress, a tawny lightweight cotton dress, moved with her as she moved around the room. Putting her dish ware on the table.

"Smells great," I said, trying to get a better response out of her. She seemed frazzled. The way she rushed to get Ella. I instantly remembered Freddy's warnings and my heart dropped. "They coming, ain't they, Ma?

She said nothing. She wouldn't even look at me.

"What is it they want?" I nearly shouted at her. She paused in her tracks, her eyes narrowed in on me.

My father reprimanded me for raising my voice but my mother took a softer approach and told me not to worry. Neither parent denied my claim. Neither parent answered my question.

"Is they coming for Mr. Waters? For the Andrews family? For us?" I continued on. I needed an answer.

"You think a bunch of overweight men on horses in bedsheets is supposed to worry us? You've nothing to fear but the Lord, son. Now eat. Enough talk."

My father's attempt at minimizing *their* threat did not work. Because of Peter. Because of all I've seen. The mark *they* left. Pa knew as I knew but I sat in silence, unable to fully enjoy my Sunday dinner, my favorite part of the week. I couldn't relax knowing when the moon replaced the sun, *they* would be here.

When it was time for bed, Ma, Ella, and I all packed into Ella and I's shared room. Ma spent extra time with me because she knew I was worried. She knew I would be up all night, sick with fear. She knew it because she knew she would be, too.

Ella, without a care in the world, fell asleep quickly as she did every night. Oblivious to the world around her. Ma laid on the spare cot in Ella and I's room. I could tell by her shallow breathing that she was still awake.

"What's Pa's plan?"

"Sleep now, Elvin. You've school in the morning."

"What's Mr. Water's plan? What is it they want?"

"Nobody wants nothing but for you to fall asleep."

Time passed and neither Ma nor I slept but neither of us said another word. I could hear the record player in the main room and could smell more cherry tobacco wafting in from under the bedroom door. These are comforting sounds and comforting smells and knowing Ma was staying by my side until I slept was comforting. But I knew no rest would make it to me tonight.

EVENTUALLY, Ma left the room and joined Pa in the main room. My bedroom was pitched black save for the gray moonlight that shone through the single window. The window that faced the street and faced the Water's house.

I cracked the window, allowing the cool evening air into the bedroom, and sat back in my bed. But I really cracked it so I could listen knowing I would hear them before I saw them. And heard them, I did.

The ground vibrated as the sound of horses' hooves grew louder the closer they came. Horses, a beautiful and innocent creature forced to do the devil's bidding. The light from under the door suddenly went dark and the record player stopped playing. I knew Ma and Pa were on alert, no more sounds came from the main room.

As *they* grew closer, my heart continued to sink. What was the plan? Ma and Pa pretended as if there was nothing to worry about but we all knew this was a lie. *They* were all the reason to worry. My teeth chattered from fear.

"Come on out now Waters! You knows we here!"

A tangy voice called out. Acidic. Foreign. Not one of our own. But one of *them*.

I peeked out of the bedroom window. Only 60 seconds before, the night air was still and peaceful. Solitude and peace, these are things we deserved. But now, nothing else could be heard but yelling and horses neighing.

"Get down!" Ma appeared in the room behind me and nearly gave me a heart attack. "I just knew you'd be in here awake. You want them over here next?"

She left the room and I carefully raised my face back to the window.

My eyes were lit up by the fire torches *they* carried. *They* circled Mr. Waters' home, which was pitch black like our own. Soon enough Mr. Waters came outside. His hands in his pockets. Casual. As if the commotion was no big deal and it was a typical Sunday night. As if he was used to the harassment.

From up the road, I could see Mr. Andrews walk down with a shotgun on his shoulder. Next to him, were Mr. Johnny Brown and Mr. Granville Jones. Each with their own shotguns, resting on their shoulders.

Mr. Johnny owned a fruit stand that had the sweetest apples every Fall. Mr. Granville Jones was an older man and a deacon in our church. Neither he nor Mr. Johnny lived on our road. They were both a good twenty-minute walk away. Everyone knew this was coming and everyone was prepared.

"What can I help you boys with?" Mr. Waters said to *them*.

There were just under a dozen of *them*. In the street. On his lawn. One of the men on horseback fired a shot in the air. Another threw a rock in Mr. Waters' window.

"Surely that was an accident." He responded.

Mr. Waters was mocking them. Even in the dark of night, I

could see his face showed them no fear. His face was calm and no emotion was displayed on it but slight amusement. The other three men who showed their faces outside, all looked furious. No fear in their body language. Only anger. Only disgust.

"Wasn't no accident—"

Racial slurs and curses flew from their mouths as *they* started laughing and yelling. The fire crackled on their torches.

"We don't like what you been doing. And we taking some action."

Cheers of evilness radiated throughout the small crowd of *them* all dressed in white hoods.

"Elvin!"

Ma re-entered the room and scolded me once again.

"Will the Waters' be alright?"

"They sure will. The Lord got them. He has got you too, now."

"Then why didn't the Lord have Peter?"

Ma lectured me about questioning the Lord. That I should be trusting in Him. But watching the look on Mr. Andrew's face, in my soul I knew none of this made sense.

Ma and I heard two more shots and dropped to the ground.

"Stay on this floor you hear me? Stay 'way from that window, Elvin. The Lord got us but He don't got no fools. You hear?" Her voice was coarse with worry and fear. She was deadly serious.

Ma crawled back into the main room with Pa and I crawled behind her.

Pa stood in front of the window with not a care. His own shotgun leaned against the wall next to his foot

"Elvin, why is you not sleeping?" He asked.

"What's going on out there? Who is shooting?" I asked.

"Shit," Pa cussed.

He moved away from the window and hurried out the back

door. He was running towards the well because what Ma and I did not know yet was that the Waters' home was on fire.

Ma followed Pa to the backyard and I watched from the front window. The fire, that not long ago danced on the torches, now engulfed Mr. Water's home. I knew no pail of water was going to slow it down.

Some of *them* were on the ground, surrounding someone. Someone who presumably was shot. I could no longer see Mr. Andrews. Or Mr. Waters. But I could see Mr. Granville Jones' small old body walking towards the woods behind the homes across the way. Maybe that's where everyone went. To the creek. For water.

I saw Pa come around our front yard. Two old tin buckets sloshed with water. He walked past the devils, as if they did not exist, and threw the water on the home. It was as if the buckets were teardrops. The effort was there. Both the pain and the gesture. But it was wasted. The fire only continued to grow.

"Come here, boy. You a friend of Waters? You a trouble-maker, too?"

One of the men shouted at Pa who walked back towards our house. I began to cry as I glanced at Pa's shotgun, still in the house, leaned against the wall.

"Elvin."

Ma came up from behind me in frustration but she knew if I looked away, my fear would only grow with what I couldn't see.

"They's nothing but a bunch of fools. You've nothing to fear, Elvin. You should go back to bed."

Her reassurance was wasted.

"Where are Anna May and Mrs. Waters?"

"Safe. No one in there."

"You hear me talkin' boy. Someone gonna pay!" The man shouted at Pa again and I watched Pa stop dead in his tracks. Through the darkness, he and I locked eyes through the window. He slowly turned around to face the group of white men.

I grabbed his shotgun.

I had no business holding Pa's shotgun. It was heavy in my arms but no heavier than each step I took toward my father. My fear had no ceases but I knew my father was no match for a group of hateful men when he only had his fists and two empty pails.

I managed to reach Pa, I snuggled behind his back. Unsure of what was transpiring in front of me. Evil faces. A raging fire. But resting my head in the small of Pa's back put me at ease.

"Go on, Elvin."

I heard Pa's voice low. Forced. Spoken through gritted teeth. He did not want me out here. He knew he was in no position to protect me.

I heard the men continue to shout.

"Take the gun, Pa."

Pa turned around briefly and grabbed the shotgun from my hands. I stayed behind his back.

"Time to go home now. You done caused enough damage boys." Pa said to them in an authoritative voice.

"We ain't going anywhere!" One shouted.

A shot rang in the air. My body hit the ground on instinct. My father still stood strong and I didn't see any other bodies dropped.

Mr. Granville moved slowly up the road. The shotgun pointed in the direction of *them.* The remaining men of our community held various containers of water. Their efforts mute.

"It's time to leave." Mr. Granville raised his voice but did not shout. He did reload and shoot again. Missing again.

"Now I know you a decent shot," Pa shouted towards the deacon before he also aimed his gun towards the men.

The men, many with *their* own guns, began to retreat.

Putting *their* fallen partner in crime on the back of a horse. Satisfied with the disrupted sleep of the community and the house set ablaze.

I remained on the ground. And Pa remained focused with his weapon.

Mr. Andrews joined the gun stand-off. Mr. Waters and Mr. Johnny Brown, too.

Soon, several shots rang. The deadly sound ricocheted off the windows of the homes on our road. The heat of the fire and loud bangs were enough to make me think I was going to pass out. I was directly in the line of hate and deadly fire. It was too much.

"Shit."

Again, I heard Pa cuss before he ran away from my side.

The rest of *them* ran and retreated from *their* crime scene. *They* provided enough damage and trauma for one night.

I looked over to where Pa headed and saw the other men, the other ones of us, huddled around Mr. Waters. What *they* came to do, *they* accomplished. Mr. Waters was hit and bleeding out like a Christmas hog in the middle of the road.

Behind me, Ma came to my side to comfort me. She held both my shoulders as she ushered me back into the house. She instructed me to stay in the room with Ella. And she wept as she moved about the house gathering supplies to help Mr. Waters. But like the home on fire, it was useless. *They* took a pillar of our community. *Their* jealousy, fear, and hate haunted our street once again.

If I had gone to sleep like Ella, I would have woken to my father's exhausted and serious face. I would have witnessed Ma's desperate weeping. The charred remains of the home across the street were in view as I brought in the milk bottles from the front steps in the morning before school. The horse dung on the street and the smell of anger in the air. And eventually, the lack of the friendly face with a palm full of candy.

Yes, *they* came at night, when the moon replaced the sun. *They* were gone by morning but *they* always left a trace. Whether it was a swollen body in the creek like Peter Andrews or an innocent body swinging in the wind. Whether it was a few broken windows or a completely destroyed home and family. *They* always left their mark.

16

A DEATH'S BALLAD

CARMEN DE WIT

She was a half creature from the sea, and she intended on destroying a man's life.

She tried giving human men another chance after her best friend convinced her to do so. For the past few months, Signe had been together with a man, but him cheating on her was the last straw in a string of countless other disappointments.

"I'm glad I dumped his ass," Signe said as soon as Cara slid into the chair opposite hers.

"Hold on a second, I need a drink before you start ranting." Cara waved, and a waiter came over to take up her regular choice: a white wine.

Signe let the ice cubes in her own ice tea spin around while she waited for Cara's drink to arrive. The bar tonight wasn't too packed. Only a few regular customers were lined up at the bar, empty glasses spread out before them. The bartender serving them had a rough look about him, but appearances, Signe discovered, were often misleading. A soft song played in the background, soothing her nerves somewhat.

Cara laid her hand atop hers. "Why are you glad you dumped Owen?"

"He cheated on me." Signe had no idea how her voice was steady, as her knees wobbled and her hands shook. She could collapse any moment, really. "And I want him to regret that he did."

"Oh sweetie, I'm sure you do." Cara trailed off when the waiter came back with a glass of wine. He smiled shyly as Cara thanked him. She leaned in closer when he left. "What do you need for your little scheme?"

Signe grinned. "This is why we're best friends."

THE MOON OVERHEAD illuminated her as she stepped out of the sea and into the smallest town possible: there was only one street lined with several houses, two stores, and one inn. It was completely deserted, which was normal considering the late hour, but Signe still thought the sight was kind of eerie. Hiding here would certainly be difficult, but she was sure she could manage it.

So into the forest next to town she went. No one reasonable would be awake in the middle of the night so it didn't make any sense to knock on someone's door right now. A thin layer of snow covered the ground, her shoes leaving behind a trail. Signe had no time to worry about it. With little to no magic in her veins, she wasn't able to get rid of it. She first had to find some kind of shelter for the remaining of the night.

A wolf's howl echoed in the distance, followed by several more. The wind swept through the barren trees, some of its branches coming dangerously close to her head, and Signe had to duck out of the way more than once.

"Those damned branches," she muttered angrily to herself. Huddling inside the collar of her coat, she didn't spot the figure coming her way. Signe just passed them when they called out to her.

"What's your business at this hour?"

She whirled around in surprise, then slipped on a patch of ice hidden from sight by snow.

"Ugh that hurts," she groaned when she landed on her butt. The stranger offered her a hand, but she turned it down by getting up herself. It was weird enough to be approached by someone at three in the morning. She rushed off and didn't dare stop when they yelled, "I'm just here to help!" after her.

Like hell you are, she thought.

HER MAGIC TRICKLED BACK into her veins just as the sun rose in the sky. It always made her feel good when the moon released its hold on her. As a half-siren, her magic didn't disappear completely at full moon—unlike full-blood sirens. On those days, she still felt a sliver of her magic linger during the night.

With a confident stride, she walked into town, her clothing changed with a snap of her fingers into normal human attire. The merchants were already up and about, their wares displayed on their stalls. Seagulls flew around town, cawing loudly while finding leftover scraps to gobble up. No one paid attention to her, and she was grateful for that. The less conspicuous she appeared, the easier the plan she and Cara came up with yesterday could succeed.

It was perhaps not entirely in line with her character, and while she had some doubts about it, they were washed away when she spotted *him*, casually strolling around the market with his sister in tow. Her claws threatened to burst through. Everything inside her demanded that she go over now and confronted Owen about cheating on her, but that alone wouldn't bring her satisfaction. Her anger could wait for a little bit longer.

Owen once told her that he was afraid of spiders and while

she hadn't been able to get her hands on spiders on such short notice, it was something she could use to her advantage. Cara had suggested an illusion that would last for a day or two. Signe, however, had bigger plans than just a simple illusion: she was planning on conjuring a tarantula the size of an elephant.

"That can work if you're powerful enough." Hanna, his sister, came up to her. Signe turned to her, alarmed. She hadn't heard her at all and she also had failed to remember that Hanna was able to read minds—magic was extremely rare among humans, and she was only of the few who possessed the gift.

"I need a distraction for that though," Signe said, glaring at Owen's back.

"A power outage should do the trick." Hanna followed her gaze. "I do hope you're over him. He didn't deserver you in the slightest."

Signe huffed. "Why would *you* help me? You're his sister after all."

Hanna eyed her a for a moment. "You're not the only one whose trust he broke."

That shut her up, though she recovered after a tense moment passed. "Prove me I can trust you then."

NIGHTFALL HAD JUST SET in when Signe left the forest, its safety chipping away with each step she took. She glanced around before she entered the main street, then gestured to Cara that it was safe. Signe would lead the way to the inn while Cara made sure they weren't followed. A narrow alley led them to the back of the inn, where Hanna stood leaning against the brick wall, a cigarette dangling from her fingers.

The stench here was unbearable. Rats scuttled out from trash bags carelessly thrown by owners and flies swarmed around her head. Signe almost gagged. "How did you survive in this town? The smell is awful!"

"I didn't," Hanna simply replied. "You just get used to it."

Signe couldn't find the strength to respond.

"You guys are the loudest people I've ever heard though." Hanna trampled the cigarette with the back of her shoe. "Never been on a heist before, huh?"

"Bold of you to assume we never have," Cara said. "We actually do have some experience."

Signe remembered all their missions going horribly wrong. She always had been the quiet one between the two of them while Cara always managed to rig their heists somehow when they were so close to not getting caught. She wasn't going to mention that though.

She nodded in agreement instead.

"Let's get on with it then," Hanna stated. "Did you manage to get the key?"

Signe dangled the brass key in front of her face. "Of course I did. I'm not an incompetent thief."

Hanna snatched the cord from her hands. "I don't have time for your silly antics."

With a smooth turn, the door to the backyard opened. A short walk through the overgrown garden—all sorts of wildflowers, some nettles near the fences lining the property, and a bench shoved against the window—took them to the back door, which also opened easily with the same key.

A light went on the left house, and they halted, their black clothes blending in with their surroundings. Hopefully, they wouldn't call the cops on them for trespassing on private property as they ignored the glaring sign hammered to the back door.

Signe took the lead, an orb just floating above her palm to light up the kitchen. It was eerily quiet in the building, as if it had been abandoned just for this night. She remembered a time the inn had been packed with people all over the world, stopping by for a night before continuing their journeys.

Butcher knives hung in racks above the sink, glinting when her orb got closer. At first, Signe thought water glided along its blades, but on closer inspection she saw it was blood and recoiled, almost crashing into the stacked crates behind her. She barely held in her curse as Hanna twisted her body away just in time.

"Watch where you're going next time, will you?"

Signe didn't have time to respond, as Hanna had already turned away for the staircase. A second light orb flew behind her by Signe's own doing. It was Hanna's task to get the key to the cellar, where the fuse box was. She silently followed Cara to the living, noticing bloodied feathers spread out on the tiles on her way out.

Her stance grew tense, restless. A sense of foreboding overwhelmed her, and she tried to shrug it off at first, but it urged her to not go further.

Signe just yelled "Stop!" when a figure rose in the dark, dagger in hand to attack Cara. Shrieking, she pushed him away, but she wasn't quick enough; the damage already had been done as Cara clutched her side, blood gushing through her fingers. She rushed to her side when Cara whimpered in pain.

Licking his dry lips, the man advanced Cara again, his hands going for her bleeding wound.

She immediately understood. "He's craving blood!" His eyes blazed red as soon as she mentioned blood. His movements became more predatory, and his hands transformed into claws rivalling her own. Black fur began sprouting along his arms and legs until it completely covered the human skin.

The apprehension she felt earlier wasn't misplaced at all. They were dealing with a demon on the loose.

She swooped Cara in her arms and moved her back to the kitchen. "Stay here please." She then examined the wound, ripped off some bandage from an aid kit near, and firmly applied it to her injury. Signe hoped the bleeding would stop soon.

"We'll get you real medical attention when we've caught the demon, alright?" Signe gently brushed Cara's sweaty bangs out of the way. Cara gave her a determined nod as if to say, "Go kick that demon's ass."

The room flooded suddenly with light as Signe left the kitchen. Shielding her eyes with her arm, she carefully found her way to Hanna, who had two keys around her neck. The demon screeched loudly, his claws scraping over the wooden floor in an attempt to get away.

She used this opportunity to perform a containment spell to trap the demon. He trashed and shrieked against the bonds holding him in place. Saliva dripped from his fangs onto the floor, burning instantly through it. Wondering why no one had come downstairs yet to investigate, she boldly approached the demon, staring into his red eyes. His features looked oddly familiar, almost like she had encountered the demon before, but that was impossible.

"No one dares to summon a demon after the practice got banned," she muttered to herself.

"I dared to anyway," Owen said from behind her. "Don't worry about the guests though. They won't wake up anytime soon." She turned around to face him. He held a leash in his hands that clearly was meant for the demon. She released the containment spell as soon as the collar was fastened around the demon's neck.

Hanna was bound and gagged in a corner, her eyes widened in fear. Signe ignored her own anguish and finally allowed her siren nature to surface. It was the only way the three of them could leave this place mostly unscathed.

Her legs and arms grew longer, iridescent scales appearing here and there. Until that moment, Signe didn't realise how much she missed those, but missing them she certainly had. Her hands transformed into claws capable of tearing through flesh, her eyes turned a murky yellow and her hair now reached past her hips, flowing behind her as if they all were underwater. Only her tail was kept at bay, as it would only appear in the sea.

"I'm curious," Signe said, once her transformation was completed. "How you summoned that demon without alerting my mother's warriors?"

"I got her rival's permission to do it. He simply turned off the alarm for a day."

She swore under her breath. "Of course he did, that asshole."

Marius was her mother's first love, and even though they were equaled power-wise, he always craved to have more power than her mother. From the moment they met, at a meeting during a period of peace, Signe saw him for what he was: a greedy bastard who was willing to do anything to undermine her mother's position. Their relationship was tense at best.

"Similar people always find her each other, don't they?" A humourless laugh emerged from her lips.

He didn't offer a response.

The demon snarled viciously behind Owen, who held its leash casually in his hand. It would take only one slip for that demon to get loose. Signe cracked her knuckles and widened her stance for more stability.

She smiled widely, showing her sharp teeth. "Show me what that pet of yours got."

"With pleasure."

To her surprise, the demon lunged for Owen first. One claw tore through his shirt, shredding it effectively. Blood welled up at the gaps, and Owen fainted almost immediately at the sight of it.

Then the demon shifted his attention to her. He lunged for her left side. Signe ducked out of the way just in time. She leaped in the air, a chair giving her momentum, hoping to get on his back. For a moment, she thought she might succeed until the demon grazed her leg mid-air.

A pained grunt left her lips, hands flying to her leg immediately. Unlike Owen, blood didn't make her nauseated. A healing spell cured most of the wound, though a scar would remain.

She swiftly returned the attack with a strike of her own. He shrieked angrily, his moves becoming more brutal. He slowly crept up to her, waiting for an opportunity to charge. Signe wouldn't take any chances now, not when he had become feral.

Panting, she threw a chair at him, buying herself enough time to craft another containment spell. She was getting tired, not specifically from the fight, but it had been a long day planning all their heist.

She would end the demon this time.

He howled and fought against the bonds holding him in place once again. With one ruthless strike, she cut open his throat. Yellow blood bubbled up, frothing and, she realized with horror, crawling with tiny insects. She quickly wiped off her claw on the curtains.

Signe untied the ropes around Hanna's hands and feet and removed the gag. Owen recovered at that exact moment too. Hanna rushed to her feet and firmly poked Owen in the chest. "That was incredibly reckless of you and not to mention dangerous."

"Ugh," he said. "Why do you even care."

"I'm your older sister, that's why. I also promised our mom I'll always protect you."

"I don't want to hear a word about mom." Owen tightly clenched his fists.

Hanna huffed. "You never want to talk about mom, because you still feel guilty about what happened and I can only imagine what you're going through. But it isn't your fault and it never was. You couldn't have known that day that armed men would enter the store and would take everyone inside hostage."

He was shaking now, Signe noted. This was something he never shared with her before, and it made her feel bad. It would be the perfect time to get revenge, but it wasn't in her nature to kick a man down who still was ridden with guilt about something that happened years ago.

It made her realise that getting revenge wasn't just as important as before, though he still cheated on her. Owen needed some comfort, and by the looks of it, Hanna wasn't about to provide it.

She approached him slowly, carefully. She then gently rubbed soothing motions on his back, between his shoulder blades. Soon enough, he relaxed. She took a moment to examine his gashes and saw that the bleeding had stopped, but he still needed some stitches.

"Come on," she said, grabbing his hand. "Let's get you somewhere comfortable."

SIGNE AWOKE WITH A GROAN, her body covered by a white sheet. Her clothes were neatly stacked on a desk facing the window, where sunlight fell in broad strokes in the bedroom. Glasses filled with paint brushes lined the windowsill. In the corner was an easel with a painting of a woman positioned on it, left by the artist to dry. She assumed it was Hanna. A string of leaves hung from one end of the room to the other, and more potted plants were placed in the room. Her toes curled into the soft fabric of the rug as Signe swung her feet over the side of the bed.

It was oddly cosy.

The door opened with a soft click, and Hanna stepped into the room. Cara followed her like a shadow. They both looked anxious. Signe worriedly clutched the sheet to her chest. "What's going on?" she asked quietly, since the mood in the room had visibly shifted. The tension was so thick, that it effectively put a stop to the loud thoughts in her head. "Did something happen with Owen?"

Cara shook her head and rolled up her sleeve, her movements stiff. Her upper arm was black, gradually turning grey until it stopped just past her elbow. The veins running through her arm weren't a faint blue anymore either, but a stark gold.

Signe gasped, her hand flying to her mouth. She blinked a few times, hoping the sight would disappear on its own.

"Don't bother," Cara said defensively. "It won't go away."

Signe awkwardly embraced her from the bed. "My mother might know how to get rid of this."

"Have you gone absolutely mad?" Cara shoved her away. "Don't try to pretend you're still welcome at court. Your mother banished you two years ago!"

Hanna looked between the two of them, assessing the situation with indifference until she promptly walked out of the room.

Her best friend poked her in the chest. "Don't even think about consulting your mother for this, do you hear me?" She rolled down her sleeve, hiding the demon's mark. "You don't deserve an ounce of that serpent's attention."

Signe sighed. "You're right. I'll ask my brother instead. He might know something."

"That sounds like a great start," said Hanna, reappearing in the doorway, a book tucked under her arm. Owen hovered behind her. He hesitantly stepped into the room just as Hanna continued. "We really can use all the help we can get." She turned to Cara. "Unless you want to turn into a demon eventually."

She placed the book on her desk, flipping through the pages until she found what she had been searching for. She pointed to one of the images. "This might help cure the demon's mark, as you call it."

Signe read the spine. *An Analysis on Demons*. She eyed the

book curiously and stepped closer. Her hip accidentally bumped into Hanna's. They both blushed furiously as they looked at each other.

"I didn't know you were into this kind of stuff." Signe coughed, trying to hide her reddened cheeks.

Heat crept up Hanna's neck. "I was obsessed with demons when I was a kid."

"Didn't we all have an unhealthy obsession during our youth? I was always looking for my mother's approval when I was younger. And guess what? Turns out she didn't really care about me at all."

"I was always leaving spiders in my sister's bed," Cara said, smirking.

"And I was the annoying little brother," Owen added quietly. "But spiders? That's wicked."

"I was one hell of a devilish child."

"I bet you were." He smiled.

The conversation smoothly glided into idle small talk and soon they were all joking around. It brought her solace, to spend time with her friends like this and not give the world around them any attention for a moment or two. She wanted to experience more moments like these more often, once they dealt with the demon business.

A message lit up her phone, distracting her. "Cut the chit-chat," Signe said, once she read the text. "My brother will meet us at sundown."

SIGNE'S LEGS dangled just above the water. She counted the waves washing ashore with care. Just as the sun cast its last rays upon the earth, a male siren disrupted the sea's calmness. It immediately alerted her, the way his eyes blazed into hers. The displayed fury would be enough to sack cities with a single thought, were the emotion sincere.

She waited patiently for him. His mock anger would pass once curiosity took over. Crossing her arms, she watched as he swam closer to the shore, his features becoming clearer in the fading sunlight: a broad nose, downturned eyes, and a black blob of hair that refused to stay in shape.

"What do you need me for, sis?"

"Bold of you to assume I need you for *anything*," she crooned.

"Signe," he sighed." I know you better than that, unfortunately."

She made a rude gesture with her hand.

He laughed, his eyes crinkling at the corners. "Ever the polite heir."

Signe beckoned him to get closer. She didn't want anyone to overhear what they were speaking of. "Someone here—" she gestured to Owen, who in turn glared at her. "—Successfully summoned a demon last night. Even worse is that Marius is involved as well."

"Okay, slow down. Are you serious?"

"Very so. I killed the demon myself," she said, showing him her recent scar. "But that's not why you're here, though it's related to the demon. It managed to bite Cara, and she's been infected now."

"No way!" His eyes widened. "That's the most interesting thing I've heard for a while."

She punched his shoulder. "Quit fooling around, Thom. We're talking about a life or death situation here."

"Alright, alright. What can I do for you?" He held up his hands in surrender.

She quietly explained their plan, giving him clear instructions on what to do. She knew her brother: it was easy for him to stray from a task so she even wrote the instructions down in a notebook, a waterproof spell woven into its pages.

Hanna and the rest were a comforting presence at her back. And to her utmost surprise, she was somewhat glad that Owen was there too. His knowledge of demons could be useful later on.

"AT THIS PACE, we're not going to find a cure anytime soon." Signe slammed shut the book she had been skimming through for the past hour. She let out a frustrated sigh, going through the tome once again. Maybe there was something she missed before.

A gentle hand, however, prevented her from doing it. "You really need a break."

She looked up at Cara. "We're running out of time. I can't take a break."

"It's not healthy to be in the library every day, from dusk till sundown." Cara grabbed her hand. "Don't you wanna enjoy the sun for a bit?"

Signe reluctantly let her lead out of the dim library. Once she stepped outside, the brightness blinded her, and she blinked a few times, letting her eyes adjust to the change of light.

The corner of her mouth lifted involuntarily once she spotted the rest sitting around a picnic table in Hanna's beautiful garden. It was a peaceful sight. She wanted to preserve this calmness, this easiness they settled in. Whatever discoveries her brother soon shared with them would change all that.

For now, however, she joined the ongoing conversation. They welcomed her with comfortable smiles, and soon a beer bottle made its way to her. She took a careful sip, savouring the fruity taste. She downed the rest in one go and slammed the bottle on the table.

"Can I have another one?" she asked no one in particular.

Usually, Signe wasn't one to smother her problems with alcohol, but today she needed it.

Hanna placed a second bottle in front of her. "There you go."

Signe tilted it towards her in thanks.

An hour passed when her brother approached them, his magical abilities preventing them from noticing his presence. She was used to it by now, so she didn't give a shit when he sat down next to her. The others stopped talking almost immediately. She simply offered him her untouched drink, which he also downed in one go. He wiped away the foam with the back of his hand.

"I did some asking around." He addressed all of them. "You can't cure it." His attention shifted to Cara. "I'm sorry."

"What else can we do instead?" Hanna asked, spinning her empty bottle.

Thom's throat bobbed nervously, hesitating a moment before he quietly said, "Death is the only way to stop it."

"Fuck that." Signe stood up. She refused to believe that death was the only solution. She started to pace, attempting to silence the roar inside her head. Hanna watched her with a worried look in her eyes. She ignored her. "Did you think of every possible solution? There *must* be something or someone that can help." She was breathing hard now. Unwanted tears gathered in her eyes, and she angrily wiped them away with her palm.

Cara started crying too, which was enough for Owen to get up and pull her in a hug. He whispered something to her, but Signe couldn't hear it. The two of them soon disappeared to somewhere in Hanna's house, perhaps to look for a glass of chamomile tea.

The devastating news still had her reeling, but at least Cara had someone who managed to look after her well-being right now when she couldn't.

A sudden roar in the house disrupted the silence. Owen ran

through the open doors, panting. His eyes were wide; it was clear something had rattled him. It was then that Signe noticed three new gashes, presumably from Cara.

She pointed at his arm, her hand shaking. "Was that Cara's doing?"

Owen didn't have time to respond. With a roar, the creature that was Cara burst through one of the windows on the second floor. She descended with a graceful landing as glass rained around her. It didn't seem to bother her at all.

Everyone scrambled out of the way, except Signe. She remained standing in the middle of the garden. She never abandoned Cara before, and she wasn't planning on doing so now. Cara bellowed again, burning saliva flying through the air.

Thom rushed forward, tackling her to the ground. "You are an utter *fool*," he snarled into her face. "Cara doesn't exist anymore." He gently brushed her hair out of the way once he saw the tears in her eyes. "There's no saving her now. I'm going to put an end to this."

"No," she said, shoving Thom off her. "Let me kill her. It's the least I owe her."

Determination fuelled her steps as she walked up to Cara, halting a few metres before her. Her brother threw her favoured sword at her, which she caught with ease. Hanna and Owen watched her from the shed. Thom gave her a grim nod, silently wishing her good luck before he joined them as well.

Cara's claws scraped over the grass, specks of glass glinting in her black fur. They flew through the air as she barrelled forward. Signe saw it coming and rolled out of the way. She crouched when Cara came flying overhead, the momentum of her run-up carrying her body. She swung her sword upward and sliced her neatly across the stomach.

Cara screeched angrily as golden blood spurted out. Her following attack wasn't as precise. Bloodlust no longer drove her. She was furious, and anger always had been a bad motivator. Her movements became sloppy and thus was it easier for Signe to strike hit after hit.

She ended the fight by chaining Cara with her infamous binding spell since it worked well enough with the other demon too. Her body collapsed in the grass, the impact destroying most of it. Only then did Hanna and the rest leave the shed.

"Finish it now, before she breaks loose," Thom instructed her.

Signe only had one thing to tell her now. "I love you so much."

She shoved her sword effortlessly through Cara's chest with a yell, and she watched as the brilliant light slowly died in her best friend's eyes. They both refused to look away until Cara slumped over, her body limp.

17
THE SKIN BETWEEN MY TEETH

MAGGIE STANCU

It's October, grey and grim about the edges and beginning to catch the scent of its own death. Taps and cracks echo from the birds splitting shells against the bark of the old oak while babies cry in their nests, begging for mum to come home. An unnamed creature battles in the ocean, screaming as it struggles to free itself from the morning tide. It will suffocate just as the sun breaks the horizon.

This is bearable.

Everything is ravenous. Something claws at the back of my skull.

It's morning, he says. *Roll over.*

I'm lying in the meadow (her meadow), a small patch of long grass and lavender just a short walk from the beach below where we used to picnic. The ground is soft and uncomfortable, and I am being used as a misshapen platter for my friend, an admittedly derivative Crow, who feasts upon the worms writhing through my mud-soaked beard. With great effort, they try to escape his clutches.

They will not succeed.

He shudders a little as he swallows them down. *I don't enjoy them,* he tells me. *I prefer something with a little rot. A little sick. A little death to have a good, long suck on.*

He gives me a nip as he goes for the last fellow squirming just beneath my chin, taking a bit of my flesh with him.

Sorry, old chap.

He turns away a moment before twisting his head round, peering at me through the corner of an eye black as the midnight sea. He taps his sharp feet against my chest. Eager.

You taste delicious.

I think he might eat me (I think he already has) when he grows bored of my company. For now, he hops to the ground and wanders off in search of something else to swallow.

Alone and filthy, I want to shed the scraps of man. I want to shriek until my throat has gone raw and my mind has turned slow and thinking about her doesn't feel like an act of violence. I want to dig up the earth with my bare hands, trembling, and crawl inside her grave. With an open mouth and disgusted heart, I want to taste her decay, to feel the rot on my tongue and love her harder. I want more than anything to sleep in her arms, and I want very much to die there.

Guilt finds a home behind my eyes. I weep into the mud, all worms devoured.

Hours have passed, and I've shredded my clothes trying to peel myself from the hardened ground. The sky is wounded by deep crimson gashes that dribble through the clouds, perhaps permanently staining the colouring of the world, a world for which I am no longer capable of caring.

Abandoning the bloodied heavens, I stumble along the lawn only somewhat dressed, the tatters of my shirt and chunks of my trousers consumed by the crusted mud. I am more than half-starved, all but foaming at the mouth, and yet I cannot so much as stomach even the thought of proper food. I've currently taken to the habit of sucking, sometimes chewing about the delicate flesh of my wrists, and though I ingest nothing, the act seems to satiate some hunger and oddly, a despairing need for affection.

I find comfort only in the skin between my teeth.

I am steps from the house and somewhat calm when I feel the devastating crack beneath my heel. For a moment, I consider the sympathies of the willfully ignorant and think to continue on my way, without a glance, and be spared the misery of compassion. Surely, I am owed this sin, but I have something of a penchant for self-mutilating iniquity, particularly as it pertains to my soul. One might even call it a perversion, and I have such little control.

I lift my foot off of a shattered shell and observe, with no small amount of agony, the confusion of the snail who looks at me with utter despair, a single question devouring his small form.

He does not ask me what has happened. Instead, he asks me why, and I imagine that to this poor creature, I am god. Most cruel and unforgiving by way of simple indifference, taking without thought that which I have no claim to, I have robbed him of his only home. I have caused irreparable damage to this thing that has done no harm, and I think it must be crueler to leave him this way. It seems wrong to take his home without his life, and I think I could endure the violence of it more than the knowledge that I have added to his suffering.

I lift my heel and take a breath.

I hold in preparation for calamity.

Somewhere in the distance, Crow caws, and for reasons I may never understand, it saves a life. I lower my heel, step carefully round the snail and leave him a quivering wreck in the red grass.

This is not how life should be.

With each step taken, I feel more and more certain that I have deprived myself of a most necessary, most merciful bloodshed. Fury rises in my throat like bile as panic seeps from my pores, spilling onto the cobblestones of the entranceway and spreading its vile stench. The house, dead, towers above my skull, its great wooden doors open as I left them, unbothered by the wind. Leaves have scattered themselves about the hall, tinged scarlet and despite the chill, each seems to hum with vibrant vitality, revelling in their mockery of my existence. I kneel before them, hesitantly brushing my fingers against the nearest, as burnt as the dying sun, and though it's slightly rough to the touch, it lacks the fragility I need. Clenched in my fist, it refuses to crumble. It only folds, tucking itself in with care and a desire for preservation greater than any I have experienced for myself.

I let it drop from my hand. I scratch at my beard. I walk over to a nearby vase and raise it above my head before remembering that it was one of my wife's favourites. I set it back where it belongs, gently, and give it a little wipe down the best I can, before picking up a dish I'm fairly certain she held in no esteem. With two hands, I raise it high, and with the rage of a man who has lost more than sanity can bear, I send it hurtling to the ground.

There is no great shatter. There are no shards of glass. There is nothing but a dull thud and a small indentation. It is another mockery, one I cannot entirely comprehend without shattering myself, and so I do the only thing of which I am capable. I laugh.

I laugh, and that laughter reverberates through my chest until it tears open the cavity and I cannot breathe. I dig my nails into my filthy cheeks while sobs, howls, and absolute wretchedness consume me, and I consider the word consume and how it seems to eat itself.

I seem to eat myself.

I listen to the creaking of the floorboards and at this

moment, I am certain it is the voice of god. God, who is in the gardens and the forests, though I cannot hear him. In the branches of the trees he created, he is mute and it is only after a great cut that he begins to speak. I marvel at the cruelty of a god whose voice only sounds after death and dismemberment. Such atrocity. Such beautiful music.

I weep. I weep. I weep until I laugh and that laugh sounds like the floorboards, like splinters in my throat.

I take a mirror from the wall and fling it at the stairs. I fall to my knees when it shatters, the most glorious devastation. Hundreds of sharp fragments litter the ground, glittering like rubies from the distant light of the bloodied sun. I want to roll in them, to rub my cheek against their sting. I want to swallow them whole and scream as they tear my throat to shreds.

Seven years of bad luck, old chap.

I hadn't heard his arrival. Crow flaps to my side as I admire the wreckage, the great mess of leaves and glass, and a little blood. I look down at my hands, vicious hands, caked in grime and decorated with slivers. I finally catch my own scent.

I need a bath.

Crow pads along after me, hopping up the stairs with unpleasantly ruffled feathers and a gleeful look in his eye. He gives a grating coo.

Don't look so grim, he tells me with something of a grin. *Feasts still to be had, my lad, and most unexpected excitements.*

He lets out a low chuckle. It sounds a little like god. *After all,* he says, *I just had the most deliciously despairing snail.*

"Do you like it, Daddy?"

She tugs on the left leg of my trousers, staring up at me with big, brown eyes and a shy smile that dares to mend all the pieces of me.

"Darling?" I ask, nonsensical and utterly in love.

She holds out a piece of paper, rocking back and forth on her heels as she looks down at her little red shoes. I smile, taking the page gently between my fingers. The edges are bursting with swirls of blue that cling to a soft, swooping green.

I kneel beside her. Of the two of us, she always loves to be taller. "What are these?" I ask, pointing at the blue swirls.

"Oceans in the grass," she murmurs, positively twinkling.

I'm beaming. "Oceans in the grass. Of course." My eyes return to the drawing. "They're beautiful."

The grass is longer in the middle, interspersed with bits of purple.

"Lavender."

Her voice is quiet.

No. No, that isn't quite right.

Her voice is distant, like a voice from a faded memory, something I can't be entirely certain of. It exists in a subset of reality; adjacent, but never truly touching, and it isn't as it ought to be.

I can't seem to look at her. I can't seem to look at anything. I cannot find the room or even myself, and yet I am inexplicably staring. I am staring into an absence. I do not have eyes.

"Lavender, Daddy." Her voice is a rasp. Something harsher hides in the gaps between her letters.

"La-ven-der." The sounds are stilted, almost inhuman and for a moment, I am less than myself. Gone is the absence, returned are the eyes, and she is next to me, smiling. I smile, too. This has been awfully silly of me.

I revisit the drawing, where the grass is longer in the middle, interspersed with bits of lavender. Nestled between the oceans in the grass is her meadow, and in her meadow is a family. Mum, with a picnic basket full of strawberries. Daddy, with a book titled, 'Grief'. Crow, eating Daddy's leg.

Crow, eating Daddy's leg.

I reach for my daughter's hand. It is made of black feathers.

With an inquisitive twist of his head, Crow peers at me from his seat on the armchair. I'm in my study. My hair, still wet from the bath, clings to my forehead and cheeks. My robe hangs loose. I am kneeling on the rug as I was with my daughter just now, as I was two years ago when she showed me the drawing of our family having a picnic in her meadow.

Where did you go? Crow asks.

Where did I go?

"I don't know," I say. "Somewhere...perhaps a nowhere...was I asleep?"

Crow shakes his head. *You were looking at those.*

I follow his gaze behind the sofa to the desk in the centre of the room, all but obscured by pages upon pages of her drawings.

I sink into the desk chair. Crow shakes out his feathers and flies to another room, or wherever it is that crows fly. I take one of the pictures in my hands and turn it over. My loves smile up at me, both dancing under a crescent moon.

Both.

Both.

Jesus Christ, both. The word itself is a gaping wound. It is a blunt instrument. If god had any mercy, he would have made it a noose. If god had any mercy, he would have given us better words. Such names for the sinners, the murderers, the infinitely cruel, but what name for the father who has survived his child? To the desk, the floorboards, the burning hearth, I speak. I beg.

You have given me no name, and yet I cannot name myself. I am unformed and in agony, not so much a man, but a gash where love once bled, and oh, heavenly lord, I am desperate for a drop. Bless me, father. Forgive me, father. Love me, father.

Love me.

Is that not why we turn to you? Are we not all children, abandoned, begging for a scrap of our father's love?

Almighty god, but a gross misplacement of yearning.

I am without words and once again, laughing until my eyes drift back to the crayon portrait of my darlings, dead. Both dead.

If I still cared to lie, I would think to claim some sort of possession but I am, in this moment, horrifically, unreservedly myself. I lift the drawing to my lips and begin to suck on the corner of the paper, swallowing slivers as they dissolve on my tongue. I take and taste and take again, page by page until I feel I must burst.

In another room, my friend begins to cry.

Crow weeps while Daddy eats, and little god is silent.

18

UNHAPPILY FOREVER EVER AFTER

CATHRINE SWIFT

My vampire ex-husband had dressed as Dracula for Halloween as long as I'd known him. Which was a very long time.

All these decades later, he still got a kick out of dancing scarily close to the truth in public. You would think being an immortal for nearly eighty years would grant a person time to develop a broader sense of humor. But alas, Elric Sullivan remained mentally trapped in his early twenties. Despite being well past thirty-five when he was turned.

"Hello, Ric," I said when the door to our home—well, his home now—swung open. "Blessed Samhain."

He dipped his chin toward his bare chest. No long black cape or a drop of blood; fake, or AB positive (his favorite), in sight.

"To you as well, my love."

My eyes traveled from his bare feet, up his tailored slacks, to the black leather belt and multiple rings decorating his hands. Hands currently offering me first pick of the candy-filled plastic cauldron he would no doubt dump in the next kid's pillowcase who knocked.

I waved away both the candy and the longing his words

always stirred within me. We'd been divorced thirty years of the fifty we'd known each other, but he continued using the endearment despite my many requests to stop.

"Costume shrink in the wash?" I gestured at the top half of his body.

He flexed muscles he had no business having at well over a hundred years old–if we included his human years–and leaned his shoulder against the door frame.

"At school today, I overheard the desperate housewives chatting about how devastatingly handsome I am. And what a shame it is that I'm here in this big house all alone." He sighed theatrically. "It got me thinking."

I rolled my eyes and shifted my weight to the other foot. "Uh-huh?"

I had heard those housewives myself a time or two. If only they knew who–what—he truly was, they might not be so quick to lust after him. Thankfully, they were intimated enough by me, the just as hot, equally scary ex-wife, that their fantasies would surely remain just that.

Still, it was a small town, and eventually, Ric or I would figure out some way to move on. Perhaps this year should be our last rendezvous.

"Could finally be time for me to move on?" he continued, apparently on the same page. "I thought, might as well give them a little show when they bring their kidlets around tonight. See who's still talking and wanting come Monday's lunch period."

A spark of jealousy prickled at the base of my spine, but I buried it. His games were as predictable as his jokes and stories of the old glory days. I'd heard, played along, and fake laughed to all of them more times than I could count.

"Perhaps it is."

His dark eyebrows lifted. "No objections, counselor?"

I put on my best lawyer face even though it was well past

office hours.

"What do I have to object to?"

If he wanted to use his high school history teacher status to pick up bored soccer moms, I had no right to stop him. He was free to do whatever he wanted, with whomever he wanted.

Instead of answering, he stepped aside and swept his arm back, welcoming me into the house.

"Care for a drink?"

"Sure."

As I entered the foyer, his fingers grazed my forearm, stopping me in my tracks.

"And, of course, happy birthday."

I offered him an involuntary smile, unable to stay completely aloof in such proximity.

He really was devastatingly handsome.

"Thank you."

He shut the door as I hung up my coat and slipped out of the leather ankle boots I'd worn for the walk over. His eyes raked my body, though the floral maxi dress I'd worn tonight was hardly revealing. Of course, after fifty years of seeing me naked, he knew exactly how I looked beneath it. One of many things that hadn't changed since the night we met.

October 31st, 1972.

The first time I'd worn this dress.

I only remembered the date after all these years because it had been my thirtieth birthday. And, technically, my last.

He often said he'd been reborn with me when I'd turned, but I knew now that was all romantic bullshit. Love–genuine love–couldn't truly be measured or equated by someone who lived forever. One could never truly appreciate something without fear of losing it.

I should know.

"I shall return, make yourself comfortable if you'd like."

He gestured to the overly cushy sofa before leaving me standing in the living room we'd once shared, for the kitchen.

In his absence, I scanned the space. Aside from taking down our wedding photos, he'd changed almost nothing about the decor since we had purchased this home in the early eighties.

I wish he had. Our tastes back then left much to be desired through the lens of decades passed.

Without thinking, my feet carried me toward our former master bedroom. The door was open and when I flicked the light on I was met with a pristinely clean space. I knew he hadn't slept in this room since the night I'd left, and I couldn't blame him.

Not wanting to feel like shit was precisely why I hadn't kept the house and kicked him out. Instead, I'd kicked myself out, but unfortunately, a bed still felt very empty at night whether you'd shared it with someone before or not.

When he entered the bedroom a few minutes later, one crystal tumbler in each hand, I was running my fingers over the dresser top, collecting dust where my jewelry box had once sat.

"There you are."

I accepted the drink and swirled its dark red contents. "Thank you."

He watched me as he sipped his and I eventually followed suit, tasting the wine and blood cocktail.

"B-negative?" I asked, surprised. "Where did you find this?"

"A few towns over during spring break."

"That's lucky."

He toasted me. "Only the best for such an important day."

I drained my glass, hardly tasting it. He continued watching me and sipping, so I moved to the window, drawing the curtains closed. My fingers stayed curled around the linen, unable to release them.

Why was I so nervous? And what exactly was I nervous about?

After a minute, he set his tumbler aside, pulled back the comforter, and crossed over to me.

"Are you alright?"

I nodded.

"Are you certain?"

I nodded again.

"My love. If you wish to–"

"I'm not looking for a way to get out of this if that's what you're thinking."

He chuckled. "May I touch you?"

I inhaled a shattered breath.

"Yes."

Gingerly, he wrapped his arms around me, bending over me, lips on my throat, fingers gripping the fabric of my dress. Hopefully, this year he didn't rip it. It was vintage, and who knew how many more times it could be repaired.

"I missed you, my love."

I chanced a look back at him, losing myself in the comforting shade of his eyes.

"I missed you."

"It feels so good," he whispered, squeezing tight. "Having you here."

"We only have six hours," I reminded him, slightly uncomfortable with the deeper feelings trying to work their way to the surface. "Until midnight."

He scoffed.

"I hate that rule. If you're going to cut us off, we should be allowed to start earlier."

I knew myself well enough to know I couldn't handle more than a few hours in his company. Staying one-minute past midnight put me at risk of never leaving.

"I hate *this* too," he muttered, kissing my neck, his nose brushing along my shoulder. "I shouldn't already be missing you when you're still in my arms. Where you should be here every day."

I couldn't disagree, so I side-stepped the subject completely, turning myself around to face him. Before he could speak again, I tugged him close and sought his kiss, desperate to forget this was only for tonight.

He guided me to the bed, laying me down on the cool sheets and pushing my dress up to kiss along my stomach. I lifted my hips willingly, assisting him, already aching to be consumed by him. He shoved the dress even higher, up over my breasts, and closed his lips around one nipple. Now that he was allowed to touch me, he couldn't seem to help himself. He flattened his palm against the rise of my other breast, relishing in the soft skin, still silky after all these years.

Lavender lotion and immortality really couldn't be beat.

"Any requests for the evening?" he asked, kisses paused. "Anything you've spent the last three-hundred and sixty-five days wishing for?"

"No, I don't think so."

He quirked a brow at me. "Been fully satisfied then, my love?"

I smirked. "I didn't say that."

"Well, I doubt there's anything new for us to try after all these years. Unless this latest generation figured out a new sex position."

His fingers danced along my rib cage, his mouth sucking and nipping–fang-less–between my collarbone and shoulder, finding the spot only he knew about. And he exploited it mercilessly.

"I haven't heard of anything new," I struggled to say, forcing my tone to stay even. When he gripped my hip and massaged his thumb into the muscles there, I failed. "I su–suppose we'll have to have boring old-people sex."

He huffed out a laugh. "Ah yes. Good ole missionary. No ropes, no toys. In and out, hey?"

I thought of the Halloween we met. The sharp edges of the brick wall as he thrust into me, cutting my back except where he'd bunched my dress around my ass and his hands held me up. I thought of the pulsing rock music from the club pouring from the back door we'd left cracked open with a beer bottle.

Never once in our entire relationship–alive, dead, or undead–had we engaged in boring old-people sex. And we certainly weren't going to start now.

He cradled my face, drawing my attention back to him and I was surprised to find my fingers were already curled around the dark strands of his hair. The following kiss was short but intense, and I let it end only because I knew more would come.

His fingertips floated down my cheeks and chin, to my neck, where he swept my hair away from my shoulder. Then I waited, heart pounding, as he ran his thumb along my jugular, like he had the night we met.

"Do you remember?" he whispered.

Of course, I did.

I slipped into another part of the memory, this time from before we'd gone outside. There had been hundreds of bodies crowded onto the dance floor, mostly strangers, but a few friends who'd come along to celebrate my birthday. It remained unclear who'd bumped into who first–me or him–but the moment our eyes met, I'd been bewitched. I'd thought the intense and immediate attraction was solely a vampire thing, but if his recounting of our meeting was to be believed, he had felt the same about me.

We'd had a connection from that first moment. One, supposedly meaning we were supposed to be together forever. One that drove him to boldly ask for a taste of my blood mere hours after meeting. And, two weeks later, it inspired me to beg him to turn me so we would never be apart.

Of course, I knew now, forever is a very, very long time. And immortal beings or not, there was only so long two people could spend together without wanting to kill each other. Metaphorically and literally. It had come to sharpening stakes or signing papers by the time I finally gave in and packed my bags, exhausted and heartbroken. We'd tried everything, but no connection, not even a blood bond, could keep us together.

He could never know how sometimes I regretted it. After all, he'd barely put up a fight when I'd walked out the door.

"I remember," I finally said. "The first bite."

He pressed a little harder, making me swallow.

"I still don't regret turning you," he whispered in my ear. "I hope you don't regret it, either. Even with how everything turned out."

He really meant *everything,* not just us. Before answering, I thought of the hell on earth we'd seen as decades passed and the humans learned zero lessons from their endless list of mistakes. Then I considered the fact we were hardly any better. The repetitive fights we'd had over the years were proof enough.

Of course, there was always the distracting and inexcusable savior called beauty. The fashion and music. The cities we'd visited. The bursts of hope for humanity And of course, the love we'd shared.

"No, I don't regret it."

His touch moved feather-light across my collarbone, pulling me back once more. Both recalling our past and being with him now held the same welcoming warmth I rarely allowed myself to feel recently. But tonight I could sink inside it guilt free and stay a while. Perhaps long enough to hold me over until our next anniversary. Or maybe forever, so I could stop coming back and putting us both through this.

A nice, but ridiculous thought.

I loved the sensation of being a vampire on my own, but *with* him... It was freedom. Pleasure, raw and unfiltered. As much as it was death and unnatural, it was life. And no matter how many decades we spent apart, I would forever love him for gifting me the opportunity to experience the world this way.

He kissed me again, and all thoughts evaporated as need expanded between us like hot air. We moved through it, closer together, his fingers trailing down to hook my knee and bring my leg up over his.

He was hard, I was desperate, and it was the perfect combination. But we didn't rush. Not yet.

His touch ghosted over my lips, between my breasts, and then further, where he slid one, and then another finger inside me. I gasped, and then moaned when he twisted his wrist around and up. He knew my body and my cravings, better than perhaps I knew them myself. My next, louder moan he captured with a kiss, drinking it down like water.

Or, in our case, blood.

"You're going to take this pleasure I give you, my love." His fingers stroked faster. "When I give it, how I give it. Just as you always have. And when you think you're done, I'll make you beg for a little more."

"Yes," I whimpered, not caring as his thumb brushed my clit how pathetic I probably sounded.

No matter how many years I spent with the powers and strength of a vampire, Ric could forever be trusted to strip me back to the bare bones of existence. And I loved him for it.

I also loved the ways he took advantage of the fact I wasn't a fragile human.

"You'll remember what it is to be loved by me," he said, pinning me to the mattress, his kisses traveling to my navel.

As if I could ever forget.

Lightning fast,—thank you vampire speed—I was on top of him, taking advantage of his distraction. He caught his breath, chuckling as I shimmied down to straddle his hips. Eyes squeezed shut, fingers digging into my bare thighs, he took a moment of my teasing hips sliding back and forth over his trousers before attempting to take control again, possessing my lips and hands with his. I didn't protest when he trapped me beneath him once more, just pulled him closer and nibbled along his neck.

I loved the battle and the showing off, his strength, my speed.

I could win if I really wanted to, one of us would imply. *And I will surrender, but not yet,* the other would wordlessly answer.

Until one of us did surrender—not only to one another, but to our cravings and desires.

I loved this side of us, but it was all too much after a year apart. I wasn't conditioned to it anymore. It was also the farthest thing from being enough. I wanted more, always. And so did he. Maybe it was less of an *us* issue and another one of those vampire things? But no matter how many times we made love or fucked, or something in between, it was never truly *enough*.

My lips trailed down his arm, my pointed fangs leaving faint red marks in their wake. When had they dropped? I hadn't even noticed, too distracted by him.

He should be equally distracted at this point, and far more out of control than he was. Why was he holding back?

I dragged my nails across his shoulder blades. That usually did the trick, but he must have spent the last twelve months preparing for this. His resolve was iron clad as he captured my hands, holding them above my head. His tongue and teeth moved over my ribs next, leaving a wet trail along the dip of my waist.

Slowly, he released his grip on my forearms, sliding even lower on my body.

He was trying to prolong this. Drag out every moment until the last.

"Please, Ric." Tired of the torture already, I was a mess, squirming and fisting the pillows, then the sheets.

I ached and burned.

I hated begging, but he liked it, and I had to get the upper hand somehow. I couldn't let him leave me shattered again. . . Last year, it had taken me weeks to think about anything other than his touch and taste.

"Yes?"

He didn't have to pull back for me to register the cocky expression on his face. The simple, three-letter word dripped with taunting, his own desire, and mischief.

At that moment, he was more than my former lover. He was pure vampire; a wild hunter and a skilled seducer. The monster one reads about in fiction. And fuck, if it wasn't painfully arousing.

"Everything," I hissed, gripping his hair tightly. "I want more of everything."

His fingertips brushed the inside of my thighs, followed by his velvet soft lips, framed by the stubble of a beard he'd neglected to shave off after work the last few days. A long, hot lick of his tongue followed. It felt good against my skin, but it also felt miles away from where I needed his attention most.

Would he bite me now? Would he–

No.

He was already moving back up my torso, but the familiar sting of fangs scraping my skin was a promising sign he was finally beginning to lose control.

Fucking finally. Now maybe we could get somewhere.

A telltale moan escaped him when his tongue soothed the red marks. He must have broken skin. Only *my* blood made him react quite like that.

And now it was my turn to take advantage again.

I guided him onto his back, a little slower this time, should he want to stop me. He didn't. He surrendered, arms above his head and dazed, glittering gaze expectant. I was only a little disappointed he wasn't fighting back, but I chose to enjoy the submission while it lasted, sliding my hands over his chest, shoulders, and biceps, around the curve of his elbows, and up to his hands. I guided them beneath the pillows, releasing when he gripped the headboard rails.

"Wise move," I whispered. "You'll probably want to hold on."

He grunted, eyes squeezed shut, probably trying to compose himself by reciting the alphabet backwards in Hebrew or Latin. But that wouldn't do, now would it?

He was going to lose control whether he liked it or not.

I shimmied down again until I was kneeling on either side of his left knee. After letting the heat from my breath dance over the tip of his cock, I swiped my tongue along my bottom lip, just barely, *barely* grazing him.

The headboard squeaked as he tugged on the rails.

I grinned, proudly.

"You torture me, I torture you. All's fair, right?"

He didn't answer other than to thrust his hips up.

Message received, with pleasure.

I wrapped my fingers around the base, letting my tongue flick out once, twice, three times. "Have you been so busy screwing all the neighborhood housewives you've forgotten how we work?"

Somehow, he managed to smirk at the roof through his locked jaw and gritted teeth.

"I knew you were jealous."

I licked him again, this time as if his cock was a melting popsicle on a hot day, complete with a short but hard suck at the top.

"Hardly."

He looked down, trying to be cocky, but his heaving chest and blown pupils gave him away.

"Not even a little?"

"We're divorced."

My hand pumped up and down his length, squeezing various pressures here and there, testing his arousal level, and what he craved right now that I could give him.

He huffed and puffed, and the headboard squeaked in protest again. Good thing we'd reinforced it to both the wall and the floor a few years ago. Poor thing put in just as much work as Ric and I.

"I-I do recall something about signing a paper or two once upon a time." He glared, but the anger melted away when I swirled my tongue *slowly* all the way from the base of him to the tip. "Bu-but that's just papers," he choked out. "They say nothing about my heart. Or, yours."

This time, I took his entire cock into my mouth, if only to silence him. I didn't hate the power surge I felt either, watching his eyes roll back as he melted against the pillows, so I sucked harder.

"Gods," he groaned out, a deep guttural sound from the back of his throat.

Then his hands were on me and he was hauling my body up his, attacking my mouth with his once more. In the rush, my fang grazed his top lip, and I lapped the drop of blood greedily, feeling the spark of his power entering my system, but I didn't try bringing more blood to the surface.

That would have to wait.

"Why did you stop me?"

"I'm also done being tortured."

He rocked his hips against mine, grinding us together. Fuck, that felt good.

"You needn't worry," I teased, grinding against him in return. "I need this—*you*—too. I know you can feel how badly."

This fight for dominance had ended. He would take me, and I would gladly let him. I had learned over the years that surrendering to him was not the same as giving him away my power. It was a beautiful, balanced dance of give and take.

Together, we worked our bodies around so I was on my back beneath him, both sighing, first in desperation, then lust, as he slid back and forth, just missing his destination. Fangless, I bit hard on his bottom lip and he jolted.

"Stop fucking around and–"

"Fuck you?"

"Yeah."

Now, more than ever, the intense need to feel him inside me tore at my heart. At my soul. I couldn't take one more second of not being one with him. Midnight was coming, and we had to stop wasting time. He seemed to agree because he quickly shed and deposited his pants to the floor.

When he was back on the bed and naked between my legs, I lifted my hips, rocking them back, shifting up, and then rolling forward, my legs wrapping around him. He slid smoothly into me, *finally*, and my mouth fell open, but no sound escaped.

A year could pass in the blink of an eye for someone like us with so many years behind us, and so many ahead. But the time apart always felt heavy and long once we were joined together. It was like the absence of him was made all the more obvious by his sudden presence. And it never failed to shake me to my core. To make the longing I could quash every other day impossible to ignore.

Thankfully, pleasure distracted me from the cracks in my heart, pulling my attention to the familiar orgasm coiling low inside me, and I released a high-pitched moan, shockingly close already. He had no right to be this good in bed, but of course, I shouldn't have expected any less. Decades of fucking and making love in every position imaginable, on every continent on the planet, provided the experience and knowledge needed to quickly find a rhythm that worked for both of us.

And with it, we rediscovered our reason for why, even

though it hurt to come together once a year, it hurt far more to never be together at all. There was nothing more sane, more right, more true than how incredible this felt.

Decades of history, of fights and make-ups, of separations and reunions, it always came back to this. This core connection we shared could never be fully squashed thanks to this carnal spark of humanity remaining within both of our reanimated forms.

At least that, I knew, was true. As proven by thirty years of failing to find someone else to love. For me, it would always be him.

"I love you," he whispered, as if he knew my thoughts. Which he probably did. "In 1972, in 2022, in 2052. I will always love you."

I would allow myself to say it once. Only today.

"I love you."

He sighed, relieved, and then he was hiking my leg up, moving a little deeper, a little faster. Bringing me closer to release, higher and higher, the coil within spinning tighter and tighter.

My nails dug into his biceps, both of our fangs fully extended now.

Lust and bloodlust combined with love, longing, hate, and loneliness into a whirling vortex I dived straight into the eye of. *This* was the sanest form of insanity I'd ever known.

"I'm close, Ric," I gasped.

"I know." He gritted his teeth, holding me tight. "I can feel you."

His thrusts held new purpose, each movement shattering my remaining resolve as a fire within expanded, licking at my flesh from the inside out, a familiar spark building inside me. I opened my eyes and our gazes connected, and there it was. That soul mate buzz.

That's what the old witch we'd met in the nineties had called it. She'd called us soulmates. What a foolish term. But. . .in moments like this. . . perhaps it wasn't so foolish after all. What else could rock me straight to my core like this?

I clung to him as I came, nails scrambling and scratching at his back, knowing he was whispering curses and praises in my ear, but barely able to decipher them. The scent of blood told me I'd broken his skin, and I salivated for it, torn once more between human lust and bloodlust.

"Go on," he choked out, gripping my hips tightly, and I eyed the vein in his neck pulsing beneath the surface, waiting for me. Begging for me.

Ric was the most delicious thing on the planet. His blood was the equivalent of all my favorite human foods–chocolate cake, biscuits and gravy, and sweet potato pie–all rolled into one. But it wasn't only his taste that made feeding from him a beautiful experience.

As my fangs sunk into his throat and his blood flowed into me, I was swept under. This was deeper than love, greater than devotion. The pure trust it took to blood share with another was indescribable. He was sharing his very essence with me–the literal thing that kept his undead body alive. More than that, he was allowing me the privilege of looking inside his mind. His very soul. I saw his memories, hopes, dreams, and fears. Most I'd seen before, but there were new flashes this time. Moments of his life from the last year I'd missed.

I saw him as a child, standing in a log cabin and peeking around the corner as his younger sister was born. I felt the excitement and smelled the crackling wood.

I saw him, still human, kissing a bronze-skinned man in Paris and felt his confusion and joy. There was lavender in the vase next to them.

I saw him walking down a dark alley, felt the unsteady cobblestones beneath my feet, and suddenly a gun was pointed at him out of the darkness. I felt the pain of the gunshot, the shock, and finally the peace of death.

I saw his first kill and felt his fear and self-disgust, and also the pure high of first blood lust. I could smell the blood and hear the echoes of his victim's screams as they faded away into nothing against the crisp white walls of the hospital room.

I heard the music that played on our wedding day as though I was physically back in the moment again, but instead, I saw myself through his eyes and felt the way he'd felt looking at me in the long-sleeved lace gown. I felt his heart stop and all the oxygen leave his body as he was flooded by intense love.

I saw our wedding night, and how delectable my still human body had looked to him as he slipped off my lingerie in the moonlight.

I took his breath away and drove him mad. And I absorbed it all as I drank him in, savoring every drop he granted me.

"Slow down," he finally murmured, easing me back.

"Join me," I sank my fangs back into this skin, deeper this time, and a millimeter over from the first bite.

I was getting greedy, keeping his self-healing skin wounded and open. He could have stopped me, but he didn't. Instead, he brushed my hair back once more, tilted my face, and kissed along my chin and cheekbones.

"Ready?" he half whispered, half growled into my ear.

I nodded, my fingers in his hair, tugging and pulling and twisting so he could get closer to my throat.

When his fangs pierced my skin I muffled a cry with my free hand, letting the pleasure take over as I felt our minds join, along with our bodies. It wasn't quite as intense as the first time we'd blood shared as vampires. Nothing would ever be that intense again for as long as we lived, not even if we did it with other vampires, but the pleasure was there, and a hum ran through my veins like an electric current, just as I knew it ran through his.

Blood sharing was probably the reason we couldn't fully let go of one another. As vampires, all injuries healed, leaving us without marks other than the ones received before being turned —but the fang marks from a mutual blood share bonding session remained. Almost like permanent wedding rings.

It was more than my heart that belonged to him. It was my mind and body, too. And, even, my soul.

Ric had been correct when he said the divorce was just paperwork. We *were* forever because of this.

I wasn't sure what he was seeing of my past, but I opened my mind fully to him, allowing him in everywhere and anywhere he wanted to go, and after a few moments I had to stop drinking to fully enjoy the experience. Nothing outside these four walls mattered right now, only how utterly we belonged to one another at this moment. It was all-consuming, taking over my mind and my body.

He pulled back, my blood dripping from either side of his mouth, and smiled at me. I had licked my lips clean, but he didn't bother, as usual. He was far more focused on hitting *the* spot again and again.

My fingers slipped on his sweaty back as we moved, my spine arching for him.

"Come for me," he said, a plea as much as a demand. "Please, my love."

I turned my head, burying my face in the pillow, muffling my screams, as his fingers dug into my hips, holding me in place, giving himself more leverage to move. His other hand was by my head, supporting his weight, and I could hear the blood pulsing through his veins, just beneath the skin my nose kept brushing. I put my arms around his neck, offering either of my wrists to him.

"Again," I gasped out, and he didn't hesitate, biting me once more, drinking slowly and easily this time as his wall of self-control crumbled and he came inside me.

I joined him, savoring him as he savored me, the hum of our blood bond starting at our toes and creeping through our veins and muscles. My skin felt warm, but it didn't burn, not even where Ric's fangs had pierced my skin again. The hum continued to travel up into our minds, curling around and through our synapses like live wires sprouting.

When I could no longer focus on how he tasted, and only on how he felt as he tasted me, I knew the re-bonding was complete. Like an engine tune-up, we were, for all intents and purposes, recalibrated to one another.

How dreadfully wonderful. How utterly, destructively perfect for two people who were no longer together.

The worst part was I wouldn't take it back, even if I could.

Our fangs retracted simultaneously, our bodies satiated and content. And utterly spent. I knew he was at least when his arm collapsed out from under him. Quickly he rolled off me and away, the power, control, and possession he'd felt a few moments ago seeping from his body now that it was all over.

I hated this part. The regret. The hope. The dread. It was like whiplash after being so deeply connected as we'd just been.

Silently, I grabbed the sheet we'd fucked onto the floor and pulled it over us both, my hand hovering over his chest. Wanting to touch him, uncertain if I should or not. Ultimately, I said fuck it and wrapped my arm around his waist.

He released a shattered, pained exhale as my cheek settled on his ribs, but he didn't pull away.

"How much longer do we have?" he asked, probably as afraid as I was to check the time.

"I don't know."

"Don't look."

I wiggled closer to him.

"No, not yet."

"Let me fall asleep first. It hurts waking and finding you gone, but not as much as watching you leave."

"Alright," I said softly, my voice quivering like his was.

Neither of us spoke again.

I lay there, listening to his breath even out into nothing, and his heartbeat flicker and fade. He was sleeping like the dead, and it would be ages before he woke. I was free to go, and yet I stayed well beyond my self-determined curfew.

It was only when the sun started rising that I forced myself to slip from his arms, my own limbs and eyelids heavy now. He slept on as I redressed and headed for the door, hesitating for a moment between in and out.

I wouldn't look back. If I did, I would find myself in bed and in his arms once more.

No wonder he didn't want to watch me leave. Leaving was fucking hard. I took a deep breath I didn't need–a human habit that somehow still slipped back on occasion–and let the door shut behind me.

I wanted to tell myself this would be the last year. That tomorrow I would pack up the little townhouse and get on a plane. Go anywhere in the world besides this impossibly small town. I'd be doing us both a favor. But those kinds of thoughts were a waste of energy.

Even if I somehow found the strength to leave, he would simply follow. He wouldn't even have a choice. We were bonded. One.

A couple in love who couldn't be together, but also, couldn't be apart.

Unhappily forever, ever after.

19
NOT JUST A NIGHTMARE
KAYLIE NOEL

My eyes dart back and forth between the unopened champagne bottle in my trembling hand and the lifeless body splayed out on the kitchen floor. I didn't mean to kill him.

It's not unlike us to turn what should be a fun, joyous evening into a fight, especially when there is alcohol involved. It's my fault. It's always my fault. But I didn't mean to kill him. I love him.

Feeling uneasy, I set the champagne bottle down and lean onto the counter to steady myself. I close my eyes as I try to recall how I found myself here.

Burke and I were meant to be celebrating his promotion at work tonight, but instead, here we are. I shouldn't have brought up Bree again. We had finally worked through the most recent cheating incident. He was drunk. It meant nothing. I had gotten too comfortable and let myself go. We both agreed that I needed to make some changes so he wouldn't do it again.

I was working on losing weight and I even had an appointment scheduled to cut a few inches off of my hair, just how Burke likes it. I was trying to be less opinionated, or at least be quiet about my opinions. "You're so much prettier when you're not talking."

But Burke went out with his friends after work to celebrate, and when he came home already drunk, I was worried he may have made another mistake. Sure, I was already drunk, too. I may have overdrunk a little while I was preparing for our night and stressing over everything being perfect. I turn to alcohol during times of stress. That's another thing I am working on.

When he came home, we were going to celebrate, just the two of us. I had a charcuterie board overflowing with all of his favorite cheeses and fruit, a chocolate tart with caramel drizzle for dessert, and a bottle of champagne ready for us to pop. I was really looking forward to our night together, but then he stumbled through the front door and knocked over my grandmother's vase that was sitting on the entryway table.

I heard the crash and knew immediately what had happened. Determined to not let it ruin our night, I took a deep breath in, held it, and slowly let it back out as I rounded the corner to the entryway. This was a new technique I learned from my breathwork classes and it had really come in handy lately. Burke thinks the classes are dumb. "Why do you need someone to teach you how to breathe?" He always mocks me about it. It's hard to explain to someone that tries to stoke the flames of their emotions by pouring alcohol on them.

When I came around the corner, there he was. It didn't matter how drunk he was, he was still so incredibly beautiful. As he looked down at the broken vase on the floor, a dark strand of hair fell in front of his left eye and when he looked back up at me, I was done for. Every single time. He just had that effect on me. On everyone really.

As his eyes met mine, my heartbeat quickened. I parted my lips and sucked in a breath. I love this man. He walked down the hallway, grabbed my face, and kissed me like he hadn't seen me in years. He slipped a hand into his pocket and I just knew he had something for me. I put my hands on my face and grinned like a little girl who just learned her crush liked her back. His hand emerged from his pocket with a bag of the little chocolate-covered gummy bears from the candy store down the road.

Those little gummy bears are my favorite and he knows that. This was his promotion celebration and he was still thinking about me. I don't deserve this man. He grabbed my hand in his and danced me into the kitchen, straight to the champagne. But first, I wanted to clear things up so I wasn't worrying all night.

"Did you have fun out with your colleagues?" I flashed a small, sweet smile.

"Maybe a little too much fun. Everyone was staying out longer, but I couldn't wait to get home to you, my love." He kissed my forehead. I loved when he did this. My smile grew bigger.

"Was she there?" I didn't want to think about it, but I knew I had to ask. Waiting with anticipation, I twirled my hair around my finger like I always did when I was nervous.

"Was who there?"

"Don't play dumb, Burke." The smile dropped from my face. "Was she there or not?"

"If you mean Bree, yes she was there. To support me." My heart quickly fell into my stomach, like one of those rides at the fair.

"To support you? You don't need her fucking support." Beads of sweat formed around my hairline. I was furious now. He knew this would upset me and he did it anyway.

"Just get over it. I drunkenly screwed my hot coworker one goddamn time and now you won't just leave it alone!" Droplets of spit landed on my face as he leaned forward and yelled.

"Get over it? Are you fucking serious, Burke? You are such an arrogant asshole!" I adore this man, but our fights can get intense. It's only because our relationship is so full of passion.

He'd only hit me once. I deserved it then. A bartender was

getting a little flirty with me and I didn't immediately shut him down. I didn't tell him I was happily in a relationship with the greatest guy in the world. I should have told him. He punched me in the face that night when we got home. He felt really bad the next day, and he never hit me again. Yeah, sometimes he shoved me against the wall or grabbed me a little too aggressively by the back of my clothes, but nothing I couldn't handle. I knew he felt bad when he hit me that one and only time and he would never do it again.

Then why did I feel so scared? It was then that he grabbed my hair and yanked my head back so I was looking directly up at him. I didn't know what else to do. My eyes darted around, but I couldn't move my head. Panicking, I reached for the counter and felt around for something. Anything. Anything that could stop him from hurting me. My hand found the unopened bottle of champagne and without even thinking, I just grabbed it. I grabbed it and I swung it directly at him. As the bottle made contact with his head, his grip on my hair came undone and he fell to the floor. He did not get back up.

I take a deep breath and push away from the counter, bringing my thoughts back to this moment. Surely he is fine though. He is just knocked out like I was when he hit me. I've seen him deal with much worse in the many bar fights he's been in in the years we've been together. Now we are even. He is going to be so pissed at me when he wakes up though. Or maybe he is so drunk, that he won't even remember what happened. He hardly remembers much when he gets this drunk.

I squat down and try to pick him up, but I can't. He is so much bigger than me. I grab him by the ankles and pull him into the living room, falling over several times along the way. There is no way I can get him all the way down the hallway to our bedroom. I leave his body on the floor next to the couch.

Hopefully, when he wakes up he will just think he rolled off the couch. It wouldn't be out of character for him. I kneel beside him and put my ear to his chest. I can hear his heart beating and feel his chest rising and falling with each breath. At least I think so. Unless I am feeling my own heart thumping with anxiety. No, no it's his. He is fine. And I can't linger otherwise he might wake up and remember what really happened. I lean forward and plop a kiss on his lips before standing back up. "I love you, my dear. I am so damn proud of you," I tell him before I turn and stumble out of the room.

I walk back into the kitchen and pop the champagne. After pouring two glasses, I quickly chug one and set the empty glass on the coffee table next to Burke. I grab the other glass and the charcuterie board and pad down the hallway to the bedroom, sloshing champagne onto the floor as I go.

I must have passed out after scarfing down the contents of the charcuterie board and finishing off the champagne because the next thing I know the room is shrouded in darkness. I hear footsteps approaching from down the hallway toward the bedroom, followed by the door creaking open. I feel the covers fold down beside me and the weight of Burke's body climbing into bed. I hold my breath, afraid of how he might react, but he scoots his body behind mine under the covers and puts his arms around me, enveloping my body with his. Trying not to give away any signs that I am awake, I quietly let out the breath I have been holding in.

He seems to have either already forgotten what happened, or he has forgiven me. I don't deserve his forgiveness, but I will gladly accept it. If a conversation is to be had about what happened, I would rather wait until morning anyway. I let myself drift back off to sleep, this time in the arms of the man I love.

I awaken to my stomach turning. Quickly jumping out of bed, I run to the bathroom to let the contents of my stomach out into the toilet. I must have had way too much to drink last night. I scratch my head as I try to remember our night celebrating Burke's promotion. That's when I recall the memory. A champagne bottle and Burke lying on the floor. I recoil at the thought. Not my finest moment.

I slowly tiptoe back into the bedroom, hoping to see Burke still sleeping, but his side of the bed is empty. That's odd. I can still see the indent from his body, so he couldn't have gotten up very long ago. Probably just getting some water. I look at the clock. It's only 2:32 am, so I start getting back into bed. That's when I see something concerning. Blood on Burke's side of the bed. Shit. I must have really hurt him, and he's definitely not going to forget about this. I see a faint trail of blood and I quietly follow it out into the living room where it ends, but I don't see him anywhere.

I'm torn between feeling worried that he is severely hurt and terrified that he's pissed at me. Just as a teardrop rolls down my face, the front door slams open. I jump up and run toward the door. "Burke?" I call in desperation, but there's no answer. I get to the door just as a clap of thunder shakes the house. The wind is really picking up. Maybe he left and didn't latch the door on his way out. I quickly close it and make sure both locks are secured.

I give him a call, and just as the phone starts ringing on my end, I hear the faint sound of his ringtone in the distance. Following the sound, I find Burke's phone on the floor in the hallway among the shattered pieces of glass from my grandmother's vase. I pick it up and look at it. The background is a picture of the two of us from three years ago. We were so in love and happy. My smile looks so genuine and I looked so hot in that dress. Red and skin tight. Burke loves that dress.

I lock the screen, set the phone on the entryway table, and head back to my room. I open the closet door. Where is that dress? If I put it on before Burke gets home, he won't be able to be mad at me. I just need to find it. The hangers make loud screeching noises as I slide clothing along the rack to look for the dress. I don't see it. Frantically overturning bins, the floor quickly becomes covered in clothes. That's when I see a glimmer of red. It must have fallen off the hanger. I quickly rip my clothes off and step into the dress. When I pull it up, I can't get it over my hips. This can't be right. As I force the dress up even more, it completely tears up the side.

"You could stand to lose at least 15 pounds. Lose 20 and I won't be able to keep my hands off you," I hear Burke say in my head. I think. I look into the full-length mirror and immediately scream when I see Burke's smirking reflection behind me.

"You scared me!" I quickly turn around… but he's not there.

I must still be drunk. Or maybe this is all just a nightmare. What a night it's been. I look back into the mirror, hating what I see. And I know Burke does, too. I just want him to love me and be attracted to me. Without bothering to even try peeling the dress back off of my body, I walk into the bathroom. Something catches my eye. A pair of scissors sitting next to the sink. Picking them up, I finger the blades.

I feel the soft touch of a hand on my shoulder. "You look like a child with that long, stringy hair. I would find you more attractive if you would just cut it." It's Burke's voice, again. I whirl around. No one is there. Letting out an ear-piercing scream, I chop a chunk of my hair off. And then another. And another. Until the floor is covered in big chunks of blonde hair. I look into the mirror at my new short hair and touch my reflection. "Will you love me now, Burke!" I scream at the mirror and throw the scissors across the bathroom, knocking a picture off the shelf.

It falls to the floor and the glass shatters. It's another picture of Burke and me. This time we are at the beach. I am wearing a teeny tiny bikini and his arms are wrapped around me. Those were the days when he couldn't keep his hands off of me. As I stand up to leave, I notice blood dripping onto the floor. I must have cut myself on the broken glass without even noticing.

I start to walk across the bathroom to the sink, when I kick something hard covered in my hair that I chopped off only moments ago. When I pick it up, hair falls all over my feet and I can see what it is. My heart plummets into my stomach. It's a scale. I think back to when I was skinny, like in that picture on Burke's background and the one lying on the bathroom floor. When he used to look at me with such love in his eyes. He hasn't looked at me like that in so long. I'll look like that again someday. I have to if I want to save my relationship.

A scream emerges from deep within me and I throw the scale at the mirror. It cracks. Tears trickle down my face as I lean forward to inspect the glass. This night is just full of broken things and broken people. I close my eyes and wipe the tears. When I open them again and look at my reflection, it is not tears running down my face, but blood. I shriek. I blink and when I open my eyes the blood on my face is gone. Only tears are left on my face and blood on my hands. Shaking my head back and forth, I try to make sense of what just happened.

Sweating and crying, I walk out to the living room with chunks of hair stuck to my skin. I know I look as disgusting as I feel. I am still wearing the too-small dress, ripped up the side and my hands are covered in blood. I am a mess. No wonder Burke left. I don't deserve him. He is too good for me. Falling to the ground, I dissolve into sobs. And then lightning cuts across the sky, followed by a loud crack of thunder, and I am plummeted into the darkness.

When I open my eyes, rays of sunshine are peaking through the blinds. Looking around confused, I realize I am in my bed. I look beside me, but Burke is still not there. Pushing the covers aside, I get out of bed. I hold my hands out in front of me; there is no blood. I sprint to the bathroom. There is no broken picture frame, no broken mirror. The scale is sitting on the floor and the closet is not in disarray. I look into the mirror and my hair is long again. I touch my reflection and my eyes well up with tears. I hear footsteps coming down the hallway and I freeze.

"Good morning, my love," I hear just seconds before I see my boyfriend round the corner, smiling and looking completely unharmed. I must look upset because his face quickly changes to concern. "Everything okay?" He comes over to wrap his arms around me from behind.

"Yes, thank God. I am so glad to see you!" But as I say those words, something doesn't feel right. I'm not glad to see him, but I don't want him to know that. Not yet. "I had a terrible nightmare. It just felt so real." Instead of letting myself relax and fall into him, my body stiffens as I recall my dream and all the terrible things Burke has said to me.

"I've got you. It was just a nightmare. I'm here now." But these words don't provide me with relief like they used to. I cannot forget what he has done and how he has made me feel. And I don't want to. He made me think I was a hideous monster. I know better now. There is only one monster in this relationship, and it is not me.

I look up into the mirror and just as my gaze meets his in our reflection, a single drop of blood falls from his eye.

ABOUT THE AUTHORS

Amanda Havill Adgate is a writer and lifelong voracious reader. Her formative years were spent building blanket forts, scribbling scenes into notebooks, crafting imaginary worlds, and cooking meals based on favorite stories. When not writing, Amanda can be found drinking copious amounts of tea and coffee, homeschooling her four daughters, wandering antique malls, or laughing with her husband, usually with a book close by. She currently lives with her family near the mountains of North Carolina.

Ava Lynn Beck is a paranormal fantasy author and lover of all things dark and bitter. When not writing, you can find her reading, drinking coffee, or at a café doing both. For updates and other content, follow Ava on Instagram (@ava.lynn.beck) and TikTok (@avalynnbeck).

When Ireleigh is not explaining how to pronounce her name at Starbucks (like the beginning of Ireland put together with the name Leigh) she's reading her stories out loud to her adorable puppy who couldn't care less about them but puts up with it anyway. Together, they live in Philadelphia, terrorizing the bookshops and streets in their wake. You can find her on Instagram as @ireleigh17

Felicity Devoria is a new author currently pursuing a bachelor's degree in media production and three English-related minors. She dreams of writing books and movies about people who go on magical adventures and lust after each other. You can find her as @felicitydevoria on Instagram, where she posts occasionally helpful writing tips.

Alexandra Faszewski has been telling stories before she could even write them down. These days, she can be found accessorizing with a mug of English Breakfast tea, cuddling with her Pittie mix, or nose deep in a book, of course! She also loves to spend her time traveling and exploring new places. She's on Instagram as @alexfaszewski

---

Author of too many (currently unfinished) stories involving dragons, magical chaos and castles, Kimberley has a degree in Creative Writing and English Literature from the University of Winchester. When not reading or writing, you can find her out in nature with her camera working on combining her love of animals with photography. Known to her friends as Kimmie, she lives on the south coast of England with her family. This is her first published story since her university days. Find her on Instagram @kimmiefordwrites

Laura Gulbranson is a native Arizonan who has been writing since 3rd grade. Laura writes about characters caught in between worlds and between cultures. Although a little dilettante across genres, Laura finds her home writing literary contemporaries and fantasy genre benders that mix magic, mystery, adventure, and romance. When she isn't daydreaming about fantastical worlds or dreamy romances for her novels, she is working her mortal job, hanging out with her fur-children, and traveling. Her Instagram is @thebookthalovedme

An avid reader with a vivid imagination, Hasfariza Hassan is a writer who resides in the busy state of Selangor in Malaysia. She is 19 years old, currently studying A-levels at Sunway College. She has a fascination with questions and likes to analyze things from different perspectives. Hasfariza loves exploring other cultures and languages, especially since she grew up in Malaysia and Indiana, USA. Her overactive imagination inspired her to write at the age of four, plunging her into the world of fantasy, and she hopes to use her writing as a platform to give a voice to those who are unrepresented. Hasfariza's poem *The End of Us* is published in *Collecting Dust* by Hudson Warm, an anthology featuring voices from around the world and she was the recipient of the bronze and silver award in the Queen's Commonwealth Essay Competition in 2015, 2019 and 2021. Instagram: @Hasfariza_hassan

After a near-fatal car accident, Julia turned to writing as part of recovery. Having studied YA fiction at the University of

Toronto, and becoming an alumni of Adrienne Young's Writing with the Soul, her coping skills turned into writing. Julia has had more surgeries than Frankenstein, is a creature of the night like Batman, and creates memorable heroes and monsters of her own. She's on Instagram @juliajacksonauthor. Her website is juliajacksonauthor.com

---

Gabriela Lavarello has been writing and telling stories since she was a young girl. Perhaps it was inevitable that she would call grappling with words and making writing-related videos on YouTube a career—and love every moment.When not writing or filming, you can find Gabriela reading, cuddling her dog Raven, or riding and training horses. Of Liars and Thieves, the first installment of an upper YA fantasy trilogy, is Gabriela's debut novel, published in September 2021. You can find her on Instagram as @authorgabrielalavarello and TikTok as @gabrielalavarello88

Anaïs Milo is an author and storyteller from the Southern US, working primarily in the horror and mystery genres. Though an avid horror writer since childhood, "A Crow's Call at Night" is the first spooky story to be written by her in years. Anaïs is currently in college and studying psychology, with plans to become a psychologist later in her career. In her free time, she enjoys bird photography, language learning, and of course, writing. You can find her at @katspandemonium on Instagram.

Maddi Neuenswander, an author from northern Utah, believes in the healing power of stories. Readers who enjoy fantasy with relatable characters and relationships will love her unique combination of wit and whimsy and fall in love with reading all over again. Her Instagram is @writermaddineuenswander

---

Xyvah M. Okoye is an epic fantasy author and believer. When she isn't tinkering with the mechanics of another story, she might be refueling her magic in a pool, on the beach, or close to some other body of water. And at times like that, with her pointy ears twitching and her button nose buried in a book, if you look close enough, you just might see the shimmering veil around her… The veil between this world, and hers… Between what is, and what possibly could be.

To find out more, visit www.xmokoye.com

Follow her on social media: @xmokoye

Raised in fantasy and sci-fi, and after ten long years of absorbing every available piece of knowledge, Mireya G. Parra realized writing should be done on the page, not only in the mind. With this short story, they've promoted themself from writer to author. You can find them on Instagram as @mireyag.parra

---

Tiffany Paige is an aspiring author who lives in the suburbs of Philadelphia with her husband and sons. This is her first published piece of work. In her spare time, she writes novels that she hopes will inspire marginalized groups of people. Her Instagram is @seventhpaige

---

Carmen de Wit grew up in the south of the Netherlands, where she spent her childhood pretending to be a princess. Nowadays, she creates fairytales of her own. When she's not writing, you can find her cuddling her cat or drinking tea while watching Netflix. You can find her on Instagram @gunsandstories.

Cathrine Swift is a Canadian indie author and Youtuber, passionate about writing steamy romantic fiction embedded with responsible representation and diversity. She wants to help fill the world with books bursting with characters of all religions, races, sexual orientations, and identities. When she isn't writing, she can be found taking care of her daughter, decluttering a closet, or reading fanfiction and drinking a matcha latte. Her favourite trope is enemies to lovers and if you ever want to talk about Star Trek, Star Wars, Marvel, or Doctor Who, she's your girl. She's on Instagram as @authorcathrineswift

---

Maggie Stancu (b. 1997) is an author of fiction and poetry, whose work ponders the nature of morality, mortality, and those who exist on the borders of society. She resides in Ontario, Canada, where she spends her free time engaging in photography and watching her favourite fantasy/period shows. You can find her on both Instagram and Twitter as @maggiestancu.

Kaylie Noel is new to the writing world, but has been a lover of words her whole life. When she isn't creating, you can find her either spending time with her human kids and cat companions or enjoying an iced mocha and vegan donut while she binges reality television. You can keep up with her shenanigans on Instagram @kaylofthewild.

ONE LAST TALE GLOSSARY

Appa - Dad in Tamil

Ma - An endearment used affectionately in Tamil

Amma - Mom in Tamil

Akka - Older sister in Tamil

Lah - A Malaysian slang used at the end of words and sentences for emphasis

Pengawas – Prefect

Standard six and three – Sixth grade and third grade

Pengerusi - Class monitor

Perhimpunan - Assembly

Karangan - Essay

Bagai langit dengan bumi - A Malay proverb about how different two people are

Kan - Right (usually used at the end of sentences)

Aiyah - A Malaysian expression to express dismay

Encik - Mr.

Puan - Mrs.

Cik - Miss

Pengakap - Scouts

Tahu tak apa yang I nampak - Do you know what I saw?

Pelik - Weird

Memang - Really

SMK Mujarab – The school's name

Manuk pansuh – A traditional Iban dish

Terkejutnya - That surprised me

Padan muka dia - Serves him right

Rumah sukan - House practice

Koperasi - Cooperative store

Surau - A designated room for prayers and at school, it's used for Islamic classes

Baju Kurung – A traditional clothing for females in Malaysia. However, it's also worn as a school uniform.

Cepat lah - Hurry up

PJ – An abbreviation for Pendidikan Jasmani which means physical education.

Abang - A form of respect for a man older than you , but also refers to your older brother

Some more – A Malaysian slang used to emphasise something such as the presence of the assistant head prefect

Penolong ketua pengawas - Assistant head prefect

Abak - Dad in Iban

Dage - Eldest brother in Mandarin

Ayat Al- Kursi - Usually read by Muslims for protection and in times of danger

Tu melampaulah - That's too extreme / much

www.ingramcontent.com/pod-product-compliance
Lightning Source LLC
Chambersburg PA
CBHW030604310726
48979CB00003B/566

* 9 7 8 1 7 3 6 1 3 6 3 8 6 *